Create a
Desired Future
by Working on Your
Own Dream

IDOWU KOTILA

PAGE PUBLISHING, INC.
Conneaut Lake, PA

First originally published by Page Publishing 2020

ISBN 978-1-64701-401-8 (pbk)
ISBN 978-1-64701-402-5 (digital)

Printed in the United States of America

DEDICATION

This book is dedicated to the glory of God, the greatest author of wisdom, knowledge, and understanding. To my late parents, Chief Emmanuel Ayeni Kotila and late Chief Mrs. Elizabeth Omoladun Kotila.

CONTENTS

FOREWORD

I dowu Kottila is a man of principle, passion, energy, and commitment. *Create a Desired Future by Working on Your Own Dream* is about personal change and creating something great—your future. Idowu is an energy coach and a mentor in his own right. A premise he lives by is *"don't be smart, get smart."*

Merriam-Webster says that *energy* is a dynamic quality, the capacity of being active, a positive spiritual force, and the exertion of power: *effort.* To move from where you are—in spirit, mind, and body—you are going to have to exert effort. You are going to have to work on yourself. Gregg Amerman says that "if you work hard on your job, you'll make a living. If you work hard on your business and yourself, you'll make a fortune." Step 1 is to figure out where you want to be in life, then you can figure out how to get there.

Learn to be a winner, not a whiner. The difference is commitment to yourself and having zero doubt in being able to achieve your goals. Throughout your journey, you must control your thoughts and emotions, because in the end, what you think determines how you act. How you act determines what you get.

People will judge you on your perseverance and consistency. In other words, do you believe enough in your dream to stay the course? Enjoy the lessons from Idowu and learn from his experiences. Don't judge.

—Dr. Larry Erickson

Dr. Larry Erickson is an associate professor of ethical leadership, entrepreneur, and business strategy in the MBA and DBA programs at St. Mary's University of Minnesota. He's the co-owner of Essentials 4 Life, Health, and Wellness (physical and financial) with his wife, Darla.

PREFACE

I have noticed that many people are living in penury and dying of poverty, working like elephants and eating like ants in the midst of plenty, just because our people lack financial orientation and wisdom. Moreover, the majority of family problems and divorce among Christians and the people in the secular world are due to poor management of family finances.

The observation above, and my desire for entrepreneurship, prompted me to go about writing this book on the need for an individual to work on personal dreams. This book intends to teach people practical solutions to financial problems and what to put into consideration while starting or planning a business or considering a business model. It is written to remind people on how to think and grow rich and to encourage people on the need to be an entrepreneur and ways to go about it. It is another attempt to remind people that a borrower is a slave to the lender, and that knowledge without practice is useless while practice without knowledge is dangerous. People must know that where they are today is a result of thought they had and steps they took yesterday.

Part of the basis of this book is to open the eyes of the people to the fact that investors invest today in order to buy a lot tomorrow with convenience, while a poor man buys today and pays a lot tomorrow under pressure and lack. That investment rather than work produces wealth. This book is to remind the reader that jobs (salary) are meant to maintain the current living situation and can't make one rich. People should know that they should place their interest on investment and not on conspicuous spending on clothes, gadgets, and all unprofitable ventures. In addition, this book is written to let people realize that talents and skills needed by everyone to succeed have been inbuilt in individuals by God. Your success will depend on how you use your talents and what you use your time and talents for.

Moreover, I am trying to emphasize on the fact that working for people will only provide a living, but Investing in business will create a fortune. There is a need to open the eyes and reasoning faculties of people to what poor people and billionaires think about money, and what makes the difference between a billionaire and the poor man— investment. Among the goals of this book is to wake people up on how to judiciously use their time and teach people on how to take stocks of what they invest their time and resources on.

Lastly, this book is to remind the reader that in order to be a helper of destinies or to be able to help other people around you or in your communities, your thinking should be far more than receiving salaries but working on one's dream and investing on what individuals have passion for.

ACKNOWLEDGMENTS

Writing this second book has made me believe more than ever before that indeed, with God all things are possible. I would forever be thankful to some different individuals who saw possibilities of getting things done in me by always reminding me that I needed to work fast on this second book, having written the first book some years ago. The grace of God and their encouragement really energized, motivated, and helped me in making sure that this second book came to reality while the third and fourth one is in the making.

Many thanks to Pastor Mrs. Jumoke Olowokere, RCCG Strong Tower Parish Minneapolis, Minnesota, United States of America, for consistently reminding me about the needs for me to make the second book a reality and that I should not be too distracted from working on my talent.

I would never forget all the encouragements and productive advice from some uncles like Lawyer Toyin Abe (Nigeria), Lawyer Gbenga Agbaje (USA), Toba Adeyeye (USA), and Akin Ayoola (Canada). Kudos to Prof. Akin Bamigboye, the Founder and CEO Louis Med Hospital Lekki Phase 1 Lagos Nigeria, who I always look forward to as a role model. His life's styles are an inspiration to me.

Great thanks to Mr. Christopher Akinremi, Mr. Charlie Oribamise, Pastor Olufadeji Amele, Prince Samuel Adejuwon (Sr)., Mrs. Funmilayo Oluwole, and Mrs. Mogbonjubola Adetifa for their words of encouragements all the time.

The links and the professional advice received from my brother from another mother in the person of Mr. Akinjide Falaki cannot go unnoticed. Thank you, bro. To my uncle and mentor, Lawyer Mayowa Ojo, I recognized your immense contributions. Dr. Ayo Adeniyi advice can never be ignored so meaningful! My personal brothers Biddy Oluwole and Taiwo Adefajo words of encouragement cannot go unrecognized. Thank you.

To my senior Pastor Ghandl Olaoye of RCCG Jesus House Washington DC USA who after reading my first book told me "my brother, you have potential and what it takes to be successful, you just need to package yourself, follow your dream and disallowed distractions. This your book I read can make you millions". The lessons I learnt and still learning from Senior Pastor Tola Odutola of Jesus House Baltimore USA anytime I am opportune to be under his ministration cannot be left unused.

To my mentor and professor of entrepreneurship who was my professor in graduate school of business at St. Mary's University of Minnesota, USA, Dr. Larry Erickson. He was the one who made me known one day during one of our private discussions after classwork that "you can only make a living while working for people as a salary earner, but possibly make fortunes while working on your own business." He said to me another day during our hang out at coffee joint that, "Do you know borrower will always be a lender's slave, and that he who control your time [employers] have great influence and control on your future? Idowu, start follow your dream and put more time on what you have passion for and stop busying on things that are not necessary".

I really appreciate the unmeasurable contributions of my Spiritual father, Pastor, mentor and most importantly the important bridge and links between most of the important people that matters in my business dealings who will not only support with words of prayers but with financial commitment to any reasonable project in person of Senior Pastor Emmanuel Olusola Olowokere of RCCG Strong Tower Parish Minneapolis Minnesota USA. You are highly recognized sir. Thank you, sir.

I deeply appreciate my best friend (my wife), who is the lifetime and the most viable investment I ever invested in, for her incredible support and sacrifice to make sure that we have a balanced family most especially when I am making some risks and decisions about my dream which might not make sense to an ordinary woman, she still supports me because she believes.

My appreciation will not be complete without acknowledging the three awesome dividends (my children) from my investment, Hannah, Abisade, and Adeteniola Kotila for being good children. To all my friends, families, and well-wishers who time will not permit me to mention, I say thank you. May God bless you all amen.

INTRODUCTION

At any point in time, if your present condition is unacceptable to you, you have two important decisions to make for a better tomorrow. Firstly, you can accept the present unacceptable condition. In other words, you can give up and let go of your future desires and dreams by pitching your tent with what life has offered. Remember, in most cases, life will not offer you your desires but what is available. Secondly, one can refuse to accept the unacceptable and look for a new direction. This I call a life-changing decision which can shape up your life and move you forward speedily to achieve goals and to fulfill your destiny in life. After living in America for over ten years and working for different employers from different business sectors, I tried various possible shifts available and worked several hours of overtime as much as I could. I received different kinds of paychecks. All my efforts to save some money at the end of the month proved abortive due to a lot of recurrent expenditures like bills and other unforeseen contingences because nothing is free. You pay for everything. These are common challenges apart from other problems from co-employees, supervisors, and in some cases, the manager of the company. These are frustrating indeed. To make it worse, I discovered there are several restrictions in working for people. While at work, we usually have specific designated times for both breakfast and lunch, which was never enough. Any attempt to spend extra time after the company's designated time may be the beginning of the end of the job for the employees.

No one dare received personal phone calls while at work regardless of how important the call is. Some places of work will never allow you to bring your phone into the work area; phones will either be in the locker, gown, or coatroom. To those who are able to bring their phones into their table at work, they dare not use personal phones until after working hours. Another strange, horrible, and challenging situation I experienced was that we hardly had more than four weeks of vacation per year. Exhaustion of your vacation before the end of the year may mean that you have to use the next vacation without pay in case you've been hired at work. In case you are a temporary worker, you will not only go unpaid, but you might be penalized by receiving what employers called *occurrence*, if luck is not on one's side. Each company has various numbers of occurrences allowed, after which an employee will be terminated. Come rain, snowstorms, or sunshine, you have to be at work at a stipulated or appointed time without excuse, or else you will be shown your way out of the company.

I also noticed that majority of the family feud and divorce that happened among couples is due to lack of time for their spouses. We all know that communication is important in building and solidifying good relationships. Many homes in the Western world lack good communication due to the nature of couples' jobs. Thank God for understanding, my wife would resume work as early as 6:30 a.m. and get back after 3:00 p.m. come rain, come snow, Monday to Friday! I usually work at home most of the time. I usually felt uncomfortable anytime she woke up ready to leave for work. We know that the early morning is the best time for a husband and wife to think about the way forward for the family. As head of household, I knew that it was not right for my wife to continue in that way. I believed we could have a better life than what we had now because, practically, I knew some few people that were living a pressure-free life.

After I went through the circle of working to pay taxed and bills for a long time, seeing my wife waking up too early, it dawned on me that the majority of people lived under pressure and fake lives to make ends meet. I began to look for another possible way of living a good life by looking for possible U-turns or exits from my current insufficient highway of life. One of the exit signs that I first discovered that really blew me off was that millionaires don't sweat to get money anymore when they arrive at a certain stage. Though it may look tough at the beginning, but at a latter stage, they don't work for money but their money works for them. They were familiar with selling ideas, and people see them as a group to trust. People meet with them to discuss viable business ideas. This time around, money works and talks for them. Every little effort they make turns to millions for them. I also discovered that *the poor serve as tools for rich men to make further fortune.* While rich people are busy playing golf, flying in private jets, and buying expensive materials, the poor (employees) are busy working in their companies to enrich the rich people's bank account.

Don't get me wrong. I am not saying working to pay your bills and taxes are not right, because that is what keeps government of the land going in meeting up with their financial obligations. The Bible does not even support idle hands. Moreover, I got to know that millionaires, too, pay taxes as required by the law. But the criteria for paying taxes are much more different from the poor people. Poor people pay under pressure with agony and pains, while the rich rarely feel the pinch because they have lots of resources and investments to use in write-off taxes. Although it appears to the poor as if they were paying lots of taxes when they heard about the figures, but the truth of the matter is, what millionaires are paying in taxes are minimal compared to their yearly take-home as gain. We cannot blame them because they pursue their dreams, and it is working fine for them.

The inability to save for the future among the poor people is the critical issue in this society. Many can't live independently without credit. Everything is all about your credit level. The more your ability to accumulate debt, the more many people think they are secure financially! That is why people sign for thirty years' home mortgage and many years of car notes packaged with high interest. An average individual with a five-year car repayment and or a thirty-year home mortgage must have paid triple the original price he or she signed for at the end of the payment period. There is a slang that *an average American is one paycheck ahead to be homeless.* Why? Because if you miss one paycheck or salary, you might not be able to meet up with all your financial obligations for a certain period of time. (*Terrible life experience of American federal government employees during the brief government short down known as* Trump short down *in 2018 is a typical example.*) For whatever reason at all, any human being falling in between any of these categories must check him or herself and try as much as possible to create time and work on his or her dream.

If you are working for people and not with people, working on your dream is important. *If you are receiving an appointment instead of setting appointment, or perhaps you have a talent but you don't know how it can work for you, you have to wake up.* If you are standing in group meetings where your employers address lots of you while you are all standing instead of board meetings at your place of work where you ought to sit around the table facing each other, making and agreeing on decisions affecting your company(s), you need to wake up. *For you to receive your paychecks (salary) and begin to cross-check if your hours are fully paid, you need a solution to your challenges.* If you can't take a day off unless you have somebody who will cover your shift for you, you need to think twice. If you can't meet up with your bills unless you work overtime, you should know something is wrong somewhere. If you are living in America and you are soaked in poverty like somebody living in a third world country, or in war-torn countries, I will recommend you for orientation. *If you are the types that develop high blood pressure because you are worrying about how your tomorrow would look like financially, you need to go back to the drawing board and replan your life.*

If you are among the people that develop high blood pressure because your financial condition is not in order, and therefore your children cannot switch on the light, run the tap water, or switch on the heater in winter or air-condition in summer because of oncoming bills, you should remember it is high time for you to reexamine your present level. *If you are in the category of those that compete with others in acquiring material things instead of competing on investments, you definitely qualify to meet with a financial counselor.* As an immigrant, if your family back home in your native country don't know your kids due to lack of air fare or transport fare or no time off, or you have three or four kids and they can't travel with you at once and you end up setting a time table or schedule for them one after the other to travel home due to financial incapability, you need a deliverance from anointed men and women of God. You seriously need God's intervention.

If you are traveling to anywhere in the world, you have about three to four stopovers due to cheap ticket which eventually turns ten hours journey to twenty-four hours. You need to get out of your roof and look up to see there are many stars in the sky. *Peradventure, you dare not pick phone calls from home or distance because of the fear of what you will give out financially. You need to assign quiet time for yourself as frequently as possible to think about the way forward.* If price of travel ticket determines when you can travel, to the extent everybody around you knows exactly when you want to travel because people have to shop for tickets for you, you need to move closer to people who can show you what to do to better your situation. If you are the one who had not for once been to airport or have no cause to travel out of your domain not because you are comfortable or you choose not to but because you don't have the financial capacity or connections to succeed in life, you need to pray that the helper of destiny should locate you.

In case you are mingling among the poor when God says you should stand out, I guess you need God's intervention. *If only monthly or Friday or weekend of your paycheck (salary) is when you are happy because you are sure you will have some money in your bank account, I advise that this is the best time to work on your dream.* If you are living in Europe, America, and any of the foreign countries and it is your habit that anybody going to your home countries must help you bring native clothes with different styles only for you to wear the clothes once or twice in a year or you work overtime or charge your credit card all the time because you want to buy attires for a wedding or birthday ceremony, you need to attend money management class. If you have started budgeting for next year's trip because of traveling ticket fare or because of personal time off (PTO) at work, you need to work on your talent. *If you just started a new business only for you to go and lease a car for hire purchase (car notes) or move to a bigger house because you have some money extra to make monthly payment, you need to read the financial management books and the stories of successful people.*

Perhaps the free food you are eating in group homes or assisted living homes where you are working is blindfolding you and derailing you from working on your dream. You need to learn how to bail yourself out of self-inflicted urges for free food. I would strongly recommend you for eating disorder therapy in order for you to be able to work on your talent and dream. If you are the type that still needs to get approval for you to go on vacation with your family, you are under financial and your boss bondage. You need to work on how to break loose. You lived in an underdeveloped country, graduated after a long time, applied endlessly for jobs that are not available. You better wake up and work on whatever you have passion for and stop wasting your time.

Peradventure, if you are the type that relies on godfathers or run after political post holders, it is high time you invest in your future and save your generation from poverty. *It is also important at this junction to know that relying on your father's wealth or your uncles or aunties abroad cannot help your dream.* Many spent lots of fortune in processing visa to advanced countries looking for greener pastures. I would advise you to spend your time and money in establishing a business of your dream and possibly what you have passion for. Who tells you that you can't prosper in your present location? You better be looking for opportunities and what people need in your locality and try to meet their needs.

I know you are a manager at your place of work; you can hire and fire other employees based on your judgments. That's right! But mind you, you don't have the final say. Your boss on top has the final say. *Can you please remind yourself how many managers you know that have passed through your company since you were hired?* Remember there can be downsizing, and you can get fired. Remember the 2008 global economic recession? *Did you have plan B? If yes, what was your plan B?* It's true that your company promised to invest on you so that you can be a better tool for them. I presumed, for you to have risen to the managerial level at your current job, you must have either worked in various companies or possibly you must have been serving your present company for a long time. Don't deceive yourself. Work on your personal dream and try to develop and work on those skills and connections you've made since you have been working on other people's job and move on with your life.

Ooh, you are a software and or hardware engineer. You can code and decode, lock and unlock programs. You can log on to your office computer wherever you are. You were assigned a pager to keep you alert about what is happening at your place of work at all times, meaning you can work at home or on your mobile devices at any time at anywhere. You are the type that logs in to business phone conferences with other colleagues in your sister companies or at the corporate office at the other side of the ocean (continent). If you've been complaining about sleepless nights due to long hours of conferences, it is time for you to reexamine your choice. *My question is, does your take-home at the end of the month measure up or better compare with what you were contributing to the company with your talent?* Can you please familiarize yourself with the history and genesis of all companies you've once worked for and use them as a template to start your own company?

Are you not tired of bringing office work home to do during your personal and family time just for you to impress your boss and to move the dream of other people forward? Oh! I don't have enough capital to start. *I know you are used to free cups of coffee and bagels plus other treats and freebies you are getting during board meetings and holiday season. Come on! You can get better than this if you have your own company.* Please don't place cost on your dream. Start small; it will grow bigger. *Stop acting as a pillar that holds other people's dream while your own dream is left inactivated! Dust up your talents and wake up from your slumber.* Times are not on your side. Oh ye of little faith, try to do something.

In case you have a business before and it failed, note that you are not a failure. What will make you fail is your inability to continue to try. All you need is to seriously work on your own dream. If you are convinced that riches are not beyond your reach, that you can still be what you wish to be, that money, fame, happiness, recognition, and independence can be had by all who have dreams and pursued them or use their talent wisely.

If you have ever been discouraged, if you have tried and failed, one single change may prove to be the oasis in the desert of lost hope for which you have been searching. If you are ever handicapped by illness or physical affliction and feel depressed or tired, you need to make changes. In case you ever considered yourself disabled, which you think may serve as a roadblock for your progress, I will advise you to watch *Nick Vujicic's* life on YouTube. Nick Vujicic is an Australian born without arms or legs. If that would not convince you on how to find your ability in disability, I would suggest that you watch another video on YouTube which showcases the life of *Richie Parker.* Richie Parker, who overcame being born in South Carolina, United States of America, without arms to become a chassis and body component designer for Hendricks Motorsports. Despite all odds against these men, they have achieved great things in life. After watching these videos, I guess this change may find you literarily swept into success. *There are solutions to your problems.* The major solution is that you need to work on your dreams and not on other people's dreams. For instance, if crying is what you have passion for, try to package your cry in a professional way. It will eventually lead you to success. Use your experience to craft out something that will advance your dream.

Mr. and Ms. Manager, please wake up. Time is not on your side. Start something today. Regardless of how well you can manage people's wealth, companies, and human beings, as a manager who depends solely on monthly salary or biweekly paychecks, you need to grasp the meaning of average for you to better understand the necessity for a better future and the need to work on your personal dream. When you survey the entire spectrum of wealth, you will discover that there are various categories. At one extreme, you will find *the poor*, who can never make the ends meet. Next to the poor is *the comfortable.* He is the one who makes ends meets but has no savings. Next to this is *the rich.* Under this category. we have people whose needs are met with added luxury of some savings. After this are *the wealthy.* We can identify the wealthy because such people do not only have some savings, but they are so rich that they can afford to put their surplus in fixed deposits. At the extreme end of spectrum of wealth is *the flourishing.* These people are so rich that they can lend to nations. Having looked at this survey, individuals must know where he/she belongs. It is left for you to choose in which group you want to belong to.

For as many people that desire the last two groups, which are *wealthy* and *flourishing*, getting a paycheck or salary every two weeks or monthly should never be your option. I would suggest you work on your dream and what you have passion for so that you and your generation will not become moneymaking tools for the wealthy.

It is important you do not deviate or shift from what you've heard, because the Bible says *"the man who wondered out of the way of understanding shall remain in the congregations of the dead"* (Prov. 21:16).

POVERTY

The Bible tells us, "The rich man's wealth is his strong city; the destruction of the poor is their poverty" (Prov. 10:15). *Poverty can be defined as a desperate shortage of spending power. Poverty occurs when resources fall far short in relation to daily needs.* You can be short in finance or other resources. A person can also be said to be poor if he does not have any tangible possession. Poverty, as we all know, is not a new problem, and it cannot be solved easily unless we follow divine orders. Although poverty in the land cannot be eradicated, it can be reduced or alleviated because the Word of God says there will always be poor people in the land (Deut. 15:11). Poverty, in most cases, has to do with dreams. *One of the obstacles of your dream is poverty.* Poverty does not only occur when you have financial shortfall. You are said to be poor when you are short of freedom and ideas. You are considered to be in a poor state if you have ideas and you don't know how to make it work for you or you can't use it to your own advantage. Likewise, *a person without a dream, vision, or mission is said to be poor.*

Poverty is said to be in operation in your life if nobody wants to listen to you or you can't give a directive to people or you gave a directive and nobody was ready to obey your directive. You are an apartment for poverty if your family and friends can make vital decisions concerning you, your friendship, or family without caring to keep you informed because your contribution will mean very little. *You are short of freedom when other people control your time.* People control your time when you can't go off work unless your boss approves it. After approval, if there are repercussions in case you failed to resume to work as approved by your boss or your employer, you are in poverty.

You are a poor man if any of your family members is sick and need medical attention but you have to give your job a priority at the expense of your family. You are also in poverty if you can't live comfortably for two weeks without a paycheck or salary. If lack of regular paycheck or salaries for some time prompted you to spend your savings, your 401(k), or your cooperative money, I consider you to be in a serious financial dilemma. If you are such a person that has no savings, whereby losing your job causes you to borrow money from friends and relatives to survive, I would say you are completely poor. *You are considered to be a poor man if you cannot pick up your phone when those that are in need called you, just because you don't have anything to give. You are in poverty class when creditors are harassing you with phone calls and other messages because of your outstanding bills.*

Fighting with your spouse or any member of your family whenever they are in need or requested financial or material assistance from you is a sign of poverty. Telling stories or giving excuses where and when you're supposed to spend or give out money is another sign of poverty. You still don't have financial freedom if your only source of income is your salary. *If you are not yet reaching the level of making money, why you are sleeping? You are not yet in the group of people who have made it.*

Interestingly, poverty does not just fall from heaven. Poverty can be caused by personal error, and people around you can also cause poverty for you. It can also be caused by situations beyond personal control. Other personal causes of poverty include laziness on the part of the individual. The wise are industrious and willing to work diligently to provide for their needs. *Excessive sleeping at the expense of work is bad. The result is poverty.* Other personal causes of poverty are foolish spending and excessive love of pleasure. Bad influence, peer pressure, imitation, and greed are causes of poverty. *You cannot expect to have any leftover for investment if your appetite is bigger than your income.*

There are some other human causes of poverty which are beyond control of an individual poor man. For example, bad government, dishonesty, corruption, bad employers, wars, and production of substandard goods for the public use can also cause poverty. There are, however, some of the agents of poverty that are beyond human control, like disease and bad weather. Sad enough, problem associated with poverty are so many. Poverty causes national, family, and societal problems we are facing today. Sickness, disease, and unhygienic accommodation and feeding are part of poverty problems.

Poverty in some cases causes divorce, child labor, and juvenile delinquencies. Most of the immoralities like prostitution are signs of poverty. *To break the backbone of poverty, it is highly essential to work on your own personal dream inasmuch as working for people who cannot make you somebody in life but enslave you.* However, it is essential to have an idea of what poverty really means and to be able to work out of it. The best possible way is by diligently and carefully working on your dream. I hope it will serve as a flashlight in the darkness for the reader of this book on how to focus on what it takes for a person to work on personal dreams in order to create a better future as demonstrated by the chapters in this book.

A DREAM

A dream is a clear picture of a better future. It is common among the construction engineers to draw a picture or plan of the next building or complex they want to build (plan) and stage it on the board in their site for people to see and let people know what the engineers are planning to build. You don't need to tell people your dream if you have the clear picture in place. People will perceive it in your actions. The picture may represent so many things to people depending on your dream.

You may decide to put it in your own word by saying or projecting whatever you wish yourself or your children to become in future. *The saddest and the poorest man in life is the person who doesn't have a dream.* In other words, if you don't have a dream, you are considered poor. It doesn't matter if you have money or you are poor. If you have hope and a dream, there is every possibility that you can gain the success you are dreaming about. *The most frustrating person in the world is the person with a dream but not realizing that he has a dream.* Likewise, if you own all the money on this earth without a dream and hope, you may go bankrupt one day.

WHAT A DREAM IS

A dream is irrespective of your status, age, class (either low or high), social status, education, and any other conditions. A dream is about the future. Abraham still became the father of nations at an old age. Google and Facebook guys are young originators/founders. Your age and your present condition do not prevent you from contributing to your generation. At an age above seventy, you still have a lot to contribute. Even when you are younger than twenty, you can still contribute. Remember David started young while Abraham (seventy-five years) and Moses (eighty years) started late, and they still made their significant difference in their generations. Moses saw a burning bush. David was young when he killed Goliath. Don't say you are too old or young. Even Jesus started at a younger age—thirty. He performed all the wonders and preached words to the world. It is not how far but how well.

Don't say if only you have migrated to an advanced country when you were young or not married, or had I known I would have studied medicine or do other courses. Now I keep hearing people talking about different training and courses, but I am over forty. Forget about that. You can still make your own contribution now. *You don't have any excuse for not contributing your own quota.*

The dirt on the dollars does not make dollar devalued. The dollar note may be dirty, yet it is not devalued by dirt on it. The value was determined at the mint. The dirt in the marketplace cannot devalue the value that was placed on dollars from the mint. Your value was determined by God, so your present situation cannot devalue you. Philemon 1:6 says, "The communication of thy faith may become

29

effectual by the acknowledging of every good thing which is in you in Christ Jesus."

You can still make a unique contribution in life. You may say you are an old man or woman over seventy, but you can train your grandkids, and you can give advice or counsel people. Bishop David Oyedepo was raised by his grandmother; likewise, a grandmother raised President Obama. Most grandmas cannot read, but they have ability to reason and give good advice because what they know about life, we the younger ones don't know. Don't use age as an excuse not to contribute to your generation. Those who had made it in life are those who did something about their dreams. They attempt the impossible, waiting and discovering what God can do. Do something about your own dream today.

Confidence. In pursuing your dream, you must believe in your ability to accomplish the dream. Realizing your dream is about having confidence in yourself concerning whatever you are doing. *There is no profession that is guaranteed from heaven to become successful without human effort and hard work.* Why must you be timid about your own profession and try to mimic other people's career while you can as well do well in the area you have trained and have passion for? If you know how to sing, you don't want to envy the person who is talented in playing keyboard. You should have it at the back of your mind that there is no profession that is better than the other one. For instance, a medical doctor cannot perform the duties of a security man or a janitor in the hospital, while a pilot in an airplane cannot do the job of the people sitting in the control tower or the job of the hostesses.

A basketball or football player cannot do the job of cheerleaders on the field at the same time. As father who is the head of a family, you can't perform the duties of a woman, most especially in the area of childbearing. Your eyes cannot perform the duty of your ear; likewise, your knees cannot do what your hip will do. In other words, toes cannot do what a thumb will do. God created man and placed those parts at different locations to perform different functions. But the most important thing is that they are all working together as a team to achieve a common purpose. Why then, as human beings, we tend to feel inferior or envious of another man's profession?

Divine compensation. It might look funny that working successfully on your dream can look like compensating. Yes, it is! Why? Because when the time of compensation comes, God can use your dream, gifts, or talents to compensate you. *God may not compensate you on what you have but not used.* Using your talents or gift will bring you connections, increase fortunes, and upliftment you don't imagine. You should not forget the story of the talents where the master rewarded those who traded with their funds by adding the portion of the one who failed to trade with his fund to the portions of those who actually used their funds. When the time of accounting comes, *God may open the door for you, but God will not drag you into the door.* When you have the opportunity or you have doors of opportunities open, you must be wise and make positive use of the opportunities. *You should not let opportunity slip in your hand, but you should make use of the opportunity very well.*

You should not behave like Mordechai who misused the opportunity. God compensated Joseph through his talent. Joseph was a mere dreamer; he used his talent (dream interpreter) in the prison. Because people knew him for what he was, when the time of compensation came, he was called to interpret the dream for the king. He could have chosen not to let people know that he could interpret dreams while he was in prison. But as destiny and compensation time would not go unfulfilled, God made way for him in the palace through the dream he interpreted.

Working on your dreams and using your talents and gifts can make things work in your favor through divine compensation at the appointed time by God. In 2 Samuel 6:6–11, there was an error which turned in favor of Obed-Edom. The Ark of God was carried into Obed-Edom. For three months, everybody envied Obed-Edom. *Compensation gets into your past and gets what belongs to you that has been denied from you.* Obed-Edom was a poor man meant to die in poverty. David knew that the Ark was the cause of death for Uzzah because he put his hand into the Ark of God. As a result, David was afraid to keep the Ark, and instead he chose to keep the deadly Ark in the house of poor Obed-Edom. Obed-Edom was already dying in poverty, and David's next line of action was to keep the deadly Ark in Obed-Edom's house. Instead of death, Obed-Edom was blessed with his household.

Not many people will accept keeping such a deadly Ark, but through the gift of obedience that God Installed into the heart of Obed-Edom, he did not reject the Ark that was meant for evil for his family. As a result of Obed-Edom's willingness to accept the Ark, God turned what was meant for evil in favor of Obed-Edom. David did not know what God wanted to do with the Ark in three months. Obed-Edom's status changed, and he became one of the advisers in David's palace. The same thing happened to Mephibosheth in 2 Samuel 9:10. Some people usually want to advice people against helping you in life, while some want to bring confusion that will compound your problems into your door as David did to Obed-Edom. *When it is divine time to help you, the wise men become fools for your sake and will commit an error that will work in your favor.*

God might as well decide to increase your capacity in order for you to face or withstand your adversaries and challenges. God can also do so to showcase himself by telling your oppressors that he is the Lord, and let your testimony show clearly to the world that he is the Lord over all situations. God increased the capacity of Obed-Edom to be able to carry and keep the Ark in his house for three months. As powerful and influential as David was, he did not qualify to carry the Ark, because God did not empower him to. It is not by power or might but by destiny. What are we talking about? *God can use your talent to increase you in all areas where you so much need uplift-ment if you make wise use of your talent.* It is very wrong to leave your talent inactivated. Inactivated talent is like debit or credit card you have on your bank account and name. No matter how much money you have in the account, if your debit card is not activated as directed by the card issuing authority, the card cannot give you access to any cash at the ATM. Neither can you use the card for any business trans-actions. An inactivated bank card is compared to an ordinary plastic. Likewise, any good dream you did not work fervently on will remain just a mere dream. *Any talent or gift you did not use will be eventually withdrawn from you as in the case in the story of the talents.* Where people who used their ten talents judiciously were credited with other talents, the single talent was withdrawn from the servant who failed to use his own talent!

Life gives back to you what you gave. It's not proper for you to go and harvest what you did not sow. Many businesses are not growing because of the little effort business owners put to them. When some businesses open at 6:00 a.m., you open yours at 12:00 p.m. and close by 4:00 p.m., and you keep complaining that your business is not growing. How are you running your business? What are the functional principles you put in place to guide your business? Have you ever read any book on money lately? *Many work so hard. They work eight hours a day, and some do overtime but don't have an idea how to utilize the money.* Many keep saying money doesn't matter but guess what? They work Monday to Friday to seek money. Some even work over the weekend. Despite the labor, sometimes they have nothing to show for the long hard labor because of lack of proper planning or poor financial management.

You need to be serious with whatever you are doing. *Don't be late to work and get out of work early and be expecting promotion.* You cannot be promoted beyond your level of competence and productivity. Life is about give and take. A person cannot be promoted beyond his level of competence. In other words, *life will compensate you based on your contributions.*

Attitude. "Attitude is a little thing that makes a big difference" said Winston Churchill. For you to reach your goals or achieve your dreams in life, good attitude is important. *Whenever competition is tough and things look so close, good attitude is the key needed for you to stand out.* Attitude makes a difference between two marketers who are selling similar products. While those with good attitude make a lot of sales, those with bad attitude to customers may not make good sales. *Your attitude to your helpers of destiny will determine if you will get the actual help needed by you or not.*

A friend of mine was able to secure his dream job through his positive attitude to the job he wanted. There were more than twenty applicants for one job position. After a series of interviews, the applicants were trimmed down to two. The management was left with a tough choice to make in choosing the right candidate out of the two best candidates for the only job opening. The chairman of the company resolved to offer the job to any of the two with the best attitude toward the job. The two candidates were scheduled to come for the final interview the next day. On getting to the company, the management delayed the two candidates till the end of the closing hour without the interview taking place, thinking one of them would be frustrated and leave early, but none of them were frustrated. Another interview date was scheduled for 8: 00 a.m. On the appointed date, the first person to show up at work on the interview date was awarded the job. That is what attitude can do.

"People may hear your words, but they feel your attitude" (John C Maxwell).

"Keep a good attitude and do the right thing even when it's hard. When you do that you are passing the test, and God promises you, your marked moments are on their way" (Joel Osteen).

"Take the attitude of a student; never be too much to learn something new" (Og Mandino).

Fulfilling one's goal in life has to do with individual's attitudes. In life, your attitude can break or make you. For instance, if A B C D E F G H I J K L M N O P Q R S T U V W S Y Z is equal to 1 2 3 4 5 6 7 8 9 10 11 12 13 14 15 16 17 18 19 20 21 22 23 24 25 26, let us try some numerical exercises. Let us examine the following terms and qualities: hard work, knowledge, love, luck, money, leadership, fame, position, and attitude.

Then,

Hard work

8 + 1 + 18 + 4 + 23 + 15 + 18 + 11 = 98 percent

Knowledge

11 + 14 + 15 + 23 + 12 + 5 + 4 + 7 + 5 = 96 percent

Love

12 + 15 + 22 + 5 = 54 percent

Luck

12 + 21 + 3 + 11 = 47 percent

None of them make 100 percent. Then what are the qualities that make 100 percent?

Is it money?

Money

13 + 15 + 14 + 5 + 25 = 72 percent

Leadership?

No!

Leadership

12 + 5 + 1 + 4 + 5 + 18 + 19 + 8 + 9 + 16 = 97 percent

Fame?

No!

Fame

6 + 1 + 13 + 5 = 25 percent

Can *position* make your life 100 percent successful? Absolutely not!

Position

117 percent

Your position will never qualify you to achieve 100 percent success inasmuch as you lack good *attitude*.

There is solution to every problem provided you have a good *attitude*.

Attitude in our table will give 100 percent score!

1 + 20 + 20 + 9 + 20 + 21 + 4 + 5 = 100 percent. It is your *attitude* toward life, work, and things around you that makes your life 100 percent successful. Zig Ziglar said, "Your attitude, not your aptitude, will determine your altitude."

Principle. A principle is a fixed law that is established to guarantee performance of a product. Principles are established in the life of individuals to make life simple. In actual sense, if we can learn the principle that guides our daily activities, we will simplify our lives, and there will be fewer difficulties. *Anybody in life that doesn't know the principle that guides anything will definitely end up in experimenting.*

Everybody on earth has one dream or the order in his/her lifetime. Many are at an old age; they have been dreaming right from their youthful age. But the reason why many dreams are not coming to pass is that many have not even learned to exercise the principles that are designed by the creator for carrying out an individual's dream. What a lot of people don't know is that there is difference between the principle and the fact. *A principle simply is the law that is established to create successful function of a particular promise or action.* In anything that was created on earth, there is always a guided principle that will make it work. But if not clearly followed, it will lead to malfunctions of such a product or system. Every manufacturer of every product manufactured his/her products guided by established procedure. It is an established procedure that you cannot browse on your computers or any other electronic gadgets without being connected into the Internet, because that is the format. Without the Internet, you can't do much of surfing on your gadget. Likewise, for a ship or boat to work perfectly fine, it has to be operated on water and not on the ground like a car or in the air like an airplane. That is the principle that was associated with the ship right from the manufacturer.

Your wristwatch was designed to be placed on your wrist for effective functioning. *Success in life is based on the obedience to principles.* Parents don't expect your kids to be successful without following the guided principle which says, "Teach your child the way he should go when he grows up. He will not depart from it." The spouse should not expect the marriage to work out without following the marriage principle that says you should respect each other.

Success in marriage, profession, business, and career is not a matter of being lucky or fortunate but is in following the established principles of success. *Success and effective or sufficient performance in life is literarily a result of keeping to principles.*

Lack of principles in life leads to trial and error. Because the pilots know the principle that guide the effective functioning of an airplane, they don't operate an airplane on highway but in the air; likewise cars were not operated on the sea. *Human beings tend to depend on other people in getting things done most of the time because they don't know the principle that guide what they want to do.* If you understand the principle, you will definitely go for it. Principles made it possible for birds to migrate from one region to the other as the climate changes every year without any navigators or instructors.

In order for you to achieve what you are supposed to do in life, you have to know the principle by which you are born to function. The good thing about principle is that if you obey the principles that guide something, you can definitely predict the outcome.

One of the reasons why we have problems in life is because we keep using other people's words, which may backfire. You cannot be doing wrong things and keep putting the wrong things in your life and be expecting excellent results. You can't plant a seed and wet it with hot water and expect good yield. I believe we can all predict the outcome of an event or our action most of the time when we know the circumstances and conditions under which the event or action took place. Myles Monroe once said that *"prophecy is meant for people who refuse to listen either to God or to the secular instructions."* You don't need anybody to prophesy to you that you will remain in poverty if you don't work. Likewise, a student did not need anybody to prophesy that he or she will fail if he or she did not prepare for his examination.

Furthermore, you don't require any counselor to tell you that you are most likely to die of cancer or lung diseases if you are a reckless chain-smoker. A womanizer should know in his mind that STDs are not far from him and that he may likely die earlier than he should be due to women-related problems. If you obey the principle that guides whatever actions you want to take, the result will be surely fine. By and large, people are said to fail in life simply because they don't obey the God principles that are in holy books, the Bible and Quran. The Ten Commandments in the Bible are not there for fun. You either obey them and live longer or disobey and face the consequences. The choices are ours.

When we read books, we need not to be too concerned about the facts in the books but the principles that were used in the books. Why? Because the facts can change anytime, but the principles can't change. *A fact is just a description of a present state of things, action, or event. While a principle is an everlasting truth which is said to be fixed.* Principles, in most cases, remain constant and do not change, but the facts may vary and be subjected to changes based on the trend of events or circumstances. *Fact is temporal, while principle is constant. We are not created to live by the fact but by the principle.* That is why the law of gravity doesn't care where you are. It works all over because it is the principle and the truth. One thing about principle is that a *principle is not a respecter of any opinion.* No matter how prayerful or non-prayerful you are, if you put a stone on water, it will surely sink. Any object we throw up must finally come down. It is a law of nature, period. You need to respect principle lest it will destroy you. If you really obey the principle of God, and those that guide our daily activities, we don't have to worry much about our lives. Not touching a live electric wire without an insulator or with wet materials to avoid being electrocuted is a principle that is constant and cannot change all over the world. If you touch a live wire anywhere in the world, the result will be the same.

An airplane that was flying was able to maintain its position up due to the principle and law of aerodynamics. The aerodynamics law was possible simply because of the principle of jet fuel that was in the airplane. This makes the airplane act contrary to the principle and law of gravity. Guess what! As soon as there is no gas in the airplane, the aerodynamics principles will stop working, and the force of gravity principles will definitely set in, and the airplane will surely come down. When you lock into a principle, nothing can stop you from achieving the goal. When you lock into the principle of God, success is inevitable. If you understand fully the principle of God and lock into it, success is a sure bet for you regardless of any resistance.

Being a born-again Christian or believer does not make you a success in life. What will make you a success is your respect for the principles that guide success. *If you don't understand the principles that guide success, you will collapse under pressure.* That is why we see many unbelievers who understand the principles of what they are doing in life progressing and successful all the time. Many don't go to church or mosques, yet they prosper and lend money and materials to the believers. The simple reason is that they know what to do and are familiar with the principles that guide success. *You need to get familiar with the principles that guide success for you to be successful.*

Persistence. In order to be successful and to fulfill dreams in life, you need to be persistent in every good thing you are doing. *Persistence is a consistent insistence that you must have and maintain in pursuing the good things you are going after.* You are said to be persistent when you refuse to listen to the noise in the market and concentrate on your bargaining in the market! You refuse to give up to whatever obstacles that come across your way in pursuing your goals. When you refuse to give in to anybody that can abort your goals, you are persistent. A person who is persistent must stand against every opposition and discouragement. Not that opposition will not come; you will see them as a temporary detour. They are not permanent. *One thing about a person that is persistent is that he will irritate opposition due to his persistency.* He will keep doing what he knows how to do without looking back. It doesn't matter the level of oppositions; he will forge ahead.

You need to be steadfast and be persistent in doing what you know your dream is. Whatever you are born to do will not come to you cheap even though it is easy, not until you stand up boldly for your right to get it. *Freedom in America did not come cheap until human right activists like Martin Luther King and others stood up for the people's right.* You can't be a master of your dream without proper and consistent practice. I once heard Dr. Myles Monroe said, "Whatever you are born to do is behind the locked door. For you to get the locked door open, you have to be irritated." To be irritated does not mean you have to be stinking. But you have to keep knocking and banging the door until the person who is in charge of the locked door is not comfortable with you and your action and therefore give you what you want from him.

In order to achieve irritation, persistency must be at work. Why must you settle for less in life? Please note the fact that your business was not successful last year does not mean it cannot be successful this year. If your business is not successful in one country, state, or continent due to bad economic policies, you should endeavor to take it to another country, state, or continent. *Who tells you that you can only succeed in one particular location?* If you have a dream or desire to start up a business but money is your problem because banks refused to give you loan, don't worry! Try to work on your credit and look for viable collaterals and go back to the banks and request for another loan. Your persistence and confidence will surely secure you the capital needed to start up your business. *Because you failed once does not mean you will continue to fail.*

You should not stop because resistance comes against you. That is why God said, "Knock. It shall be open to you." God does not tell us to turn back by the door (obstacles), but he said we should knock and wait there for the door to open. *Majority of our women will agree with me that many of them marry their husbands because of the man's persistence.* Persistency in most cases has to do with prayer. One of the purposes of prayer in relation to your dream is that prayer will keep you closer to the author of the dream. Likewise, prayer will always revive you when you are so tired and getting beaten by the challenges of life. In order to fulfill one's dream, it is essential to stay closer to God in prayer and supplications, most especially when the things of life challenge you. By the time you finish seeking the face of God, all the challenges will bow to you!

Persistence has to do with your perception. Perception has to do with the ways you see things. *Whatever you cannot perceive, you cannot receive it.* You should not let people change your perception about the ways you see things. *If people can change your perception about yourself, they will succeed in changing your future.* If you agree with the people's opinion that you are useless or nothing good can come out of you, eventually you may not make it in life because everything you lay your hand upon will look like a mess. Don't let people confuse you about who you are and what you are capable of doing. Let your mental faculty be at work all the time. Don't let anybody take your dream out of you. *If you can perceive your dream, you will eventually realize it one day.* Let your dream be big. You may start small but with a goal for a bigger future enterprise. Have it in mind to have a mega business that more than three generations will benefit from. *Let your dream be that you want to put an end to poverty in your generation.* See yourself walking as a success and not as a failure. Reject the perception of man about you. Perceive that you are not poor but blessed. See that you are not down but up, not a tail but a head. *As a man thinks, so he is. So be positive about your perception of yourself and things. Be optimist.*

Measure of grace. Why do you want to stand in when God says you should stand out? Consider your calling and know your ministry. Don't be surprised that the next person beside you might be the one to dethrone you if you don't mind your calling or if you don't do what you know well. *Place the right value on your calling and do it well.* How you see your calling will determine how you do it and will affect your product. *What determines your gift is the grace you have.* You don't have to step on to another man's grace. We all have our own measure of grace. *The best you can only be when you want to be like another person is a second best!* Whatever you do in trying to be like the other person will only make you a carbon copy of the other person. People will say he does things like the other man.

Knowledge without practice is useless, while practice without knowledge is dangerous. We should live in integrity. Integrity comes from *integer*, which means "whole." Be whole and not a fraction. *I do pity some people that will rather prefer to do what other people are doing rather than doing what they know how to do best.* Unless you are deceiving yourself, there is nobody who doesn't know his or her areas of weakness and strength. Why then are you trying to copy other people's profession? You need to fulfill your life assignment, lest you die as a poor person who does not fulfill any destiny. *The fulfillment of your potential is based on your assignment. If you are not on your assignment, you can't reach your potential.* There is no way you will succeed on any other person's assignment.

During the last recession, there was a massive layoff in a particular organization/establishment. There was a woman who was not affected simply because she enjoyed smiling at work. When the owner of the company was asked why she was not laid off like other coworkers, the man enthusiastically replied, "She is the only one that makes me happy at work whenever I am down or depressed about situations at work. This woman always smile at me and asked me if everything was okay!" The boss went further to confirm that the woman did the same to others at work. And for this reason, he could not let her go or lose her smiling face. This is a very revealing testimony on the power of keeping a smiling face as much as possible.

A combatant soldier cannot perform well as a Navy Seal, while a Marine officer cannot perform the functions of a Naval officer, and vice versa. There is no way an accountant will succeed in doing the work of an architect unless he does architecture. If you know that you are good in organizing parties, meetings, decorations, and so on without anybody telling you, you should know that the area of event planning is your area of interest. You should not venture into the area of catering just because you see a colleague of yours getting frequent contract for cooking for parties! Doing this, you already know that you will fail because you do not have the skill for cooking.

Physical profiling does not mean success as well. For example, because you are tall does not qualify you to be a professional basketball player just because you see the likes of Hakeem Olajuwon, Michael Jordan, and Kobe Bryant excel in that field. You must, in addition, develop necessary skills of flexible movement fast enough for you to be able to play basketball. Many judged the mode of living of people by the cars people ride, houses they live in, and the materials things people wear. Make no mistake. *The financial capabilities of people cannot be judged accurately by what you can see in the physical.* For this society, many live on credit, which they struggle to pay at the end of each month. One day I saw a lady who drove one of the latest Mercedes Benz jeep who bought five dollars' gas at the gas station. I did not need anybody to tell me that she was riding the car under some sort of hardship and duress.

Another day, I was next to a guy who drove one of the expensive Escalades at the drive-through ATM in one of the banks here in Twins Cities, USA. He left his receipt by the ATM machine. Since I was the next person to him, I was able to see the available balance. Guess how much? The available balance was seven dollars and fifty-five cents! On our way out of the bank, the guy stopped, still on the stop sign. I was forced to honk at him. Perhaps he might have been carried away and thought about the available balance in the account. Can you imagine somebody driving such a car with expensive chromes and tires left with such an amount of money in his bank account? I suspected that the lady with the latest Mercedes Benz who bought five dollars' worth of gas would have loved to buy more if she had the financial capability to do so.

I guess there might have been somebody out there who is using an old 2004 Highlander Truck, not as fanciful as those of the luxurious narrated above but without heavy monthly payments and who can afford to buy gas up to half thank. Ordinarily, he might feel the ones in the latest models is better than him without knowing what they are passing through. That is why it is not good to judge people based on the material things they have. A new car or house, most especially in the Western world, does not mean that one is in a more comfortable position than the other. History shows that. Warren Buffet does not use fanciful cars nor does he live in a mansion, yet he is one of the richest people in our generation.

Another important issue is that of raising a family. Different cultures treat reproduction differently. However, most cultures value reproduction as part of success. Learn how to produce after yourself. You will ultimately reproduce after your own kind before you can become successful. *If you don't like what you see in you, change it and reengineer yourself, but don't try to copy what you see in other person because your purposes in life are different. If you want to be great in life, you will pay a great price.* If you want to grow, you must go for the best. Don't run your business on a part-time basis.

What a Dream Is Not!

A dream is not wishful thinking. A dream is different from a wish because a wish is something that comes and goes. *You can forget a wish you thought about yesterday, but you can't forget your dream.* When you are under pressure, you may have a wish. You are at work and you are frustrated by the nature of the job you are doing. You may wish to start your own job and employ people. When your car broke down on the highway, most especially during winter period or at odd times, you may wish you have job that can make you afford good and road-worthy cars. Furthermore, when you are traveling from one state to the other and you board a bus or train instead of boarding an airplane due to your financial situation and the journey became so boring to you, you may wish to have a good business that can let you afford airfare.

I wonder if you ever board a commercial passenger plane where you were to be seated in the economy carbine, which is not comfortable for you for the fact that you have to bend your legs and endure distractions from other passengers and the offensive odors from the lavatory section while those in business and first class are having a nice time. you might wish to have a good business that can qualify you to be in first class or business section. But as soon as you alighted from the plane and feel a sign of relief, you forgot about the pains, the wish you had when you are under pressure, and the uncomfortable condition in the airplane may quickly fade from your memory.

Have you ever slept in a nice hotel where you wished your house looked like that? Anybody who ever lived in an apartment or condominium where other tenants are smokers and usually smoked by the door or hallway will wish to own his or her family home. *When you are tired of one thing or the other, you may have a wish. That is a wish under certain circumstances, but it is not a dream.* As soon as you get out of that unwanted circumstances, your wish is forgotten. It eluded your mind. You might not think about such wishes until you are under such unwanted circumstances again. But in case of dream, *no matter the condition, you can't forget your dream. You can't deviate from it.*

If you are a manager of a company with a dream to own your own company, no matter how much salary you earn or incentives you get from that job, you will still work on your dream. *Your dream will forever follow you around because it is inbuilt.* In the place where I come from, it is very common for people to buy cars without inbuilt air-conditioners (factory built air-conditioner). To upgrade such a car, you need to install AC with the help of roadside technicians, but the truth of the matter is that such adjustments have problems. While the engine of the car with inbuilt AC from factory run perfectly well, the other one does malfunction, and in most cases, it develops mechanical faults. It can be removed by the car owner without think much about it, while the factory-built AC will work perfectly according to the design. It does not involve a lot of refurbishing or any mechanical adjustment because that was what the AC compartment was wired from the factory to do. The same thing happened to your dreams and wishes.

The talents you need to succeed in life have been wired in you. You therefore don't need much encouragement or motivation to pursue your dream, while much persuasions, motivation, and encouragement are needed to achieve your wishes. You must learn to see ahead. A man who sees ahead will always be ahead.

A dream is not a selfish ambition. A selfish ambition is an ambition to use all the resources available to help yourself alone. A selfish ambition is for you to want buy exotic cars worth thousands of dollars to show off and cruise alone with your wife or children while there are lots of people around you who are very poor that they cannot afford two square meals a day. Of what economic sense does it make for you to buy a house of half a million dollars with just three or four bedrooms while many around you are homeless! That is a selfish ambition. A selfish ambition is for you to send your children abroad to study or send them to expensive schools when you have lots of children around your children or in your communities or village who can't afford to pay tuition fees in public schools, and you close your eyes on them or pretend as if you don't know such things exist.

Do you ever realize that those kids you don't help today when you have the ability to do so can turn around to be a great problem and cause confusion for your children in future even when you are still alive? A good idea or dream is to use your resources to help others in need. Sending generational kids to schools is a dream. Setting up businesses for the needy are investments; established companies in your village is an investment. *Do you ever realize that money alone is not the only mode of investing? Advising people is also an investment.* Do you ever think connecting people with their helpers of destiny is a dream? It is in helping other people that God will lift you up. How helpful are you? God has given us different talents. It is one thing to have a talent and another thing to use the talent. In Acts 8:5–8, Philip shone for the Lord and brought joy to a city. How many individuals, families, or communities have you delivered joy to? If Philip in the

Bible could singlehandedly deliver joy to the city during his lifetime, you have no excuse not be a source of joy to others.

On the other hand, if you considered the aftermath of not trading with the talent given in the parable of the talents, no person with talents or gifts who is in his right mind will like to go through what happened to the unproductive servant in Matthew 25:28–30. Instead of receiving commendation, the unprofitable servant received a rebuke. I pray that God will not rebuke us for not positively using our talents or gifts to profit others. Beside the rebuke, the servant who received one talent lost it to the servant who traded with what his master gave him originally! Do you ever know or think that talented or gifted individuals can lose his or her talents and gifts to others who are ready to trade with it? This is one of the major reasons why you should use whatever talents or gifts that God has given to you in a productive way to glorify God and humanity while you are still alive and not bury all the glory, talents, and gifts in you.

Today, there are many gifted and talented individuals who once have had certain talents or abilities, but because they failed to use these talents well, the power and grace to operate such endowment was withdrawn from them. *Their only achievement is that they can only point to other people they see using the talents they once had.* I pray that will not be the portion of the reader of this book in Jesus's name. *What change or profit has your presence and involvement brought to the life of others?* Can you please, for God's sake and for the sake of humanity, rise up and dust your talent and begin to use it for mankind? Go and establish that petty business, write the books, the magazines, articles which you have proposed to help people to become gainfully employed. Write the book of poems or the book for kids for the benefit of the younger generation.

The major reason why many politicians especially in Africa and in third world countries don't deliver is because of selfish ambition and lack of conscience. When they are in position, they will do all they can to favor their favorites and relatives while those who are not in line with them are on their own. Can somebody tell me why a public office holder should have millions of foreign currencies in foreign bank accounts while unemployment rate in his/her country is high? Many choose to buy houses in a reserve area as soon as they make it. Many send family abroad, forgetting that sending relatives abroad is not the solution to their problems.

Anything you call a dream that does not help other people is selfish. We had a self-ambition from Lucifer in the book of Isiah14:12–15. He wanted to become this and that. Why did he want to do all these things? He never told anybody. Your dream must be the one that will bless other people. One of the good examples of unselfish ambition can be found in the Acts 16:9 where *Paul had a dream, and he helped the people of Macedonia.* In this case, his dream was to help other people. Everybody has one dream or the other inside him/her. What is disturbing you from carrying out your dream? Please, you have no excuse. Wake up and deliver God's sent message to your generation by helping the people out of their predicaments.

Your dream is not about numbers. Your dream might be to help only one person, and that person may go ahead to help others. Your own assignment like Pharaoh's daughter might be to help Moses from drowning by taking care of the baby Moses to prevent his death. Why not go back to your village and look for your own baby Moses by taking some bold steps and pay examination fees for some children whose parents can't afford to pay? Help people in your village who have business ideas but don't have money to execute the business. *Do you ever realize many of the touts, armed robbers, drugs dealers, sex workers and other less privileged children would have made it in life if only they could proceed further beyond high school? But they were unable to go further because nobody was ready to pay their tuition fees!*

To many of us abroad, traveling back to our villages is an abomination simply because we have all our immediate family abroad, or our thinking is that there are some witches or wizards that are waiting to devour us. But the truth of the matter is that was where we grew up. That was where we learned the ability to endure hardship, which kept us going through the entire siege abroad and in the cities, even in our marriages. None of our children even know our origin.

I pray many of you will not end up like a man in our village who was a successful businessman and acquired a lot of wealth in his lifetime, but his children did not know anybody in the village.

47

To those of us who knew this man when he was alive, we saw this man as money. I mean money! But unfortunately for him, he died suddenly. His corpse was brought to the village. Most of his friends were amazed to see that despite his vastly acquired wealth in the cities during his lifetime, he has not completed his house in the village. To make things worse, his children did not know anybody in the village. This man was buried like a stranger in front of his uncompleted bushy building. Ever since that day, I am talking of about twenty years ago, none of his kids ever returned to the village. The house still remains uncompleted and desolate.

If he had thought of his last minutes or six feet, he would have tried and made things right in his lifetime by helping his community with his wealth. You should ask how you can help people. It is not enough to point to someone else and blame him/her for what is wrong. We should accept or take responsibilities. It is not enough to say somebody ought to do something about a situation. You may *recognize that you are the somebody to do it.*

Slothfulness. Your dream is not about slothfulness. *Slothfulness is a certain degree of unwillingness to commit to oneself.* It can also be an individual inability to work on himself or herself, thereby leading to time wastage. Achieving your dream/goals is about not giving room for procrastination or slothfulness at all. You should be inspired and be thirsty to get to the top. You should remember that the Bible says, "A slothful man hideth his hand in his bosom and will not so much as bring to his mouth again" (Prov. 19:24). If you overly become too selective of the opportunities that come your way, or you are wasting time in deciding what to do, you may lose the opportunities with all the consequences of inaction. As a businessman who wants to start a business and employ people to work for you, you must go extra miles than your peers. *You must learn how to wake up at night while others are sleeping and do what others will not have time or thinking of doing.* By the time you are awake during the day, you will teach and mentor those that were sleeping most of the time. You will make your money and fortune through them, and they will worship and adore you. How? Because when they were sleeping, you were awake thinking of how to find solutions to the problems they have in their businesses, health, family issues, and so on. Someone earlier asked one of the millionaires, "What is the shortest way to get rich?" The millionaire's simple answer was "Produce or invent what people need." That was what Apple did to become what it is today!

You must be able to think faster than others; you must strategize a means of connecting with people who know better than you do. You must quickly make a wise use of the connections you have. You don't have to connect with many people but few people who can help you out of your predicament. Connections with helpers of destiny is not about numbers, not how many people you know, or how long you've known them but about how well they know you, how fast, and how smart you turn the connections to your advantage. *You need to ask sensible and constructive questions. You don't make any unbusinesslike jokes when you are with your helpers of destinies or anybody who know better than you do. You don't talk when your helpers are talking. Instead you ask questions.* You will gain much from their conversation. You don't first sit down or sit down in the front row by yourself without being ordered to do so when you are meeting with people who can help you. You must be looking at all problems and challenges as opportunities and be sensitive to your environment and whatever situation you meet yourself. We are told that Chinese see problems as money and investment opportunity, and that is the more reason why they all spread all over the world today.

As a student who either wants first class or the first position, you must be prepared to study far more than your peers. There is no success without hard work. *To graduate from the school of failure or poverty to school of success, you must meet the requirement that can transform you from college of poverty to that of success.* For any core courses you want to register for, you must meet up with the prerequisites. If you are lazy or failed to work hard when you had the time, you must be prepared to get the reward meant for failures. You don't want your life to be like that of those who always referred to olden days as their good days. I have heard some people several times always referring to their heydays as the best days Why? Maybe because they let opportunities slip away from them. *You should aspire to inspire before you expire.*

Many immigrants in America and in the Western world find it difficult to travel back home. Not that they don't want to go, but they did not have anything they can fall back on at home. Why? Because they have been soaked in the Western world's life to the extent that none of their families know their children at home. Many don't even have kids. Some have kids and broken homes because they were not happily married, and their spouses or girlfriends have the custody of their children. Discouragements have set in. Now they are getting old, all they can see is the bad pictures of their past.

An old man in his sixties from Africa once said to my hearing that ever since his parent died, he didn't have anything to do with Africa anymore. All of his kids are married, and they have not, for once, been to Africa. They are not even ready to go because none of them married an African, and their mother was a foreigner too. This elderly man was so confused that the only thing this man knew about Africa was bad news. He knew how many people that were killed by bombs and how many people were kidnapped per month. How much money was wasted by the governments at all levels? He has the video of ghastly motor accidents that happened in African countries. He's up-to-date on the statistic of how many people that are hungry; he can forecast the reason why there are political unrest and ethnic clashes in Africa. He knows the deplorable conditions of the African roads and bridges. He concluded in a conversation with me one day that "anywhere you are that you can have your daily bread is your home," and that he would prefer to die in group or nursing home here in America. These are what he is using as a parameters, reasons, and consolations to back up the reason why he should not go back home. But for those who know him well, they've said that he had missed a lot of opportunities. *He did not make hay when the sun shone.* This man had forgotten that most of his classmates are kings' makers, ministers, past governors, retired CEOs, past and current chairmen and women of companies in Africa!

What is your attitude to your studies, business plan, investment desire, and the dream in you? Are you the type who's always late for meetings and appointments? *Are you used to rescheduled appointments that would have liberated you from being an ordinary man to somebody?*

Do you ever defer what you should have done today to the nearest future? *Do you realize that the so-called future is your next seconds?* You are only making room to fail if you don't wake up. The truth of the matter is, you can't stay on the fence. *If you are not prepared to pass, you will definitely be prepared to fail.* Change your attitude today and not tomorrow.

Slothfulness, laziness, and procrastination are crucial factors which can prevent people from achieving their goals or realizing their dreams. What will be your excuse for not working hard to achieve your dream? Is it your immigration status? When you have ideas that can turn to billions of dollars! Did you realize that as an undocumented individual in a foreign land, if you were able to demonstrate that you can contribute to their economy positively either by using your skills, talents, ideas, or working on your multimillion-dollar dream, or if you have a certain amount in your bank account, you can be permitted to be a lawful citizen of such country without much *problem?*

If you want to excel, you must be prepared to work hard and be disciplined. In order to overtake obstacles, challenges, and intimidations, you must wake up from your slumber. You can be great for sure! *There is a crowd at the bottom but too few at the top.* There is plenty of room at the top for the best and the disciplined. But the issue is whether procrastination and discouragement will let you work hard and do the right thing at the right time which will qualify you to have a room at the top. Will your level of procrastination earn you a credit rating that will make you worthy of being accommodated on top?

Anybody who wants to mount up like the eagle must be strong and determined for the height. Are you ready to pay the price? You can't get what you don't pay the price for, unless you are a thief or a robber. There is a severe punishment for the two. *The quality and quantity of what you will get will be determined by the price you pay.* You need to identify whatever makes you a slave to laziness and procrastination and eliminate them. For many, discouragement is the root cause of their problems. Discouragement many a times can be the foundation for procrastination. You should stop looking around for people who will comfort you. *The truth of the matter is, there is no time discourage-*

ment will cease to happen, but what you need is for you to manage it as a necessary evil in your determination to advance.

The faith you have in achieving victory in your challenges should be enough to keep you going during the siege of life without waiting for peoples' sympathies. There is nobody on earth who doesn't have something to thank God for despite all the challenges. It is a gift and grace of God for us to even know our state of being. Many have their reasoning faculties without being useful to them. Many are in pains but can't feel the pain. For you to feel pains in your body and to know that you are cold or hot is even enough for you to thank God. Do you want to tell me that you don't have one or two people you know in the past two years that had died? You are alive in your house, not in jail or on a hospital bed. Still you complain when people on hospital beds and in jail are thanking God because they believe that when there is life, there is hope.

Pastor Adeboye of the Redeem Church recorded in his book *Open Heaven* that in 1975, he went to Kirikiri Prisons (Lagos, Nigeria) with an elder to minister to the inmates when he saw a young man playing the organ and dancing with so much joy that Daddy Adeboye could not ignore him. He asked if the man was about to be released. It was revealed the man bagged a life sentence for slapping a friend to death. Initially, he was sentenced to death, but after an appeal, his death sentence was reduced to life imprisonment, hence the causes of his joy. Since he met the Lord, he believed there was still hope for him. The man was not discouraged despite his ordeals, challenges, and barriers.

Discouragement is a terrible thing. Apart from beclouding one's vision, it drains one's strength. *When you are discouraged, there will be no energy to do good things you had earlier set out to achieve.* Many of us are battling with different levels of discouragement which can slow down our morale, desire, and ability to accomplish our mission or which can lead to inability to achieve our dreams. Christians and Muslims are equally affected.

Discouragement is a spirit. It is scientific in its attacking people. It is capable of providing you with facts, figures, faces, photographs, and other physical evidences to buttress why you should give up hope and the reasons why you must not be successful or make it in life. To counter this spirit, we should not operate by sight, fear, or by copying. *Anyone who operates by sight, fear, or copy will be an easy prey to the spirit of discouragement.* A discouraged man will always look down. If you are looking down, you can't look up at the same time. If you can't look up, you can't look unto Jesus. In other words, if you are discouraged at all, it is evidence that you have taken your eyes off Jesus, the author and the finisher of your faith (Heb. 12:2).

Remember that *what you have that you don't value, or what you are getting discouraged about is what some people are praying and working day and night to have.* The position you are today that you are still moody about is a dream for some. The husband or wife you have that you don't appreciate is what some are ready to accommodate outside. The types of job you have today that you are complaining about instead of working not only hard but smart and seize whatever opportunity you can tap and move on to establish your own business is what some people are posting résumés for and waiting for somebody to call them for interview. Having a green card in America is an asset, but many don't realize or appreciate it as an opener to wider and greater opportunities for success.

You may not understand what I am talking about since you live in the United State of America or in the developed world. People outside America or in the third world countries who spent their fortune in processing American visas will appreciate it better. Having an American blue passport which gives you the right to fly around the globe without visa and with exceptions in some countries is an asset for business, but many don't realize that. Many have not even traveled out of America or out of developed countries where they lived for the past ten years because they don't realize the grace they carry. All they keep complaining about is high taxes, bad weather, and giving unprofitable excuses for their inactivities.

You need to ask businessmen and women from the third world countries who are looking for visas to do business. *What we don't appreciate will depreciate.* Discouragement will not let you see what you value. Common language of discouragement is depreciation. Why? Because when you are discouraged, you don't see value in whatever you have or situation around you. That is why you keep complaining. The calamity that befell you is not just about you but about your destiny. The devil and the dream killers around you want to use your circumstance as a ladder to derail you from your right part to fulfilling your God-given destiny. The devil has nothing to do with your green card. A green card is merely plastic. After citizenship, your green card will be useless. Your inability to secure your green card is not about the card itself and not about physical you, but it is about your destiny and your spirit man. What controls the physical is within. The devil knows if you have a green card, your status will change. You may go to places and your destiny will shine. The devil doesn't have anything to do with your bareness. Not having children doesn't make any meaning to the devil. *What the devil wants to gain is your ability to get discouraged.* When you get discouraged, other negative things will fall in place to scatter the good plans you have and make you unstable and lose focus.

Discouragement usually leads to procrastination. When you are discouraged, you will keep on postponing what you ought to do right now till other time. That is why you can't, up till now, start working on the business dreams you have ever since. Many through discouragement fail to pray but keep flipping channels at night, hoping to relax a little bit and pray later but to discover that you just sleep all over the night and wake up in the morning. *Discouragement can blind your eyes of understanding. It can also prevent you from seeing clearly. You cannot hang on to your bad manners, mistakes, or misdeeds of yesterday if you must enjoy tomorrow.*

Intimidation. Intimidation is intentional behavior that "would cause a person of ordinary sensibilities" to fear *injury* or *harm*. In other words, *an intimidated person has a tendency to die before death comes closer to him. Likewise, he must have made up his mind that he will fail before failure comes.* You need to know that you are a special and peculiar person. It is important you know that you are an important creation of God. You need not to believe in what the secular world, parent, or anybody is telling you that you are common. *You are not common because your fingerprint is different from others.* To achieve your dream, you don't have to be intimidated by any circumstances or situation. *In order to succeed in life, your desire for success should be greater than fear or failure.*

During the life of John the Baptist, the Bible says that people came to ask him different questions about his identity. They asked, "Are you Elisha? Are you one of the prophets? Are you the Messiah that is coming?" They kept guessing who he was. He kept saying *no* to all their questions about his identity! Eventually, John the Baptist then answered and said, "I am the voice of one crying in the wilderness." Because *he was the one that was giving the assignment to point to the messiah. The Lamb of God that takes away the sin of the world which no other person can do.* Elisha and Moses could not have pointed to the Messiah. His own assignment was in John 1:29, which was to point to the lamb of God. The next day, John saw Jesus coming unto him and said, "Behold the Lamb of God who takes away the sin of the world."

Don't look at your personal account, immigration, or marital status and any other challenges like foreclosure, divorce, or what you are going through now or in the past. And don't let that discourage you or tell you that you are not qualified to pursue your dream. You need to forget about your past and move on. Anything you lost in the past is considered not yours, because if it was yours, God would not let you lose it. You can't lose whatever truly belongs to you. Close your eyes to other people's profession and face your own profession. We can't all be lawyers, doctors, or IT guys. Don't be intimidated because you see somebody doing well in one profession while you are struggling in your own area of chosen career. *We are all wired to do well and be successful in different fields and careers in life. Your duty is to discover your area of strength and follow it up.* I know a brother. He was an illegal immigrant in our church for over fifteen years but has companies which even donated a van to the church. Not many people were aware of his immigrant status until the pastor shared the testimony of how the brother was incarcerated by the immigration officials and how his green card was finally approved. Despite his illegal immigrant's status, the guy worked hard that he was able to donate a van to his church. In contrast, there are many American or British citizens who remain mediocre despite all the opportunities surrounding them because they cannot see beyond their noses. What they think of is bad governance and uncomfortable weather conditions. They can't see beyond their noses. Such behavior needs to stop if you really need to achieve your dream.

A dream is not about well-wishers. You don't need anybody to cheer you up before you can pursue your dreams if you are determined. There is a story of a young mosquito who went out flying for the first time in its life. The father asked him, "How does it feel?"

The mosquito replied, "It was great! Everyone was clapping for me."

The father replied, "They weren't clapping for you. They wanted to kill you!" *The more they clapped, the more the risk of your death.* The inexperienced young mosquito was perplexed. The lesson here is that *not all the people who celebrate you are well-wishers.* So you need to be careful and not let the human praises act as distraction for you in the course of pursuing your dream. *You should not expect that everybody will support you when you are pursuing your dream.* At any point in time when it seems that everybody is singing you praises and everything seems to be working for you, you should watch out and reexamine yourself.

People will not be attracted to you unless they have something to gain from you or they want to harm you! That is human nature. Many times, disappointed or unsuccessful people move together rather than to their successful fellows. This is because birds of the same feather flock together. As is said, iron sharpened iron. The unsuccessful people may read about the achievers and their investments and may become critical of the success instead of recognizing effort pointed into the success. *The more your opposition, the more likely you are doing well more than your critics. The more people are singing your praises, the earlier you should know that you have not yet arrived.* As soon as you cross the poverty line, the game will change. Because they know you are no more in poverty circle. The level has changed. *Your success will always act as a repellant to the poor.* Rich men will never be attracted to the poor. The rich man's success is a poor man's headache, most especially those that are allergic to success and have the mentality that anybody who is rich gets rich in a dubious way. The unsuccessful person become sadistic and forgets to appreciate the sacrifices which the successful ones must have made before the present success. Unsuccessful people look at successful men as those on top that they cannot mingle with. They believe the ladder to success is what can only be climbed by specific set of people. *Some well-wishers in some cases might be crowd in your life.* Because their noise is enough to cause distraction for you in moving to your next level of success.

A dream is not about religion. Achieving success in life is not about your religion's background. Regardless of your religion, what will make you successful in life has been inbuilt into your life right from creation. It is so amazing today that some people are so reluctant to do business with people out of their religion's belief. If you are in that position, it is high time you change. Failure to change may compound your lack and poverty. Do not listen to people who are trying to convince you that you could have made it if you have been a member of one congregation or the other. Joining a congregation or the other in my own opinion does not determine how far you will go in business. Why? Because God has put in us all we are destined to be.

Attending one particular congregation or the other cannot change the purpose of God for your life. Don't get me wrong. *Your location at times may determine your allocation.* But at the same time, what would be would be, regardless of any congregation you belong to. Don't be myopic by sitting down in a place under the pretense or belief that your future will be bright under a particular pastor or imam when you ought to have moved on to a viable location where you can better improve yourself for success. God is omnipresent. Unless you hear from God or from a viable man of God that your present location is the right place for you to achieve your dream, don't shortchange yourself by listening to other people who do not know the purpose of God for your life. Being an active member of a particular congregation or being committed to serve in a particular congregation is a different ballgame from achieving your dream and fulfilling the purpose of God for your life. Be wise and be truthful enough to yourself by identifying what exactly is good for you.

A dream is irrespective of place of birth. Examples have shown that success can be archived irrespective of the place of our birth. For example, Nelson Mandela, the late president of South Africa, was born in a village called Mvezo and grew up in a small village next to Mvezo called Qunu in the Eastern Cape Province in South Africa. Population census of 2001 estimated the whole population of Qunu to be 213 people from fifty-six households, comprised of 122 females and 91 Males.

Another example is Bill Clinton, who was born in a small town of Hope, Arkansas. As of the *census* of 2000, there were 10,616 people; 3,961 households; and 2,638 families residing in the city. In year 2012, the town has a population of 17,264.

Barack Obama was born in Honolulu, Hawaii. As of 2013, the population of Honolulu was estimated by Census Bureau to be 983,429. The lesson here is that even though these great men were born in villages or in remote areas, they are successful individuals. We should therefore not allow anybody or circumstances of our birth limit our effort to be successful. Success is not limited to only those born in the cities. You have no excuse not to be successful as a village person. *You should aspire to inspire before you expire.*

HOW DO YOU KNOW
YOUR DREAM?

Dream is what is seated deep in you. It is what you always think about. Either you are sleeping or walking or at any age, it doesn't leave you alone. You are frustrated because you are not pursuing your dream. It is only the right steps that will give you expected results, not just any steps. Nobody needs to beg or persuade you before you can pursue your dream if you are serious about it. Michael Jackson was successful in singing because he pursued his dream with a great determination. It is the same with the popular professional basketball or soccer players who put everything into what they have chosen to do as their career.

Tiger Woods, the popular golfer, does not need any encouragement to play golf once he has chosen golf as his passion. You don't struggle doing what you are wired to do. *When you see people struggling in one profession, skills, or the other, it means that is not what they were wired to do.* When some people who claimed to be men of God hold microphones, you know they are not meant to be a pastor. The functions of heads is different from that of hands. *You will not be successful by doing what you are not made to do.* If some who are supposed to be hairdressers go on to sing because they see others successful in singing, they are likely to fail.

Some people may be in different professions or jobs today not because they like to be in there but because they see others prospering in such professions. If care is not taken, such individuals may end up not enjoying their second-choice profession. The lesson here is that parents should not force their children to study a particular profession simply because the profession has some money incentives or because you see some other kids prospering in that field. It is not proper for you as a parent to impose any career or profession on your children unless they have passion for such career and the thought for that career is deep-seated in them.

Anything that makes you joyful can also be your area of assignment. As a parent, you need to have a dream of what your children should become and know what your assignments are in making them achieve it. That is one of your biggest assignments in life.

A dream is what invokes very strong emotion in us. Our passion will always be in line with our gift. If you have no strong passion about your gift, you might be doing something else. Some people may very passionate about something before, but with time they may change and do something else. That something may lead to frustration. *You will always need external motivation to do something which you may not have passion for.* Lack of passion for what we do has been identified as a critical factor for frustration. For example, if the foundational background before coming to America or any other Western world is either in the business line or in engineering. But on getting to America or other destinations, we change direction to nursing or car selling business without knowing much about cars. One may run into difficulties including operating at great loss. On the other hand, if you are in an area of your calling, you will be internally motivated and pursue your dream with commitment and determination. This is adequately summarized by Steve Jobs (2011). *"The only way to do a great job is to love what you do. If you haven't found it yet, keep looking. Don't settle. As with all matters of the heart, you'll know when you find it."*

As a lady, you need to have your dream before you find your husband. Love is blind, but marriage will open your eyes. If you find a husband before your dream, the husband may kill the dream. It is wrong to think that because you are a woman, you must not have a dream. Your dream cannot prevent you from getting the right husband at various levels. If you are an illiterate, apprentice, a student, etc., you will find your mate. No matter what level you are, you will always see somebody at your level to marry. That is why many people in high positions still get husbands. Great women like Hillary Clinton, Margaret Thatcher, and very many notable women are happily married despite their accomplishments.

You'll meet the right man during the course of pursuing your dream. *Any man you meet outside your dream is not the right man.* God will never give you a dream you cannot handle. Your real husband cannot be intimidated by your dream. The husband should let the wife dream. God gave grace to both men and women to carry out divine assignments. God's grace is a divine resource given to man to fulfill divine assignment or divine mandate. The assignment that God placed in our hand has nothing to do with gender. *Your gender does not really determine your assignment.* Every human being made by God is in his image, either male or female. God rested on the seventh day so that his creations could continue the job. There is no male or female who is a subset of God's image. That is, we are created equally. *God had not left the assignment for male alone to do, but he committed the assignment to both male and female to do. Why then are some men feeling intimidated and insecure when they see some women carrying out some strategic duties?* Why are some husbands not happy when they see their wives progressing? Some become uncomfortable with the progress of their wives. That shouldn't be so.

On the other hand, *some women, for cultural reasons, have been reported to leave certain duties for their husbands to do even when they know that they can perform better in certain areas than their husband.* The question of gender, intimidation, inferiority complex, or respect is different from the real ability to do a job well. Women should not leave some sensitive matters for their husbands or other men when they know that the men don't have better ideas than the women! Don't get me wrong. I don't mean that women should not give due respect to their husbands, but I am emphasizing the need to get the job done by whoever has the better ability or knowledge. We are not competing. *Anybody that is complete in Christ does not compete.* Nobody should have dominion more than others. A pilot does not have dominion over the plane he or she is flying, but the computer does. Because in most cases, when the airplane computer shuts down, many pilots are confused about what they are supposed to do. That is one of the major causes of plane crashes. Having dominion does not mean you have power over all but only on your own section. *Your dominion is exercised over your own assignment.* The car transmission can't do the work of a car engine, while the brake pedal cannot do what a radiator in the car will do, and vice versa.

Your assignment started right from the womb, and it is irrespective of your gender. An individual's assignment varies. There are some ways and signs that you can follow to know exactly what are related to your assignments or what your assignments are meant to be. Something you enjoy doing can relate to your assignment. *Something you have passion for could also be what your assignment is supposed to be.* If there is any particular problem that you love to solve, it can be the area of your assignment.

If one is fired from a particular job, it does not mean you are done. It might mark the beginning of a new era in your life. *Bill Gates had to quit his job before his Microsoft ideas became established.* Leaving a particular job is not a dead end. It may be the genesis that will lead to your dream. *Don't think that only leaders and your boss have dreams. I wonder how you can be following a leader without asking the direction he or she is leading you.* Never assume that your leaders can be right all the time. Leaders are not God. Never in your life should you think that your present situation can predict your future. Things can change for the better with determination on your part. Some people have moved from poverty to prosperity through hard work and use of available opportunities, whereas some with the minimal success remained at that level because they felt satisfied.

A dream is not what you are looking for outside you. It is not about guessing. *A dream is an inbuilt attitude in you.* You can't be silent about your dream. If you are too quiet or slow in taking action concerning your life, it is either you don't have a dream or you don't take your dream seriously. You either have a dream or not have a dream at all. *You don't look at your surroundings for dreams. Dreams are very powerful that they can't be left unnoticed.* A good dream must be the one that can help other people. Think about the rich man in the Bible at whose gate Lazarus sat. We all know the consequences of his inability to use his talent to help the needy. How many people benefited from your riches? How many school fees are you paying? How many people are you feeding? How many homeless people are you clothing and providing shelter for? How many orphans have you sent to school? How many people have you put food on their table? How many foundations have you founded or funded? You have to be practical and be physical with your dream and talent.

KEYS TO ACHIEVING YOUR DREAM

*U*nderstanding the power of examples. If you don't understand how to follow an example, it might be difficult for you to achieve your dream. Philippians 3:17 testifies to this fact. Another example was Elisha, who followed Elijah into the sea and copied him on how to part the sea. Elisha was able to part the sea with the rod by following the example of Elijah. There is nothing you are doing or about to do that somebody has not done before you. *It will not be that easy to see the likes of Steve Jobs and Bill Gates in our generation.*

Read and find out the story of people who are successful in what you are about to do and build on it. As a mother, you can raise powerful kids. You will make many people to be poor in life if you fail to fulfill your destiny. You are destined to be an industrialist who is supposed to employ others who will sit on your management board. But you refused to work on it. Imagine if Steve Jobs did not invent Apple. You can imagine how many Apple stores there are worldwide and how many people are employed through Apple products. Many are Apple distributors, retailers, technicians, and managers in various stores. What about online transactions about Apple products both at Amazon, eBay, etc.? Do you ever think about it? That the guy who invented Microsoft found jobs for millions of people through his invention?

We have a lot of churches and organizations which you belong to, spending money on hospitality, car rentals, consulting, etc. during programs. Why can't somebody start those businesses? You can be a consultant in any field. All you need to do is to package yourself and look at the way others do their things. Usually, a consultant in most cases just need a pencil and papers to draft. To make presentations, you can start by first cutting and pasting your points. After six months, you will master it and do it in your own ways. You can do this because it is your calling.

The important thing about a dream is that the *devil is afraid of the dream.* In Genesis 37:19–20 in the Bible, it tells us that the brothers of Joseph conspired to kill him. They told each other that the "dreamer is coming." *People will fear you if you have a dream.* You will be the talk of the town. Pursue your dream and don't let anybody stop you from your dream. Martin Luther King says, "I have a dream." His dream terrorized oppositions. Till today, his legacy lives on. His dream makes him a hero in our generation.

Don't let your dream die in you unfulfilled. You should not let your dream be buried in the grave. Anytime I pass through a graveyard, I began to feel sorry for as many people that were buried in the graveyard, most especially those who died young or the elderly that died in poverty and lived unfulfilled lives. Why? Because they ended up depositing their unused talents in graves.

The graveyard is the richest spot for ideas and talents on earth, simply because there are lots of unfulfilled dreams, talents, and gifts buried in the grave. Lots of magazines are unwritten, lots of poetry and elementary school books unwritten, lots of inventions unfulfilled, and lot of industrialist died as employees because they didn't even think of establishing a single company in their lifetime. Lots of potential lenders died and were buried there as borrowers. As a matter of fact, many were buried with their credit cards, student loans, mortgages, car loans, child-support, and internal revenue debts despite the fact that they were destined to be CEOs of generational banks.

A lot of counsellors and advisers died as single parents with broken homes. Lots of mentors died as touts. Lots of generational politicians died as beggars, while many motivational speakers died frustrated. Their dreams were buried with them unfulfilled. In other words, they died filled up! Why? Because they did not empty the dreams and the gifts in them before they died. *It is a good thing for a human being to die empty by fulfilling his or her promises and destiny as ordained/written by God.*

Avoid putting money first. Many place cost on their dreams. So as soon as they hear about dreams, they think about money. How much will it cost, and how am I going to raise the money? But money must not prevent you from having or fulfilling your dream. What about the Google and Facebook guys? Money is never an obstacle if you have the right dream. You don't need money to dream. What is required is to have an idea and start setting the time for achieving the set dream.

The only contribution that a mediocre man will always add to an achiever is criticism. Criticism of your dream will surely come from people around you. Do everything to ignore criticisms but not the critics. Remember that not all criticisms are bad; some are productive. Moreover, some critics may be doing you good in disguise. We just need to be careful, because in life, *there is every purpose for every person you meet. Good people will give you happiness, bad people will teach you lessons, and the best people will leave you with memories.* Many a times, God doesn't bring the people we want but the people we need. Some people are there to test you. Some will teach you, and some will bring the best out of you. It is your duty to trust in God and appreciate everyone he brings into your life.

You may fail once or even twice, but that does not make you a failure. *Not trying at all or not trying again after a failure makes you a failure.* After all, it was said that the guy who invented the round ball (Charles Goodyear) failed many times before he finally made the ball. Somebody who started an exam and failed is far better than somebody who failed to try at all. If you fail in one business, try another one. There is nothing bad in trying two or more businesses before finally discovering the one that will bring prosperity for you. If one business partner fails you, you should try another person. If your relations, friends, or business partners failed you in one business, endeavor to try again and go through another route. There is no sin or crime in trying several ways to find success.

In the Bible, we read how Peter tried to walk on the water but began to sink and cried to Christ for help! What about the other disciples? They did not make any attempt! What's their name today? *Don't allow the situation in your bank account today to disallow you from dreaming big.* It is not possible for you to have all the wealth and money in this world. Why? Because there is no way you can afford it. Likewise, *it is absolutely true that you can't afford all you want or need.* But don't be intimidated because of that. To have a vision and ideas is not enough to make you a successful man in life. What makes you a success story is to support your vision and ideas with necessary and appropriate actions.

What you need to have as a plus is for you to *learn how to find and use somebody else's money in supporting your goals and ideas.* Mind you, doing this does not mean you are trying to involve in shady things or play upon other people's intelligence. But the truth is that there are lots of rich people who don't have the genius visions and ideas you have but who may be ready to support you for mutual benefits. You should get out of the mind-set that you are nothing without money and that you cannot dream nor do something because you don't have money once you have achievable goals/dreams. *Work on your good ideas and vision so that money can come.*

Place your vision and ideas on the table. Sponsors will definitely show up. You should stop thinking of ending your career or intending business ideas because you don't have enough money in your bank account or because you don't have a godfather. You should stop laying emphases and putting your hope on celebrities, stars, and people you think can help you because you may get disappointed if they do not share your dream/vision. Have it at the back of your mind that nobody is perfect. It's only God that will forever keep his promise. Ninety-nine percent of the time, human beings stand the chances of disappointing you. *Why then are you so comfortable in placing your dream and vision online by relying on individual's promise of helping you to be somebody?* Although you might be on the lucky side. If that is your story, congratulations. But it is not common. This does not prevent you from having big dreams or being hopeful and ambitious.

You should learn to dream with your eyes open. When you see it, you should aspire to get exposed to it and go ahead to achieve it. Remember that it is not lonely at the top. If you can get to the top, people will surround you. Success has so many relatives and friends.

Avoid laziness. Laziness is one of the most common causes of failure that can prevent you from achieving your dream. Lazy people are people usually with the habits of quitting when they were overtaken by temporary defeat. You must know enough to seek expert counsel before you give up. You must not stop to pursue your dream any day, time, or in any situation because men say no to you. *You must not settle for no from people whom you know will always say no.*

For success to come in any person's life, he or she must be ready to meet with disappointments, temporary defeat, possible frustration, and some failures as challenges without giving up easily. Majority of those who failed in life are those who gave up easily because of temporary failure or frustration resulting in a lifetime of poverty and impoverishment.

You should learn lesson from the ants. Ants never quit. If they're headed somewhere and you try to stop them, they'll look for another way. They'll climb over, they'll climb under, and they'll climb around. They keep looking for another way. They never get intimidated and discouraged. They believe that any roadblock is not a full stop for them. So they don't give up easily. One thing about success is that *the greatest success usually comes one step beyond the point at which defeat overtakes people.* That is why many quit or turn back at the intersection of their breakthrough.

Failure is so dangerous that it takes over people's confidence, encouragement, and desire at the point where success is almost within the reach. No to your dreams, ideas, aspirations, and confidence does not necessarily mean no. It is important to keep on no matter how hard the race, the going, and the challenge may be. Don't give up. Try and try again; it is not enough to say I tried. Search within for strength to try and try again. *Remember, life ends when you stop dreaming. Hope ends when you stop believing.* This is an important lesson to learn before we can succeed in anything we want to achieve.

You need to find time to study and analyze your past failures and defeats in order to see the lessons they taught. Unfortunately, many are so lazy or ignorant that they fail to look to their past for lessons to learn. *A man who has no time to study failure or no knowledge that may lead to success cannot learn the art of converting defeat to stepping-stones for future success and opportunities.* Riches come only to those who work hard consistently and smart. Riches begin with a state of mind, with definite purpose and more hard work. You must take one step, then another. It is not enough to begin. You must, step by step, commit yourself to follow through and make yourself come through.

If you are the type who has the mind-set of laziness, riches might be far from you because achieving your dream might be difficult due to your inability to take up the matter concerning your dream and destiny with seriousness. You should work toward acquiring the state of mind which attracts riches, or else poverty will be forever your flatmate. *If you were once a failure, never give up because the word* failure *can mean "first attempt in learning under real experience." It is another opportunity to make additional effort to succeed using the past experience to your advantage.* END *should mean to you "effort never dies," and* NO *"next opportunities."*

You need to be positive. In everything you are doing in life, you should try as much as possible to avoid being lukewarm. One of the reasons that caused Peter to deny Jesus is lukewarmness. The Bible tells us in Mark 14:66–67 that when Peter got to the place of the high priest, he sat with the servants and warmed himself by the fireplace. At this point, one would wonder what Peter was still doing in that place after he had been confronted not once but twice about the fact that he had been with Jesus. The answer is simply because Peter was enjoying the warmth of the fire in that environment. Beloved, *you should beware of the comfort zones in life because they may be physically comforting but not ideal for your progress and promotion.*

Climbing new heights in your assignment will require new level of diligence. To attain a greater level in life, you must be ready to work hard. I mean real hard work and not mediocre work. You must be ready to take on more volume of work and welcome fresh assignment and avoid being lazy. It is very sad that what is pegging the promotion of some people is what they have already accomplished. I mean past achievements. If you meet them, they will tell you to go and check their records. Ask them, "Is there any present testimony?" The answer will be "No, but in the past, I achieved this or that." It is good to give yourself a pat on the back, but it is better to tell yourself that you have more in your store to show.

While most people were envious of Paul and some were wishing they could do a fraction of what he did, he was saying he had no record of past achievements, as his major concern was what he could further achieve then. *Many people want to move to higher level in life, but they don't have capacity to cope with the assignment needed to get them to higher level.* If you really want to go up, you should be ready to prepare yourself in so many ways. You should be ready to acquire more education, attend more seminars, workshops, and trainings to equip yourself more. You also need to find better ways of doing what you do. How ready are you to go to the next level? You action and decision will tell.

Avoid impossibility. An average or poor man is too familiar with the word *impossible*! He knows the entire thing which cannot be done right and the reason why it can't be done right. He knows all the rules which cannot work. One of the ideas that kills dreams and causes weakness is *a lot of people have the habit of measuring everything and everyone by their own impression and beliefs.* These are the sets of people who have already made up their minds that they want to live in poverty, demotion, failure, and wants. Brian Tracy once said, "Never consider the possibility of failure. As long as you persist, you will be successful."

You should embrace every possibility and believe that nothing is impossible. God is in the business of making champions out of men, and he is already making some people champions. However, *there are some people who may not want to become champions. You may wonder or ask me why. The answer is simply because the cost of becoming a champion is very high.* Because of that, many don't want to dare it. They are not ready to pay the price. To become a champion in any of the sporting activities like boxing, basketball, soccer, American football, and all other sports involves lots of tasks. You will first wake up at 5:00 a.m. and do some road walks. You beat the air while you jog, and you cannot eat certain food when you are preparing for a championship.

Likewise, to become a great person in a corporate world, you need to go to school and pay some vital price. *To become a champion is not an easy thing. To remain a champion is even harder than becoming a champion.* When you become a champion, there are several people who will be seeking to dethrone you. You should take your life seriously. Life is not just about bread and butter. As a divine champion, *after you prosper, your prosperity must not for any reason replace God in your life.*

If you want to be great, you must realize that wealth is not for you to begin to build material things around yourself. If you obey and follow all things with humility, you will always be an overcomer and sing joyfully. People around you will truly know that. You will see an evidence of dreams being fulfilled in you. As a dreamer, you should not be cut up doing the wrong thing. If you really want to impact the world with your ideas and vision, you should be obedient to God. True success requires you to represent the possibility of good things that can happen to you through what you can do with your life and your career. You should not allow impossibilities to be in your record as *other peoples' successes in life represent the possibilities of what you can do in life.*

Seeing lots of people successful in their various careers and businesses are an indication that you also can be successful. Other peoples' successes are the physical examples of millions of songs and records you can produce, the magazines and books you can publish, the types of what you can invent for generational use, the types of designer clothes you can produce, the types of toys and educational games you can manufacture, and the types of architectural drawings and buildings you can build to make millions, even billions. But if you don't believe you can do anything, you are going to become a junkyard, lazy and depressed, troubled, sick, hostile, and selfish person. You may possibly die of poverty.

You should not ever think of becoming a pitiable person for everybody around you to pity you. Don't let people feel sorry for you because you grew up in a dysfunctional house or grew up as an abused or molested child. Stop thinking about all those things that had happened to you in the past which can make you sick psychologically. Avoid something that can cause you to sit down in the pity party and cause you to swim in misery and make yourself dysfunctional in life. Strive hard. It is not enough to want better things. *You must come with concrete ways to make things better.*

You can redeem your glory by getting out of the pity party, get out of your house and your closet, and mix with productive and active individuals. Get out of your antisocial life. *Nobody is going to offer you something good if you are not on their radar.* You will lack connections or signals if your antenna is not spread wide. *You may never pick up any channels if you are not on the part of good radar. Out of sight is out of mind.* You can't be living in a jungle or in remote areas and be expecting to meet with people in the city or in Hollywood. You have to be closer to where things are happening. No one would ever show you the path to success if you are not closer to the person. Nobody will ever know your dream, aspiration, and ability in you if you failed to show it.

Deceits from egoism and pride are the biggest killers of dreams, marriages, careers, and businesses. *Stop boasting about your ideas and dreams in the presence of your friends and people who cannot be of any help to you in any way.* Going to ghetto, your village, or local areas and boasting about your ideas, or the promise some helpers of destinies have for you will not lead you to anywhere. Instead, it will just shatter your dream and make you unfulfilled in life. *You should also stop boasting in the presence of your helpers of destiny.* Instead, listen and learn from whatever advice they have to offer you.

Avoid procrastination. Procrastination, people say, is the thief of time. Procrastination will deprive you from speeding. Without speed, you may not get your miracle. Likewise, it may be harder for you to speedily fulfill your dream. You need to gather speeds to achieve certain things. In Mark 5:26–27, the woman with issues of blood speedily ran and overtook others to speedily touch the garment of our Lord Jesus Christ. You can imagine if the woman with the issue of blood was procrastinating in touching the garment of the Lord Jesus. I can imagine how she would have lost her chance of receiving her healing. What the man beside the pools of Bethsaida lack was speed. What he needed to get healed was getting into the pool. He has been seated beside the pool for a long time, but because of his slow speed, people overtook him to enter the pool. This eventually prolonged the years of his suffering.

Another good example was that the blessing that was supposed to be for Esau was given to Jacob because their mother, Rebecca, helped Jacob to gain speed by asking Jacob to quickly provide the meal needed to get the blessing of their father before Esau came back from the field. Likewise, the Lord slowed down the Egyptians and caused the Israelites to run faster across the Red Sea, only for Red Sea to swallow the pursuing Egyptians. David was quick enough to throw the first stone into Goliath's forehead. David said, "We cannot afford to be slow lest the Absalom will catch up with us."

Never schedule life-changing appointments and reschedule or get there late. Because others are ready to take care of the job, we should not be slow. If you are to submit a proposal, don't use many years to write the proposal. Don't delay. You can't be so childish to think that this opportunity will be forever, or you think the position will be waiting for you alone for life. You need to learn a simple lesson from ants. Ants think winter all summer. *You can't be so naïve as to think that your summer will last forever.* So ants are gathering food for winter in summer. It is important to think ahead and make hay when the sun shines!

Ants also think summer all winter. During the winter, ants remind themselves, "This won't last long. We'll soon be out of here." And on the first warm day, the ants are out. If it turns cold again, they'll dive back down, but then they come out the first warmth without wasting any time. They can't wait to get out. Every second in life counts for ants. Likewise, ants know exactly the measure of what they need in life to succeed.

How much will an ant gather during the summer to prepare for winter? They gathered all they possibly could. The lesson here remains that *we should look ahead, stay positive, and do all we can when we have energy and chance to do it. Harvey Mackay* once said, "Time is free, but it is priceless. You can't own it, but you can use it. You can't keep it, but you can spend it. Once you've lost it, you can never get it back."

Avoid low self-esteem. Don't let anybody tell you how low you are or compare you with anybody when you know that you are wonderfully made by God. And God created you not as a carbon copy but as a unique original. What is happening to a common person cannot happen to you. Whatever you are doing or wherever you are going, you have the mind of specialty in you and behave special and prove to people that you are special without an air.

You may be black or have an accent; it does not matter. *Don't allow your shoulder or head to drop no matter what situation you find yourself.* Because there is something special about you and in you. There is a unique contribution special about you that you need to make. *Please do not feed the fear.* Never be afraid to pick up your broken dreams and move on. If you have made mistakes, there is always another chance for you. You can have a fresh start any moment you choose to.

Going back to the word failure *as in page 50, the essential element for us in failure is not the falling down but the danger of staying down.* If one's dream should fall and break into pieces, one should never be afraid to pick up those pieces and begin again. When you feel like giving up, remember why you held up for so long in the first place. Soon you will have a breakthrough that will upgrade you and silence your mockers. *Create your own happiness and be yourself.* Don't ever give up. Try to cherish your every memory, then follow your bliss. Enjoy the little things and work hard. *Be the change you wish to see in the world by following your heart and be your own kind of beauty.* Be truthful to yourself. Believe in the power of your dream. And remember that if you can't dream, it you can't become it. Believe and you will never get lost. *Do what you love and try new things and avoid being a copycat if you want success.*

You must be a thinking man. It is said that being handsome, sexy, having good clothes, shoes, different hairstyles, and being merely talented cannot make you fulfill your dreams. If you ever think all these attributes without proper thinking will help you get to the promised land, you better forget it because they will not lead you there. *You better be a thinking man or woman who has strategies and ideas.* Think of the best way to do things and to navigate for success. These are all about planning and focusing. Although there are some situations which demand spontaneous actions, in most cases, planning ahead will see you through the situations.

Stop the worry. Worry is a state of uneasiness or anxiety in the mind. Somebody defined *worry* as thinking with one emotion. In most cases, worry does not allow one to see God's mercy around. *Worry also does not allow he who worries to see opportunity around.* Neither does it allow one to see or notice the helpers of destiny. It could also lead to depression and low self-esteem.

The level of worry depends on individuals and situations. *Many worry because of their care of life*, what to eat, drink, or wear. Majority worry over children and care of life. Many times, *worry may push people to go into unreasonable debt to buy worldly materials.* Many worry and fear about the possible challenges that may face them. Many run their daily life activities based on what other people do or say. People worry about what people say or would say about them. What will happen to family members after they must have departed this earth is the worry of many parents.

There are people who worry about their beauty, looks, and even status. Another source of worry is lack of riches. After all, Matthew 6:27 says, "Which of you by worrying can add one cubit to his stature?" *Major solution to anxiety is to cast all burden unto Jesus and put into mind God's assurances.* Remember the Lord's Prayer in Matthew 6:11. Learn to live one day at a time and remember that there is nothing too hard for God to do. *Don't count the minutes; count the life. Remember nothing is worth more than this day.* Life is beautiful, so you should live for today. If God can bring water out of rock, he can definitely solve your problem. Since God can wake up Lazarus after three days, why will your situation be too hard for him? After all, you are still alive. He can easily solve your problems.

Another way to overcome anxiety is to be satisfied with whatever you have. *Don't worry when you cannot understand everything.
The truth of the matter is, you can't know everything, and you cannot
solve everybody's problem.* You should not feel bad if you cannot find
solutions to every problem or you cannot meet everybody's need.
Stop thinking too much. It is all right not to know all the answers
because you are not alpha and omega. Anxiety will not bring solutions to your problems. Be happy and smile because you don't own
all the problems in the world.

Remember that *there is one happiness in life. That is to love and
to be loved.* If recently you've been worrying about joblessness, having
spent too much, and your expenditure is getting more than your
income, you need to put those worries behind you. Why? Because
there are plenty of opportunities that could bring increased income,
possibly a new job, even a new career. A lot of phone calls, e-mails,
or other communications could bring news of these possibilities your
way. All you need is for you to record the one that seem most prom-
ising and follow it up.

You should have in mind that fear incapacitates. The first time
you are confronted with a golden opportunity that will catapult you
into greatness, you may think that your end has finally come. They
may be so big that you may not recognize them because they may
camouflage as problems. Don't be scared but rather rejoice that your
change has come at last. *Remember that after David was anointed king
in his father's house, Goliath showed up to take his crown.*

Henceforth, learn that certain problems that come your way
after a prophetic word from God on your promotion, success, victory, or breakthrough are out to legitimize your blessings and usher
you into a higher level. When people were in doubt about how
young David could ever qualify to be so honored, by the time he
killed Goliath, all their doubts were dissipated. His brothers and
others who were challenging God's decision acknowledged that even
though he was younger, he was outstanding since he could accomplish what they could not.

Are you a child of destiny? If truly you are, you should show it
by not being scared of problems. Welcome problems that come your

way and see the advantage they will fetch you when you are used by God to solve the problems. A child with a dream does not run away from problems. *The greater your challenges, the bigger your joy should be because the end result will definitely bring you greatness.* If you really want to see success and want prosperity to come your way, you must not shy away from problems. You must attempt to start new things and be able to take risks. *Success doesn't come easy in any form. No success will come without examination. No event, no history.*

Why are you hiding from the hot spot in the battlefield? Doubt not God's ability in you. Why are you afraid for your life when you don't have to? A great person sees every mountain as a potential testimony. Arise today and confront all your giants and challenges. You should cause them to be afraid of your God and the destiny that God had wired you to fulfil. The greatest hindrance to reaching your destiny is fear. It is an enemy at the door of opportunity. You should step forward and do more in order for you to receive your victory.

Manage your time. One thing you should know about time is that *everything happens now and not in future.* Many relate to time as if they were standing in the middle of a timeline. Many pretend as if they stand in the present. You look back at the past as if the past is past. We look forward into the future as if it is in the distance, which can be matched into with expectation and hope. *Many relate to the future as if it is a destination to get into.* Many look at it as a city which can be located on a map and get to it through GPS. But the truth of the matter is, the past is gone. You will never have your past back. *Your past is a spent resource.* Why are you still holding on to what is no more available?

One thing we should know about the future is that *the future is an illusion that will never come to pass.* The future will always appear to be now and then. It will also appear as the past. Remember every past moment once occurred as a present moment. *I want you to believe you can't live in the past or the future; all you have to live in is now.* All that you ever had was now. All you are going to have is now. All you are going to achieve is now.

Many a times, most of what human beings do, say, think about, and worry about do not make any meaning. Dr. Joseph Juran, a management consultant, studied what executives did every day. He found out that 20 percent of an executive's activities, thoughts, and conversations produced more than 80 percent of the executive's results. Based on Juran's hypothesis, *only 20 percent of a human's current activities produced 80 percent of human results.* Eighty percent of our time is typically spent generating less than 20 percent of what we got as result. In other words, *80 percent of our time is wasted on thoughts, conversations, and all other activities that do not make much difference or contribute to our progress.* There is an adage which says that time wasted can never be regained. We should endeavor to spend our time on those things that will reasonably benefit our life and that of the people around us.

When it comes to the importance of time in relation to our daily life, it is very important to note that *God gave us the same time, which is twenty-four hours in a day and 365 days in a year.* But the difference in time relative to individuals is how we spent our time, what we spent our time on, and what we achieve during the time frame we have. The same time the CEO of a company spent in the office where he makes his millions of dollars is the same time the cleaner of his age in the same office used per day at work. But their take-home wages are quite different. What makes the difference is that while the CEO was busy developing himself in going to school and attending different academic programs that will better his life, I guess the cleaner was busy channeling his efforts on entire things which did not contribute to the building of his dream.

Circumstances and other issues of life might have prevented the cleaner from developing himself right from onset, but that is not the issue now. The issue is, what are you doing with the little time you have on your side? A lifestyle of a professor of gynecology with a name withheld really energized me on the need to judiciously spend time on profitable ventures that can promote upliftment and move someone to another level rather than forever be a subordinate to the boss. Sharing the story of his life with people in my own opinion will serve as a motivation for many who have dreams but fail to pursue the dreams. It will also serve as an energizer to those who always spot fears at the onset of their breakthrough.

This gynecologist was working with the government. At the same time, he was given another opportunity to work with the United Nations. This opportunity to an average human being will look like a breakthrough. Many would have thought they have arrived for working with United Nations. During this period, he established his own private clinic. He discovered that most of his attention was on the United Nations job rather than that of the government. He was quick to resign the government work. He accepted the United Nations work and continued his private clinical business, which he did as part time. His assignment with the United Nations involved traveling a lot. This served as a big distraction for his private business.

At a point, he realized that he did not have much time for his private practice where he earned more than the United Nations work. He quickly realized the economic reality of the situation, and he resigned from the United Nations job to devote his time to his private practice.

He was so determined to devote all his time for his private business. He said most of his colleagues working with government and other organizations usually reminded him about the benefit of working for government ranging from retirement benefits and some other incentives which may be absent from private practice. He told me that since he knew how much his colleagues working for government set aside as a retirement fund every month, he also opened a fixed bank account to which he put a fixed amount every month for his retirement. What blew me off was what he said—that the retirement benefits and all other incentives needed for his saving monthly provisions were usually paid for by just two to three patients. He made it a tradition that the bills paid by the first two or three patients in a month were being deposited into his own personal fixed retirement account. Aside from that, he set a salary scale for himself per month in the same manner he paid his employees.

After practicing for some years now, with clinics in two countries, he was so convinced that it is far profitable for one to work on his dream rather than working in support of other people's dream under the pretense of paying you salaries and other peanuts incentives. At the end of our conversation, he emphasized critically to me that it is important for people to know how to make wise use of their time. The same time he spent working for the United Nations receiving "peanut" was the same time he was spending at his own business where he was a boss with a lot of freedom.

The most fascinating aspect of his testimony was that he didn't have time to collect some of the salaries he worked for at the later stage of his working for others, simply because he didn't have time to go and fill the paperwork needed to get those salaries and allowances meant for him. He said to me, "My time is so valuable to me now than to go and queue and be signing documents for some thousands of dollars when I can make triple of such money while working in my clinic within that time." The money has been sitting there more than five years now, he said.

What I am saying is that time is precious, and once lost can never be regained. To achieve your dream, you need to be conscious of your time and manage it very well. My question is, What are you doing with your time? Many spend their time gossiping, sleeping, drinking, partying, and some use theirs to promote the dream of others by working for them. *Stop being busy on big things that are not profitable. Use your little time on little things that can add value to your life.*

Longevity. You should have the mind of longevity in all things you are doing. Longevity is the ability to see further ahead. You should think generationally. Plan big on whatever you are doing. Let your plans and projections go beyond now. *True vision must be a long-time vision.* You don't plan a business that will not last you more than five years. Don't get your office in a location that will not attract customers. Make sure that your office is spacious for future expansion. Plan ahead and get a better place.

PREPARE FOR GREATNESS

What is greatness? Greatness means to stand out. To be the dominating one. Greatness may mean largeness in size. It means to be preeminent, imposing, grand, distinguished in importance and remarkable in ability, character, and achievement, and of course in the anointing of God. *It must be understood that every form of greatness begins in a small way. There is no greatness without a fight.* But when the battle for greatness will come, may God give us victory. Zacchaeus was short, but he climbed the tree in other to get a better view of Christ above everybody in the crowd. He did not prepare according to his stature. Even Jesus Christ who does not look up to anybody looked up to see Zacchaeus on the tree! Why? Because Jesus was prepared to bless Zacchaeus. Thank God because Jesus did not take advice from anyone before he blessed anybody. So he asked Zacchaeus to come down, and he went to his house. Even those who were taller in the crowd now looked over to Zacchaeus. Every child of God should be guided by the motto "it is not over until it is over." *Note that it cannot be over until you are fully blessed and truly great.*

Greatness is influence. Greatness as we all know cannot be achieved on the platter of gold. Greatness in life requires some prerequisites. Some but not limited to the prerequisite you need to fulfill in readiness for greatness is an honest identification of personal weakness. *Weaknesses are not an excuse not to be great.* The truth is that one should properly manage personal weakness in order to achieve greatness. For example, you should not allow your weakness to make you lose your focus. *The devil cannot manufacture but can use what is already manufactured against you.* Weakness is part of it. Identify what your strength is. Your strength is in your talent, gift, and ability to follow examples. Whatever you need to become great is already in you.

Availability is part of the way to greatness. Your greatness is in your strength. *Your greatness is not to make strength out of your weakness.* You can only become average in your weakness. You should not put much focus on your weakness but on your strength. By working on your strength, it is possible for you to be at 90 percent. While working on your weakness, you can't get more than 50 percent! *You have to give room for your strength to manifest.* You must be ready to celebrate good things that God puts in your life. You can't be great by pulling yourself down. It is the work of the devil that makes you forget about miracles in the church and focus on things that cannot profit you.

Reposition and reassigning. They are so important. You can't be great if you always want to do what is convenient. By deciding to stay in your comfort zone, you may not be great. You need to move out of your shell or cocoon. You don't sing because you love to sing, but you do it because you are good at it and God gave you the grace to do it. You must be ready for reassigning. *No matter how talented you are, you need to be ready for reassigning and changes.* You must not live a life of assuming anything goes. You must be in order in your entire daily endeavor. As God deserves the best, you, too, must be at your best.

Holy Spirit. Be careful of what you think you know how to do, because if you're not careful, you may not have required anointing to do it. Without anointing, the devil might steal your ideas from you. The Holy Spirit is important. The Holy Spirit can make life easy. *Nothing good like the one who knows the answer to give you answer to your question.* The Holy Spirit can tell you what to do. The Holy Spirit really wants to help us all the time. We need to be ready to allow him to help us. Our helper, which is Holy Spirit, is already in us. But we don't really use it or encourage him to help us. We need the Holy Spirit to become great. If we are going to be great, we should get to the level where the Holy Spirit will be speaking with us. Without our only spirit working in us and with us, it might be difficult to attain greatness.

Faith. You need faith to prepare for greatness if you must fulfill your dream. *Faith allows you to see what is in the other side even when you are not there.* Because other sides are always better than here. Great people are never be satisfied where they are. Some people moved to other side (in the Bible) because they decided in their minds that they preferred to proceed forward and die rather than die where they were staying currently. But they went and prospered. God is the source of greatness. Therefore, to achieve greatness, you need to please God. *It is impossible to please God without faith. Faith is therefore the master key to greatness.* Jesus Christ, Isaac, Joseph, David, and Abraham have an unshakeable faith in God on their way to greatness. God promised us his greatness already, and his promise is yea and Amen. Faith in God gives us the external activator which gives life, power, and action to the impulse of thought. Faith in God is the only known antidote for failure. *Having faith in God contains the seeds of achievement and greatness.* Have faith *and* plug to God's promise. Do not ever quit even if there are delays and discouraging circumstances or physical contradictions. Faith in God will encourage you to sow your seeds no matter the prevailing economic situations.

Patience. Patience is another characteristic of greatness. Patience in this context means waiting on the Lord for his time to become manifested in you. In the Bible, we learned that Joseph waited for thirteen years for the fulfillment of his God-given dream, and Moses waited forty years until it was God's time for him to rescue Israel. Jesus waited thirty years before he fulfilled God's promises as Messiah. God has a reason for his timing. It might take long, but it will surely happen if God has ordained it. *The time of waiting is a time of preparation.* Proper or appropriate *preparation precedes greatness.* You do not become a boxing champion overnight; neither do you become a professional footballer in just one day. No one can become a great man of God in just one day. It takes process. Greatness that comes suddenly or that is gotten by surprise will be lost suddenly or by surprise. If you don't wait for your time patiently, you might become great, but your crash from greatness will equally be great. *Greatness* comes to people who maintain good attitude in the period of waiting. You must have an attitude that with God, all things are possible in addition to honoring God, the giver of all good things.

Recognizing the source of greatness will help you get connected to the source and to tap to the covenant of grace, wisdom, empowerments, humility, and anointing for greatness. God has made every provision in his plan for you to be great. *Your duty is to not write yourself off by choosing greatness.*

Priority. By having too many options at a time, you may not achieve anything great. Instead of having a particular thing done, if you go all over and look for what is not lost, you may achieve nothing. That is why many are not marrying today because they have lots of brothers and sisters they are eyeing without them making a choice. Many have lots of ideas and projects going on in their minds without taking action to choose the one to work on. It is recommended that we should prioritize our ideas and work on them one after the other. Lumping ideas together will not lead us to anywhere great!

Diligent. Greatness in life requires you to be diligent. This will surely set you on the part of greatness. Likewise, you must be courageous to take some important decisions. Bravery in the face of negative circumstances, boldness to confront obstacles that are on your way to greatness, and heroic feats will all lead to greatness. *David's greatness began on the day he confronted and defeated Goliath the giant.* While King Saul and his soldiers saw Goliath as a great problem to face, David saw Goliath as an opportunity not to be missed. Here we see a single problem but two different perspectives.

In the physical, that is how the issues of our life look like. What many count as problems or roadblocks to their progress may fade into manageable challenges if only they can sum up courage boldly to confront the challenges. Life is full of battle. No wrestler or boxer became a champion without fighting severally. *Greatness comes after overcoming challenges.* If you do not fight a war or without war, you can't become a winner. It is also said that "no event, no history." Don't let the fear of what could happen make nothing happen.

Greatness has to do with strategic planning and thinking and good attitude. As stated earlier, we are wired and calibrated for greatness right from the time we were formed. However, it is the inability to understand who we are and what our purpose is in life that often leads to our failure. Greatness requires that individuals should be prudent in behavior. Prudency requires us to be discreet, careful, wise, and circumspect in order to avoid undesired or undesirable consequences.

Greatness eludes so many people in life because they say God is in control and refuse to do things decently and in an orderly manner. *To achieve greatness, we have to be prudent in our finances and in taking financial decisions.* It is also essential for us to be comely in nature. To be comely is to be fine looking, to have some charisma, to speak well in private and public, to have good courage, and to have an attractive personality. People in this category do attract favor easily. *Greatness can be easily linked with favor from God and favor with men.* You need to know how to greatly package yourself in order to receive anointing and favor for greatness.

Sacrifice. Sacrifice is another area to consider for greatness. *If you don't have passion and cannot make sacrifice for any business, you should not do it.* You should be ready to sacrifice. Sacrifice is all about giving. Not in terms of money alone but in giving one's time, skill, and in using one's talents. *If you are not ready for making sacrifices, it will be impossible to be great or achieve set dreams. The sacrifice you refuse to make today can deny you of future success or greatness.* For example, the sacrifice to train or acquire academic skills will give us good foundation for future success once the appropriate skills have been acquired. Sacrifice is not in speech but in action.

Consistency. Consistency is an achievement of a level of performance that does not vary over time. Consistency brings a life without contradiction. In 1 Corinthians 15:58, the Bible says we should pray without ceasing. You can't be silent about your dream. A dream is what will enforce you to cry out consistently. There are several lessons you need to learn from the Shunammite woman in the 2 Kings 4:18–26. In her time of need, she cried persistently to God until she got help. Moreover, when she got to the man of God, she grabbed his feet, resolving not to leave him until she got an answer.

The reason why you are still nursing your problems till today is because you are too quiet and comfortable with where you are now. If you are too quiet, your helpers of destinies might be thinking you are comfortable at the present position of yours and do nothing about your case. A widow of one of the sons of the prophets had a serious financial problem that could have led to her untimely death if she had kept quiet. It was when she cried out that God raised a helper for her. Whatever situation you find yourself, you need to cry out to whoever can help you out in order for you to fulfill your dream.

Marriages are broken not because they are not started well but because there is no consistency. A runner who wants to be a champion must run fast and hard to the end of the race, mindful that those behind him could overtake him. Act 10:1–4 shows us that things we are doing occasionally without consistency cannot make us great. But what we are doing consistently will make us great.

We need to build our consistency muscle but not like a jellyfish. We should be thankful to God for the things God gives us freely. If God should judge us based on our inconsistency in giving or obeying his commands and on many other things we are doing deliberately openly and secretly which run contrary to the will and purpose of God for our lives, we should not be alive today. The man by the pool of water was there for about thirty-eight years. He persisted and stayed there until God blessed him. The man at the beautiful gate was there for a long time before he got healed.

Zacchaeus was consistent in waiting patiently on the tree for Jesus to pass by. His persistence and endurance made Jesus look up to him and to bless him even when Jesus never looked up to anybody except to God. The Bible says that we have a spirit in us. So why are people looking for God all around? What we need is in us. Why then are we looking for what is not lost?

My people have a saying that what we are looking for in another state (Sokoto) which is far from us is in our pocket. You need to maintain consistency. Consistency builds your character. It doesn't matter what you are taught or learn if you don't put it into practice, regardless of the school you have attended. You need to practice before you become good. Knowledge without practice is useless, while practice without knowledge is dangerous.

Greatness will come when you are ready to be unpopular, ready to face persecution. Your ability to make progress and fulfilling your dream may also be triggered when you are ready to change friends and ready to cross some lines and get out of your familiar territory, cocoon, or comfort zone. Greatness may as well involve doing away with certain things. In some cases, you will let go of some things which you previously considered precious to you but which were in fact setting you back from achieving the purpose of God for your life! The only contribution mediocrity can make to your life is criticism. Those who criticize your ability and every step of progress you make must be ignored before you can move ahead and fulfill your dream. Greatness does not come on a platter of gold. It comes with great and costly price. Nothing great, special, or valuable comes cheap.

You must be consistent in doing what is right and what is appropriate to achieve greatness. You don't just stop drinking, smoking, womanizing, and gambling today just because you have financial challenges or health issues only for you to go back and do the same when you have some cash on you or after you got healed.

Don't you know that living a fake and flamboyant life at the expense of investing in your life, children, and your communities just because you want to impress some people or you want to belong to certain groups is throwing a spanner to the wheel of your fortunes, dreams, and destiny? Why do you want to stand in and feel among the poor when God designed you to stand out? Why must you lease a new car from a car dealership and pay car notes every month when you know your income is not enough to maintain it? What about living in an expensive house, using designer clothes, shoes, bags, wristwatches, and glasses when your take-home pay cannot sustain you?

Have you ever thought about it for a second that the house you are living in and the car you are ridding are the cause of your high blood pressure? Because when you fail to make monthly payment, all the flashy things will disappear. To avoid that happening, you must work hard. In the process, your work may not allow you to have enough time for yourself and for the family! Many divorces and broken homes today are due to lack of communication between couples caused by too much working hours. Majority of couples break up because they have no time to discuss and iron out their differences because of long hours of working.

Do you ever notice that the more your daily life and time you spend serving other people as a worker regardless of your position at your job, the more you are likely to waste your precious time and destiny? And the faster your age goes, the less you are able to think deep about your life. Some people, because of little baits (incentives) given to them by their employers, keep ignoring and postponing the gifts, talents, dreams, and the businesses that they have passion for at the beginning.

Some people take jobs hoping to use the jobs as ladders to their own business but later decide to stay on, without even bothering to move further afield. Why? This may be because of the fake satisfaction they enjoy when they are promoted as managers, supervisors, quality controllers, analysts, chief financial officers, treasurers, secretaries of the companies, and all other manners of big names on paper with offices or partitioned cubicles assigned to them as offices. The provision of the facilities kept their spirits alive and kept the individuals working for the companies without adequate remuneration, leading to a lack of funds at hand or in their bank accounts. The owners of the companies or the employers may sing to the bank at the expense of the employees. Many fail to realize that there is no way they can be at their best when they are still under any boss. An employee cannot make as much as the boss or employer.

Some big companies use payment of tuition fees as a bait to tie down many of their employees who want to further their education under the agreement that they will work for the companies for certain a period of years after graduation. This I believe in my own opinion is the genesis of another slavery despite the employees' education. The employees may become comfortable and forget their personal dreams because their promotion will bring more workload, leaving them less time for their personal plans and families

I was once a factory worker in one of the reputable medical equipment producing companies in America. This company specialized in producing medical devices for solving a lot of medical issues. I worked in this company for a year as an assembler in their clean room. Although I liked the job based on the work environment, it dawned on me one night that I was just wasting my time in supporting another man's dream.

It was Christmas period, precisely December 23 of that year. The chairman of the company decided to appreciate all employees for the good job done since the beginning of that year. It was a winter period; the weather was so cold and not friendly at all. I was on the night shift. The employee appreciation ceremony started around 2:00 a.m. The president and the vice president of the company were brothers. They didn't live in Minnesota but in Hawaii, simply because of the cold weather. They already appointed some people to take charge of the company whenever they were not on ground. They made barbeque and served all employees with hot dogs, bread, chips, and drinks. The company gave all employees one free embroidered shirt each with company the name and logo on it. In my own opinion, the shirt was meant for free advertisement anytime we wore the shirt. Many of my coworkers believed that the shirt was a free gift. But I knew in my mind that all employees were running the commercial we were not getting paid for.

My turning point from working as tools for making money for these two brothers and others came when the president of the company was addressing us after our midnight meal. In his speech, he appreciated everybody for the job well done and dedication to duties. He announced the multimillion-dollar profit the company realized for that year. As if that was not enough, he altered another statement that triggered the anger for freedom in me. He said and I quote, "We apologize for flying in so late from Hawaii today. You see, we are no more used to this terrible cold weather. We feel for you guys. My wife and the kids sent their greetings. They would have loved to come but for this terrible cold. The vice president and I are so grateful for your dedication to this job. Having made this millions of dollars in profits in this fiscal year, we deem it necessary and important to compensate you employees with fifty-dollar grocery gift cards for the Christmas with a T-shirt each. We will also raise your pay by fifty cents to one dollar per hour depending on your years of service in this company."

Everybody clapped. I did not clap. Within me, I saw that moment as a moment of change which I had been waiting for. I began to think differently from that moment. Starting from that night, I decided to walk away from the company. Consequently, I did not go back to that company the following January. After many years of leaving the company, there were many of my coworkers who are still working, only for them to be getting a dollar or less raise every year. This makes me belief that, indeed, men can be used as tools for making fortune for others.

Imagine, the owner of the company you are working tirelessly for is living hundreds of miles away. All he does is to log on into the computer and check his bank account to know how much money has been credited into his account while some people are working tirelessly day and night to make sure that the money was deposited into his account. He could spend the money as he pleases. During the day, he may be at the golf course or in other places, spending his profit on cars, boats, and on his mansion lavishly. I did not see anything bad in that if that was how he chose to use his own money and time. The same thing is applicable to all other employers or chairmen and founders of various companies.

The truth of the matter is, we are all born naked. Nobody was born to be an employer. Employers are made in life. My question now remains, Why are over 95 percent of the world population who are considered to be poor chose to work as moneymaking tools for the so-called 5 percent of the population that are wealthy? Why are people not waking up from their slumbers? The good news is that it is never too late. That is what this book is all about.

A friend of mine once told me that since he finished his master's degree, his workload at work had increased geometrically to the extent that he worked at home during public holidays like Christmas and Thanksgiving!

In the country where I was born, the security man (gatemen), cooks, and drivers of rich men didn't normally get rich. The only favor they enjoy was to smell the wealth; they carried the money in bags and boxes for their masters to spend but will never get access to the wealth. The only consolation the drivers do have is to drive the exotic cars that belong to their bossed and hold the key while at service, only for them to drop the keys and take bikes to their houses after the day's job. Some drivers even trek home. The circle of driving nice cars during the day and walking home at night continues for many drivers for a long time without being able to think on what they can do to improve their lives.

The same situation is applicable to those that are working per hour or as salary earners who work five or six days a week all year round, only for them to have four weeks of vacation in a year and file their tax returns early in the year to have little savings. Many people are in this type of a living which I want to describe as a hook of slavery. To get out of this hook of slavery, one needs to consistently think about one's dreams, talents, ideas, and all other things and how to turn them into prosperity.

You need to stand out in order to become noticeable. You can't be noticed easily in a crowd. Are you noticeable to God and others in your congregation? Which type of workers are you in your church? Are you a Sunday churchgoer just to warm the bench? Be careful not to give priority to your dream over your God. You should be able to give God your time without complaints or excuses. Abraham in the Bible succeeded in his life journey because he was obedient to God in all ways.

At your place of work, how high or low are you rated? What are you contributing to your community and generation in general? Are you like a snake that just passes on a rock without people tracing its track on the stone? You must be a thinker, an inventor, a contributor, etc. before you can impact the life of people around you positively. You must be committed, dedicated, and factual in whatever is committed to your hand. You have to set your priority right. You should be able to build goodwill by working on your dream.

Desire. Desire is the suggestive feeling of possession of something. Desire may be called craving, longing, yearning, request, or wish for something. It is the driving force behind any greatness. You are said to experience greatness when you desire to be great. Having a good desire is another way of greatness.

For you to be great, you must have a definite purpose. That is, *you must have a good knowledge of what you want and a burning desire to achieve it.* Desire is borne out of need and dissatisfactions with your present status in life. What you are pursuing in life says a lot about you. Your life will always gravitate toward the desire of your heart. Desire also inspires and motivates. The proof of definite desire is a determined pursuit of a goal irrespective of current situations and circumstances. *Mere wishing to be great alone cannot lead to greatness,* but desiring greatness with focus of mind and appropriate planning with defined ways and means to achieve the goals will bring greatness.

Desire is like a living organism. It is born, it grows, and it can die. People with strong desires to be great should know that every setback along the path to greatness must be registered in order to overcome. You must desire to be great in life because greatness is your heritage. Many people are just living day by day because they are satisfied with their present positions and conditions. You must refuse to stay on the edge of blessing because there exists greatness on the other side. A strong desire to fulfill one's mission in life will fire one to greatness. *If your desire is in line with the will of God, and one concentrates on it and does not associate with small thinkers, one will definitely achieve what one desires.*

Obedience. Obedience is another driving force behind greatness. Obedience in the spirit realm simply means readiness to do or follow whatever God instructed us to do notwithstanding the circumstances. In the Bible, we were told that Abraham obeyed God when God instructed him to go out of his country to the land that God was to show him. It moved from certainty to the uncertainty through obedience to God's order.

Dream. Successful people have achieved success because they believed and worked hard on their dreams. They can be described as tomorrow thinkers. *Dreams motivate you into action.* What you see in your dream is what you become. *Unsuccessful people are motivated by today alone, and they are not tomorrow thinkers.* Who are you? Are you today or tomorrow thinker? *Vision and dreams are the sure path to greatness when properly executed.*

Know The Secret
To Success

*S*uccess is getting and utilizing new ideas, concepts, and perceptions for profitable products.* It is also the progressive realization of worthy ideas. Success is realizing God's desire for us and responding obediently to it in order to reach our maximum potentials. This will definitely please you and bring success to others. *A major factor in achieving success is proper planning and management of time and resources.* To achieve success, we must diligently plan and continuously manage available resources. *There is no one who can go far on the ladder of success without dedication to hard work.*

Let me share with you a motivational message about the answers someone found while he was meditating on the secrets to success in life. He said he found the answer right there in his room. He said that the fan said, "Be cool." The roof said, "I am high." The window said, "See the world." The clock said, "Every minute is precious." While the mirror said, "Reflect before you act." The calendar said, "Be up-to-date." The door said, "Push hard for your goals." The mat said, "Kneel down and pray." The toilet said, "Flush the haters that don't want to see you come out to anything good in life!" The seat said, "Sit down for a minute and think deep about your life, past, present, and the future." Pen and paper said, "Be accountable for all actions and steps you take." The TV said, "Watch me only when it is necessary or else your precious time may be wasted on me." The computer said, "Don't get carried away with all my contents. I may serve as a distraction." The Bible laughed and said, "Read me for directions."

For your dream to come to reality, you need to find out and know the secret to success. Someone once observed that *there are at least two indispensable requirements for success. These are creativity and innovation.* Creativity involves thinking up new ideas and developing new concepts while innovation is described as doing a new things and creating new products and processes.

Success comes with a price. Although, the price is far less than the value of success. *For example, if you think that education is expensive, you may try ignorance to appreciate the value of education. We achieve success only when it is intentionally searched.* It cannot be given; it cannot be purchased by money. Formal education, in most cases, may be very important for success. For example, Thomas A. Edison, who became one of the world's leading inventors, was said to had just three months of schooling! Knowing the secrets to success and determination to succeed are more important for success than mere acquisition of knowledge through formal schooling or education. We should know that *riches are not beyond our reach and* that money, fame, recognition, happiness, joy, and financial freedom can be obtained by all those who are ready to make the sacrifice and determination to have them. All we need to do is to set proper priorities and be focused on our dreams and ideas. Remember that *all achievements, earned riches, fame, and financial freedom began in good ideas turned into practical action. Truly thoughts will remain abstracts until they are turned into practical actions to produce measurable assets.*

Success is the turning point where opportunities meet actions. We must consciously seek opportunities and work for success. We should not just sit down and wait for people to encourage us to succeed. While looking around for success, we must let the spirit of God lead us in all our ways. Whenever we see opportunities that can bring success, we should be ready to seize the opportunities without being rigid in pursuing our goal for success. We should avoid anxiety because *being anxious can aggravate a problem. Anxiety is also a product of worry.* Be careful of what you are anxious over. *Success comes to those who are success conscious, while failure comes to those who allow themselves to become failure conscious.* We must learn how to change our minds from failure to success consciousness. When your desire is not ordinary, no one can stop it. In order to be successful in whatever we do we must make up our minds and be determined to succeed. Every success in life depends on appropriate knowledge. Knowledge can be divine or acquired. What we know and whom we know and who know us with God's support will determine the success we can attain in life. *Understanding makes us outstanding in life. A successful man will never lack good things.* We can build ourselves up by using or adopting the success of those before us. We must also be ready to start from a point and follow the proper part in order to achieve success. The beginning may be small, yet the end will be great if we follow due process without cutting corners or jumping the queue. The Bible says that *we must not despise our little beginnings.*

Whenever we are getting ready for a mission of success, we must put on our best appearance. Many a times when opportunities comes, they may appear in different forms and from different directions. That is one of the tricks of opportunity. *Opportunity has a habit of slipping in by the back door, and often it comes disguised in the form of a misfortune or a temporary defeat.* That is why so many fail to recognize opportunities. Great assets can be acquired through our definite knowledge and intangible impulses of thought, which can be transmitted into material rewards by the innovative application of known principles.

In other words, you need to imbibe the spirit of what some scholars called *stop and start. We should stop mourning for the past but start molding for the future, stop thinking of the loss and start thinking of God's love and how to reclaim all our losses.* Furthermore, we should stop thinking about disgrace but focus on God's grace that should be enough for us. We should stop wondering, Why me? "Start watching for new us." Stop wishing for the best and start working for the best. Stop talking and thinking about the problems but start talking and claiming the promises of God's solutions.

Stop lying down in despair; start rising up to glory. *It takes determination to be successful in life, business, marriage, and in the ministry.* How determined are you about making progress in life? Added to determination is endurance. To endure means to suffer, to undergo pain, hardship, difficulties, problems, and all sorts of hard situations without giving up. Some people, while in their problems or challenges, wonder if God is still in existence because they wondered why God could make them suffer such magnitude. But *the truth is demonstrated in the case of an invigilator or teacher who kept quiet when the students were writing an exam in the exam hall. But after the exam, the teacher could decide the fate of the students as to either the students will fail or pass the exam.* Same thing is applicable to God. God will allow us to go through some challenges while he folds his arms, looking at us like teacher/invigilator. Mind you, God has his purpose for our lives.

There are always prices for success. Endurance requires discipline and self-discipline. And to enjoy spiritual and physical success, we must discipline ourselves. Our appetite for food and our desire for sleep and comfort must be controlled. We should also discipline our tongues. *Our speed toward the selected goal must be measured.*

Another ingredient for success is seriousness. This is the active part of determination. Seriousness means acting purposefully for success. Someone who wishes to be successful and endure pain, hardship, and difficulties without being serious may never achieve success. We must identify those things that will make us successful and act on them with seriousness.

Another important aspect of seriousness is faithfulness. Faithfulness denotes being completely loyal to a cause. Firstly, *you must be faithful to God, the author of success. You must also be faithful to yourself and the assignment entrusted to your hands.* You must also be faithful to others. Faithfulness to other does not mean you have to please everyone. Bill Cosby once said, "I don't know the key to success, but the key to failure is to try to please everyone."

Although it takes strong will to be faithful. The one who aspires to be faithful must be diligent. Diligence means wholehearted searching. In your quest for good success, seek the Lord with all your heart and serve him in holiness and truth. "Behold I will do a new thing," said the Lord. You may not have anything to start with at the onset of your success, but you must have the capacity to know what you want and the determination to stand by that desire until you realize it. You can think yourselves into fortune.

Knowing the secret of success has to do with knowing or understanding the law or principle that guides success in life. The law in the physical realm has so many definitions; it might be the guide that was put in place by some group of people for people or objects to obey. For instance, for an individual to travel from one country to another, it is the law that one must show a valid international passport to the immigration officers at the point of entry of the country one is traveling to. In other words, it will be impossible for one to travel to another country without valid traveling documents.

The law of gravity says that anything that goes up must surely come down. Meaning nothing stays up forever. It's a law in America and other Western worlds that man must not abuse a woman regardless of her offence. It is also a law globally that you must pay your utility bill when it is due or else you will face an interruption in the supply of utilities. The law may be the principle which must not be broken if success is to be achieved. Success on its own has laws that guide it and which must be obeyed to achieve it. The principle of success is on maintaining a balance between hard work and sincere praying for success.

Many people appear not to know that we have to live a balanced life between hard work and sincere and faithful service. The lack of this basic knowledge often made many Christians to make mistakes of praying and fasting without doing other things that can make them succeed. On the other hand, they may devote their time to working hard without involving God, believing they can naturally make things happen on their own! The truth of the matter is, *anybody that brings God and the law of success together would be a double winner.* Many wonder why many Christian businessmen and women fail in their businesses despite their apparent commitment to the things of God, while the so-called nonbelievers who appear not to know God are successful in their own businesses. The reason is simply because the *unbelievers may know the secret that guides success and follow it meticulously.*

We need to know that there are certain laws of success which will work for us when we discover and apply them in our daily activities. We need to apply the law of success in our homes, businesses, and communities. *God want us to succeed, but we must apply the law of success for us to get good results!*

One of the laws of success is the law of sight. It means that our destiny can only be changed with the size of our vision. *Whatever we can see in our spirit is definitely what we can get in reality.* It is difficult to take us into vision which we cannot see or perceive by ourselves. It is difficult to execute what we cannot see in our spirit. When you see things in your spirit, it is very easy for it to come to pass. It is very important for you to have the power of sight. Arnold Schwarzenegger ones mentioned *vision finding* as one of the rules that guides success in life. To be a successful person in life, you must have your vision clearly laid out. When you discover your vision, the rest will follow.

This time, it is not the physical sight but the spiritual sight. It is very important to see in the spirit what God has in store for our future and what God is planning to do in our lives. The usefulness of this is that when people come around to pull us down, we will know that their opinions don't matter. *What should matter to us is our vision and not the opinion of the other people who can look down, underrate, belittle us and rubbish all our intentions and aspirations.* Many can look down on us because of our color or stature but should not discourage us from pursuing our goals.

Inability to see with the spiritual eyes can stop people from moving forward and get to where they want to be. The Bible makes it clear that what we see are temporal while what we do not see are eternal. *It is possible not to see everything physically, but we can see most thing spiritually through the eyes of the spirit!* We should henceforth see ourselves as lenders and not borrowers, as helpers of destiny and not as help seekers! We should look forward to how our businesses would expand into mega and multimillion-dollar companies and how we would be employers of people. Our spiritual sight and vision will protect us further. We should also know that as a man thinks, so he is. *If we can see it, we can feel it, receive it, and can surely be it. Once we envisage it, it will surely come to pass.* How we see ourselves determines what we will say about ourselves. It will also determine how we will behave and what we can become. *We cannot rise beyond what we are able to see.* Many are the eyes that look, but few are the eyes that see. We should be able to see beyond what the ordinary eyes can see. Where other people cannot see opportunities, the determined mind should be able to see opportunities and success.

You should see beyond limitations. Many of us tend to keep memories of our past in our minds and in our houses. There are pictures of where and how we failed one exam or the other, how we failed to make profit in the business we first embark on, the pictures of our grandfathers, our childhood, weddings, and birthdays, but *we fail to develop and keep or have the picture of our future in our minds. We need to hang the picture of our future on the wall and in our minds and begin to act according to what we see about our future.* If we fail to have all these in our minds, we will begin to listen to what people say to us and begin to act according to what people say about us. *Success has other price tags on it, and the price tags on it reads courage, determination, discipline, risk-taking, perseverance, consistency, and doing the right thing for the right reasons.*

Successful people would always do whatever it takes to get the job done, whether they like it or not. They also understand that it is not a single attempt or push that makes success achievable but the total accumulation of efforts and the consistency in making efforts. *In most cases, successful people form the habits that feed their success instead of habits that feed their failure.* Naturally, the path to success is not convenient. If you ever see anybody making it easily or conveniently, watch out; it may not last. The path to success is not easy as it is marked with discouragement and easy excuses not to perform! Most people find it easier to stay in bed rather than wake and work hard and smart for success. Many may prefer to see the weather outside as not being conducive for them to make it in life. They may refuse to get out of their comfortable place to try to work under the inclement sky! *Getting on the path and being able to stay consistently on the path to success requires courage, determination, and faith.* Standing boldly on the path makes you a hero and champion. One of the characteristics of the champions is that while they don't know exactly what is out there, they still boldly go out there and make an impact. *Champions are so courageous.* To be courageous means to have purpose and live to face all the obstacles which may be present.

A critical element in achieving success is to start on the right path and to remember that no matter what we had passed through in the past, we can begin fresh with greater determination to succeed. *We can begin on a new slate at any time.* However, the problems many are facing is that they put much emphasis on their past failures and forget to focus on the future with hope. We can start building our new life today by starting on the right note. *The most powerful force for change from failure to success is time. Time can either promote one or work against one.* We need to understand the secret of time, which is that if we stay firm on the path of success long enough, we will definitely get whatever we want once we do the rights.

Ability to commit yourself for a very long period of time to whatever you are doing is one of the keys to achieve success. To make it in life, one must learn patience. Just as the pregnant woman has to wait for a complete nine months to deliver a baby, we must stay for a given time before seeing the result of our hard work even though we are in the jet age when we want things to happen now or never. We are in the era of microwave where we want our frozen food to get hotter within seconds. Life is not like that. Persistency with good attitude for a short period of time will never get the job done. We need to be persistent for a long time with good attitude combined with patience in order for us to accomplish the positive change we want.

Presence and consistency matters in your race to success. "For anyone to be successful in life, the 80 percent of success is showing up!" says Woody Allen, the famous playwriter. You have already won the battle if you commit in showing up yourself every day on the battle you are about to win. The rest of the 20 percent is left to your skill, knowledge, drive, and execution. For any problems, challenges, and tribulations facing us in life, the best option is not for us to run away but to wait and face them squarely. *We must stay and face the challenges. Whatever you don't fear will definitely fear you.* This is applicable to all areas of our lives. Be consistent. Tom Seaver once said, "In baseball, my theory is to strive for consistency, not to worry about the numbers. If you dwell on statistics you get shortsighted; if you aim for consistency, the number will be there at the end."

As important as showing up is, consistency is what is needed to do the finishing. A great choreographer who wants to win the applause of the audience and win the show must not only regularly practice every day but must run the same play over and over until every step has been properly mastered. All that will be left for D-day is execution. The same principle applies in the game of soccer and in many other sports and also in academics. We must master the fundamentals of any game before winning in the game.

If we aspire to be motivational speakers, reading motivational books and listening to the tapes of successful people must be a priority. As simple as it looks, it is also easy for us not to do it. It is very easy for a student who does extra research and read in the library after leaving the lecture room to be on top of the class because of his more consistent working than all others who do not care to work hard! *It is sad to see some people fall off the right path to their success by not doing any more of what they were thought to do every day because they don't have anyone to tell them exactly what to do.* In other words, they are said to be deficient in the principle of consistency.

Malcolm Gladwell, the author of the book called *Outliers*, once said in his research that most of the important industries like software, education, military, and many other manufacturing giants usually spend an average of ten thousand hours in making good products ready for the open market. The lesson here is that we should be ready to put in several hours into whatever we are doing in order for us to produce good things. We should not be too much in a hurry. We need to make provisions for long hours to produce high-quality products we can be proud of.

We should give ourselves time for whatever we are doing to materialize. Most people are looking for quick actions and forget to learn the truth that success doesn't come overnight or even in a few weeks or in months. *It usually takes a lot of time and hard work for success to come into reality.* One thing about successful people is that as soon as they find something that works, they repeat such an action over and over again with a good attitude over a period of time until they are successful. A common problem with some people is that most people are not willing to put in adequate time which can ensure success of whatever they do.

The best advice to reach one's goals and dreams in life is to stay focused and keep away from distractions. There is no doubt about it that distractions may come from many angles and at any stage of one's life, most especially as one wants to progress. *Negativity may show up at your door step every single day, seven days a week, with or without your permission.* The negativity or distraction we are talking about here is not limited to human beings alone; it may be from what we are seeing in the media or the trend of events in our environment. Many a times, we are constantly bombarded by negative messages from the media and other sources that can impact the way we look at life.

The reason why we always find magazines and the newspapers in the grocery stores, restaurants, bus stations, and all centers where people visit regularly is because those are the places they can easily catch the attention of the masses. Many of those nonmotivational magazines and newspapers have nothing positive to offer. They are just there to distract our attention from working on our dreams. What lesson do we want to learn from a celebrity magazines that 80 percent of the pages showcase celebrity divorce after spending over five million dollars on a wedding that lasted for less than a year? Of what help is the story of a celebrity that bought a ring of over twenty thousand dollars with a dress worth more than ten thousand dollars when there are some people that are homeless and are struggling to have their daily meals?

Of what use is reading auto magazines that showcase two-passenger cars worth over one hundred thousand dollars to someone who cannot afford a bicycle? Unfortunately, when some people read such magazines, they lose their focus and begin to see life in a negative way as if they cannot make it in life anymore. *Many forget about their dreams and get focused on entirely wrong directions.* The truth is that there is nothing in those magazines we need to know. Do we ever notice that most of the distractive advertisements on television stations come in the middle of most of the popular programs that caught the attentions of millions of viewers? Many have derailed completely from their dreams by watching unproductive advertisement. The truth is, there is nothing in those advertisements which you need to know because they will not motivate you to your next level and may not contribute a dime to our better life.

Distractions are not limited to magazines and other media outlets alone. Majority of the people that work and associate with us on a daily basis can also act as a distraction for our progress. Don't get me wrong, there are few good friends and associates that can help us reach our goals in life, but they are scarce and very hard to find. *There may also be many people who may not want to see you move to a higher level because they themselves have no better place to go or they may have no future to hope for.* They are like stagnant water in the pond that stinks. They are called *naysayers.* They are the set of people that take your attention from the task at hand; they will derail you completely from your track if care is not taken. They are professionals in taking people's attention. They will talk you off your dream. We have this type of people in various places of works. They assemble by the water cooler in the lunch room and gossip about who is doing what and make fun of those who are trying to be dedicated to their jobs. They are also common among our families and friends. No matter how small, big, and genuine your dreams are, they will have every reason to tell you that your dream can not be possible. You should not listen to the dream killers and enemies of success. Whatever they see as impossibilities or liabilities in you will become assets if you follow your passion.

The truth of the matter is, we are not going to change such people from the way they are. Some people are born to distract peoples' attention from making progress. We should devise ways of getting around them because they will surely appear. We just have to manage them. *It is left to us to decide whether or not to allow those people to dictate to us who and what to be,* or would we let people shape up our lives for us? The problem with this set of people is that they will not readily go away as they will usually attach to us like parasites or desperate associates.

To be great in life, your attention must be far away from those who are not ready to contribute positively to your life. However, one of the best ways to move a step away from distractive elements according to Jeff Olson is to "form a mastermind group of like-minded people who see things in the way you see it." Jeff stressed further by saying, "If you do opposite of what majority does, nine times out of ten, you are going to be right." To back up Jeff's philosophy, the great German philosopher and businessman Arthur Schopenhauer once said long time ago, "Every truth passes through three stages before it is recognized. In the first stage, it is ridiculed. In the second stage, it is opposed, while at the third stage, it is regarded as self-evident." Like I mentioned earlier, opposition and ridicule will come. But *you need a right attitude to go through the public ridicule and the opposition of naysayers telling you that your dreams are not realizable.* Don't let small minds tell you that your dreams are too big.

You should work your ass off if you really want to become successful in life. You never want to fail when you work hard enough. The ability to hang in there when things are tough is one of the keys to success in life. When bad things are happening to us in life, we have to embrace them and be determined to succeed/overcome. *Don't quit, because quitters don't win and winners don't quit. No pain, no gain.* When we are in the middle of adversaries and an adversary is in front of our door, we must step up to the challenges. It will only make us stronger. Remember, no event, no history. *You may not appreciate a sweet taste unless you had once experienced a bitter taste.* Likewise, we may not appreciate happiness if we have not experienced sadness! Life and other circumstances in life are going to batter us, but we must remember that there are thousands of people who are in the same shoes. If you can manage your adversaries or challenges, it may change your life for better.

Author Shawn Anchor once said, "Happiness is the precursor to success not mere result." If you are happy, your brain is more alert and engaged, free to create, and will eventually lead to productivity. Happiness and optimism actually fuel performance and achievement. *Waiting to be happy limits the brain's potential for success.* Whereas, cultivating positive brains will make us more motivated, efficient, creative, productive, and drive performance upward. *It is easy to achieve your personal dream when you are happy than when you are sad.*

Success in life has to do with the mood. The more you are in a good mood, the more the tendency for you to see opportunities around you to be plugged into for success. *Although, hard work and consistency usually enhance success, yet good attitude and a happy disposition are additional factors for success.*

Great desire to be great and determination to achieve the set goal are important factors to make it in life. Ninety percent of times, people get whatever they desire. Desire is the basic motivation that gets us up early and keeps us up late. When challenges and discouragement show up, it is the burning desire that will keep us matching forward. Mind you, I am not saying the road to success is going to be easy. We will meet lots of obstacles on our way to success. But the desire in us will surely see us through. *The level of obstacles we face on our path to success will determine the level or outcome of our success.* The value of our success will be determined by the quantity of challenges encountered. We have to change our orientation and philosophy about problems because problems will always be there, because they are part of everyday life and they will not go away. What is needed is to develop strategies to manage whatever problems that are present. We must also be prepared to forge ahead and believe like the traditional *Chinese, who see problems as opportunities to make money.* The Chinese can quickly adapt to any situation inasmuch as it will bring forth money. That is why Chinese are scattered all over the world.

Having faith in God is one of the best tools you need to succeed in life. You seriously need faith. You may know what to do and don't have the instrument to do it. A surgeon cannot carry out any operation if he doesn't have proper tools. He may know all what to do, but without tools, he can't function. Every man needs tools to succeed. *Without faith, one of those success may be difficult to achieve.* Faith will surely help us achieve our goals. Why? It is faith that keeps one going when there are discouragements on the way. Hebrews 11:1 *tells us that faith is the substance of things hoped for, the evidence of things not seen.* We need faith as a good companion to move forward hopefully and expectantly to please God. All other things must be an addition to our faith. *We can't go empty-handed from a task if we have faith as our foundation. When we have faith, we will have virtue, knowledge, and a brighter future.*

We should know that Satan doesn't have anything to do with a car crash or with any accident, neither was he (Satan) responsible for the house that got burned down! *The motive of Satan is to get us discouraged by stealing the faith in us.* We will never be barren or unfruitful with good faith. Your faith will keep reminding you that you have a future. In other words, every mountain that stops others will not stop you, because you will see mountain as a stepping-stone to your future. Faith gives you sight and insight to achieve your dream.

Favor is another tool which can activate your success. You should pray that God should give you necessary favor anytime you need it. *No matter how much you labor, you need the favor of God to make you successful.* Being a hardworking man doesn't mean one will be successful. Success is a favor from God. We learned that the biblical Esau was hardworking and that he worked all through the night to hunt for food for his father. But before he came back home, his blessing has been given to his brother! If labor profits a man, Esau would not have missed his father's blessing. I pray we will not miss our blessings in Jesus's name. Again, we will not labor in vain by God's grace. Labor disappointed Esau. Labor is the first curse that God pronounced on man. God said that in his labor will a man live while for the woman God said that the woman will give birth in great labor.

Favor is the secret that made Esther get to the palace to become a queen. For Esther whose richest man in her family was a gatekeeper, it takes the favor of God for her to become somebody in life. For the richest man in the family to be a gatekeeper, who have depended on him to succeed, it takes the grace of God for all who depends on such a person to make it in life. Why? Because the gatekeeper himself is already at the low level; therefore, there is tendency for those who rely on him to be below the lowest level in life. *When we are in a low level in life, it will be very hard to fulfill our dream.* We will need God's intervention to make it in life. *Favor makes what is not meant for you to be yours.* It makes people give you what is supposed not to be yours.

You also need anointing in your life to become successful. Your head must not lack ointment. *The anointing is divine empowerment that helps you do what your natural ability would not have allowed you to do.* In whatever career or business you are, the anointing of God matters in pushing you through. It was the anointing that put Samson through in all his achievements; he killed lions and won lots of battles. It was not by his ability but by God's anointing. *Anointing makes you outstanding among your contemporaries.* While others are striving hard in vain without anointing, one with anointing goes forward with success. The anointing of God gives one an advantage over the others.

CRAVE FOR SUCCESS

I n everything we do in life, we should know that we are the masters of our fate and captains of our souls because we have the power to control our thoughts. *Human brains are said to become magnetized with the dominating thoughts that we hold in our minds all the time.* These magnetics in our minds attract to us the forces, the people, and the life issues which are equivalent or have something to do with what we are thinking. In other words, before you can accumulate riches or be successful in a greater way, you must let your mind be magnetized with intense and serious desire to be rich. In other words, you must become money conscious until the desire for money drives you to create definite plans for getting or acquiring money! *You can't graduate from the school of poverty until you meet all the requirements that can promote you to the school of success.* That is to say, you can't let go of your poverty situation until you must have been provoked by the poverty itself to seriously seek success. If not, you will still hang in there in poverty.

The requirement you need to move on or to wake you up is simple. It is called provocation and irritation from poverty. When you are still seeing poverty as a good friend or neighbor you desire, it is possible for you to still pitch your tent with it. For example, when you are earning thirty dollars per hour and you consider that as normal for you when your employers are making millions through you every week, you will still keep on doing the job and put 80 percent of your effort and time into it, while the remaining 20 percent is meant for your family. For those that have family, it means you have no personal life. If it is still all right for you to be smelling adult poop and lifting people who are twice as heavy as you are and you still continue to pick hours and double your working hours. If you are not tired of waking up with alarms at specific times, not mind people setting or programming your time as per how many minutes you can use for lunch, or what time you can pick or not pick your phone even when you are not in a prison yard, I guess you will still ride on.

If you are a manager with university degrees, good résumé with vast knowledge, you are the one who determines who to hire or not to hire at work. You fire people when due, you evaluate the working progress of your co-employees, and the outcome of your evaluation determines who is to be promoted or left out, please don't be carried away by your position. I want to challenge you that if you put 60 percent of the 80 percent of the effort you put to other peoples' work into your own personal business, I believe that your take-home may be much better than the current take-home. Not that alone, you will regain your freedom. *As a manager, do you ever realize that the more your status at work, the more your responsibilities and challenges*, the more tax you pay despite the little increase to your take home due to your new position? The less your ability to focus on your family issue, the more money you spend on those activities that you used to do or supervise when your job was not all that time-consuming. If you are not careful, your position as a manager or supervisor may affect your family and even your relationship with God because you will always have reasons to get tired after a days' job. If care is not taken, you may be frustrated and transfer your aggression to people around you, including members of your immediate family!

Pastors are not left alone in this situation. That is why it is common nowadays to see among pastor children those are wayward because their parents have no time to take good care of the family. Without a good wife as backup for a pastor to hold the family when the pastor is away or undergoing challenges, the children will be at the receiving end. It is common to hear of managers who take home their office work during holidays and weekends. What a professional slavery and bondage! As a manager, do you ever realize that you stand the chance of taking the blame and praises of your department or units? Have you ever thought of being fired one day? You should because there may no longer be full assurance of security of tenure in today's corporate business. You are a good manager who is well loved by everybody at work, including the CEO, and this gives you confidence that you are not likely to be fired and that you hope to retire in your present company!

Please remember the economic recession that shook the global economy lately. In case the worst happens, what is your plan B? You need to prepare for a rainy day. It is easier and better for a cleaner to lose his or her job than a manager. I know of a man, a banker, who used to work in one of the reputable banks in America who according to him worked and served the bank for over ten years. Toward the last months of his career in the bank, he was assigned a post as a trainer in order to train new employees who technically are hired to replace him. After he had trained the new employees, he was let go. I was so curious to ask the man why he was let go by the bank despite his loyalty to the bank. His answer was, "I think I was let go simply because of my old age." I asked the man the way forward. His answer was "I am confused, and my plan was to invest my retirement benefit on a business that will sustain me for the rest of my life. But with the discharged letter coupled with four kids in colleges and my old age, I don't know the way out yet." This I hope will be an eye-opener for as many that depend and plan their life around salaries and wages.

Whatever the mind of a man can conceive and believe, it can be achieved. You must make sure you make a place for yourselves no matter the economic situations or obstacles you can have on your way which may tend to bow you down. I had earlier given the story of a brother who worked hard and smart to buy cargo van for his church despite his immigration limitation and challenges. What he did was to make ways for himself where it seemed to be no way! He refused to be pulled down by immigration challenges, and he forged ahead to use his talent productively.

Desire can be turned to success and reality by being specific and be definite. To achieve your dream, it is not good enough to merely say, "I need or want plenty of money." But *you must be definite and specific about how much money you want and in what time frame and know exactly what you want to do with the money.* You must know definiteness of your purpose. That is, you must have the knowledge and know exactly what you want and place all your energy, power, effort, and burning desire to achieve the goal. Failure to do this might cause you to work amiss. Working amiss is so dangerous that you don't want to really have anything to do with it at all. Working amiss is laboring more with few or no result. It allows you to work hard for what you are not supposed to work hard for. To pray it should not snow in the midst of winter season is a form of praying amiss. It involves using your effort in the wrong directions. Working like an elephant but eating like ants involves wasteful effort and time.

Setting time for yourself is necessary in meeting your goals and reaching the point of your dream. *You should set a time you want to achieve your dream and get the money you desire.* Not being able to set a specific time for yourself will make you feel that you have enough time when time is not on your side. Drawing your plan toward your dream is very important. You must draw or map up a realistic plan to be used to achieve the dream. The plan must be followed, giving no room for procrastination. You should write down the amount of money or wealth you want and what you want to do with it. Paste it where you can see it easily. This will surely remind you of your dream whenever you see the posted message.

You need to read aloud the statement you wrote down at least two times in a day—once when you wake up and when you are retiring to bed. As you read it, you should see it, feel it, and act as if you have already achieved the goal. These steps are not only meant for acquiring wealth but can be useful in achieving or sustaining any goal. Although it may look crazy or impossible for you to see yourself as a millionaire, CEO, or a successful businessman before you get there or in possession of huge money before you get it, that is where the burning desire becomes a critical factor and a driving force.

If you have a burning desire of being a wealthy man or woman, it will be easy for you to convince yourself that you can have it and you will go for it. That is exactly what happens when civil engineers draw the exact plan of the building they want to build on billboard in the site for everybody to see. Anybody that sees the picture will know exactly what the builder has in mind to build on the plot.

PREREQUISITE FOR A GREAT FORTUNE

Some vital and necessary steps must be taken before a dream can come to reality or a goal can be reached or achieved successfully. To have a dream is not enough but to achieve it. In order to realize a goal or a dream, one must have clear ideas on how to achieve the goal, must be committed, must be ready to make necessary sacrifices, and must be very determined not to allow any obstacle or discouragement to dampen his determination to achieve success.

You can never have or acquire riches in large quantities unless you plan well and work very hard and smart. A desire for money cannot in itself bring money until you plan and work very well for making money. It is possible for one to work hard without a dream. *Working hard without a dream is like investing in an unprofitable venture.* You can never fly if you remain on the ground without flying equipment or without a confirmed ticket.

Many people may want to be uplifted when they are not ready to put in necessary efforts. If you do not put on necessary efforts, the upliftment will not be achieved. On the other hand, it is said that we must take action in order for purpose of God in our lives to be realized or fulfilled. Dr. Martin Luther King said, "If you can't fly then run, if you can't run walk, if you can't walk then crawl. But whatever you do, you have to keep moving forward." In this statement, the critical element is movement...movement toward a greater position or desire location.

Many have to get out of their tents for them to achieve great things. The tent is a place of familiarity, a place of procrastination. It's a place of management, frustration, and a place of never enough. It is also a place where people lost their values and respect. The tent is a comfort zone where many people who are struggling don't want to leave. People under the tent are familiar with doing the same thing again and again and keep getting the same result. Your own tent may be your present place of work, or it may be the environment where you are living currently, which does not add any value to your life because nothing profitable is happening there. To some people, their own tent might be their association with some unproductive friends. Bad habits like smoking, womanizing, drug addiction, and procrastination are some people's tent. *Some like Peter in the Bible need their boats to be rocked and troubled before they could make an urgent move about their lives.* Until you get up, you cannot take off. After a while, you need to grow up and stop fighting or complaining about the same issues. Without getting out of the tent, you might not be able to see how your vision will go or work for you. Get out of the tent and mingle or move closer to where you want or aspire to be.

To get out of tent is to do something different. Do something that adds values to your life. Zacchaeus did something that added values to his life by climbing onto the trees to see Jesus. When you get out of your tent, you will see possibilities and progress. In 1 Samuel 23:16–18, it is revealed that despite David's anointing, he went out of his tent to the wilderness before he was later found by Jonathan. He would have stayed in the palace with Pharaoh. But he was feeling uncomfortable and went to the wilderness first to do what he needed to do. David knew the wilderness was not a comfortable place, but he still managed to stay in the wilderness for him to fulfill his purpose. His promotion and blessing met him in the wilderness. When David went back to the palace he went back as a champion. *To get out of the tents and become relevant, we have to do something different. We have to do what is unusual.* There is a time in life when you have to make some decisions that don't make sense. It may look unreasonable in the beginning, but it will definitely pay off. Peter in the Bible attempted to leave his tent by making bold steps to walk on water, although he was about to sink before he finally got help. His name was heard among the great people in the Bible today while the name of his colleague who stayed in the boat was not as popular as his name today.

VISION

Vision is an internal exercise in which one sees or conceives an idea. Vision is the basis of survival. It is also the beginning with an end in mind. Vision can be further described as foresight with the benefit of a hindsight. Where there is no vision, people perish. *Vision is the product of effective thinking. Vision is a painting of what we ought to be or become in the future.* Whenever we talk about vision, we need to rise above where we are presently because vision is not about where we are now but where we are going. Vision is superior to ambition because while ambition is what you want happening, vision is what God wants to happen. I once heard somebody say, "Great men think because they are great, and great men are great because they think," and I believe him.

A man of vision sees what God has for him before its fulfillment. Vision is no doubt one of the most powerful forces available to man on earth today. Vision gives meaning to life; it keeps us alive and conditions our lives. *An aspect of thinking that differentiates great men and women from mediocre ones is the ability to handle a vision.* How important is vision to renowned men and women? It is very critical. Action springs out of what we fundamentally desire. *A man with no vision is at best a living corpse. He desires nothing and so achieves nothing.* Every great man in history is a personal owner of a vision. A man or woman of vision achieves success in his or her endeavors. *What would be worse than blind is to have sight without vision.* You need vision for your business; you need vision with God's help to run your family.

Every success starts in the womb of serious opposition. Vision takes time, resources, and challenges couple with various setbacks before it become reality. Part of the problem we have in the world today is that when we see people prospering and doing good both financially and in other ways, we expect ourselves to be in their shoes suddenly or overnight. Many assumed some people succeeded overnight. That is not true because it is impossible. There is nobody who can succeed overnight without prior efforts or thinking. It will not happen suddenly. All what people see now is the glory but have no clue about the story behind the glory.

Having a vision does not depend on your location or background. *Place a man with vision in a desert where it seems there is no opportunity, he will survive. But place a man without vision in a fertile ground or in a palace full of opportunities, the mediocre man may end up lacking.* A man without vision is like a bird without wings. Without vision, you can't amount to anything, you can't fly, and you can't become great. The vision speaks and does not stay silent. Vision is the basis of living. Vision is the key to provision. Provision is meant for the vision. Make sure you have big plans and vision; small plans attract small people while big plans or visions attract big people. Small people cause big problems. *The size of the vision you have will determine who will be attracted to you.* What you see is what you get. What you get is what you can acquire.

You need to train your mind to obtain money that is to recognize business which can create wealth. *Working at a particular job should not make it a permanent stage for you if you have a vision. It is your vision that speaks for you and showcase you and not your job or your employer.* You should show and work on the product of your vision and not on the vision of another person. To be a vision builder, you need to ask yourself a question. Which vision are you going to work on?

If you are going to actualize or fulfill your vision, there are some steps you need to take. The first step is for you to catch your vision. Your vision can be caught from God. It can be caught from your pain, and your vision can also be caught based on compassion. You must be able to catch your vision by yourself. Many of us are looking for people to catch the vision for us. When you catch your vision, there should be no argument about it from anybody. Whatever vision you see about yourself in regard to where you want to be or about the good things you want to do in future should not be a matter of contest or argument between you or anybody. Don't be intimidated. You may tell people one of your greatest vision which seems to people unachievable. Nobody has right to contest your vision with you.

You should not be looking at people's faces when you are talking about your vision. Your vision doesn't belong to anybody. If you don't celebrate your vision, nobody will celebrate it for you. Therefore, you must catch it, embrace it, and be comfortable with it. Even though what you are saying seems as if it's not going to be possible, it doesn't matter. It's still your vision. *Having vision is a critical stage because it's not at the realm of reality but at the realm of thought. Many cannot see it.* That is why when you are sharing your vision with people around you including your spouse, they tend to look at you and size you up based on where you are or your present situation and resolve to doubt your vision. It is not their fault. Their problem is that they can't see where you are coming from. *People will oppose your vision, but the greater the opposition, the greater the chance of your vision becoming successful.* You must be able to know and be convinced that your vision must come to pass despite the opposition. *You must be careful of making deals when you are hungry or have serious opposition to your vision so that you don't reduce your vision to zero.* You should refuse and reject the spirit that tells you to manage the present position you are.

You must cast your vision. This happens when you start building a network of people around you who would supply what you need to build your vision. You need people around you to help you cast your vision. *Don't form the habit of telling people you don't need their help. You can disagree on issues, but don't tell people you don't need them.* You must know exactly when to cast the vision you already catch. *Testimony is not good enough when your vision is not yet achieved.* At the meeting point of catching and casting the vision is where the devil is trying to abort the vision. So you must be careful. In casting your vision, there is always a cost that is attached to the realization of the vision. There is emotional, human, materials, and timing cost. In casting the vision, we have to be careful so that we don't cast everything at a time.

We must speak out our vision. A vision that is not spoken is most likely to die. You are probably not able to be accountable for such a vision. Many visions die because they were never spoken out. *When you speak out your vision, destiny helpers may jump at it and make it come to reality. But be careful of where and when to speak out your vision.* Don't sleep on your vision. Act like the *Nike* slogan: "Just do it."

You must be ready to cut the vision. You must be ready to cut everything that has nothing to do with your vision. If you are going somewhere, you need to be careful of whom you are hanging around with because not everybody is going together in the same direction and at the same speed. If you are at the airport traveling to America and you meet your old friend of twenty years old traveling to the UK, when it's time for passengers to board the plane traveling to America in which you are one of them, I believe you dare not wait and continue discussion with your friend traveling to the UK lest you will miss your flight. You don't have to be spiritual to know what will happen in such a situation. That is the challenge many people are facing in life today. *We hang around and bond with many people that are not going to where we are going*, until you miss your train or flight and begin to ask yourself what happened.

There is need for energy and passion in achieving your vision. You need to be careful on who and what you devote your energy on. You must choose your fight in achieving your vision. That is, not every fight is worthy of fighting when it comes to achievement of your vision.

There is something or some people you should let go even if they offend or cheat you, while there are some people you should be carefully dealt with despite their emotional state and loyalty to you. *Loyalty does not confirm ability.* Some might be loyal and not able to perform what is needed of them to do. We must be able to know when to draw the line between loyalty and ability. It's true. The guy might be loyal to you and stay around you all the time, but when it comes to getting the job done, he is not the right guy. Such unproductive people must not be put in charge of any project. You can allow them to be among members of a particular committee but not the head or in charge of the committee. *You should be careful about what you are doing in achieving your vision.* It is very easy to get distracted from the line of vision. *Don't leave uncertainty for certainty when it comes to vision actualization.* Cutting people and materials off on your way to vision actualization might be painful and costly, but you need to focus. You need strength and grace to do that. *You must secure whom you are in God for you to know how to cut your vision distractor off.*

You must be committed to your vision. Real vision takes time to build up. Commitment is required or else it is going to fail. Commitment is the key to the realization of every dream. Commitment is embedded in faithfulness. You must be faithful to your vision and keep constant practicing. In moments you stop committing yourself and stop practicing, your vision will die. You cannot set up a business and operate the business in the same manner your employee will operate the business. You don't want to close the office the same time your employees are closing. Likewise, you don't want to wake up at the same time with employees lest your business will collapse.

For your vision to come to reality, you must connect the dots. That is, you must know what to do at the right time. You must ask yourself what you need to do to make things straight and know who you need to talk to in order to make things right. *You must not place yourself at high level and stay in a bubble without knowing what is going on about your vision.* Your legs must be on the floor. Don't stay in the bubble. It will take people and you connecting the dots before the vision can come to pass.

You must also care for your vision. This is where customer care comes to play. Vision without care is not good. *If you can't handle and care for a business worth thousands of dollars, how would you care for the business that's worth millions?* God will not bless you with a bigger business if you cannot handle a smaller one. Your attitude to your vision is essential. Attitude will cause your vision to grow wings.

Every building must have a designed plan. You can't build vision without working effectively on your desired dream, unless the vision will turn to confusion. You need to operate with strength. *Life will always draw lines for you. Spouse, children, economy, environment, circumstances, and many other things will draw lines for you as you are working on your dream.* But if you are focused and persistent about your dream, you will surely achieve it.

Without the vision, you can't build anything. Vision is good and important for you to get the work done. No matter how good your marriage is, there will be a time when you will feel like you don't want to do it again. The same thing is applicable to our career and our jobs. *There will be a time when we may lose our focus, but as soon as we remember what our vision is, we will be energized to move on.*

Good foundation is important in vision building. People can be frustrated if the foundation of their vision is weak. *The higher or taller the building you want to build, the stronger and deeper the foundation should be.* You can't build a skyscraper on a weak foundation, lest it will crumble. This principle is applicable to the secular world. For you to be on top or to be rated extraordinary, you need to be smarter than your contemporaries and do what they cannot do. That is, you need to go the extra mile to achieve much more. Although, going the extra mile can be a burden, yet the truth of the matter is, you can't be a vision builder without necessary and associated burdens.

Your burden may look like a wall of a building which you might see as roadblock to your vision and dream. The wall of the building can represent so many things which you believe in such as lack of finances, helpers, and conducive environment.

Procrastination, fear, carbon copying, or imitation can serve as a wall for you. In any case, no matter how strong the wall of a building is, it cannot be too hard for a caterpillar to demolish. You must stand firm and be strong like caterpillars against the wall that can hinder your progress. A friend of mine used to make a joke by saying, "You should not rest your head quietly on the wall or barricade that stand as a stumbling block between you and your progress in a bid to endure the barricade. Rather, you should hit the wall forcefully with whatever weapon[s] you have for you to have your way to the other side, lest the wall will eventually fall on you, and you may remain stagnant forever." It takes leadership to build a vision. *You may not maximize your potential until you have a crisis. Many are destined to prosper in the midst of crisis. You need to be sensitive to time and* events. This is crucial in fulfilling one's dream. Unfortunately, many see crisis as problems instead of opportunities. Many have great potentials but are unable to fulfill or maximize their potentials because they do not learn from their past mistakes.

Some are destined to help the poor and the needy before their breakthrough can come forth. If you fall in this category, no matter what you are doing, you have to go back to where you came or originated from and contribute to their improvement. *Your dream can be achieved regardless of whether you are living in the city or village.* Many who stay in the city just want to enjoy the weather and other social infrastructures without vision. They will rot and not achieve their dream. *If you don't see the potential of succeeding in yourself, you might not achieve breakthrough.* What you don't see, you don't achieve because you will never think about it. Even if you feel it, you may not care about it. *You must set new targets for yourself for your vision to come to reality.* You need to give an accurate appraiser of yourself to see what next to do better. Aspire to go out and see things and set new targets for yourself. It will allow you to set a game plan. You must be ready for lots of pain and challenges. Many may want to rise but may not be ready for challenges, want to marry but not ready for the marital challenges. In fact, *whenever you set your mind to build anything, you must be ready to pay the price.* The enemy will always show up to destroy your vision, but it is your duty to ignore such enemy.

To be successful in life, you must have a clear vision for your life. A personal vision comes from a glimpse of your destiny and destination. Vision can also be a glimpse of your reason for living. *Your dream has to do with your purpose.*

When God shows you your purpose, you need to sometimes keep it to yourself or else people may cut you short. That is the case of Joseph with his brothers. *Vision gives you the address of where you are supposed to go, and the same vision will navigate you to your rightful destination.* Vision gives you a goal to accomplish. Without a definite vision, you will follow any route because every place may look alike. With a clear vision, you will know exactly where to go, who to carry along, and when to start off your journey and possible stopovers. If you know where you are going, you will definitely know the route that can lead you there even without anybody guiding you. In other words, you don't have to depend on anybody as your GPS to get to certain destinations.

Clear vision will make you not to drive off the road at the wrong exit. If you don't know where you are going, any road will get you there, but the difference between you and the person who knows where he is going is that you will definitely get there late. When you are late to a destination, anything can happen to you. If you know where you are going, you will not take the wrong exits if they look right to you. That is why in life, we have good friends who may not be right for what we want to accomplish. You may have beautiful things around you which may not be good for your purpose. You can do all what you want to do, but the truth is that not all you want to do may be profitable.

When you offer yourself unto God, he will surely show you the way to go. Anything that can disturb you of your vision and purpose is not good for you, and you must abstain from it be it fornication, drinking, smoking, peer group influence, imitation, fraud, and so on. Try to flee from such once they are not good for your purpose. Your vision and destiny are much more different. What works for your friends might not work for you. Don't shoot yourself out of your vision.

Line crossing is necessary for you to make it in life; life will draw a line for you. Your wife or kids may draw lines for you. Line crossers are always the winners. If you don't cross lines, you may not make it. For every addition to the family, there is a pain experienced by everybody in the family. The mother will experience pain during pregnancy and delivery. A responsible father will experience pain by taking care of the mother during and after pregnancy. People usually stay and refuse to not do anything because of the fear to do something. Overweight people can't control it because of the pain they will face at fitness centers.

Many refuse to seek help from those who can help them because their egoism and cocky habits will not let them go low to meet up with their helpers. You need to be in good accord with almost anybody that comes across your way in life. It might be at you place of work, church, your community, and schools, and so on. Do you hear me say it is easy? No! It is not easy. But you need endurance to do it.

Among the Christians in the churches today, a lot of people have their own caucus. Many chose caucus based on career, gender, social, ethnics, material possession, society you belong to, the type of school they or their children attend, immigration status, and lot of criteria which have deprived many from moving forward in life. It will be hard to seek help from anybody you don't have good relationship with.

Building relationships is a gradual process and not spontaneous. You don't just develop interest in somebody you have no good relationship with before just because you realized suddenly that he or she might be of help for you in one area. *Nobody will like to render help for you based on the conditional love you have for them.* There is an adage commonly used where I come from: "You don't begin to process your palm oil on the market day." Many have forgotten that *in life, achieving one's dreams has to do with who know you and not who you know.* It is possible you know your helper of destiny and lots of people that are making it in life, but they need to know you before they can volunteer to render any help for you. A president of any nation is well-known by so many individuals, but it will not help everybody but those he knows. Who you know doesn't matter, but who knows you matters most because they will link you to success.

Likewise, there are some people who don't know you, and you don't have to know them because they will affect you adversely. Likewise, *your progress can be determined by who you meet because they will help you to move up, and those you don't want to meet because they will pull you down as soon as you meet them.*

How cordial is your relationship with people who know you? Are you still holding grudges and keeping malice with someone who was supposed to help you simply because you can't see beyond your nose? Or do you think he or she cannot be of help to you based on the current situation he or she is now or because you were once offended? Make no mistake, you need to think twice and forget about the past and think about the future and learn how to let go.

You need to develop shock absorbers that can resist pain. You need capacity. *If you don't go beyond your pain, you will become bitter. Many may suffer as a result of increased pain.* Recently I was watching a documentary of two different families. A daughter from one family was ill, and her lungs needed to be replaced while there was another family who lost their son to an accident and was ready to donate their son's organ to the girl in need of lungs to ensure her survival. After the surgery, both parents met to appreciate each other. I can see the boldness, composure, and courage of the parent that lost their son while the other girl survived at the mercy of their son's organ that was donated to her. Despite the ordeals the family went through, they were not bitter. Many parents would have not made the organ donation possible and allow the other girl to die. I began to imagine where this family got that courage from.

Achieving your dream has much to do with how close you are to people of increased capacity. You must work with people of increased capacity. *If you were in one particular environment or place of work including church where you were not taught on how to grow, or you were not given room to grow you better leave.* The paralyzed man was lifted through the roof by his friends and relatives whom I considered as helpers of destiny. This was made possible not by himself but because of people of high capacity known as helpers of destiny. Note that nobody can build alone. *How far you will go will determined by people around you or who you hang out with.* It is virtually impossible for you to succeed without having somebody who can be of help for you or without you passing through some people as mentor or helpers who know better than you do. It all depends on who you are hanging out with. A tree can't make a forest.

In most cases, the salaries of friends or people that think alike are almost the same or similar since birds of the same feather flock together. If you want to increase your salary, you need to change your friends. Your friend in this case might mean so many things; it depends on individuals and the situation surrounding you. For many of you, the friend you need to change can be your present job, the types of houses or cars you are using, your mode of spending money, your advisers, societies you belong to, your lifestyles. Your place of abode might be what you need to change by relocating to another place in case the city you are living in doesn't have all it takes to sustain your business or the dream you have. If you have anybody that you are looking toward as your boss at work, mentor, or your leader who cannot show you the path to success in life or does not want you to stand on your feet but only to be given you crumbles, pennies, peanuts out of his wealth upon your hardworking and loyal to him or her, you need to reroute your journey with him or her before it is too late.

You don't want to be like a security man, gateman, and drivers working for wealthy individuals in the part of the world I originated from. Drivers are the closest and the confidants of their masters, the rich man, because they travel together. He is the one who knows all the business plans and follows his boss to trips more than anybody else. Many drivers know the secret of their bosses than any of their family members. Unfortunately, drivers in most cases, are known to die as poor men, with exceptions of the lucky ones who are able to invest on their children. Most drivers are familiar with borrowing money before the end of the month. They are familiar with cash, I mean a bunch of cash, but not have any access to the cash. They served in the millionaire's mansion(s) during the day, but they end up sleeping at night in another house that does not measure up to the standard. They drive nice cars in the day, but later at night, they go home in a taxi or bike. Some even walk home. Gatemen will always open the door for the rich men, both day and night. But the gateman will not have a place in the mansion but at the door post. Upon all, they usually run errands for all members of their boss's family, including their friends.

You have been working more than ten years in a particular job, only for you to get a raise with less than five dollars per hour once in three years after your performance was reviewed. The question remains, *Why are you staying long with a master who is using you to make his own money?* Why are you allowing your boss to play golf and invest around the world with your talent when you are not dumb? How come your boss only comes to office once in a while and you work twenty-four seven, only for him to collect reports and updates from you, but still you can't feel the impact in your bank account?

After you've worked your full-time Monday to Friday, you still bring your office job home at weekends and holidays. You don't have life, and you neither have time for your family nor think deep on the way forward.

Why can't you work on your talents, gifts, and dreams? After many years at work, you know the ins and outs of the company. You've worked in all departments. Why can't you study the company and see what you can work or improve on in order to establish your own company after so many years of your professional slavery? Since your boss cannot help you out, you need to gradually plan your own life or else you might die as an instrument or tool for the rich men. "Life is inherently risky. There is only one big risk you should avoid at all costs, and that is the risk of doing nothing," said Denis Whitley. If you don't take risks, you will always work for someone who does.

I pity some people who follow leaders blindly without caring to ask the directions to where they are going. Not many leaders are capable of helping you to reach your goals and achieve your dreams. Working for people is so dangerous that it will make you lose focus on your personal plans. Your mind will always be on your paycheck or salary. Many people will be professional slaves forever because they can't afford to miss biweekly paychecks or monthly salaries. Most of their attention will be on how to receive what they consider full paychecks or salaries. They will never have time to reason about the way forward. They will rather go for overtime than to think. You must be able to review your performance. The bigger your dream, the bigger the possibility for your project to come wither or water down. Because if care is not taken, distractions and confusion may set in. You should build yourself up according to the vision you have; you can do this by reviewing the vision. *Whenever you don't review your performance, you are playing with failure. If you don't embrace your performance, you will celebrate mediocrity.*

The fact that your grandfathers labor much to get money does not mean you should not sit down and evaluate yourself to improve more. Sit down and look back from where you are coming from up to where you are presently. What are your strengths and weaknesses? What are the statistics and the records of people who had, at one time in life, progressed in your family and community from the last two or three generations? What did they do right or wrong? What are their strengths and weaknesses? What do you think you can improve on? Which ideas or methods of the elders in your family and community can you emulate in order for you to move ahead? Compare them to the groups of families and communities that are really making it in the society. You must get yourself a mentor in the area you are trying to increase your capacity in. Everybody needs mentor(s) at one point in life. There is a reason why God put some people ahead of you. A tree can never make a forest. *The questions your mentors ask from you are to raise you up.* Don't be intimidated by their questions, corrections, and any criticism they make about any action you take. For every vision you have, somebody has done it before, so you need to ride on their backs to avoid their past mistakes. Apart from avoiding making mistakes, do you ever realize that having a good mentor can act as a catalyst to your progress? Elisha repeated exactly what Elijah did even after Elijah was gone. Elisha smacked the rod on the water in order to part the water. Don't be afraid to look for mentors. Look for a good one. That is the reason why we have coaches who coach men and women in various fields of sports and other areas of life endeavors.

The ability to compose yourself when you are with your mentor is very important. *As a mentee, you have to keep quiet when you are with your mentor(s) or people above you. You need to understand when to talk and when to keep quiet. Likewise, you must not sit down when you are supposed to stand up. It is also important to let somebody usher you to sit down and show you where to sit rather than struggling to sit in the front row or choose a particular seat for yourself.* You should also recognize when it is time for business. You don't crack any jokes that is not businesslike when you are in a gathering to discuss what can change your destiny or what can move you forward. It will be even better to keep mute and listen to your mentor's discussion rather than contributing when your contributions add no values to the meeting. You will make them feel comfortable by not proving to be their competitor. More also, the Dalai Lama said, "When you talk, you are only repeating what you already know. But if you listen, you may learn something new." In order for you to truly achieve your dream, you should not let your past experiences weigh you down. If people ask you of your past, you don't need to tell them the past of your past, because it will not help matters. Let your life show results. *As a husband at home, you don't fight for respect or supremacy. What your wife and your children need is good results of what you are doing. Women will easily submit and respect you when your ways of life yield an excellent result.* Many do business for a long time without results. People like to associate with achievers. In the area where I came from, there is an adage which says, "Success has many relations." No one wants to support you at the start of your journey, but once they see your success, they all want to be friends again. Without results, many people can't follow you for a long time. They will dump you.

Everywhere Jesus went, people followed him despite no advertisement, flyer, or radio announcement. Why? Because there was a good result in what Jesus was doing. Nehemiah showed good results. That was why people in his time couldn't mock him. David's ovation was loud after killing Goliath. As a businessman or professional in any field, you need to be on top of anything you are doing. When you are at your best, the best in town will look for you. You will be attracted to success. People with good business ideas will seek to be your companion. You will dine and wine with successful people. Creating more rooms for yourself is one of the keys to acquire and sustain a better future. The more room you make, the more comfortable you are and the more likely for you to prosper. Majority of those who are very busy in their various professions and jobs are the ones that are getting more responsibilities in our churches and communities today. Majority of the executive committees in the landlord associations are the people who are doing well financially in that community. Not that wealthy landlords are looking down on other landlords who are yet to make it. But the truth is that a *majority of the poor people don't want to shoulder any responsibilities at home and in society.* This is their lifestyle. They are so comfortable where they are. They don't want to shoulder any responsibilities. They are so used to a parasitic mode of life. You should involve yourself in some community activities, volunteer at various churches, organizations, both profits and nonprofits, and companies. You might even volunteer in your kids' schools.

In your community, try to behave responsibly by attending the community meetings. Let people know who you are in your environment. Familiarize yourself with your community. Try to get out of your shell and cocoon. Doing this will give you the opportunity to connect and open your eyes to business opportunities. Likewise, this will increase the trust people have in you inasmuch as they always see you around as one of them. Some may ask, "Do I need to engage myself and multitask?" No! But you need to be as social as possible with the people in your environment. Why? Because many will not do business or get along with whoever they don't know or trust.

As a businessman who wants to be greater in life, you need to get familiar with the latest business techniques and technologies that can help move your business forward. Go out there and ask questions. Familiarize yourself with the latest technologies. You don't want to keep using typewriters with ribbons of many colors when there is a new generation of computers and printers that can do better jobs. Upgrade your phone and all the electronic gadgets that can help you in your business. You should be accessible to your e-mails and all other vital information necessary wherever you go. You don't want to wait until you get to a cybercafé before you access vital information about your business. *Ignorance is not an excuse when it comes to vision building. Act like somebody with a vison.*

CHOICE

A chieving dreams and goals in life is about choice—the most valuable gift of all that we always have. The gift we can and always have is a gift of choice. We can choose to live a good life or the opposite. Likewise, one can choose to be a player or a spectator. *One may as well choose to be a celebrity or celebrate people. To become rich or poor is a matter of choice too.* We are all born with virtually unlimited potential. We have 86,400 seconds a day, which is meant for individual use. Where you end up in life is not determined by where you start. It's what you choose to do with the seconds you have that matters; it is what you choose to do with your potential that shapes your end. You can choose to be selfish, or you can choose to make a difference in life.

There are two things that will create your dreams in life. They are your *choices* and your *commitment* to those choices. *Your choice will definitely make or break you.* There are some choices that can lead you to an amazing life. You need to be kind to everyone, including those who may ordinarily not deserve it. Smile at challenges because there are divine gifts hidden in them. Try to embrace change because it is what is sure in life. Resisting it will only lead to frustration. Always accept responsibility and try not to shift blames. Believe in your dreams. If you don't, nobody else will. Encourage, commend, and celebrate yourself before anybody does. *Be happy on your own before expecting anybody to make you happy.* Strive every day to become just a little better. Soon you will be a master at what you are doing. Protect your dream and don't give testimony about your dream and achievement. Don't let anybody steal your dreams. They are your great assets. Be part of the solution and not the problem. Be courageous when the problems arise. Don't be intimidated by problems or challenges. The bigger problems you are willing to solve, the bigger the rewards you will get. Open your heart to strangers because they may be the new friends you are about to meet. *Confront your fear boldly and you will overcome it.*

Choose to make a difference unlike many people who just choose to stay alive. Don't let yourself be influenced by negativity; instead constantly seek advice from people who have more experience, knowledge, and success than you do. Surely, it will tremendously speed up your journey to success. Don't focus on the past but learn from the past to secure a better future. Always keep your world. Chose to believe you have the power to create and change everything around you for the better. Complain less and take more action. Don't accept mediocrity and choose excellence. Nobody is born mediocre. It's a choice. Forgive and let go; it will liberate an enormous amount of energy and creativity in you. Stand up for yourself and your beliefs. Hug someone every day and create a better world. Together we can do it if we choose to. It is a choice.

You should try as much as possible to stay away from anger. It hurts only you more at the end of the day. If you are right, there is no need to get angry. And if you are wrong, you do not have right to get angry. *Patience with family is love, patience with others is respect, and patience with self is confidence, while with God it is faith. Never think hard about the past because it may bring tears while negatively thinking about the future may create fear. Live this moment with a smile which will bring cheers.* Your tomorrow starts from now but not a journey to a destination. Every problem comes to make us or break us. The choice is ours whether to become victorious or be victims. Beautiful things may not always be good, but good things are always beautiful! Do you know why God created gaps between fingers? I wish to suggest that the gaps are created so that someone who is special to you may come and fill those gaps by holding your hand forever. *Happiness keeps you sweet and being sweet brings happiness.*

Consider the making of a choice in life as a basketball game in which some players sit on the bench based on the manager or coach's decision or choice, which the players may or may not have control over. But they are holding on to the empty promises that they will soon get to the game any moment, or they do not have any hope that they will take part in the game. Some are standing by the sideline encouraging the players even though their efforts will not count in the game. It is not sure that they will be rewarded. Some are known as cheerleaders cheering the players on, but people don't recognize them because they are not the players at the center. Their financial reward is minimal compared with what real players will take home, despite the fact that they spent longer time in the game arena clapping and cheering the players. Those who are in the court playing the game are the real players. Among the players, some hold the ball as if they are tired of throwing the ball into the net. Some hold the ball and pass it to other players to shoot it into the net for points because they believe the game is for the team. Some of the players may strive hard by making attempts to throw the ball into the net because they personally deem it important to score. Regardless of how a player can dribble, it is only when the ball is put in the net that a point can be scored. It is he who throws the ball into the net that gets the highest points credited to his name. The points will not be credited to those that pass the ball or hold the ball, even though they will all share the victory as a team. The most valuable players which will be chosen based on the points scored or other outstanding performances still stand out among his teammates at the end of the game. The ongoing life challenge is your personal game; you can't afford not to be the most valuable player. *You should not sit on the bench and seek permission from someone for you to play the game when the clock of the game is ticking.* What game of life are you playing that procrastination and self-indulgence is depriving you from making your quota? Please wake up. You should take a shot.

Many a times, making choices is not going to be easy. But making a good choice with endurance is rewarding. *A person on the top of the roller coaster preparing to slide down the hill and roll around the tracks at faster speed will not find it so easy to accomplish the roller coaster journey.* But upon the storms, screaming, and the fear gone through during the course of rolling around, coupled with the tendency for their hair to get roughened by heavy wind, majority of the time, people who survive riding roller coasters always confirm its fun. For women who go through childbearing, it is not easy, but they endure the hardship and the risk of childbearing just because it's their choice to have more than one child. *There is no action leading to success in life that is going to be easy. Good and valuable things do not come cheap.* The road to success is usually narrow, rough, discouraging, and challenging. All one needs to do to be successful is to endure the hardship, be steadfast, and be focused on the goal. *You don't have anything to lose in trying, but you prepare to lose when you decide not to try!*

Talking about the choice of making progress in life can be compared to an observation and touching of an elephant by several people. For example, looking at an elephant from the front will show it to be so scary and frightening. But looking at it from the rear side may make it look somehow funny and friendly. Touching the elephant trunk (the elongated and coil substance for breathing, smelling, for sound production, and for grasping substances) feels rough and bumpy. As for the ear, the base is thick, and the tip is thin. The skin at the back of the head is thick and hard while the belly part is a little bit soft. The limbs (legs) are strong and hard. Individual's comments or perspective about the elephant's body texture will vary according to part one touches. In the same way, people have different feelings and reactions to being successful in life depending on their experience and exposure. *People see success from different perspectives. Some find it easier to be successful in life. While to some, making headway in life in their own opinion is hard.* Many look at certain avenues to become successful as "no go" areas because they see or perceive danger in the avenues. Some look earnestly for windows of opportunities. As most people cannot afford to face an oncoming elephant or vehicles at high speed, many have phobias for success. They can't face any challenges or obstacles on the way to their breakthrough.

Some people are so allergic to the path to success. Regardless how easy or permeable the path to success is, many will not pass through it. *Many already inflict themselves with poverty and lack based on their actions and negligence.* That is why some generations are in a deep financial mess up to the second or third generation. You are the architect of your own fortune or misfortune. *No matter your mistakes or what you have done wrong in life, no matter how backward you are, you can always start a fresh as a beginner.* You can start and follow the patterns of success at any given time. The most important motivation that will keep you moving ahead is having faith in whatever process you are taking in your quest to rise because you may not see the success coming initially or spontaneously. *It is important for you not to base the evidence of your success on what you can physically see now but on your personal choices, your philosophy, and what you know.* What you are seeing now is temporal, and it is possible that you may not see your success coming at first. The secret things are from the above. If you want to understand and apply faith in creating the life of your dream, you can't make your choices based on physical evidence but based on what you know and your philosophy.

Let us look at success and failure in two different dimensions as the pairs of two sides of a balance scale held by the Lady Justice (*the statue symbolized justice in the field of law*). Let us assume that when you are in bad and deplorable stages of your life, like when you are financially down, sick, or your marriage, family, or your career is not working properly, the scale tilts downward. For the downward failure side of the scale to lift up and get to the equilibrium, many would expect it to happen suddenly or sporadically. I guess this can only happen in the movies. Remember, your life activities cannot be better compared with a movie. Having said that, what then is the solution for lifting up the lower failure part of the scale? You can begin by adding little possible actions to the success side of the scale. Initially when you started adding the positive action to the success axis of the scale, you may not see or feel anything. The more you keep adding weight to the success side positively, you will see the failure side of the scale shifting, and it will finally swing your way and bring the scale to equilibrium. Irrespective of negative weight you have on the failure part of the scale, adding little grams of success one after the other at a particular time to the success area without adding no more weight to the failure area will definitely shift in your favor. Remember this. Initially when you first started adding the positive attitude to the success side, it may not make any difference because your eyes may not see the progress being made. But in truth, there is progress. That is why it is not good to judge your choice by the evidence of your eyes. You may be frustrated if you don't initially see the scale moving despite your efforts in making things work. That is why majority of people get frustrated and quit prematurely before their breakthrough. That is why many may remain in poverty forever.

You have a choice about what you speak, and the word you speak becomes your reality. You are where you are today because of what you've been saying about yourself. *Words are like seeds. Ehen you speak something out, you give life to what you are saying.* If you continue to say it, eventually that can become a reality. Whether you realize it or not, you are prophesying your future. It is okay when you say something like, "I am going to make it. I want to be a helper of destinies. I would like to pay the school fees for as many students as possible, and I am blessed. I will be a ruler of a nations. I am coming out of debts." That is not something that is impossible because what you succeeded in doing was that you were prophesying victory, success, and new levels to your life. *Your life will move in the direction of your words.* Unfortunately, so many people are used to prophesying bad words like "Business is slow. I don't think I can make it. Nobody has done this in my family and my community. My educational background cannot qualify me for such an appointment. I don't have proper connections, and I'll probably get laid off from this job. Flu season is here. I always get it. I have an allergy." They are saying these words without realizing that they are prophesying defeat. *You can't talk defeat and expect to have victory.* You can't talk lacks, not enough, can't afford it, never can't get it, and expect to have abundance. *If you have a poor mouth, you are going to have a poor life.* If you don't like what you are seeing, start sowing some different seeds. We all have these negative talks that goes in our heads. There are enough people out there that are telling us that we cannot do it. Why then do we want to tell our souls the same negative words? We need to get our own self-affirmation. Barack Obama's self-affirmation in 2008 election was "*Yes, we can.*" Eventually he became the president of the United States of America. *There must be a quiet moment or time in our lives that we have to reaffirm and remind ourselves that we are the captains of our own ship and the masters of our faith.* Nobody is going to confirm great words and assurances to us. If we don't believe in ourselves, nobody is going to believe in us. We should develop your own confidence and get away from people who can pin us down. We have the responsibilities of making it happen by ourselves. We should live strong as a brand. The free and common gift we have in life is the gift of choice. We all have our own choices to make.

IDENTIFICATION OF TRUE FRIENDS

Who are true friends, and why are they necessary assets? True friends' identification in life is necessary in achieving one's dreams. We must be careful to distinguish between bad and good friends. In trying to do so, there are some vital signs and characters to note in order to identify whether your friends are really true friends or not. This is really important in a bid to move your life forward.

True friends will enter into your experiences and situations. They will want to feel what you are feeling at critical periods. The relationship between Jonathan and David in the Bible is a good example. The Bible says Jonathan arose and went to David in the wilderness. Jonathan was in his comfort zone. He was hospitable in the palace, but when he noticed that David was in danger, he quickly went to David to alert him.

A true friend will not distance himself from you when you are under one challenge or the other. True friends will not only tell you that, he will also be praying for you when you are in distress. He or she should show up for you in time of need more than prayer. Prayer is important, but other actions are equally important.

A true friend will enter the wilderness with you. Your real friend will not only be with you when you are right, but he or she must also be with you when you have challenges or when things are not going well. When things are right with you, I guess you may not need any friend to stay with you. You need somebody beside you when things are a little bit rocky. *A friend who can only stand with you when things are rosy with you already has a policy that is contrary to the policy that Jesus has for humankind in the beginning.* We were told that *even while we were yet sinners, Jesus accepted us and died for us.* (Rom. 5:8). Jesus does not walk away from us when we are going through our difficulties.

If you have a friend who walks away from you when you really need him/her, it is left for you to delete his/her name from your friends list! If, for example, you have a friend whom you stood by when he was in need but decided to keep distance from you when you are in problems, it is better for you to run from such a friend. Such a friend may throw a spanner to your wheel of progress. True friends will surely encourage you to endure any difficult situation you may be passing through. Jonathan arose and advised David when he got to David in the wilderness.

Some friends can show up, but the problems with some of these friends are that when they show up, their advice or statements may make the situation even worse than what they meant! In some situations, some friends may show up for you, but their presence may not be of any help to you. You will feel as if they should leave you alone and get out of your sight because of worse complaints.

Many of the bad friends will want to show up simply to find out what is wrong with your life. The truth of the matter is, *you do not need any friends to do critical analysis about what is wrong or going on in your life.* If your friends' presence does not encourage you to endure but is used to compound your problem, it will be time to let friends off your sight! Your true friends must not be the ones that will be jealous or envious of your elevation.

You should pray that the Lord should deliver you from friends who cannot handle your elevation. *You will definitely know who your real friends are when God elevates you.* If any particular friend of yours happens to be uncomfortable with you whenever you have a promotion, a new car, a good job, huge contracts, a new house, or when you have a good spouse, and if that friend cannot handle the new and marvelous things that God is doing in your life, it is better you cut him/her off before he/she can do damage to your fulfilling your dreams.

Although, *people around may feel you are cocky and arrogant, but you just believe that not everybody should have a seat on the front row of your life.* That is why it is important sometimes that you should have an usher's ministry whereby the ushers will walk some notorious people into the back rows of your life and tell them that they should sit back and watch you afar from the back row, since they do not deserve to sit closer to you. When they are jealous and envious of what God is doing in your life right now, I wonder what they will do when God enlarges your coast more than the way you are now. Therefore, you must call a spade a spade and distance yourself from them.

ORDER AND STRUCTURE

*O*rder is a condition of logical or comprehensive arrangement among separate elements or group. It can also mean to be a sequence or arrangement of successive things. Order is to regulate; it is to tidy up. Order is to do things according to priority. A life of order is to finish one project before moving to another one. We must put order and structure in place in order to move forward. Many darkness in the lives of people in our society today are due to lack of order. An orderly life does not get intimidated by other people's success. Likewise, *there is no room for inferiority complex in the calendar of a man who is organized.* Why? Because he has directions and purpose for his life. He doesn't have time to bother himself for what he doesn't need or bother for. Structure can also mean to put things together in the order it should be. It can also be placing things in their position by not modules things together. An object can be well structured when it is held or put together in an orderly way. *A well-structured life does not allow you to put the round peg in square holes; neither does it procrastinate by leaving what is supposed to be done today till tomorrow.* You don't do what is supposed to be the first as the last thing, which is contrary to a well-structured life.

In Mark 6:40, Jesus instructed the apostles to instruct the crowd to sit down orderly before they began to serve the bread and the fishes. They sat down in ranks, by hundred and by fifties. *Orderliness, in this case, surely will prevent confusion and chaos. It determines how things can get done fast in a timely manner.*

Every leader must learn how to compartmentalize challenges in order to move forward. You don't let the challenges you faced yesterday affect you today; likewise, your present difficulties should not be a determinant on how to face tomorrow. *Each day carries its challenges. There is no way you will be free of challenges except when you are dead.*

Because you failed to win a contract does not mean you should not submit a proposal for another one. Neither does it prevent you from executing the one you are doing presently very well. Just because you were involved in a car accident does not mean you will not ride another car. I guess you'll need a car to survive the current accident. Because you had a bad day at work does not qualify you to transfer the aggression to your family at home. And because you have a family feud at home does not license for you not to perform to expectations at your place of work. Family and work are two different compartments that must not be mixed. They are two different things that demand different attention.

Orderliness makes you a finisher and makes your goals not only achievable but achievable on time. Orderliness tells us that there is a right way to behave. There is a way of doing things right and another way of doing things wrong. If you don't put yourself in order, it will make it difficult for you to receive what may happen tomorrow. *Orderliness gives us a template of how things should be done. Orderliness erases confusion.* It makes you see beyond your nose. It also puts things and people in their proper places. *Orderliness gives values to our resources.* It also helps to unify people and teams. *Growth is also promoted through orderliness.*

Orderliness and maturity work together. They are like five and six which cannot be separated. Without maturity, it might be difficult for you to achieve your dream. If you have a knee injury and you do a kneecap replacement with heavy body weight, your knee may not mature or be strong enough to carry your body weight. It's the same thing if you are to be blessed by God and you are not mature enough, you may not be able to absorb the blessing. In the physical realm, if you are not mature enough, it might be difficult for you to turn opportunities to your advantage. Lack of maturity may possibly let your time elude you because you might not be sensitive to your time. *You don't need to know many people if you are well organized.*

Divine connection is not about numbers but your ability to utilize those connections you have. In life, a business and marriage that are out of order will never maximize their potentials. *We should try to learn what it takes to put our life in order. We should learn our lesson before we are forced to learn it.* It is very advantageous and cheap to put things in order for yourselves rather than letting circumstances or events force you to put your life together. If circumstances should force you to put things together, it might be hard. So you can take the easiest route by putting things in order on your own voluntarily.

LEADERSHIP

T he action of leading a group of people or an organization is known as leadership.

In order to fulfill your goal in life, having leadership traits and abilities is important. *If you can't lead people right, you will have to struggle to make it in life.* The difference between a leader and a follower is in our attitude. It is a unique attitude that distinguishes leaders from followers. You should have the heart of leadership before leading the people. *True leadership is not a method, technique, or science but an attitude.*

Your leadership attitude comes alive when you become aware of your true nature. The belief and convenience of a leader regulates the nature of his or her leadership. The truth about true leadership is that *leadership is not about control; it is about service delivery. It is not about power but empowerment. Leadership is not about manipulation but inspiration. More also, leadership is not about people but purpose. Leadership is about becoming more than doing.* There are serious and urgent demands for leadership in our present day. This is very important for the smooth running of affairs. Leadership is the number one need of the twenty-first century. It determines everything. *Leadership is the source and solution to all problems in the society.*

More nations, companies, organizations, and corporations are overmanaged and underled for lack of leadership. For you to become successful in our modern age, you need to know the boundary between a leader and the followers and choose which categories you want to belong to. Leadership and followership are two vital subjects that demand attention and need to be put into consideration for an average individual or nation to become successful.

Leadership, as small as the word is, determines the qualities of the followers. It also determines the mentality of the followers. The level or types of leadership leading the people will determine the attitude and morality of the followers. Leaders determine the destiny of the followers. Steve Jobs said, "Innovation distinguishes between a leader and a follower."

To become successful in life, you need to have leadership traits, characteristics, and qualities. *Leadership quality is irrespective of age, color, tribes, and location. Nor does it have anything to do with numbers and gender.* How much you take or achieve through your leadership depends on your expectations. The fact that we have a lot of people in a particular circle or parties following a particular leader does not mean the leader can lead. *When you lack order in your leadership, your leadership will be limited.*

You have to be submissive as a leader for you to lead your followers. To be a good leader, you must have a guided principle which you must follow in carrying out all your achievable or proposed plans. *In all things you are doing, there must be somebody whom you must fear. That is, answerable to somebody.* You have to include ability, consistency, and be vigilant. As a leader, you are bound to reveal your personal story to the follower in order to encourage or motivate them, while it is possible for you not to know their own history. So if leadership is void of loyalty, followers can use the leader's story to kill or go against the leader. One needs to know where and when to share personal stories. Using your story against you can be dangerous for your progress. There comes the need to be careful. God operates in the order of principle in all his dealings with men and other creations. Having basic principles to follow is so crucial for a leader who's aiming at attaining greater heights. We have natural and spiritual principles. Principles work everywhere in the physical. But the intervention of God in many cases may change or alter the earthly principle. But this will not work for everybody in most cases. Inasmuch as ability to live a desired future requires a good leadership ability, a good leader with a desire to succeed must have some leadership principles which will serve as a navigator in his route to a successful path. You must have self-mastering ability. As a leader, you must master yourself.

Respect is not to be asked for but to earn; great people like Nelson Mandela, Martin Luther King, and Bill Clinton do not need to struggle for respect. But they earn it. You need to improve yourself to lead people. Leaders must be corrigible. A good leader must be ready to accept productive criticism from his/her followers. It is not a crime for subordinates to suggest useful ideas to their boss. But what matters most is where and how the suggestion is made and the motive behind the advice. Good leaders do not lead by positional authority. A title does not make you a leader because leadership goes beyond charisma or position. Leadership does not stop in your ability to talk and brainwash your followers. Leaders need to understand the need of their followers and know how to meet the need at critical time and in a timely manner. Not that alone, a leader must be a person that people can bank on and vouch for in anything he/she does.

Whenever a good leader is taking an action, the followers should be able to go and sleep and close their eyes without suspecting the leader. You don't want to wait till you are ready to lead before you start doing or behaving well. To earn respect and trust of people is neither a day's job, nor does it happen spontaneously. It is a gradual process. It is easier for people to remember your wrongdoings and mistakes than to remember the good works you have done in the past.

President Obama would have not been able to become the American president if he did not perform well in the previous positions when he was an ordinary person. Furthermore, none of the many allegations that were levelled against him during the presidential campaign in 2008 was established. While Obama could be considered lucky to have crossed the hurdles, none of the contesting politicians in the 2012 presidential election on the other party was able to cross the magic line due to their horrible past and simply because they could not give good account of themselves. Likewise, many people in authorities around the globe have been stripped of their positions, while many were not able to attain the level and positions they aspired for due to inability to give accounts of themselves.

Inability to perform or behave well may not let some people get to their promised land. Although, they might be looking at their promised land ahead, but lack of good morals may deprive them from getting there. The promised land may vary according to individuals. To some, their promised land may be how to meet with their helpers of destiny. It may also be a life-changing contract or job. To unmarried people, it might be their spouses. Political post might be a promised land for some. Many reach their promised land but do not last enough due to their past life. There is need for one to be focused; it takes a lot of courage and determination to press on. There is always a process before you can come out the best. The road to success is so rough that only those who are focused are the people who can pass through it and trail it to the end.

To come out with nice clothes, it needs proper ironing which in itself requires much heat. To make a real gold, it has to pass through ball of fire. Good things do not come easy. Focusing involves a lot of maturity; if we are going to succeed and end well, we need to get proper focus. No matter what happens, you must not let distractions derail you from your dream. When it is your best, you will know this is your best. If you don't get the business you are aspiring for, don't get discouraged. Note that your best is yet to come. The path to success is full of confusion and challenges; there is no doubt about that. Ability to work with people is one of the best qualities a good and ambitious leader should have in order to fulfill his destiny. You can't work well with people if you don't know or study them. In that regard, you need to know who your followers are. Know the weaknesses and their strengths. It is advisable to focus on their strengths rather than on the weaknesses of followers in order to get the best from the followers. Why not forget about those things individuals don't know how to do and focus on those they can dot and teach them how to do it better in order to get the best from them?

The truth of the matter is, not all followers that leaders perfectly train or shape up to become exactly what the leaders may want them to become. Moreover, the weakness of Mr. A might be the strength in

Mr. B. It is important to coach individuals on their areas of strength. That is where encouragement for teamwork is recommended. The more people practice, the better they are. We should note that not everybody in a movie can play the same or every role. Likewise, in the secular world, we have categories of people with different characters and mind-sets with specific areas of expertise where they can perform best.

In the hierarchy of leadership, followers are usually categorized as follows:

(a) *Wonderer. These are the set of people that don't really get anything you are doing. No matter how you train them, they will not catch up.* They usually get frustrated at the end. The good thing about them is that they usually make the numbers.

(b) *The follow us. They understand what leaders want them to do, but they don't want to do anything. They know what is right, but they will not do it.* They are the people with ordinary leather boxes in the house. They don't care or bother if the house is on fire because they don't have anything to lose. They are always mobile.

(c) *Achievers. They are the set of people who usually understand what leaders want them to do, and they do it right.* You can count on them. They work alone; they don't usually want to work as a team with people in their department. They like doing things alone in order to achieve the goals and become champions alone. They always want to take the glory but not want to share the glory with anybody. They are known as one-man brigades. Anytime they are not around in most cases, they have nobody to fill the vacuum they left. They always work to protect their selfish interest. They always want to put others at a disadvantage. But this is not good enough.

(d) *Leaders. Leaders, on the other hand, usually do whatever assignment trusted in their care right. They do it and let every-body contribute in doing the assignment.* They like working with others as a team. *They always let everybody know and learn from what they are doing.* They all become champions. Everybody gets the praise. These kinds of people don't usually want publicity. They want everybody to be fine. They don't usually take offence in any wrongdoings or mistakes you made. They are always aspiring to make sure you are on the right track. These are the set of people we always need and want to stay with in order to fast forward our progress.

Communication. To be a good leader, good communication skills are an important asset. Although, the need for communication does not only end with the leaders alone. Everybody must be able to communicate. But leaders need it most. Lest you will be stripped of your dignity, position, and respect. You must go beyond speaking to people; you don't just mount the podium or pulpit and vibrate and make noise for nothing without carrying people along. You must communicate. You don't want to mimic any other pastor or leaders. Neither do you want to be using their styles.

You must be able to present your ideas and pass it across to people with your own conviction. *A leader who is able to communicate usually gets things done easily and faster. They don't need much campaign to win souls to their side. They usually command respect anytime and anywhere.*

During the 2012 presidential campaign between President Barrack Obama and Mitt Romney, it got to a stage where many voters were no more feeling for President Obama because they felt he was no longer communicating with them, and his opinion polls began to drop. But as soon as Bill Clinton joined the campaign train and shed more light on health care reform and some vital national issues that concerned voters, the table turned around in favor of President Obama. Not that President Obama was not a good orator or speaker, but the situation on ground at that time demanded a clearer delivery of ideas to the anxious voters.

Bill Clinton is one of the greatest men of our time who has the ability to communicate and carry people along. His influence really went a long way in the 2012 American presidential elections in favor of President Obama. His ability to communicate and not just talk made him a respectable person worldwide. That was why he was able to secure the bail for two American journalists that were detained in a North Korean prison in August 2009. That is why his foundation (Clinton Foundation) is one of the mega nongovernmental organizations in the world today.

Talk is cheap. It is easy to see what is wrong with others, but to profess solution is a big problem for many people. It is easier for the spectator watching a soccer match to criticize the players on the field, but they don't have the technical know-how on the steps the players should take in winning the match.

Every leader has to be self-driven by a set goal. Don't go around and look for encouragement and attention all the time. It will get to a point as a leader when you need to motivate and work on yourself, or else you will become high maintenance. There are some things when they get to particular level, you just have to leave it and let go. *When seniors are demanding the same attention as the younger ones, something is wrong somewhere.* You don't want to be a crybaby. As a leader with such an attitude, it will be difficult for you to attain your set goals. You need to sharpen your strength. *When you sharpen your strength, your weakness becomes irrelevant.*

Giving. Leaders should focus more on what they can give and not what they can get. Good leaders must be motivated on what they can give. President J. F. Kennedy once said, "Think of what you can do for your country and not what your country can do for you." *You are not a good giver if what you are giving does not cause you anything.*

You don't want to give people your crumbs. Don't give out your junk as a gift. Giving or seed sowing does not end with giving money or material things alone, but to help others go up and achieve their dreams without pressing them down or taking advantage of them. Many times, leaders receive calls and demand attention from followers at the expense of their families. That is another way of giving by sharing their time. Try to give to people what is right, not what you feel you want to tell or show them if it is not good for them. Don't ever let money control you. *If your motivation is only about what you can get, you will be miserable.* The truth is, without seeds, there is no harvest.

Before a man can marry a woman, he has to sow a seed of "Will you marry me?" Everything you do including your smiles, kindness, handshake, careful observation, and ability to care for others is a seed.

In the Bible story, the butler helps Joseph by sowing the seed of kindness, curiosity, and ability to observe mood. How? The butler was able to detect that the king was not happy because he noticed the king's frowning and troubled face. He was quick to ask the king if everything was okay with him. Through the butler, Joseph was connected to the king and knew he had a dream which he needed somebody like Joseph to interpret.

Indeed, Joseph interpreted the dream. Blessing of Joseph started by ability of the butler to ask questions after paying attention to the look on king's face. Through this, the door of Egypt was open to Joseph. For you to succeed speedily in life, you need to be able to care for others and try to be observant and sensitive to your environment as much as you can.

Multitask. It is essential to be able to handle do many tasks at a time as a leader. If you can't handle many things at a time, your leadership will crumble. We need to emulate good and responsible women in the area of multitasking. Women have more multitasking capacities than men. Good women will go to work, prepare dinner, and take care of the children during the day up to bedtime. At night, responsible women will try to take good care of their husbands. Still, they don't complain much despite the challenges they face at work, on the way home, and even what they experienced from the pressure mounted by the husband and the children.

To make it in life, you need to spread your tentacles. Be ready to multitask. You don't focus your attention only on one kind of business. You must learn how to diversify in case one business fails. You should think straight on which business you could do next that will fill the vacuum left by the failed business. Are you such a person who is not always ready to accommodate visitors or listen to anybody else while working on a particular project in your office? Can you be on the phone and do another thing in the office? How often do you remember appointments you set up for somebody or the one they set up for you? *Do you ever remember your last conversation with your business associates? If not, how often do you take notes or records in relation to your business?* To make it in any business, your brain must be on top of whatever you are doing. You don't let your busy schedule affect your family.

Can you still hold on to your business despite your family challenges, or are you the type that a little siege in your family can mean the beginning of the end of your business? How effective can you combine family matters with your business? *To really be successful in your business, you need to be able to draw the line between your business and the family in such a way that one will not interfere with the other.*

Awareness. Every good leader should have the sense of awareness. He/she should know the conditions of whom he/she is leading, be sensitive to the environment, and know what is wrong with the followers. *When you work long with leaders, as a follower, you need to be able to predict such leaders.*

If you are not aware of your environment, you will all share the blame. You should know the weaknesses and the strengths of your subordinates. You should know what really encourages individuals to put in their best and what reduces their efficiency. It will be to your advantage if you can understand your subordinate better by knowing what their problems are, what to do, whom to meet and, how to find lasting solutions to their problems. *You should also be on top in knowing the state of the market you are operating in at a particular time.*

Knowing your environment better is another way of saving yourself from embarrassment and improving the rate of achieving success. In Matthew 14:15–21, the five loaves of bread and fishes that the apostles saw as not enough in the desert was the one Jesus Christ used to feed thousands of people. The apostles did not know the principles that would make the two fishes and five loaves of breads multiply. Thank God that Jesus Christ the mechanism that worked with the bread and the fishes. The simple mechanism is Jesus looked up, gave thanks, and blessed the bread. That was how the great multitude was fed and there was surplus. Eventually, provisions of the food for the multitude in the desert saved the apostles from embarrassment. You can imagine what would have happened if there was no food to feed the multitude in the desert on that day. The Bible tells us that Jesus ordered the apostles to tell the multitude to sit down in order, but without any food provisions for them, commotion would have happened. *When you discover the principles that work with your talent, you will surely prosper.* The question remains, *What is your God-given talent, and what mechanism do you need to work with for you to prosper?* You need to figure that out by yourself.

Awareness is also a tool that can save us from discouragement and fruitless efforts. We can note that the same net Simon Peter had which caught nothing initially was the one Jesus said he should cast into the sea which eventually caught more than enough. What Peter lacked throughout the night was God's favor. God's favor was not in his boat and net. But as soon as Jesus, who carried favor, entered Simon Peter's boat, the story changed, and he caught more than enough that all other fishermen in the other boats came to help him out.

Reproduction. Every leader should have the abilities to reproduce after them. You can be spiritual and also be excellent. Stop giving excuses without excellence. As a leader, you need to take into account how many people have breakthroughs through you. How many people have you helped? Are you a leader without good legacy? What legacy are you trying to leave for the followers? Do you ever show others the secret of that business? Did you ever think of financing people's dream? Many leaders want to die with their skills and knowledge without transferring it to people behind them, which is contrary to the qualities of good leaders. Reproducing after yourself is another way of achieving your dream. Please, learn to reproduce.

WHAT DO YOU HAVE?

I n Acts 3:1–6, Peter said, "Silver and gold have I none," but the name of Jesus Christ which he has was used to heal the lame man. *You can't come to the table without having something. You need to see what you have and begin to use what you have.* Once you realize what you have and begin to use it, more than sky will be your limit. In 2 Kings 4:2, Elisha asks the woman what she had. What she had was used to help her and turn her life around. Moses was asked what was in his hand. He said, "Rod." He was asked to lay it down, and it turned into a snake. The same rod was used to part the sea.

Not being able to recognize what you have is a great danger and disservice to your progress. In the desert where Jesus fed multitudes with five loaves of bread and two fishes, the little boy and the apostles did not recognize that what they had at hand was enough to feed the multitude. Thank God for Jesus, majority would have died of hunger in the desert. You can't contribute to a mission without bringing something to the table. As an individual who wants to succeed in life, you must make sure you have but are not limited to the following:

The name of the Lord. We have the name of the Lord. In Proverbs 18:10, the name of the Lord is what we have, and it is a good thing. Some trust in chariots, and some trust in Horses. Psalms 118:9–12 tells us that we shall quench them with the name of the Lord. It is not good to tell people not to gang up against you, because if they don't come against you, they will not fall. It says in 1 Samuel 17:45, David came to Goliath with the name of the Lord, and he conquered.

The spirit of the Lord. In 1 Corinthians 2:9–12, if you have the spirit of the Lord and work with understanding, you will survive. If you have the spirit of God, you should not worry about tomorrow. Romans 8:15 says we should be filled with the spirit of God. With this, there is no vision we will not be able to achieve. *Don't do things alone without involving the Holy Spirit in what you are doing.* When you rely on the spirit of God in all you are doing, you will finish well.

Hope. In Psalms 31:24, if you lose your hope, you are not helping yourselves. *You can live for some days without food and water, but it is virtually impossible for an average human being to live without hope for a second.* Hope is the anchor of your faith. You can't build life without hope. Hope makes you keep going to where you are going without being tired (Rom. 5:2).

In a secular world, *your GPS in most cases usually increases your hope of getting to your chosen destinations by telling you the directions you should go and the distance required to get to the destination.* By telling you that you will soon get to your destination, it increases and activates your hope. Whatever you are going through, you should not lose your hope. It is hope that makes you go to bed today and wake up tomorrow (Rom. 5:5). Stop looking at yourself as the epidemic of failure. *You should stop focusing on what you don't have.* You must not lose hope. If Leman, the leprous man, lost hope and refused not to go into the river the seventh time, he would have remained a leper forever. President Buhari, the president of Federal Republic of Nigeria, contested for presidential election and lost three times before he finally won the presidential election the fourth time. What motivated and propelled him was hope and persistency. You must be persistent for your rain to fall. There might have been some issues that happened outside that you don't want to tell anybody at home, but you wish to keep it to yourselves. *You should not give up because of little challenges that want to block your progress. Hang in there and be persistent and let your hope rise.*

Good name. A good name is better than silver and riches. President Clinton was able to bail out two American journalists that were detained in North Korean jail due to his good name with the authorities in North Korea as an ex-president.

You cannot switch destiny with other people. Try not to be like somebody. Be yourself. You need to understand that you can't help everybody. *When you can't help everybody, don't feel bad. Just do what you can do. Don't tarnish your image because you want to help people.* Don't overstress yourself to please people. Let your yes be yes and your no be no. *Try to be honest with people. Don't let people doubt you.* This is so crucial in fulfilling one's dream.

BE READY FOR THE RAIN

I t is very important to prepare for an abundance of rain. There is something about rain. Rain refreshes, rain brings abundance, fruitfulness, rain brings food, and it cleans. It is important and so exciting to hear that abundant rain is coming, most especially when drought has been in existence for a while. Likewise, it is important to note what you hear. What you hear will grip to your mind. In order for your rain to fall, you need to do away with negative things that take God's position in you.

You must avoid everything that cannot allow you to serve God. It is very bad to note that people watch cars and detail it for hours but can't pray for ten minutes. They go to parties for hours without sleep but sleep at night vigils. Many have Sunday as their free day set up to watch all manners of games, including soccer. A friend of mine once made fun of one of our friends that she had time to work during the week coupled with lots of overtime and party till dawn on Saturday with various outfits that were bought on credit but did not have time to be in the presence of the Lord for a second and will not attend any church service on Sundays. Still she was expecting her rain to fall!

Where I came from, it is a tradition to line up buckets around the buildings when it rains. In a very serious rain, the bigger your bucket, the more rainwater you will gather at the end of the rain, provided you open up your bucket. But for a close bucket, you shouldn't expect any water at the end of the rain. Meaning, irrespective of the size of the blessing and opportunity on your way, if you are not prepared for it, you might not share from it. *Many have lost their timely blessings because of their negligence and carefree attitude.* Many have failed to be at the exact location where they were supposed to be when their helpers of destiny were ready to help them. However, you need to load your cloud with whatever you are expecting from God if you are expecting favor show favor to others. If you need money, give money out. If you need help, help others. Don't be afraid to load your cloud. If you have a lot of clothes or shoes or any other materials, give some out to people. That's loading up your cloud. By loading your cloud, God will reciprocate through somebody. Ditto, show mercy and your children will receive favor. Tilling your ground, that is get ready to enjoy the presence of abundant rain. You must get ready for the help you need to be given. There is nothing we are looking for that God will not do for us if we till our ground. Tilling the ground may be to go to school. You can't be looking for a husband and not be able to cook. You need to learn and know how to cook in order to be a blessing to your family because your mother in law will not eat pizza. Even if a man can eat pizza, his parents and relatives will not eat pizza or canned food. If you're looking for a baby, you need to work in children's church. Be a volunteer in any way you can, help children, and love kids. If you need favor, you have to do favor for people.

NEXT CHAPTER

Achieving your dream has to do with your thinking and working towards your journey of life. When Joseph was in Egypt, Egypt was his because he claimed Egypt. *Never see any place you are as not yours because with that mind-set, you may not get the best from that place, because you may not see anything good or any opportunity in the place.*

Many people live in Africa but believe that their luck/helpers are in America. Many are destined to do fine in one continent, but since they did not realize it, all their focus is on how to travel to the other continent for greener pastures, thus undermining and looking down on the pastures in their present location. They can't see opportunities which others see in their present land. They have forgotten that *there is no land that cannot be fertile and noting that the fertility of the land will depend on how we treat the land and how we define fertility and for what purpose.*

A rocky soil might not be good for planting, but we can get some mineral resources and pure water under the rock. *Whatever you don't appreciate will depreciate,* and wherever you have you don't appreciate or you don't feel you belong to the environment, you cannot enjoy the good of such land. That is why many immigrants in America and other developed countries don't make it in life because they are so myopic and do not see the good of the land. Instead they keep complaining about the tax, strict laws, the cold, and making all other unnecessary excuses. Many are relocating from the cold regions to the East Coast and warm areas, forgetting each region has its bad and good sides. Where there is no snow, there will be hurricane, while some regions are used to tornados. Outbreak of fire is the problem of some areas. *Many are so blindfolded that all they can see is how others are making it in a crude and quick way in other countries, how politicians are making quick money, how people are making money on fake and abandoned contracts in Africa.*

Some people are used to reading the success stories of others. They can't see the opportunity in the land of milk and honey where they are living. Jesus established himself and did good things in many places. *Whichever land does not belong to you by right and understanding, you have no permission to eat the best of such land.* Because Jesus knew his children will go to places, he decreed that "wherever your soles stepped, I will give to you as your possession." Possessing can also mean that such a thing belongs to you. *Whatever you don't believe belongs to you can never be yours.* As Joshua delays in the distribution of what belongs to Israel, Caleb said, "Give me this mountain." He said, "We have been passing through this place for too long. Give me the portion of my land and do not delay anymore." Others didn't know that they could make a demand, but thank God for understanding. It takes understanding for Caleb to make his demand. Caleb said to Joshua, "You can't delay me since I saw it, then give it to me in the physical." *You must be ready to take possession of whatever is yours in whatever land you are.*

Never see yourself as inferior in any land you are. Don't wait for people to come to your rescue. Never allow waiting to become a habit. Live your dreams and fulfill your destiny. You must enjoy your portion to the fullest or else your dream cannot be fulfilled.

You should have it in mind that where you are now is not the last chapter of your life, regardless of your age, gender, challenges, and circumstances surrounding you. You still have many chapters ahead, and your books are in volumes. You are moving from one chapter to the other.

You should get it clear that the things concerning you are written down already. Hebrews 10:7 confirms that the volume of books was writing down concerning the son of a man. Your life and destiny carry a book that must be fully fulfilled. You don't want to live an aborted and unfulfilled life without fulfilling your destiny. The plans of God for you are like writing handbooks. This has to do with doing God's will. God's will can simply mean living a life of divine order. *The divine order can lead you to divine plans of God for your life.*

Many of us are not living in the fullness of God's plans for our lives. Without this, our dreams in life cannot be fulfilled. One of the physical evidences of this is that you struggle a lot to get your living. You don't have enough for yourself, and the immediate family do not to talk of giving to others in need in your community. Many don't answer their phones because they don't have enough to give to the callers. *Jesus did not struggle as we men do. Why? Because the things that were written down by divine agenda was what was happening in his life while he was on earth.*

When you live in the plans of God for your life, life will know that you are living in the fullness. *No matter how good you are living now, you are not yet living in the fullness of God for your life.* Divine order is a creational guide or plan for the way your life must look like. Even before you were born, God had plans for you about what to become, where to live, whom to meet, not to meet, what to have on the earth, and so on.

Books have been written about Jesus before he was born. It has been written down that he will be born in a manger by the Virgin Mary. It was also prophesized that three wise men would visit him. When heaven looked down the earth, what was written down about Jesus was the same with what Jesus was experiencing. However, in human beings, cases that were written in heaven concerning us might be different entirely from what we are experiencing because of our nature and circumstances. We cannot live a fulfilling life when we do not live in God's way.

At times, your level of achievement in life can cause people to sing your praise and be rejoicing with you because they thought you had achieved a great deal or you had arrived. But heaven can as well be weeping on your behalf because you may be seen as failure since you have not fulfilled half of what was destined for you to achieve. *Do not be carried away with praise of the people. Set your standard and evaluate yourself from time to time.* Never be before or after your divine schedules. You can't be under divine agenda and lack anything that is good. Likewise, *you can't be under divine agenda and be a debtor. Debt takes value away from you. When you are in debt, your value is reduced.* That is why when creditors are calling you, they don't call you with respect because you owed them. *A debtor is a potential slave to the lender or creditor.* Lenders may call "Hello! Hello! Hello!" without putting sir/ma'am on your name. They will ask with attitude, "Are you Mr. or Ms. so and so?" If you say no, they may ask you to tell the debtor to call the creditor back. But if your credit standing is good with them and you are up-to-date in your payment, their tones and mode of speaking will change over the phone. You will hear, "What can we do for you, sir or ma'am! Is there any way we can better help you? Hope you enjoy our service today. We have good deal which I think will be good for you!" But *as a debtor, they will take out "sir" or "ma'am" in the communication.*

You need to pray that God will add value to your life. *Any relationship that can't add value to your life, you should let go and say bye.* There is no relationship except that of my wife that I cannot let go if I sense it will devalue my life. Why? Because God hates divorce with passion. As a matter of fact, my wife can't devalue me because all what put in her life by God for me is to elevate me and not to demote me. That is why you need to pray that God should give you your divine spouse if yet unmarried and to those who are married. I pray God will bring peace to your homes.

When you are under divine agenda at the right time, right position with right company, your debt and bill can be paid off unexpectedly without struggle. *It is quite easy for someone who is debt-free to fulfill his or her destiny by working on his or her divine God-given dream.* Because there will be so much pressure. That was the case of Peter when Jesus called him to go to the sea and catch the first fish for him to pay off his debt. Peter did not plan to pay his bills or debt, but *when Peter was under the divine agenda and he was around Jesus who could add value to his life, Peter's financial status changed. The Lord made Peter to pay his bills unexpectedly.*

Pray that the Lord will place you around those that will add value to your life. This is important. *When you are sweating and struggling or you were embarrassed by debt or any ugly circumstances, please check where you are and who your friends and partners are.* Try to audit your steps. *When you are under God's divine agenda, God's favor might turn onlookers into your helpers of destiny.* Exodus 12:36 says, "And the Lord gave the people favor in the sight of the Egyptians, so that they lent unto them such things as they required. And they spoilt the Egyptians."

Moreover, God's favors can give you the ability to convert the good of your enemies into your spoils of war. Favor can also write off your debts. Having gone through several plagues in quick succession, the Egyptians were prepared to pay any price to get rid of Israelites. So by the time the Israelites were leaving Egypt for good, the Egyptians were not thinking of the money or treasures they had given them or the debt some of them might have owed. *God's favor can definitely cause your debt to be written off. A debt-free life is definitely a catalyst to a life of destiny and dream fulfillment.*

We also learn from Exodus 3:21–22 that when God's favor comes, people who were not willing to help you will not only be too glad to help you but will leave no stone unturned in their bid to help you. The Israelites were about to set out on a journey, and they had great needs for this long trip. God gave them favor before the Egyptians. The result was that the Egyptian gave them everything they asked for concerning the trip. *You should pray and let God command onlookers to turn into the helpers of your destiny.*

Enough is enough of struggles, complaints, and bitterness. Stop blaming the government but think of what you can do to explore opportunities in available policies and programs. *Your greatness in life is not achieved by how hardworking you are but by the divine favor of God.* It takes God no time to transform you from a poverty state to an abundant state. This transformation can come in any way that pleases God. He can use anything, anybody, or situation to elevate you by allowing all things to work for you if you are in his divine agenda.

When you are under God's divine agenda for your life, people will see you as a champion. You, too, will act like a champion. Good ideas will come through you. People will consult you for solutions to generational problems. They will think you are smart. But the truth of the matter is that you are not smarter than others. *What is controlling your success and progress is not in the physical but in the spiritual level where you have divine favors.* It might also be that the time for God to divinely favor you has come. This was the case of biblical Joseph who transformed from a prisoner to become an adviser in the palace. The same scenario and principle worked for the late President Nelson Mandela and President Obasanjo who left prisons to become presidents in their respective countries. When one is under divine agenda, people of color will be willing to help, while known and unknown people will go the extra mile to help one fulfill one's dream.

Don't surround yourself with friends who are not under divine agenda and the will of God. They will not only damage themselves but they will damage you also. After they have damaged themselves, you will be the next one to damage. That is why if there is a part in your car that is bad and you don't fix it, it will end up damaging other parts. If your friends or neighbor are not under the agenda of God, or not at the right place, you might want to part with them. Or else they might not allow you to fulfill your dream because they will pull you down.

There are damaging destinies. Many destinies have been damaged because of the carefree attitude of some people. A drunkard destiny is a damaged destiny which can influence others in negative ways. *Parents who are drunkards or chain-smokers will for sure influence their kid's life negatively.* A man who likes anything under skirts is prone to damage his destiny. A man who lives a hunter's life is said to have a damaged destiny also.

Who are the hunters? *A hunter is somebody who lives on what he catches today and has no savings for tomorrow.* Hunters in other cases do not live to replenish life. They don't add value to the reserves or forests where they hunt for animals, and instead they always cause reduction by killing the animals. They don't breed or nurture animals. *Hunters are always in need, always on the move, and they will never be content with what they have.* Usually, hunters don't know for sure where their tomorrow provision will come from. They live a life of gambling.

Where I was born, hunters do not live a clean life. They appeared always dirty, and most of the hunters usually do not eat the best of the animals they killed despite the difficulties they faced in the forest, because they always sold the animals for money, which appeared not enough for them.

When you are under the divine will, God will put everything under your control and prosper you. That was the case when Jesus was on preaching engagement. He sent the disciples to go ahead of him while he was having a quiet time with God. Jesus needed to catch up with the disciples according to the scripture. God could have done three things, one to path the water as done earlier for the Israelites. He could have told Jesus to use a boat or pull the disciples back for Jesus to meet with them. But heaven said Jesus deserved speedy promotion. The Lord commanded Jesus to walk on water to speed up his journey in order to catch up with the disciples. It means since Jesus was in the right place at the right time, wonder must happen. That is why *you need to be mindful of where you should be at a particular time if you want to make it in life and live to fulfill your destiny.*

You don't want to be in a clubhouse at night drinking or womanizing when you ought to be at home thinking about your future or be with knowledgeable persons to plan the way for the next chapter of your life. The truth of the matter is that for good things to come to manifestation in the day, a lot of things must have been done at night by early risers. Who are the early risers? They are the entrepreneurs and inventors. All the technologies we use are developed and perfected by others (early risers) who worked hard while others slept or played away. *While the inventors are busy attending meetings and golfing during the day, buyers are busy working hard for the money to buy the latest products from the inventors.* Many even buy it on credit and labor hard to pay back later.

That is why people queue for Apple products before they get into the market. I like to assume that most of Apple products are invented and perfected at night by the engineers who made the design, because nighttime is the best time to think positively. Likewise, somebody looking for a husband or wife doesn't have to be all over the place but in designated places where you can find exactly what you need, not what you want. The two words *need* and *want* are different. *Need is a situation or circumstances whereby something is necessary or required some necessity while want is having a desire to possess or do something.* Don't be one size fits all, and never let all choices be your choice. If you don't know where you are going, everywhere will look like it.

You need to have standards. Anything below your standards must not be acceptable to you. You must not settle for less. You don't gamble around. You don't want to hang around with the people who cannot see beyond their noses when you are thirsty for opportunities. *Depart from those who are afraid to cross the line to other side*, determined to be a line crosser. You don't want to be in alliance with those who are used to reading the stories of successful men and women in the magazines and on the Internet, only for them to be complaining about the people in the government. These are sets of people who always believe that an average millionaire is a potential rogue. Because they are myopic about the principles that lead to success, they are allergic to success stories. They don't believe you can walk your way honestly to success.

You need to bid goodbye to guys whose mentality is that rich guys are the lucky ones and who believe that riches and fortunes are not easy to come by. You don't want to be on your bed at 10:00 a.m. when you ought to have gone for the business meeting. Likewise, *you need to be awake at night and sit by your table quietly and think of what you can produce or invent for people to use while others are sleeping.* Avoid sleeping on your bed throughout the night. You should not be too used to your comforter on the bed. Moreover, *you should not be on Facebook while you should be on your phone and have conversation with your helpers of destiny.*

What you are spending your time on and the way you spend it is so important in fulfilling your destiny. Some people during church service tweet or are on Facebook, letting the whole world know their current location. They will never jot a note on the sermon of the day. After service, their next action is to pose for a picture to be posted on Facebook for that week. When they travel, they make the whole world know where they were and what they were doing at a particular time through Facebook. Some will say, "Right now I am about to board in XYZ airport" and so on. They will never think of meeting with helper of destiny or looking for possibilities of getting business opportunities as they were waiting patiently to board the plane at the airport.

In the biblical story, it was reported that when Peter saw Jesus walking on the water, Peter attempted to copy by attempted to walk on water like Jesus but was sinking. Why? Because Peter did not possess the power to stay afloat and walk on the water nor the power to calm the wave. That is why you don't need to copy what other people are doing without asking them how they do it. You should not copy your neighbor to do what they are doing when you don't know what they are doing and the reason why they were doing what they were doing.

When you see any of your friends doing what is ungodly or what is contrary to the law of the land, like in immigration and in other cases avoid associating with such a friend. The thing might work for him, because heaven is not interested much in his case so he can take the glory himself for what he did. But if you do such a thing, you might fail because heaven is interested in your case and will want to take glory in all your success and doings. If you decided to do it in your own way and not God's way, you will be put to shame and regret doing it in the first place.

Don't try to envy anybody. It is a waste of time for what you need to succeed is already built in you. Don't see anybody's life as being better than yours. Don't see any job or carrier being better than yours. Your dream and destiny should be the best for you. Your spouse should be the best while your kids should be the best kids for you.

To be successful in life is not about copying. The destinies of twin brothers or sisters are not the same. So *you don't have to use other people's success as yardstick to measure your own success if you want to be successful and fulfill your dream and destiny.* Heaven may block your way if you remove the value of God in your life by comparing yourself with the other person that heaven does not have special concern for. That is why many people are struggling for most part of their lives. Heaven will be looking at you as somebody who is impatient and not serious. If God is concerned about you, he wants to take glory in every area of your life. Because you don't have it today does not mean you can't have it tomorrow. I am talking about staying under divine will of God as a prerequisite for you to achieve your dream and fulfill your destiny.

If you remain under the divine will of God, whatever you need, he is willing to provide it. The will of God gave Jesus the animal to ride into Jerusalem despite the fact that Jesus did not have any horse of his own to ride. But because Jesus didn't have it at a particular time does not mean he cannot have it. Jesus told the disciples to go to the city to bring back a horse that has been tied down, and to tell whoever asked for their action that the master needed it. This is the example of divine provision to fulfill a destiny.

While men go to school to get master's, Jesus got his master through the will of God. That is, when you are in the will of God, you will become the master of every circumstance, and nobody can disturb you in whatever you do because heaven is behind you. *When you are in God's will, the earth does not question you; the earth will release to you what is yours.* That is to say, nobody will owe or dupe you in whatever business you are doing. Fraudsters will never come near your dwellings. When you are in the will of God, heaven and earth will roll a red carpet for you to walk on.

It means your contemporaries will treat you as a king. you will be given priority before any other business partners. People will come and seek business ideas from you. And likewise, many will come to you with viable business ideas because they will see you as a role model and somebody they can confide in. *Don't be surprised that law of the land can change for good because of you inasmuch as you are under God's will.*

You will definitely fly like an eagle. What takes a year for some to do will be done by you within some months. You will live a ful-filled and satisfactory life when you are under the will of God. Before you needed anything, it shall show up. In order to live a satisfactory life, it is never too late for those that are not under the will of God to take some steps in rerouting their ways back to the road that will lead them to the will of God for their lives.

No matter what people know about you, they don't know your future. They may say, "Don't you know I know you very well?" Yes! It is possible for them to know you, but the truth of the matter is, they don't know much about you because the purpose and plan of God for your life is not in their hands. There is no challenge that the devil or any man who can determine your life. It is true they know your past, but they don't have the ability to know your tomorrow. They don't have the information at hand. It is now easy for doctors to know the sex, blood type, brain, and heart activities of a fetus in the womb of a pregnant woman, but they can't know the baby's destiny. The mother of the baby does not even know the plan and the purpose of God for the life of the baby she carries. *No matter how much people know about you, there is much they don't know.* What they don't know is greater than what they know. You should let your mind be at rest about that. This will serve as an engine that will keep you forging ahead of any turbulence that might want to act contrary to the will of God for your life. The best they know was your past.

You might have been irresponsible, a drunkard, a gambler, a gangster, a drug dealer, homeless, childless, and jobless before, but that was your past. That is what they knew, but they don't have an idea of your future. Though your beginning might be small, but the later end will be great. Before everybody were formed in the belly, God knew us. Though you might fail, you might not look like it, but the purpose of God for your life has been inbuilt in you. Because you failed initially does not mean that you are not carrying the purpose of God for your life, which is success!

President Obama did not look like a president initially, but that was a divine plan of God for him. Because God has planned it for him, he naturally fulfilled the promise of God for his life despite all the artificial barriers and difficult circumstances. President Obama took his time and was transformed from a young senator to the president of America and the first black American President in history. That's the plan of God at work!

PLANNING

Planning according to Wikipedia *is the process of thinking about and organizing the activities required to achieve a desired goal.* For any person in life who wants to become somebody, planning must be put into consideration. It is required. If you are alive without plans, it assumes that you are living for nothing without purpose. Proverbs 16:1–3 shows us how important planning is in the everyday life of a man. *If you wish to fulfill all your dreams in life, you must form the habit of writing all your plans on paper and make sure you are confirming and claiming whatever you have on paper as your plan.* I strongly believe God will surely let your plan come to pass.

The problem with people in life is that *many people don't know what they want to succeed in because they don't have plans written down.* People want to help God by telling him how to do his job. It is your duty to write down whatever dream you have regardless of how big the dream is. It is left for God to let it come to manifestation. *How God will execute your plan is no man's business.* What matters most is for God to get it done. The truth of the matter in life is, if you fail to plan, definitely you are planning to fail. You can't stay on the fence. If you have a plan, God will surely direct your steps as in Proverbs 1:9. But without a plan, there is nothing for God to direct in you.

No wonder why you are jumping from one place to another, from job to job. You are leaving one profession to another, one trade to another, and one city to another under the pretense of bad weather or other useless excuses. *Without planning, you will just be living a life of a kite.* People and the wind usually direct the kite to the direction they so wish. At the end of the day, they can command the kite to fall down from the high altitude it was initially flying in. You don't want to live a motionless life as a human being. *If you are not moving toward a particular goal, you might not be motivated by the success of others.* Likewise, human beings might not come up to show you the way, Why? Because it is absolutely difficult to steer a stagnant vehicle or ship. Mind you, any stagnant ship on the high sea will surely sink or capsize. Likewise, an airplane at high altitude that is motionless will definitely yield to the call of force of gravity.

Any car that is not moving will surely gather lots of dust and other's dirt. A baby that raises up his hand will surely get an elderly person to lift him up faster than his counterpart that folds his hand. God does not work on an empty promise or a life without a plan. *It is advisable to write down whatever one has planned to do in the next few years and follow it up.* Audit yourself and make the necessary amendments or corrections. It is never too late; you can still make it in life!

Many spend most of their time in making other people rich by allowing others to use them as tools for making money. Many call themselves IT professionals who can't think of establishing their own companies to offer required services which would make money. Many are traveling from one continent, country, or state to another at the expense of their immediate family to attend different conferences on behalf of the company they are working for. Many abandon their kids in the hands of housemaids and babysitters. Many go to the extent of letting their kids stay with their mothers, mothers-in-law, friends and relatives just because of their busy schedules. Recently, I met a mother who left a two-year-old girl in a babysitter's home for some days just because she was working two jobs simply because she needed money for a trip to Africa. The saddest thing is that her take-home pay did not justify the efforts she had put into her two jobs!

There are other people who were tied down to their jobs by the titles, positions, and the incentives given to them by their employers without adequate remuneration! They answered to all manners of titles like managers, treasurers, secretaries of companies, supervisors, leads, chief engineers, accountants, and so on without appropriate remuneration. Many are working toward fulfilling other people's dream at their own expense due to lack of planning. It is highly advisable for one not to work in a place where your dream cannot be fulfilled. This will let you identify exactly where you are supposed to work and not to work. *You don't just accept any appointment based on the current salaries or paycheck with other incentives if they do not promote your planned future goal or professional dream.*

One thing about employer is that before you realize ten dollars as take-home, you must have delivered a service worth hundreds of dollars. Ninety percent of employers will naturally not want any of their employees to be up to their standard financially because they don't want any unnecessary competition and they want unlimited respect. I see worker's incentives and salaries as baits with nice aromas which are usually placed on traps for catching rats or small animals while jobs are the traps. An individual who is a laborer or employee is like a rodent. Any attempt for a rodent to eat the bait on a set trap will get the rodent into danger of being caught or killed! The plan of any trapper is to catch animals from moving forward. That's exactly what the jobs are doing for employees. But there is choice to make.

Your job is to make you lose focus and blindfold you from stopping on depending on your boss. If care is not taken, you may work till your old age. In order words, if you as a worker are used to your salaries and other incentives like Christmas bonuses which are not even enough for Christmas expenses, traveling, and hotel allowances while you are supposed to be training your kids, company credit card, 401(k) matching, and your contributions known as cooperative money in Africa, company cars, drivers, and apartments as in African setting. I see you having difficulties in setting up your own business. Because setting up a business at first may not be easy; it will involve proper planning and endurance. *We should remember that Rome was not built in a day. Likewise, the journey of a thousand miles starts with a first step.* Many businesses which failed within the first two years did so because of lack of adequate planning and proper execution. Part of adequate planning is to first save for the rainy days when the new business may bring in no revenue. Many would say, "It is not easy to save money." Yes, I agree! It is not easy to save money. But if you can buy a birthday, wedding, funeral uniforms, headgears worth $150 to $400 at once, lease brand-new cars or mortgage homes with huge monthly payments, I guess you can save for your future with the same determination and commitments.

It is impossible to be rich, successful, and live a fulfilled life by going to work every day and live only on your salary. It is God's wish for you not to be employed so that you can be released and become what you are born to be in life. *You don't just want to be flowing around and be applying here and there for people to higher your gift.* I believe the destiny and the gifts you carry are so valuable than for you to go around and beg people to exchange them for a salary.

The dream you have that you are wired with from heaven is so viable and awesome enough for people to vie and compete for. You don't have to put it on sale so cheap. *You should be so valuable to the extent that nobody will be able to employ you and use you as moneymaking tools.* If you know the worth of the dreams you carry, nobody should be able to pay you because you are too much for any employer to contain. *You should position yourself in such a way that whoever you are working with (not working for) should consider themselves lucky for associating with a divine quality in you.* I wonder if you know the difference between working for people and working with people. *By working for people, you have no choice on what you can earn. It is predetermined and included in the employment contract.* That is why your employer is paying you your salary. Therefore, whatever millions of dollars your employer realizes as profit is none of your business because both of you have agreed on what you are to earn for your service. What you will earn will be determined by what time you punch in and out. *You can be fired at any time when you are working for people.* On the other hand, *when you are working with people, you are part of the decision makers.* You both sit in the board room where the business decision is taken. You both negotiate what your take-home will be at the end of any business deal. In this case, nobody can get you fired easily. By the way, all these will not happen without proper planning. *Adequate planning is one of the prices you need to pay to live like a king and achiever.*

You need to understand that every job is a temporary classroom on your way to graduate to your purpose and destiny in life. *Your current job is a bus stop which is meant for you to transit to your des-*

tination. It is also a ladder for you to climb to your business goal. Your destination is your own personal business. I wonder why the majority want to sleep at the bus stop. Why allow anybody to dictate your worth by salary? *Whatever salary your employer is paying you is exactly your worth to him irrespective of your academic statutes, age, and your efficiency.* Your salary is meant to be a token of appreciation from your employer for your service to assist him to achieve his business dream and purpose. Such a token should be worthwhile. *If you earn less than full appreciation you are due for, it is slavery.*

This of course is the case for the majority of people working for an employer Monday to Friday. This can basically happen because of lack of planning. Is it not amazing that people live round the clock without a single plan? It is important to be careful when you are making your plans; you should not make it according to your own way but according to the purpose that God has for you.

Making plans in life has to do with what is your dream or goal. What are you listening to? Are you hearing the sound of promotion or demotion? Are you hearing the sound of recession or that of economic buoyancy? Are you listening to the voice that says you can't make it? Perhaps you have listened to the voices of dream killers. Have you been brainwashed by the bad news you are hearing around you that it is not easy for somebody like you to make it or that it is not common for people to make it in your community? Maybe people have been discouraging you by saying that the probability of you making it in your chosen career or business is so slim. Kindly note that all the voices of discouragement are market noise which you should not allow to distract or disturb you. *You can choose not to listen to the market noise. It is your choice.*

You should remember that your ear is a gate to your heart. Who you listen to will determine what you become. It will determine what goes inside you. If you keep listening to those people that put you down, you will never rise. What you hear may determine what you achieve, affect your thought, and probably the level of breakthrough in life. It will also condition your future. If you have lived in the environment whereby people are telling you that all what you can do is to be a servant, a subordinate, and not a boss, or that you will be just fine with a three-bedroom apartment and buy a secondhand car and just live on your pension without thinking of getting resources to help others around you, you should wake up to achieve greater things. All you need to do is to select what you listen to, chose what you hear, and challenge and change the bad news you are hearing for your good.

Many a times we open our minds to different doctrines and opinions. Teachers can be communicators of truth and error; therefore, we are bound to select and choose what we hear if we must succeed in life. Choose what you want to hear. If somebody looks down on you, belittles you, or calls you all manners of names, you should know you do not belong to that setting. *You can also challenge what you hear by rebuking all negative prophesies about you. You must also reject the poor pictures which opponents may show to you about your future.* This is because what some people say, that you cannot succeed does not mean you will not succeed in actual fact. Furthermore, when some people say that your dream is too big, it does not mean you cannot achieve or fulfill the dream because *your success will only depend on your own personal efforts and good planning and commitment.* History shows that many great people have failed and had been rejected before their success. People like Bill Gates had faced one rejection or the other before. *Do not be discouraged by negative comments in your efforts to achieve a goal or fulfill a dream.*

Success in life has to do with selection. In other words, you don't open yourself to everything or everybody that comes your way. You have to be selective or else you will accumulate lots of junk in your domain or territory. Not everybody should qualify for your attention or be accessible to you. You should not relate to everyone on the same level. You should categorize your dealings with people. Many are full and overwhelmed with people that they can hardly differentiate how they can deal with the individuals. Some people may come to you and challenge you on the business you are doing or about to do. They may even tell you that your knowledge or experience may be inadequate for the task before you. Simply let them know that you can do it and that it is achievable.

You should know that *most of the people who criticize other people are known not to have achieved anything good in life.* Their main job is to discourage or bring people down. It is now left to you to let them have access to you. What is in their resume is just criticism. Endure not to let anybody put you down or frustrate you because you have a calling and purpose. Don't let anybody convince you that your child is good at cooking or because he has a passion for cooking therefore you should let him or her be working in kitchen or be a bartender while the restaurant owner is making the whole profit from the business. You should reject such an idea and prophesy what you, as a parent, wish for your child to become. Tell them that if they cannot see a doctor, lawyer, an accountant, and a CEO of companies in your child, you can do. You can let them know right there that your child will go for a better career. *Prophesy to your child that there is a winning spirit and a better destiny in him or her.* It doesn't matter if people don't see a better future for your child. You should have a positive future for him/her.

If you spend money, time, and affection on your child, every other good thing will follow by the grace of God. Let people know that a *balloon don't rise because of their color but because of what is inflated in them.* Therefore, there is a victory, winner, and success inside you. It is not over until you overcome. Let no man or situation run you over. Let no man mess you up. *Don't ever live by people's perception or judgments or opinion about you.* People's opinion change all the time. You should know by yourself that you are okay. Don't give people a chance to assess your outlook. Be comfortable with whatever you wear and your personal appearance. *Don't let other people's appearances intimidate you. Whatever you think is a mistake on your own part in relation to your outlook might generally become a style and later be in* Vogue.

THE NEED FOR SOMEONE

Divine connection is necessary for you to enjoy divine upgrading. You cannot be successful without people around you, by you, and for you. *For everything God will do for you, you need somebody beside you before it comes to pass.* That is why it is not proper to tell a helper that if he/she was not there to help that God will do it. That is an ingrate remark. It is true that God will do it, but God will not come down from heaven to help you. He will send somebody to help. It is true that *whatever one needs in life can be obtained through someone and that every life opportunity will come through someone.* We must therefore be current. It is when we are current that we can be correct and can have what we need. All we need is to divinely connect with someone who has what we need to move forward.

For example, it is the parents of a girl to be married who will lead her and release her to the man to marry her. Likewise, the contract you are writing a proposal for will be approved by someone. The money you are working for is in the hands of your employer while the loan which you need for a particular contract will be approved by someone in your bank. *To be successful in life, you need someone who has the resources needed at hand to deliver it to you.*

In the biblical story, the bread and the fishes that were needed to feed the multitude in the desert was in the hand of a young boy who volunteered them before Jesus blessed them to feed the multitude. For any place or position you may aspire to reach in life, you need the right connection to get you there. Pray not to meet the wrong people but to meet the right persons. When you meet the right person, they become the helpful as favors. *The next thing you need to accelerate your progress may be the right person who may facilitate the achievement of your success.*

You surely must have met a lot of people in life, but what you need now is the right persons and not the wrong persons. Who is the right person? The right person is the person who works with you to achieve your goals. The concept of the right person is not about numbers. It could relate to individuals or groups of persons. It may be a group of people who are knowledgeable about your intended goals or dream and ready to help you achieve the goal. They are always on your side and can go the extra mile for you to achieve your dream. There are also some people who may be negative, who and who may never see anything good in your plan. Such people may be so terrible to the extent that they feel that you can't do and tell you the reason why you cannot make it! They are better tagged as dream killers. They can use their negative prophecy and confessions to abort your dream.

The Bible says, "Faith cometh by hearing." *Likewise, negative decisions and bad omens, too, can come through listening to dream killers.* They can easily inject you with toxic information that can quickly cause you to abort your dreams. The earlier you stay away from them the better. *Watch dream killers carefully. They are not usually progressive.* They stayed timid and stagnant like water in a pond. Remember a stagnant pond will forever stink. This set of people have an association. They have meeting points. In Africa, a majority of them meet at the newspaper stands mostly early in the morning. They have a common name: free reader association. They read newspapers for free. All they want to read is about the progress of the achievers, the political matters, and also to criticize the activities of the government at all levels. After digesting the news, they will continue to speak negatively about what they read and pass on their criticisms. They consider themselves up-to-date in relation to current affairs. Although in the midst of free readers, there are very bright and brilliant individuals who may not be negative in thinking but majority don't use the information they acquired to their advantage.

Today, many talents in the sports world and in other careers were identified and trained by others with appropriate knowledge and skills. There are always carriers of good news who will show you what you need for your progress to manifest. You should try to meet with people of high caliber who know what to do to successfully climb the ladder. *Do not attempt to help people get to the top of the ladder when you are still struggling to climb the same ladder or else the two of you will fall with the ladder.* It is better to first be on the top of the ladder and later look back to help pull up others who are attempting to climb the ladder.

The most challenging or delicate people to have in your life to fulfill your dream are your family. I mean the people who grew up with you, your brothers and sisters. Why it is so difficult to deal with them is because they think they know much about you right from the beginning. They will treat you on the basis of the knowledge of your past because they know your genesis and background. They might tell you that nobody in your family had ever tried or succeeded doing what you are trying to do. They could advise you to remember that the grandparents died as poor people or that you don't have enough education, or you are not intelligent enough to do what you are trying to do. They may undermine your big dream by their utterances as they do not recognize that *they only know your past and that only God knows your future.* Beware of your brothers and sisters because they can end up putting you in the pit like the way it was done to biblical Joseph.

In some cases, parents can be obstacles to a child's progress. Some parents tend to help God by taming their children to become better beings. Remember anything you do out of God's plan and purpose for your life can cause you problem throughout life. I don't mean to say that parents should not suggest careers for their children, but in doing so, parents should be careful. *Any career chosen for a kid should be in accordance with the ability and interest of the child and not because some people are prosperous in such a field.* That people are doing well in one particular profession is no guarantee that another child being forced into the profession will succeed. Success will depend on the passion and interest of the child.

Another important issue is that you need to outgrow some old friends you grew with when you were growing. Some of them can cause setbacks for you, while some can lift you up. You need to check them out and size them up to know which of them is good for you to achieve your dream. *Hold on to those that go along with your dreams and drop those that appear to be a burden for you.* There is no way you can make it without stepping on toes, but at the end, you will be fine. Be careful of whom you handpick to ride along with you on your way to fulfilling your dream. It is always better to have good friends who may be better in keeping secrets.

If you want to advance in life and don't want to live a life of not enough for ever, you need to hang out with the people who are already there on top. If you want to be a millionaire, you better move closer to those who are in such a group. For you to be a great speaker, you need to spend time with great speakers. Potential businessmen need to work or be close to businessmen and women. A particular society can be described or defined by the nature of people living in such an environment. The common saying "show me your friend and I will tell you the type of person you are" may be relevant.

Your identity can be determined by the type of people you hang out with. Your level of income tends to equal to the average income of your five best friends. Likewise, the state and level of your health will be about average the level of their health. This might be applicable to all areas of your life, including the way you walk, talk, think, dress, your accomplishment, and the materials things you possess. The types of training and schools your kids attend will not be left out.

You are the overall combined average of the five people you associate with most. If five people around you are complainants who will always complain and will be looking back to their past, blaming others because of their misfortunes, or have phobias to success and living an "I don't care" life, in no time, you will find yourself in such shoes. *If you continue to hang out with those who are not successful, there is the possibility that you may not get your life straight.* Look at the people you hang out with in terms of their goals in life. Ask yourself if their goals are what you also want to achieve! Although, it is true we need people who can help us to realize our dream, yet we must be careful in our choice.

It is so sad that many people do not know exactly the quality of people they want to facilitate their success. Look at the people around you to see if they are more successful than you are or if their lifestyles look like what you want to emulate.

Your association with people around you either causes you to step up or go down. *There may be some of the people whom you need to cut your association with them from three days a week to three hours a week for you to achieve your dream. There are also some that you need to increase the time you spend with them per week for your own good.* Although, the decision to do away with old friends is not easy. It is left to you to choose your priority between hanging out with friends and remaining on the same spot and checking out to achieve your dream.

You must be aware of those who are your models or heroes. It is sad to know that the majority of people today accept heroes based on what society and conditions offer them. Anybody can become a star in their area of specialization or where one is talented. We can make movie actors, musicians, or sports legends our stars, but the question is, can we live the types of lives they lived growing up to become the legends they now are? Many a times we can make mistakes of making heroes of people who don't add values to our lives and the communities. The common societal problem nowadays is that people want to jump from an apprentice to become a master without experience. They don't care about learning the activities well enough to become skilled in order to become an expert.

Proper interaction with people. Interaction with people is another important aspect of life. However, meeting with people is not as important as dealing politely and consciously with them. The way we treat people who come across our ways and our attitudes with how we behave with them matters so much in the impression they will have about us. Remember, first impression lasts long. The lesson here is that *we should learn how to be fair or good to people because the little we do might be the one that will promote our success and prosperity.*

That is why we should smile, be nice, and do well to everyone who comes our way.

One wonders why some people find it difficult to smile. Instead they chill out and keep to themselves when they are in social gatherings and want to bear false witnesses against people instead of being real and telling the truth. One thing about people you meet is that you might think you know them, but the reality is, you don't know much about them. You don't know what destiny has in store for them. *The present situation must not be used to judge people.* To have evidence against somebody does not mean the truth. That was the case of Joseph in Pontifer's house. Pontifer's wife had Joseph's shirt as evidence, but the case was not true. If Pontifer's family had known Joseph, and if they knew what destiny had in store for him, they wouldn't have mistreated or misjudged him. For Joseph to have moved from prison to a palace involved divine connections through God's intervention before he could meet the butler who connected Joseph to the king for him to translate the king's dream. Likewise, if Joseph's brothers knew what destiny had for Joseph, they wouldn't have sold him. That is one of the more reasons why you don't look down on people.

What you need to take you to the next level is around you. It is not going to fall from heaven. It is left for you to know how to use it to your advantage. It is either going to upgrade, update, backdate, or downgrade you. *Backdate* is to make you current. To *downgrade* is to pull one down below where you are supposed to be, and to *upgrade* is to lift one from where one is to a higher level. To *update* is to keep one informed. These involve divine intervention.

You should learn not to live by availability but by desire. Leaving by availability is not good because life gives you just what is available and not what you desire. Also, it is important to get your provision not by natural means but divine means. If you get your job or contract by natural means, others may overshadow you. In the same manner, if you marry your spouse based on the physical outlook or by material things, it will take the grace and anointing of God for you not to regret the marriage. Out of all seven of Hannah's children, the only one she got by divine means was the one people remember till today.

There is no testimony in what you get naturally because it is assumed that it is normal and within human ability. Many people tend to take glory for such achievements and may not give God the glory in whatever was achieved. God deserves the glory in whatever we achieve.

CRISIS AND CREATIVITY

C risis is the cradle of creativity. We should not be afraid of a crisis. You can make it better in a crisis if you know your way. *Crisis and pressure are incubators of innovation.* Crisis is a world created by man. It is an event you can't control but manage. Crisis is a source of development and growth. Crisis creates opportunity for creativity. You should see every problem as a business opportunity. The more problems, the more business. For those who have the ability to forecast the economic future, every problem results in business. *Seeing every problem as a business is one of the fundamental ways of making it in life.* We should try to see business opportunities in crisis because crisis will bring money to those who can think and use the opportunity. The Japanese and Chinese see crisis, danger, and opportunity lay side by side. Henceforth, you should study your environment and look for problem and solve it to make money.

KNOW YOUR SUCCESS YARDSTICKS

Having hung around lately with some people who in my own opinion I called achievers, I mean the people with records of success who also perform at a high standard, I noticed one important thing which is common to them. It is their way of thinking about one word—*success*. I discovered that there is no failure in their dictionary, and that they believe that all things are possible. The way they measure success is quite different from the way average people measure success. *They know that the greatest enemy of success is the fear of failure.* That is why many people who failed to know this simple fact remain unsuccessful because they were afraid to do what could lead to their success. They believe that they might fail. In other words, they don't try to do something new for fear of failure!

Success to achievers is the completion and the fulfillment of the original intent or purpose for their existence. Success is not measured by the amount of money made, by the type of mansion or building we live in, or the many houses, private jets, or boats we own. Success is not measured by the number of friends one has, nor by being a relative of wealthy men or be the son or daughter of a present or past president. *It is not determined by how much you have in your bank's savings accounts. Moreover, success is not measured by your academic achievement.* It cannot be measured by how eloquently you can preach or by the number of people in your congregation or the numbers of your followers on Twitter, Facebook, or your other blogs. "Success is to be measured not so much by the position that one has reached in life as by the obstacles which he has overcome while trying to succeed," said Booker T. Washington.

I can define success as the ability to discover one's purpose and complete it before one dies. Success can also be defined as the potential destiny of all creative things or beings. Success must be measured basically by why you are created. It is also a way of fulfilling your purpose in life. Although each and every man's purpose is different. You should never compare your purpose with others. You have to personally define your purpose. *Whatever you are born to do is in you now, and your success in life depends on how you fulfill all that is entrapped inside you.*

In order to fulfill your destiny, you have to redefine your destiny and bring it to your purpose in life. Many at times we compete with other people in life, and because we do better than they do, we think we are successful. *Success is not outbidding or outclassing other people.* You can always find somebody lesser than you in all areas of life and think you are successful. No! That is not a true judgment. Success is not measured by what you have done or what others have done.

Success can be better measured by what you have done and what you should and could have done. In life, the only person who can really define how successful you are is God. Because he is the one who created you and knows his purpose for your life, and he is the one who can truly judge if maybe you are successful or not, or maybe you've done all what you are destined, programmed, or wired to do in life. He has the yardstick to measure your performance in life. Because your husband has a good job or business that earns good money for him which give you as a wife the opportunity to give material things to people who are less privileged around you does not mean your family has arrived or is successful.

The question is, How many jobs have you created? How many other children's school fees in your community are you paying per term or year? *How many community responsibilities have you shouldered both financially and in kind?* How many hungers have you quenched with your money? How many small business owners have you helped to establish their business? Did you realize that God wants you to do better than giving out used shoes and clothes by trusting such wealth into your family's hand? *Does it ever cross your mind that what makes you feel like a successful person in your community is because of the nature of people (middle class) living in that area?*

Don't make the mistake of measuring your success by the ability of the people around you. You will agree with me that if you relocate to another neighborhood where other rich people are living, your presence might likely not be recognized or felt because what your family had as assets might just be a peanut compared with others in your new neighborhood. At this stage, you will be doing harm to yourself than good by thinking you have arrived.

Not being able to acquire a lot of wealth or have fleets of cars or mansions at a particular time does not make you a failure. I said it earlier. Only God knows the yardstick for measuring success. What is important most is having a rest of mind.

History shows that possibilities of rich people having heart attacks and dying earlier is very high because they think a lot about their investments and the overall profit and loss on their business. Whereas an average person will just put his mind at rest and focus on the little investment or salary he is earning on a regular basis without having to panic. He does not have to think about a vessel or container on the sea, neither does he have to attend any meeting as a matter of urgency. Of course, he doesn't have any salary to pay at the end of the month. Although, that is not good enough for a man in my own opinion. Because life is not just about bread and butter.

Success must not be measured by how you compete with other people but how you compare with what you are capable of doing yourself. *You should not run your life program as if you want to beat other people.* You need to find your purpose and fulfill it. Purpose is the key to success. *What lies before you and what lies behind you are tiny matters compared with what lies within you.* Merely looking at your life one year back or can I say in this year alone, you will agree with me that one or two of the goals you set have not been fulfilled. This makes many people to be depressed, restless, and discouraged. But the truth of the matter is, *looking behind you will not really help you, and looking ahead of you can also make you afraid because you will be looking at your future as if it is not certain that you will succeed.*

What is important in your life is what is in you now. What you need to succeed in life is deposited in you already. Whatever you were born to do is inside you. The point remains, what are you doing with it for it to work for your good? *Your purpose can be defined as God's original intent for your creation. This is what God wants you to accomplish.* This is the reason why God created you. You are created by God to do things that only you can do. That is the more reason why you are so unique and don't have a photocopy. In other words, you have a unique fingerprint. What God wants you to do is your purpose for living, but when you see your own purpose in life, it becomes a vision. *Whenever you see your purpose, it is better you keep it to yourself if you want to really achieve your dream.* This is what affected Joseph when he declared his dream to his brothers. Thank God that his dream is from above and not from anybody.

At times when you have a glimpse of your purpose in life, you might not believe it. Because what God has in stock for everybody is so great that it is hard to believe. It will always be bigger than what you can ever think of or imagine. *The problems many people are facing are that society has been working against God's plans and purpose for them.* In other words, as an individual, circumstances in life will not want you to achieve your dreams.

People in life will put a limit on your purpose because they will tell you what you can and cannot do. But it is your duty to let people know that your dream is from God and that it is not stoppable. Although, they will always tell you that you are crazy because they want you to believe that your dream is too much for you to fulfil. But what society forgot is that *your dream is from God and since it is not ordinary, you are unstoppable.* The truth of the matter is, if anybody agreed with you the first time you shared your dream and purpose with them or when they heard it from somewhere else, you should know that your dream is not from God. Why? Any dream and purpose from God will always be bigger than what anybody can ever imagine. If a dream is from God, you have to be first totally rejected before you can be accepted by the people around you.

People will go against your will at first because they know you are going against their expectation for you. In other words, you are going

187

against the norms because people have already decided who you are and who you are supposed to be. *Living contrary to the people's expectation will surely disappoint them.* That is why they will always want to do everything to go against you and find faults in whatever you are doing. They will surely antagonize you. But it is your duty not to let the antagonism make you believe that you are wrong. Resistance to the opposition is a sign that you are right because you break fort to all opposition that can pull you down. The bitter truth in life is that *not many people in life have a high expectation for you.*

Without a purpose or clear understanding of why you were born, you can never succeed in life. *Your purpose in life will always separate you from anybody's opinion of you.* You cannot be successful if you don't have a master plan of where you are going and what you intend to do. *You can never be manipulated by other people if you know your purpose. One of the terrible and saddest things in life is that people don't know the reason why they exist.* That is where people try all manners of ways to look for recognition and want to get pitied when they were not supposed to be pitied.

You need to discover your purpose in life so that you can get your vision right. The creator of an object knows the reason and the purpose for its creation. You need to get your purpose from God who is the author and finisher of your faith. He knows it all.

Purpose is so powerful because you were created for a purpose, and with the purpose, nobody is mistakenly created. Purpose can be defined as the original reason of a thing. It can also be defined as a reason why things were created. Nobody on earth is born to make an experiment. You are not born to live a useless life. You are not born just to complete a life cycle and die. But *you were born just because there is something God wanted to do in life that required you to participate in.* Whatever others think about you should not be the yardstick for measuring yourself and your future. Whatever you were born to do is the reason why God created you.

Nobody is responsible for your happiness except you. Don't compare your life with others. You don't have the ideas of what other people's journey is all about. You should have it in mind that it is the will of God to make sure that you are successful in life. Therefore, success in relation to your purpose is making it to the end of your purpose. Any animal in a cage which is not allowed to do what it would have done naturally cannot fulfill its purpose. Giving birth to you as a person is one of the purposes why your mum and dad got married. Inability to have a child in any marriage does not make the marriage fulfill completely the God purpose for such a marriage. Although, many couples may wish to have children but circumstances beyond their control may not allow them to have children.

Every mango, cashew, cocoa, and palm tree is the product of a seed. *The seed is not successful until it grows and matures into full tree.* Purpose gives meaning to life with time. We were placed in time for a purpose. If you don't know your purpose in life, your life in time will have no meaning. That is why people may become frustrated. Many may wonder why they are doing the types of job, going to the same place all the time, why they were born in a particular place, or why they got married to XYZ and not to ABC?

Many commit slow suicide by drinking alcohol, smoke all manners of things, sniff cocaine, and so on. Why? Because they can't see anything more important than what they were addicted to. The reason why you should not be addicted to drugs, smokes, cocaine, and other things that can harm your destiny is because there are other things that are more beneficial to you than these things. Those other things can allow you to fulfill your destiny and the purpose of God for your life. Choices are yours. You need to stop engaging in anything that can stop you from fulfilling your dream. Because there is no value in those things. When you have a purpose for your life, it will really discipline your behavior and affect or determine your habits. Purpose gives life meaning.

The greatest motivator in life for you should be death. Whenever you think about death, you should work hard because death already set a time for you. Since you know there is a time to be born and to die, you ought to complete your assignment before you die. *If you, by any reason, die before your purpose is fulfilled, it means your destiny is killed.* The truth is, whatever you are born to do, you are given the right amount of time to do it. Many are of age right now. Still, they have not accomplished much in life, but God still gives them grace like Hezekiah. Some are living according to their time and getting things done. We are wired differently.

When you pass your time, you begin to do foolish things. That is why it is good to find your purpose and maximize the use of your time to the glory of God and mankind. You should know that your future is not ahead because God takes your future and present. That is the beginning and the end of your life, and he merges it together and implants it in you as a body. That means your future is not ahead of you but is in you at present. It is entrapped in you. *Many keep thinking they are still going to the future. That is why they keep depending on people, relationships, and connections.* Your own future is embedded in you, and so you are carrying your own raw materials.

Your future does not depend on your external environment and it is not ahead of you. People around you may not like you, but never mind. As long as you like yourself, what is inside you will carry you through. *You are not important because of how long you live but you are important because of how effective you live.* You should not be concerned about growing old but for effectiveness. Many people who impacted the life of people in most cases don't live long. Martin Luther King did not live long, neither did John Kennedy, yet they influenced lives within their short existence. Even Jesus Christ was very young when he died.

What does it profit a man that lives long without achieving any purpose or without impacting people's life positively? You should not waste any time anymore. Choose friends who will assist you to achieve your goals and read books that will inspire you to move forward. There are friends you have to drop while there are some friends you have to make if you have to get to your destination. God gave us years so that we can end and begin a new life. If some messed up in business last year till the end of December and some engaged in foolish things and made great mistakes, but it may be that January of the following year may be new beginning.

New Year brings the privilege of closure and the opportunity to begin afresh. You can correct whatever mistakes you made in the previous year and even begin on a new page. If you succeeded last year, you should not relax this year because *the greatest enemy of prog-*

ress or success is previous success. You should never let your past success enter your head or deceive you lest you will stop progressing and start falling. Don't let the success of the past prevent your present success. The future of all creations is trapped in all creations. The future of the seed is not outside the seed but in the seed. Whatever you are meant to be is already in you. In other words, the future existed before the present.

You should understand very well that there is no manufacturer on earth that will make a product without finishing it first. Before making an aircraft or any machine or product that will serve a particular purpose, the manufacturer has to draw and design the product and finish it first before restarting the one that he will introduce to the market. That is to say, those manufacturers present the future first and then go back and create the present. Whatever God has designed you to do, he has already finished it first. That means *your future is in your present and your present is going around with your future every day.*

Your future can be regarded as unmanufactured purpose. *Your future is a product of manufactured product that is passed.* No wonder people are so worried about the future that will never come. People do not realize that their own future is already in them as they are standing. But unfortunately, they are wasting their time about the future, which prevents them from making proper use of their present, forgetting that you are already in your future. What you forget to realize is that your future is better than what it is now. How do I know? God our creator will never create any substandard product. He does not create anything halfway. So you are wonderfully and fearfully made. Our God is so mighty that he cannot afford to show anybody the future plans he has in stock for mankind. Lest human beings misbehave and misuse the opportunity. Many will not even work anymore if they have the clear vision of what God has in stock for their future. That is the reason why people keep on trying and struggling to find ways to success and prosperity in life. People keep on looking for connections left and right, going to school and jumping from one profession to another, traveling from one country to another all in the name of finding greener pastures in order to become successful. In actual sense, God had already finished your own chapter of the book. *Your life every day is a chapter in your book of life. What you need to do is to make sure to read your own chapter very well, digest, and meditate on whatever you can read in this chapter that will make you come out successfully in your next life examination.* This will surely help you achieve your dream!

Individually, we all come with different and unique chapters in life. Your own chapter may be to develop the skills you have the passion for. While mine may go to school and learn a particular profession, and for many others, the chapters may be trading. Some may have singing in their chapter book of life. Some are programed to be teachers or pastors. For someone who is divinely programed to be in sport chapter's pages, if he/she stumbles on trading or comedian chapters, it is very likely that he/she might not succeed. Likewise, if you are programmed to be a teacher, it is likely you will never succeed as a politician. Why? Because leading and teaching are two parallel lines that may not meet. *You may never understand what is being taught in a chapter that you are not programmed for.* This is where trial and error come from. We keep seeing people who are reading the wrong chapters in their lifetime, struggling as if success is impossibility in life. The question remains, How do you know the exact chapter you ought to be? *It is your moral duty to sit down and discover your own chapter by yourself.* Reading other people's chapter will not do you any good in life.

Many in life are usually anxious and nervous about how they are going to read through their chapters. They have issues and concerns on how to master what is in their chapters because to some, their chapters seems to have many pages and prove to be too loaded for them. But the good news is that God, who created your chapters, is already committed to it and knows how to solve your problems. Bills payments and other unforeseen contingences coupled with some expenditures are the paragraphs in the chapter book of some people which make it too long for them to read. While family issues are the problems some are facing, to others, peer groups and wrong associates are their problems. Wrong positioning is a real headache for some.

Whatever is your concern, it is never too hard for God to solve. If God can solve Lazarus's problem, I believe he will show you the way to navigate through your storm in life. All you need to do is to move closer to God in prayer and follow God instructions, plus the advice of the achievers. If you can fulfill all righteousness, God will surely answer your prayers and provide for your needs. It is not your business to know how God is going to do it. The important thing is for you to leave everything for God and let him perform his wonder in your life. *God can finance your project through any means because he is committed to his word.* He will never wait to let his word become void. Your source is God; therefore, your resource is waiting for you.

Your future is more important than your past. Therefore, you should not worry. Try to run your own race and stop competing with others. Your own race should be more important to you than any other person's race. Your future is more valuable and powerful than your past. You can't see your past again, so you can't do anything about it. *Your future is in you right now, and you can do much more about your future than your past.* Your past is the portion of your future. It is just a small piece of your future. You still have a big piece to live with. *Don't be committed to your past failures anymore because it will restrict you from going ahead to your future.*

What a big tragedy! Your past is fixed and dead already. It's already history. While your future is still variable. You can shape it as you like to your own advantage. *The only way you can let your past affect you now is if you give your past a life. You give your past life by talking about it, thinking about it, and living with it.* You cannot change the past, but you can live a new future. The good thing about God having your future in your present is that failure will never be your portion because Jesus never fails. If you listen to him, what you are supposed to work for God can give you as a gift. In the other way around, if you take law into your hands by doing your things on your own outside God's approval, God can make you work for what is supposed to be a gift for you.

Your future in life does not depend on the economy nor on your background but on God that is working on his purpose for you. God is the owner and the maker of all things. He can turn things around and shift people from one position to another just for him to fulfill his purpose in your life. Where people say it is not going to happen, it will definitely happen for you with God. You need to be bold and have your confidence in God whom you are serving. You still have the opportunity to live a good life of no mess, tragedy, or tons of mistakes in it.

Don't ever live in your past. You cannot go into your future if you live in your past. The best and the greatest way to drive your car is not to look at the rearview mirror. If you do that and not concentrate by looking back, you will definitely crash. What are the mistakes in your past you want to improve on? For some, it's to go back to school, while to some it is to get a right man or starting a desired business. But by and large, you need to prepare and move on. Just as a seeds need the right soil and nutrients to flourish, you need the right friendship, you need to stay in the right position, and you need to meet with the right people and drop the bad people in your life. Likewise, *you need to move on and get ready to learn new things that will push your life forward.*

Your future is not to be thrown away because of bad company, your personal foolishness, and negligence. Lastly, remember *the yardstick for measuring your achievement is not by looking at your physical possessions. Not at all!*

PASSION

*P*assion is the ability for someone to have a strong desire for something. It involves having a desire that is much stronger than any obstacles. In other words, if you have passion for anything, nothing can disturb you from achieving it. As a man, you have a strong passion for the wife you married. That is why you were able to marry her as your wife. Likewise, we tend to have a strong passion for food. That is why we strive hard at all costs to get the food because we know it is good for our life. The major problem confronting the people are that the majority don't have passion for anything in life. I wonder why people refused to wake up in life with passion.

Passion is a commitment that goes beyond contention. It means anything that comes against you cannot stop your motivation for accomplish your dream. People who are successful in life have passion for everything they wish and want to do. They were always ready to die for whatever course they believed in or they were going after. *If you want to fulfill your dream in life, you must not quit going after what you wanted to do based on your first disappointment.* Passion is a kind of spirit that saves the life.

Passion in life involves finding something worthy to die for. One of the biggest problems that people are facing in life is that they don't have something in mind to die for. People gamble with their lives. They do things as if it does not matter. So if they can't achieve it, they leave it. In the real sense, *if you are not ready to die for what you are living for, it is not worth living for.* In case you have a desire to be a medical doctor or a lawyer, or you are looking at yourself as a future CEO of a multimillion-dollar company and you know what can help you to that, level is for you to go to school. Failure to get admission for the first time will never disturb you from pressing further and studying hard in order for you to get ready for your next entrance exam.

I have an uncle who is now a successful attorney in the United States of America. I remember he struggled several years before he got admitted into one of the pioneer universities in Nigeria to study law. In the first attempt, he was shy of some points to get admitted to study law. Although, he was offered admission to study another course in that university, he rejected the admission because he had no passion for the course. Of course, some of his friends settled for less or other courses which they did not have passion for just because they wanted to be on campus at all cost!

My uncle preferred to wait for the following year. He went back and enrolled in a coaching class in preparation for the next Joint Admission and Matriculation Board (JAMB) examination in Nigeria. At the second attempt, he scored more than the required points needed for him to secure an admission into that university to study law. After some years of hard work, he graduated with flying colors. Now he has his law office in one of the busiest cities in the United States of America. I once asked him why he refused to honor the alternative admission the university offered him back in the days. He was very honest to tell me, "I rejected any admission to study any course that is contrary to what I have passion for. What I have passion for is to be a lawyer." He stressed further that his passion to be an attorney originated right from when he was a teenager. His dad was summoned to court because of the money he owed which he failed to pay on time. He said ever since then, he has been looking at himself as someone who would defend people in court. More also, he said he imagined himself sitting among people in the corporate world, making vital business decisions. When he was offered admission to study what was contrary to what his passion and dream for was, he rejected it out rightly.

If you have passion for anything in life, you will never take no for an answer. If by any chance you stop doing what you are doing and you are still happy simply because you have an alternative, it means you have not discovered your purpose. In case you change your business or career for another one and it doesn't have any effect on you, it means your purpose has not been discovered. It means *what you just left undone which still satisfy and bring joy to you are not what you are born naturally to do.* What you are born to do is only what can satisfy you. When you are born and destined to do something in life, you don't retreat until you finish doing what you are wired to do. It means *what you are destined to do will surely cancel your desire for retirement until you achieve it.* If you discover what you have passion for in life, you will never think about doing something that will not profit you. In other words, nobody will press you before you do what is right. For instance, *you don't want to set an alarm to remind you when it is time for you to go to toilet.* You don't need anybody to encourage you to eat. As a responsible man, you don't need encouragement to take care of your family. Your car will not force you to buy gas (petrol). Why? Because it is your moral duty to do so when due. Otherwise, you will not get the best from the car.

The problem and the saddest thing in society today is that majority are not living according to their purpose. That is why confusion and frustration set in. When you are not living according to your purpose, all actions you take will be miserable. It will look as if you are in darkness. *You need to discover something in your life that will always cause you to do something which you have passion for in life.* You must always have at least a reason for waking up in the morning to promote your dream.

A life without a cause is a useless and purposeless life. Without a cause or purpose in life, you will be wondering around looking for what is not lost. *A purposeless life will be full of crisis.* It is a pity that some people continue to do the same thing all year round without thinking of diversifying their actions. *The reason why so many employees may not focus their attention on their God-given purpose is that many think and base their purpose on food.* People go to work and start thinking of lunchtime. And when it is lunchtime, they will be dreaming of closing time at 4:00 p.m. This is their exit and set free time based on the agreement with their employers. They are anxious to get out of the job because they are tired of the job and want to do something different as they are doing what they have no passion for.

Until you have something more important than food, you have not found your purpose.

When you discover your purpose in life, a passion will rise up in you that will keep your focus away from food and other distractions. *When you discover your purpose, your working attitude will change, and you may have "no working" hours.* A person with purpose does not have working hours. They don't punch in or punch out of the jobs. They work hard and smart. In other words, they work till they are tired. That was the style of great people who have made history. When you discover your true purpose in life, nothing will stop you because there will be passion in you that is stronger than the fear of death, intimidation, inferiority complex, discouragement, and discontinuity which are distractions.

You need to build the muscle and strength that will make you discover something that will make you have a reason for living beyond death. You cannot live to change the life of the people around you or your generation until you are ready to say and agree that distractions do not matter anymore. Meaning you must tell your affliction, opposition, critics, and all other people that don't want to see your face that you did not care about them and that it doesn't matter what they plan, say, or do. You are ready to forge ahead and pursue any dream you have. In this case, you have become a dead man to criticism. That was the case of Martin Luther King. He was dead completely to all opposition that was mitigating against his dream.

Other people's opinions are said to be too late for anybody that has a purpose to fulfil because no matter what they say or suggest to you, you will never yield to their threat because the purpose in you will not allow you to yield to whatever threat anybody has against you. You will develop a thick muscle and skin against such a threat. *If you have passion or purpose, you will be motivated by troubles* because you will develop resistant characteristics and an ability that will make you stand in the storm. *You will be consistent when you are convinced that what you are going after really belongs to you, or else you will quit in the middle of the journey.*

DEVELOP A POSITIVE MIND

Being successful in life has to do with the mind. Likewise, knowing and discovering your ability to carry out the things that can transform you from your present position to where you ought to be are related to the way your mind works. The truth of the matter is that *nothing can change for you until your mind is tuned for the change.* You can change your job, your location, your name, your wardrobes, and everything changeable in your entire life. But without a change of mind-set, you will still remain a poor person. Many are poor today because they have the mind-set that nobody has ever made it in their family's community and caucus. Because of this reason, many resign to fate and believe that poverty is normal. *Unless you have a mental transformation and believe in your ability, life may not treat you well.* Many who may have passion for certain businesses or career but saw some people failing in those businesses may be discouraged if they use the failure of others as their yardstick. A negative-minded person may never be successful in life. You should be encouraged to be positive in all your thinking.

In whatever you are doing in life, it is highly essential that you believe in your own ability before believing or relying on anybody. The genesis of many people's problem today is not because people don't believe in God but failure to believe in one's self and the ability to achieve what individuals can achieve. Mind you, I am not saying believing in God is not right. But after God, you need to believe in your personal self. *Many people do not believe in the ability to do what God has wired them to do.* You must try as much as possible to believe in yourself. One of the reasons why you should *believe* in yourself is because God believes in you. That is why God created you in his own image and wired you with all possibilities and the ability to reason.

God does not create you as a photocopy of anybody. You are made original. You should not see yourself as imitation of any mankind but as the apple of God's eye who is wonderfully made. You should begin to see yourself in the way that God sees you. You are a good product. God saw Moses and Gideon in a better light than they saw themselves. This is in Judges 6:14–15 and Exodus 3:10–11. It is so unfortunate that many people are discouraged because of the way others see them. *You need to change your thinking if things have to change for you.* Do people see you as a failure, a "never do well" person, low class, illiterate, untidy, antisocial, smoker, drunkard, former drug addict, and unserious person? Or do they judge you on the bases of your poor background? If they do, turn a deaf ear to them and do not be discouraged. That was your past. *There is nobody without a past.* What happened in the past is a past tense. You should focus on your present and future. You can no longer live in the past but focus on the future. *Do not allow other people's opinions about you determine your destiny.* All they know about you is your past and possibly your present, but they don't know your future. They don't know what will happen to you in the nearest minute. Nobody has the ability to know the plans and purpose of God for your life. Keep on trying.

You are not a failure because you try to fail. You are a failure if you fail to try more after your early failure or mistakes. Remember, people saw Peter as a reed which is not stable, but Jesus saw him as a stone which could be built upon in John 1:42. *Stop seeing yourself the way people see you.* You are more and better than your present situation. Failure to believe in yourself could be so disastrous for you. It can lead to other problems. It can even lead to an untimely death. *Many people who have been frustrated in their life schedules and committed suicide did so because they no longer believed in their ability to prosper.*

We were told that the Israelites who did not believe in God and themselves died in the wilderness. Whenever you believe in yourself and your ability to do well, your life will be prolonged. *Try as much as possible to believe in yourself no matter how challenging and discouraging your circumstances are.* One of the important reasons why you must believe in yourself is because as a person, you will always act according to the way you see yourself. The Israelites saw themselves as grasshoppers. That was why they could not move forward. If you want to progress in life, you must see yourself in a positive light. Don't ever think negatively. Negativity should no more be in your dictionary.

Remember, *it is not lack of money that causes poverty or makes people poor but lack of positive thinking and reasoning.* Many have money, but they were not joyful. Happiness is seasonal and is tied to material things. But the joy of the Lord is forever. You should endeavor to influence others positively and help them to fulfill their destinies. That is one of the best ways for you to achieve your goals and fulfill your own dream too. A family or relative you have the capacity to help which you failed to render help for may turn to be a liability for you or your children in the future. If you are on top of the ladder and you don't care about people you left at the bottom, you will surely meet them on your way down.

Are you a source of encouragement or discouragement to others? Are you saying or doing things that will help others believe in themselves? You should believe in yourself and start identifying people who should be mentors by you to fulfill your destiny. Encourage to be a positive influence on your world. A well-built generation today is the source of joy and wealth of tomorrow.

AVOID MONEY MISTAKES

In our society today, many are so poor not because they don't have access to money or lack connections, but there are some mistakes which we make in our everyday lives, and they serve as setbacks for our financial progress. This section of this book will be dealing with such vital mistakes we make with money.

Firstly, *we should avoid the "getting rich quick" mentality.* It is the idea that one can get rich fast without smart and hard work with integrity. The "get rich quick" mentality is based on dishonesty and on cutting corners! Sometimes marketers may introduce their products with some attractive conditions that if we can push the products to a certain number of people or if we can encourage a certain number of people to join the business, we will advance in the marketing system and make a great amount of money when they know that it may not be easy to achieve such a goal. However, the promise of great money to be made will draw people into the scheme.

The truth of the matter is, those that set up the scheme are just sitting at home while those that are marketing the products are busy roaming around the streets wasting time. Most times, this kind of business doesn't work. It is merely a waste of time. Remember, time is precious, and time itself is money. It is the same with pool betting lotteries and other gambling activities on which many have wasted their retirement benefits and fortunes to the extent that they find it difficult to rise in life. *We should stop spending our money and time on things that are wasteful and not viable.* The more you make money from gambling, the more you are prone to lose the money. Gambling is an addiction that you don't want to involve yourself in if you must succeed in life. The more one goes to a casino for gambling, the more addicted one becomes. Many even go to the extent of taking their paychecks and salaries to casinos to play games. Many spend days in casinos, wasting their precious time and wages from their hard labor in the name of getting rich quick. Unfortunately, majority ends up losing all.

Many are ignorant of their right to prosper in the scriptures. Many people are ignorant of the covenant God has with them on getting rich. This is the reason why many people are beating around the bushes and looking for insecure ways to get rich quickly. Many of these ways of getting rich are not very real but deceitful. We should be able to differentiate between the riches which are real and the fake. When God says the blessing of God makes riches without adding sorrow, we should know this is real. When the holy scriptures says the silver is mine and the gold is mine and the glory of the latter shall be greater than the former, it means it is real. When the Bible says the God shall supply our riches according to his riches and glory, we should know that it is real. Don't allow someone else to define or predict your blessing. *When you allow somebody else to define your blessings, that person may limit your ability.*

You should set off your mind from the belief that there is a conspiracy to keep you poor. Many who are poor may not believe that most of the mistakes that led to their being poor might have been caused by themselves. Instead they may feel that somebody else is the root cause of their poor situation. But this cannot be true because *no man can keep you where you don't want to be.* Many blame their mistakes on their parents, their origin, and background while some shift the blame for their misfortune on their friends and relatives. Many believe they would have done better if they were born in the cities or in a particular country, forgetting that different cities have different problems. Some assume that it is the responsibilities of members of their families abroad to make them successful even when they themselves are doing nothing to improve lives!

You need to wake up from your slumber and hold on to your destiny. Remember, your destiny is not in the hands of any of your family, friends, employers, and your pastors. People can only advise you on whatever you want them to advice you on but cannot impose any action on you. *Yielding to people's advice is a choice but not by force.* It is easier to lead a camel to the brooks, but you cannot force the camel to drink water. Many people like to wait for others to encourage or push and jump-start them before they can take a decisive action regarding their lives. *You don't even need anybody to encourage you on what you have passion for.* People often forget that it is not the hearer of the words that are safe but the doers of the words.

People will attach to you positively when you have something positive going on in your life. Suggestions and advice will surely come because success has so many relations. *Stop waiting for recognition. Respect is to be earned but not to fight for.* Where you are today suffering is a result of the wrong choice you made yesterday. It is your choice. You can as well make a choice to become somebody in life.

Don't have the belief that any currency is too hard to earn. Once you believe that a currency is hard to earn, it will become hard for one to get. The nickname *hard currency* that third world countries give to Western world currencies made them difficult to obtain. *You should have the mind-set that all currencies are very easy to get. This will surely alleviate the phobia that money is hard to earn.*

The concept of seed sowing is relevant to the idea of prosperity. You must sow before you can reap. *Many eat all their fruits without remembering to sow part of the seed for future harvest.* They prepare for sure hunger. Seed sowing is not limited to money contribution in churches or mosques. You sow seeds when you invest in profitable ventures like shares, estates, or property development. You create jobs, help the needy around you, and invest on your children. *Desist from the habit of fruit eating.*

Many make great mistakes by believing that jobs are sources of riches and prosperity. The truth of the matter is that jobs are jobs. Irrespective of your position at whichever jobs you are, *it will be very difficult or impossible for you to become a millionaire just by earning salaries or paychecks.* Although, some CEOs become millionaires through what they do. But the simple fact is, as a CEO, your position is not a job position because as a CEO, your position has added value to the companies you are working for. You are no more a mere laborer but part of the decision makers and a company by yourself.

Many love to write good résumés. They move from one job to another without allowing themselves the opportunities to be creative in any capacity. They become rolling stones that gather no moss. It is the creativity and invention that brings wealth and not just moving from one job to the other. Many who probably have ideas of profitable inventions but fear to use the ideas may be glued to their comfortable situation, losing potential sources of wealth. The good things around us are the results of the handiwork and thinking of some people. The clothes we wear, the wristwatches, the cars, and the airplanes we have were all invented by somebody. Most of the inventors are richer than the consumers of their products. The meaning of JOB is *just over broke.*

Saving

We need to learn how to save and save wisely. Many put their money in savings accounts with little or no interest paid. The main *reason* why people put their money in savings accounts is because the money is easy to access! But *the money put in a treasury bill and other lifetime savings are not easy to access but can earn something to benefit the investors. We cannot build wealth with the money that is easy to access and spend.* Instead we should put our money in a money market.

We should avoid investing in depreciating assets. A depreciating asset is any asset that does not increase in values. *Buying too much clothes and shoes is a depreciating asset.* Buying a big house which you are struggling to maintain is not good enough. Keeping a fleet of cars that do not earn money for you is a bad investment. Smoking, womanizing, and addiction to drugs and alcohol is also a bad investment. *Having expensive carpets, furniture, and decorations hanging on your walls when you can scarcely afford it is a negative investment.* Keeping pets when you cannot maintain it is a downward investment. *Living in an expensive apartment or neighborhood just because of peer group pressure is a bad investment.*

If we don't wake up and address our money mistakes, some external body will determine how we live, and they will hold on to some of the important documents of our life. That is why banks that own our mortgage hold the important documents of our houses. They have the power over our finances. We must device means by which the power can change hands. We don't have to wait till thirty years to finish our mortgage payments. *Until we can influence our community economically, we are still struggling to be relevant.* We must therefore do something that will improve our finances which will give us power to help our communities.

In the free enterprise society of the West, there seems to be an economic system which enriches few people by the labor of many people. *It seems as if the Western economy is designed to favor few and put the majority in bondage.* However, many can free themselves from the financial strangulation if they can avoid making serious financial mistakes. For example, by making profitable investments and savings, they can secure good a future unlike those that work overtime every day like donkeys and sweat in pains but have no financial evidence to show for their hard labor because of their financial decisions.

There is a need for proper planning for a brighter future. Many may wake up and suddenly remember that they are close to retirement age without concrete future plans for retirement. Such is a sure way to a poor future and frustration! *We must plan appropriately for our future in order to secure our future.* We are not created to be poor. *Poverty is not in our culture, but it is the financial and money mistakes which we make that may trigger the possibility of poverty.*

For instance, many poor nations today are not naturally poor as God did not make them poor. It is the lack of good leadership and the inability to properly manage their God-given resources that makes them to be poor. In Africa, Nigeria is one of the largest oil-producing countries in the world, yet the citizens are suffering from lack of appropriate employment and infrastructural facilities. *Many Nigerian youths want to migrate to the Western world, not minding the possible problems awaiting them in the Western world.* The local problems have increased the attraction in the Western world.

You need to know what you are called for by standing up to the challenges and stop making some ugly financial mistakes. *If you don't know what you are doing, someone else will redefine your destiny.* The world is listening to those who have something to offer. But *nobody will listen to you if you lack or you are poo*r. The rich are the people dictating the pace of the economy. The wealthy are the policy makers. *Do you know that the greatest form of poverty is to use every resource in one generation?* When a parent at retirement has nothing to leave for the children, the children will start struggling on their own. This will cause the chain of poverty to continue in the family. *To get out of this poverty cycle, the children must make sound financial decisions which will make them take firm control of their finances so as to free themselves from poverty.*

Did you ever realize that it is the money in your pocket that will determine where you can live in the city? Not your beauty, dressing, or connections. Neither is it your spiritual qualification. Different cities have different parks and amenities based on their design and types of people living there. *Do you realize that a majority of the people die without a will because there is nothing to write in the will?*

The problem with society today is that many are ignorant of the basic elements in moneymaking. There are few teachers who teach people about money. It is unfortunate that many work around the clock without ever reading any book about money management. *It is very important that we should endeavor to be reading money management books as often as we can and attend seminars so that our financial mentality and orientation can change.* We must make moves. It is those that make moves that can make waves in society and can have secure financial futures.

You can give money to poor people or the needy around you. Many want to give to people who have the ability to pay them back in multiple folds. But they don't want to give to the poor or those that are unpopular. Many don't want to give where it will be unnoticed. The Bible made it known to us that it is in sowing that we reap. Moreover, cheating is a great mistake in our efforts to make money. *We should pay full wages for those who serve us or render certain services for us.*

STARTING A BUSINESS

Most successful people in the world started from humble little beginnings. *We should not despise our little beginning. Starting a particular business would not come easy.*

Firstly, you need to recognize that business is meeting other people's needs. The problem that majority of people have today is that people are suffering from a common disease called *people's blindness.* You need to recognize the needs of the people and what exactly they are ready to spend money on. One millionaire once said it is simple to become a millionaire. "Just produce what people need." That is *by recognizing the needs and problems that people are ready to spend money to solve, and meeting those needs will bring money.*

Remember, to recognize money is to identify business opportunities. *How do you then recognize business opportunities? How do you recognize the flow of values?* Consider the population of where you live. Look at what their basic daily needs are. I mean what people cannot do without in a day. For example, people will need toothbrushes, toothpaste, shoes, food, and clothes. Many will also need telephones. Some will need mobility to get to their work and so on. Look at the possibilities of making all these services available to the people. *If you will be in business, you must have the capacity to see and meet the people's need.* In case you cannot discern what other people's needs are, try to look at yourself and see what your own daily basic needs are. Compare yourself with others. Definitely, your basic need will be other people's needs. *The problem we have is that most our minds have been programmed for consumption and not production.*

We need to recognize that we have been wired from heaven in a unique way to do certain things in life. It is our moral duty to find and recognize our areas of specialization which God has ordained us for and follow it up. What God divinely created and wired individuals for from heaven are different. *You don't want to copy another person's destiny.* Don't because Mr. A. is doing fine as a musician and you want to sing while God ordained you to be a trader. You need to discover what you have a passion for. God has wired our spirit concerning what we ought to be in life. That is why as human beings, we have different approaches, we have what catches our attention, and we have what we have flair for. It is your duty to combine money-making activities with what you have passion for that you have been wired to do. You should carefully take your passion to God in prayer and put it to work in order to meet the people's needs. *You need to be passionate about information and knowledge.* You need good and vast information to take you to your next level of prosperity.

The Bible says, "My people perish because of lack of knowledge." Human beings are transformed by the renewal of their minds. *The rate of change in our life is directly proportional to the rate of change in our minds.* You should know that there are moneymaking activities around information technology business. You need to recognize opportunities in problems. *There are some peculiar problems in your immediate environment or community which you do not need to wait for outsiders to come and solve for you.* It is your duty to find ways to meet the people's needs.

One of the best and the simplest ways to start a new business is to carefully look at the products that are already produced which are in circulation and find a way of improving on those products. There are no products in life that are in the final stages of development. This means we can improve on any products in life. The opportunities for improving the qualities of life of our people are so many and vast. You should not expect the government to be the front runner in developing your communities. Most of the people who brought development to your environment are not government officials. Government roles are to make rules and to enforce the rules. Most of the inventors are private individuals. *You need to take responsibilities for your lives and stop blaming governments.*

Your attitude to customers when you are in business really matters. *How are you treating your customers as a business owner?* The way you greet your customers really matters. As a trader selling goods and other essential commodities, you can't just sit down and let the customers alone to solve their problems without you attending to them while in your shop. You have to be on your feet and be diligent whenever customers are in your shop. *How do you respond to phone calls?* When you have missed calls, do you normally return calls? Are you the kind who talks politely, patiently, and softly on the phone, or you are so rude without telephone manners? You need to check out yourself.

Market Research

Research making is vital and important while aspiring to set up a business. You can go to the market and do your feasibility studies about whatever you have passion for. Interview people. Pretend to be part of the system. Ask some specific questions. Be willing to know what specific problems your intending invention or business will solve for people. What are the long- and short-term goals of your business or invention? Knowing what particular problem(s) your business is going to solve will equip you to face and answer vital questions that may arise from people in relation to your intending products or service.

You need to know who your primary targets will be. Who is going to buy your product? You need to be specific and be truthful to yourself. Some products will be bought by women, some by men, and some by those in the offices. Your target may be students or the market women. In some cases, it might be the commercial vehicle drivers and so on. Knowing your target will give you the clue on how, when, and where to advertise your products. If, for instance, students are your target, you should know that your advert will be focused on the campus. Let your advert be in campus magazines and the bulletins. Pasting your adverts on various notice boards will be relevant. You can also print fliers or handbills to be handed to the students. Pasting your billboards or banners around student's hostels will be appropriate publicity. In case women are your focus, you can place your adverts in the magazines that women like to read.

Having settled the issue of advertisement, your next question should be, Where are they going to buy it? This is so important. It is not always advisable for someone to be looking for shops before starting a business. Your business may be the one that may not need you to rent a shop at the onset of your business. *Many waste a lot of money on shop renting instead of channeling the capital on their business.* At the end of the day, they discover the shop has nothing to do with their business. For instance, there are some goods and services that people prefer you to bring to their various offices and homes for them to see and buy, because of their work schedules or other circumstances that surrounds them. *If you sit down in your shop and somebody else takes his products to the offices, homes, or campuses, he will sell his product while you sit in your shop waiting for customer to come.*

Placing price tags on your products is highly essential. In order for you to keep your business running, you must be careful on what you charge for your products. Firstly, you must figure out how much you want to charge that the consumers will be able to afford that will still give you some profit margin after your expenses on the business. At the same time, *you should not make too much profit so as not to push the price beyond the capacity of your potential customers.* You should not overprice your product or services.

Taking cognizance of the products your products want to compete with is another area that needs to be focused and placed more attention to while deciding on a business. Your own product might not be the only one in the market. Ask questions about other products and look at what those products lack and figure out how you can make your product supply whatever your competitors lack. Then move ahead and calculate the cost of doing that business. Make no mistakes about calculating only the cost that will make you start the business but also calculate the cost that will enable you to sustain the business and make profit. *It is not enough to only have the initial capital for the business but to have enough till you can comfortably make profits.*

Business Plan

Writing a business plan is essential in sustaining and keeping your business going. Habakkuk 2:2 tells us how to write down the vision in everything we are doing. There is power in writing. *When you have a vision, it is still in the realm of intangible until you write it down.* The physical expression that your vision has in the material world is in the writing. There is more power in the writing because during the course of writing, your vision touches the ground. *As your vision touches the ground, the other invisible practical expression will continue to align with your vision as you take action.*

A business plan will include your vision statement, which will show what you want your business to become and will be doing. This can be your basic assumption about the business. Assumptions like the situation in the market, the needs in the society, the people who will be the target, and the quantity people will be readily to buy in the market. *You will also need to write the source of your products or your materials.* Then write your sales projection. You can possibly write a plan for one- to ten-year plans for the business. The law of time perspective in business will come to play. *This means the higher the time you plan for your business, the higher you will rise in your business.* In that case, if you make thirty-year decisions on your business, you tend to rise higher than your peers who make just ten-year decisions because you tend to make accurate decisions today. Making year plans will surely relieve you on unnecessary pressures. Having a good projection for sales, facilities, staffing, and profit is so crucial for the business to go on. You need to make accurate calculation about these.

Identification of financial sources for your intending business is so important. Although, our provision is spiritually from above. But you need not to make a mistake of taking your prayers into God for him to show you in physical where you can get the financial source to fund the business. You need to consider the different options in sourcing for finance. You should have it in mind that God will never fail in his provision. *You should not have it in mind that your source of financing would be the same all the time.* The avenue you got financial source the last time might not necessarily be where you will get funding next time.

Your source may be from your savings. Having worked for some time, you should have some savings by not spending all your earnings. As a wise person, you should build up some savings and not behave like the foolish person who squanders all his earnings.

Your friends and relations may be good sources of your finances. Often God is merciful to you that you may not even use your personal finance to fund your business. *It is good to try to be in good terms with the majority if not with all of those you may come across in life, because you do not know the source of your future help.* Many might say, "My uncle, aunt, brothers, sisters, or friends are stingy with their money, and I doubt if they can ever lend out money to do business." Yes, that is possible, but the truth is, what have you done with the money which you collected from them before? You squandered the money in anticipation that you would receive more later. Right?

In a situation whereby you do not have savings, 10 percent of initial capital is needed to start a business. It will be very difficult for people to loan you the whole lot of money needed for the business. *People want you to be financially committed and put something on the table before they can assist you as a serious person.* Nobody will want to do business with a prodigal person. *You need to check yourself.* You must have a good record of managing finances before friends or relations can relate with you financially. This is so important in raising money for the business.

Your assets can also be another source of your finances. Assets are valuable things which you have on ground. The jewelries, electronics, clothes, houses, cars, and some other valuable things you have at home can be converted to money to start your business. In the Bible, available assets have been used to produce much more products. For example, *Jesus used five loaves of bread and some fishes to feed thousands of people while a widow used a jar of oil to pay for her debts.* All used the assets readily available on ground for great advantage.

The bank is another source of money for business, but you must have a good standing with the bank before they can finance your business. But *the negative side of borrowing money from the bank is the high interest rates the bank charges.* You must do your calculations and homework very well to avoid running into debt when you borrow from the bank.

Your suppliers can be your source of finances. You can approach your suppliers to supply you with a quantity of goods with promise to remit the proceeds as soon as you make your sales or give a specific time you want to pay back. This is what businessmen call sales return. *If you are honest and diligent enough to fulfill your promise, you can start your business without a dime by using the suppliers' goodwill to start your own business.* What is required is integrity.

The service of legal counsel is required in business information. In case it is a joint business, all the parties involved must sign all the necessary documents to be witnessed by an attorney. *You do not start a joint business with anybody based only on trust irrespective of what the person is to you, your family, friends, or church members.* In case you are a sole proprietor business owner, you need the service of a lawyer to put you through what you should know and do. *It is better you desist from doing business with your family or relatives who are not trustworthy.* This will give you a breathing space to react in case there is breach of contract agreement.

Advertisement

You need to advertise your business and let the world know what you have to offer. *You don't want to keep your business under your roof and expect people to know about it.* Nobody will light a candle and put it under the bush and expect it to light in the room. You have to put your business out and let the products or services be known. This can be done through advertisements. People may be made to know that you are there and that there is something unique you have to offer. *No angel will advertise your product for you.* This is a technological era when the Internet has made things so simple, and technology can be used to showcase any product to the world within a second.

One can say that *the network will determine the net worth of a product or service*!

Branding

Branding is a way of differentiating a product from the other products. For example, local market women brand their products with colors or numbers in order to differentiate each product from others. People selling goats in the market will put color marks or tags on their animals to distinguish animals.

Coca-Cola, Pepsi, Apple, and other notable companies have their logos as brands. You can put a logo or a catchphrase on your product in order to let it stand out so when the people see the logo, they know right away that that is your product.

Having put all these steps in place, you can now start your business. *Nothing starts until you make a move.* Many are good in planning but not in execution. Many for years have business plans but find it difficult to start. *The world does not recognize you for what you are planning to do but what you have done.* You get recognition for what you have done. We need to follow the hunter process in the bush. *The hunter process is "ready, aim, and fire."* If the hunter failed to *fire* and wasted his time on *aiming*, the animal will definitely run away. Majority of people live their lives getting *"ready! Ready! Ready!"* without *aiming*! While some people will get to the stages of *ready and aiming* but are not able to fire. *If you cannot fire, you will not fulfill your dream.* You have to *fire* before you can achieve your target. You need to strive while the iron is hot.

Don't wait for things to happen to you before you take an action. The one who observed the wind would not sow, while the one who observed the cloud will not reap. *He who waits for the perfect condition will never get things done.* Don't wait for the perfect condition before you take action. Make it perfect by yourself. Don't wait for things to happen. Make things happen. You need to take action as soon as you see the revelation, lest you will just be a mere analyst and a multimillionaire in the spirit realm and not in the physical.

Faith

Faith requires that you act as if it is so, even when it seems not to be so, because it is so. Many of us, the kind of business we are doing and the place where we are doing the business, are not commensurate with the call of God on our lies. You need to make a bold move. *If you want to catch a whale as a fisherman, you need to go to the blue sea and not just a stream behind your house.* Staying by the stream behind your house will only make you catch a big frog and not whales. We need to take action. Make that life-changing phone call. Do what you are supposed to do. Say what God wants you to say and stop procrastinating.

Nowadays, people tend to misinterpret what hardworking is. *Many believe hard work is meant to be of a physical exertion.* People forget that a major part of hard work is mental exertion. *Many have excused mental ability from hard work and replaced it with physical activities.* Many prefer activities to mental work. *People who use mental exertion are the people with mild minds.* Being a mild man does not mean you are a lazy man.

When you go into production, your products become useful only when someone needs the products. *It is possible for one to work hard and not work smart if one works hard in a wrong way.* In the physical realm, those who do hard labor with little income are said to be working hard and not smart. We all know the set of unskilled laborers in this category. *If you are sweating profusely at work before you get paid, you are in the category of those that work hard but not work smart.* That is, work like an elephant but eat like an ant.

Working hard mentality has been the challenge of many poor nations which is affecting their citizens in negative ways. We can imagine a nation like Nigeria has crude oil and cannot buy and install machines that can refine the oil. Diligence begins with sitting down and thinking about how available information can be used to one's advantage. *Those who are wealthy today do not have to work physically hard before earning money.* They only work smarter. The wealth of owners of Facebook, Apple, Microsoft, etc. came from the application of their mental work and creativity. *Work or job which makes you sweat or give you pains cannot make you a millionaire.* It will only sustain you. All you can achieve there is to continue to live at a given standard at a subsistence level.

Somebody once said that a rich man is someone who earns money while sleeping. Moreover, *when people are paying for your service even when you are sleeping, you are a rich man.* When you are out of town and your bank account is being credited with the fund from your clients or *when you are on the golf course and some people are working getting their daily bread through you, you are said to be rich.*

STRESS AND HOW TO
SHAKE OFF YOUR STRESS

S *tress is a mentally or emotionally disruptive or upsetting condition occurring in response to adverse external influence on an individual.* Stress can affect a person's health. It can also lead to increased heartbeat and a rise in blood pressure, which can result in muscular tension, irritability, and depression. Not that stress will not come, but you should behave as if it does not exist. In most cases, stress can cause distractions and make people misbehave.

People under stress can be temperamental and tend to pass on abuses to people around them. Stress can make people look crabby and hostile whenever they came from work tired and burned out. Stress can make people pass aggressions to other innocent persons. In some homes, it has been reported that stress caused husbands to beat up their wives. Stress can make many homes break apart. *The good news is that stress is a temporal. We should not destroy what is permanent in our lives because of what is temporal.*

It is so unfortunate that people who are stressed often listen to their emotions rather than listening to God of possibilities! For any stressed person, God's peace may not make any sense to them. When the troubles or mistakes com, *stressed people usually listen to the emotional voices.* Every mind is prone to stress. You need to note that having stress in life is not the end of the road to your progress. As the cloud is full and revolving around you, you should know better that there is sunshine at the opposite side. It is just a matter of time and endurance. It was the cloud that constituted the darkness. After the cloud, there is sunshine.

Your stress is for a limited time. So *you should learn how to manage your stress if you must succeed.* Many a times the cloud appears like a rock while looking at it at a distance. But try to move closer to the cloud. You will discover that the cloud is just an ordinary vapor. Take note of this while flying in the airplane. This is the way stress looks like. *The stress you are passing through is meant to create fears and set you back. Stress tends to make you lose focus. But if you stand on your feet, it cannot swallow you.* When you learn to let go and leave it for God, you will be stress free. When you are stressed, there may be a tendency to easily snap or lose one's patience or pick on everybody and everything around one. Everybody who comes across your way may look like an enemy to you. Thus losing a potential helper.

Stress uses all the energy you are supposed to use to lift yourself up to burn you down. The higher your level, the higher your stress. If you aspire to rise, you should be ready for stress. When you are stressed, it is better for you to stop whatever you are doing, relax, and go sleep and pretend as if nothing happened. Doing that will bring back renewed energy.

You should stop stressing yourself for any problem because every problem has solutions. Certain problems which can lead to sickness in our bodies can easily be solved if proper care is taken. People with stress usually go to the extent of wrecking themselves emotionally. They tend to do things irrationally and find nothing good in life. You should relax because there is no temptation that will come your way that God will not give you the strength to overcome. God knows about it.

You can come out of your stress by not worrying about the problems. All you should do is to focus on God. When you focus on God, the way and what to do will come to your spirit. At times, only one word can bail you out of your predicament. All you need to do is to speak positively to your life. *Most of the time, what you perceived as your problems may not always be problems but challenges for greater achievements.*

If there is a bad weather that demands you to stay safe at home, you should stay at home, but do not think that if you don't go to work on that day, you may lose your job. If you lose this particular job, it might be that God wants to create another business for you. He gave you the job initially. He will surely open another doors of opportunities for you.

Enough of giving yourself unnecessary stress because nothing will happen if you fail to meet the initial request. If you don't meet up your mortgage payment on time this month, you can do better next month.

You have to define your own bearing and choose the path you want to follow. *Departure at times can lead to discovery.* It is possible that you can't move forward or come across certain blessings without you doing away with some certain things. One of the best but delicate decisions a man can make is on friendship. You either make decisions that will pull you down or raise you. There are some of your friends that might suddenly separate and run away from you. You don't just give up because of that fall from your track and lose focus. People may leave you, but God will never depart from you. All you need to do is to believe in the truth in the Bible, which says, "It shall be well." If you know the truth, the truth will set you free. *It is possible for the truth to make you miserable, but it will set you free without stress at last.*

One of the major problems that people have is to meditate on the truths that may not be the honest truth about the situation they are facing. These are what are called impure thoughts that we meditate upon. Don't meditate on gossip. "He said, they said." Stop thinking that some are talking about you. Nobody is forming opinions about you. Stop stressing yourself. *The greatest thing about you is who you are in the inside.* People may know your physical being, but nobody knows what is inside you except yourself. What is in you is better than what is outside you. *Duty of stress is to assault your mind with all manners of thought that will not work for your lifting.*

Stop worrying about anything that is not worth worrying about. Don't give stress any chance in your life. *Stop thinking about things that are not important to your life.* When people are gossiping about you, try to do as if you don't hear them. *Turn a deaf ear to everything that will not promote your well-being.* If you think about someone's abuse, you may miss your blessings. If you keep rolling and eventually succeed, your mockers will surely come and apologize. Remember, *with a stressed mind, you may not fulfill your goals and purpose in life.*

IMAGINATION AND SUCCESS

*I*magination is the formation of mental images of something that is neither perceived as real nor perceived by the senses. It can also mean the ability to form mental images of things or events. Imagination allows us to perceive things as if it has happened even though it has not yet happened. It makes us think or assume. The synonym of imagine can be dream, creative power, and vision. *If you can imagine, you will have hope. If you cannot imagine something good, you might not be able to achieve success.* If you cannot imagine abundance, you may miss abundance when it comes your way because you cannot even imagine what abundance may look like. Likewise, if you cannot imagine success or progress, you may not be successful or have progress. It is therefore necessary to imagine good things for ourselves. *Lack of imagination may be responsible for why prophecies seem not to be working for many Christians nowadays.*

Many pastors would pronounce prophecy like "this is the month or year of abundance," but because many are so addicted to borrowing and lack, they cannot imagine themselves swimming in abundance and meeting their needs without borrowing. They allow the whole month or year which the prophecy is meant for to pass without the abundance. Not that a miracle is not happening, but we do not experience miracle because we do not imagine it. *For you to achieve something great, you must first imagine it.* If you can't imagine it, you can't become it.

The power of imagination gives you what is possible. Nobody can prevent you from thinking. Thoughts are things, and your thoughts become what you are. As many people that are prosperous today must have thought about it before they finally become successful. You need to be focused. If you are focused, there are lots you can achieve. Focus needs endurance. Endurance is associated with pains. *Many have great imagination but cannot endure the pains to achieve the imagination.* Nothing good comes cheap. There is a barrier between you and your imagination. If you can endure to cross the hurdle, you will surely be successful.

Men who lack imagination, dream, vision, and prophetic words may get frustrated. Without imagination, you might not have destination. Everywhere will be like a destination to you. Because you can't imagine what you desire, your imagination will produce whatever pictures you consistently focus upon. You will be whatever you consistently think about. You must produce the picture of receiving what you have been imagining. Your imagination must be a good one, and stop wasting your time and energy on imaging negatively, because the time and strength you will use to imagine good things are the same with what you will use to imagine bad things.

Whatever you can imagine will surely come to pass because it is a thing of the mind. Imagine right. The woman with the issue of blood in the Bible must have first imagined that she would receive her healing before she decided to touch Jesus's garment. This means that by imagination, she already got her healing before she touched the garment. You should not be distracted but be courageous in the pursuit of your imagination. Courage is needed in the place or atmosphere of fear. Fear comes through what we see or hear. Many who have good imagination may not achieve because of fears. Imagination brought about success. Imagination will take you to where you may never reach physically. Imagination is of the Lord.

Imagination keeps you going whenever people are attacking you. People can intimidate and confuse you, but they can't wipe out your imagination. Your prosperity and success depend on how far you can imagine. *If you think like a chick, you will definitely die like a chick. If you think like an eagle, you will soar like eagle.*

David already imagined that he would cut Goliath's head. He already imagined Goliath's head in his hand. That was the reason why the first action he took was to cut Goliath's head when Goliath fell so that his imagination could come to pass. Remember, David did not have a sword when he imagined Goliath's head in his hand. But he eventually cut Goliath's head with a sword. The lesson here is that it doesn't matter what you need to fulfill your imagination. God will surely provide it. You just go ahead and imagine positively and let God manifest his power. If you can't imagine more, you don't get more.

In order to fulfill your imagination, your body, soul, and spirit must be in unity. If your spirit is telling you that you should go for it, you can get it done, but if your body is telling you that the task ahead is hard, you may find the task impossible. On the other hand, if your spirit, body, and soul agree on a task, no stress or intimidation can hold you back. If you want to build the tower, you must first see the tower through your imagination. Secondly, you must count the cost. And thirdly, you must be ready to pay the price.

The average man in flesh will forever talk you out of your imagination. But it is left for you to perceive exactly what you have imagined and to know the process to make it a reality. Many people lose out because they don't have clear imagination. While some with imagination miss out because they listen to the noise of the market. It is not common to be a partaker of what you cannot imagine or what you imagined but did not follow up.

In the physical, many are sitting in the midst of opportunities, but they can't see the opportunities simply because they lack imagination and vision. You need to be specific and practical with your vision and what your imagination is. *You should also be careful because the devil is a counterfeit doer of what God had created.* It can make so many things look as if they are. But don't be deceived. That is where conviction has to play its role. When you are sure of your vision and imagination, it will be hard for you to make mistakes.

Many who see themselves as failures often fail. They imagined failure; that is why they failed. You must see yourself imagining and hoping for good things. Since *it is our imagination that creates what one hopes for and creates opportunities for one to recognize when opportunity comes, one must try to imagine positive things to be achieved.* But this is not easy and won't come easy and on the plate of gold. It is true that God wants us to prosper, but we have our own roles to play.

The fear of imagination killers is the beginning of wisdom if you want to fulfill your imagination. Many will discourage you by saying, "There is one lane, and you should stay within that lane." Many will say you can't do it because nobody has ever done such a thing before. Some will say you don't have enough money to carry out your dream. They might even go as far as telling you that your situation does not permit you to do what you wanted to do. They may tell you that it is not common in your community to achieve what you are about to be done. If you know the importance of your imagination, nobody can talk you out.

Don't be insane. *Insanity is for you to be doing the same thing over and over and expect the result to be different.* Making Diet Coke is an example of imagination. The invention of diet coke originated from the fact that many people don't like much sugar in their drink. In order for Coca-Cola Company not to lose the patronage of a group of people, its officials worked out a formula to produce Diet Coke! *You should ask God for creative thinking concerning everything you want to do.* You must come out of your house so that you can look up at the stars and see lots of opportunities. No harvest will come without planting. *The seed of commitment is what you give to your imagination consistently to make you prosper.* Many people give up because they did not know where they were going.

UNDERSTAND THE BLESSING SECRET

I n order to properly be on track in the journey and aspiration to fulfill your dreams and goals, it is highly important to know some characteristics and features that are associated or which come with blessings in order not to miss the blessings when they finally arrive. To be blessed is to be empowered and equipped to prosper. When you are blessed, you are happy, and things will continue to happen in your favor. Happiness is a product of happenings. It also gives you access to joy. Whether things happened as expected or not, you still have to stay positive. When you are blessed, it's likely you see things differently from the way other people see things.

A blessed man does not have anxiety over any situations because they know and believe that all is well and that there is no fear or anxiety in God. Many times, the blessed man has the ability to know the end of a particular situation before it happens. When others are panicking, the blessed man relaxes. *When you are blessed, you will not be moved unnecessarily by any situation or circumstance.*

When things are going wrong around you, people might expect you to go mad and misbehave and lose your ability to tolerate hardship, but as a blessed man who sees more than what an ordinary man sees, you will relax and be calm because you believe there is another side to the situation and that all things will work in your favor. A blessed man is said to be fortunate, because all things will work in his favor. When one is fortunate, there are possibilities of things working in ones favor as God is said to be with the person. That is the reason why when one shows up for an interview with many competitors, one is selected.

Note that you are not smarter than the others, but you are rather fortunate simply because God is on your side. *Fortune is very important for you to measure up to standard among your peers on whatever you are contending with.* When you are truly blessed, whatever you are doing, God will be involved. Whatever you are doing will be God's doing. A blessed man does not feel intimidated by any act of oppressions that may militate against him. *You need to feel enviable. That is one of the characteristics of a prosperous man.* Nobody envies failure. A blessed man still gets good result when he seems not to work so hard. *A blessed man or woman is relevant and recognized in the family and in the community because of his/her significant contributions.*

A blessed man doesn't associate with just any person or group of people. A blessed man has a discerning heart to understand that *people who influence your thinking the most will influence your life the most.* Who are you listening to? Who is talking to you? Whose advice are you taking? It is unfortunate that poor people in most cases like to listen to poor people like themselves.

One of the characteristics of a poor man is that he is an attention seeker. He always thinks that he deserves to be pitied. *The quality of your life will also correspond to or be the same with the quality of those people you are close to or familiar with.* That is why if you take a close look at say two to five friends with whom you are relating with, you may discover that you are around the same range of salary or economic status. *When you listen to wealthy people, they will challenge your mind and spirit.* They may initially put you under pressure they mentioned money in millions. You may put yourself in stress or make yourself uncomfortable until you can adjust and listen to their conversation and learn from them.

Don't pitch your tent with critics. They are those who derive joy in backbiting rather than asking about the way to make things happen from those that are making waves in society. *It is a pity that many would rather criticize a prosperous man than to move closer to him and learn the way to success.* Many see the average rich individuals as rogue and treasure looters simply because they were allergic to success and don't know that people can legitimately make it in life.

A blessed man will see these sets of people around him but should be aware of whom to associate with. *If you want to change your financial status, you must change or avoid associating with uninspiring friends.* You should not be afraid to cut off unproductive relationships. Think not of what people will say if you stop from hanging around with such people. The truth of the matter is that whatever action you take, people will still talk about you. People will forever have things to talk about. *It is better for you to take action that will be to your advantage than to stay inactive.*

You must realize that there is a time for everything. *Some relationships are seasonal that cannot be kept year-round or throughout the year, while some relationships are for life. It is your duty to know how to differentiate between what is temporal and what is permanent.* You need to seek and ask for wisdom. *When the time to break up a relationship comes, you should not hold on to such a relationship because it will not do two of you any good.*

The construction of structures has stages, and each stage requires specific skills and professionals. You don't need those who are skilled in digging the foundation of houses for roofing. You don't employ carpenters for the painting of the house. This principle applies to your relationship with people. Cutting off unprofitable friends or associations is not about being sentimental. You need to be sincere with yourself. You don't want to play with your destiny and what can affect the next generation. Life is in seasons. *If you are blessed and want your blessings to manifest, it is important to watch your association.*

THE WORD OF GOD

I n life, human beings listen to different kinds of words which eventually form the basis of what we act upon. *The important and the only word we need to listen to in order for us to be profitable is the Word of God.* You will not go far in life without the Word of God. There are many things you are stronger than, but there are so many things that are stronger than you in which you need the Word of God to overcome if you must be successful in life.

When you have tried a lot of things and it seems as if nothing is working for your good, you need a word from God as a way out of your predicaments. *If your salary can meet all your needs, you are a poor man.* Whenever you are going to be a blessing, what will define your blessing may be what you lack in the beginning. Biblical Abraham was barren for many years before he was made a father of many nations. Isaac started his journey to Rehoboth with farming. *Your problem is not the end of your journey or destination but a passing phase.* Your current problems are just bus stops, and you will surely transit as soon as your bus comes. You are not the first person to experience the problem you are passing through now. Many have gone through it before. *Never let anybody use your current situation to define you. Your present troubles are there probably to push you from where you are to where you ought to be.*

Hold on and do not be discouraged and know that not all the troubles are meant for your demotion! *The way people look at you is the problem you have. Don't be intimidated by people's look.* If you don't have a "test," you will not have "mony" because testimony gives birth to "test" and "mony." *You can't control what people say about you, but you can control what you hear. Being worried is not because of presence of evil but because of lack of information.* To achieve your goals in life, you must understand what is going on around you. Having appropriate information is important for one to make it in life.

Learn to listen carefully to the Word of God for relevant information. God's Word is a divine direction. When his words come to you, it is for divine direction. *An indication that you will soon graduate out of your farming is God's Word.* Divine direction is not about where you think you should be but where you ought to be. *Not everybody can handle many things at a time. That is the reason why God decided to start with you with small things.* If God gives you bigger things when you should be given small things, it might lead to your untimely death. When you have the Word of God, it is easier for you to continue in your journey of life.

ARISE

rise as shown in Ephesians 5:14 simply tells you to move on, to do something new, to move from where you are to where God wants you to be. It is also a way of telling you to be awake from your sleep. Arise may mean to buckle up, to ascend, get into action, to spring forth. *Arise does not end at waking up from our sleep. You may wake up and not rise up from bed. Some may kneel after waking up. But you still need to rise and be on your feet.* Many stand up and refuse to walk. The issue of sleeping, sitting down, kneeling down, and standing up represents different areas of our daily lives, in our career, our spiritual lives, family lives, our finances, our relationships, and all our life's endeavor. Individuals are at different levels, but wherever we are, we still need to arise because we have not reached the peak.

You can do better. If you are sitting down, you can still stand up. If you are standing up, there are needs for you to start walking because there are good things to achieve by mere walking. Walking is not even enough. You can start jogging. Even when you are jogging, you can move faster and run. After running, you can still fly. Flying must not be your last result while you have an opportunity to soar like an eagle. Soaring like an eagle can make you to be noticed. That is another way to arise.

You have been hiding for too long. It is time to arise and get out of your cocoon and be introduced to the world. It is time for you to come out and stand out. Start the business you have been proposing for years, go, and do the exams you ought to have done long time ago. Make the phone call you've been contemplating to make for a long time.

Submit the CVs or résumés which you have been contemplating to submit. You should start writing the books, the articles, and the magazines you had wished to write. In a nutshell, it is the time for you to do what can improve your life.

To arise also means to get out from obscurity. You can arise by getting out from where you have been hiding. Psalm 102 tells us that we should arise. Arise is biblical. God sees that many are so comfortable in the positions they are in. That is why God was telling us to arise. Arise is a commandment from God. That is why the book of Isiah says you should rise and shine.

There is an advantage for you over the people that are sitting down when you arise. *When you are standing up, you have some leverage over the people that are sleeping or sitting down.* You will develop some muscles and be easily noticed. When you start moving, you are moving to accomplish a certain goal. You can't be moving without a certain destination or goal you want to achieve.

You need to arise because time waits for nobody. *Time is such a commodity that when spent can never be recovered.* The more you wait, the older you become. Time is everything. You need to arise from your poverty, discouragement, sickness, setbacks, and lacks, not able to be recognized, intimidation, inferiority, fatigue, and all other things that are pulling you down from progressing.

Arising does not come cheap without price to be paid. Therefore, in order for you to arise, to possess your possession, to move to the next level in your career, family life, business, academics, and all other things that can elevate you, certain things have to be done by you.

Firstly, you must recognize where you are. In order for you to rise and shine, you must recognize where you are compared to where you want to be in all areas of your life like marriage, finance, academics, business, and so on. You must realize the point you are in in order for you to compare it to where you ought to be. *In case you don't know the exact point you are in, you may not know how far you still need to go.* Imagine you are on the highway, and you missed your way and you need help. The next question will be, Where are you? *If you don't know where you are when you got lost, it might be difficult for you to get help to reach your next destination.*

You can't say you don't know where you are when you got lost. If you say that, it means help will be far from you. You must therefore be aware of your state. This is the case of the prodigal son in the Bible. The prodigal son discovered where he was after he had spent all his portion of inheritance. He quickly traced his steps back home after he got to his senses and realized that he was in a bad spot. He realized that he could be better than the way he was. He woke up. He quickly ran back to his father to settle the discord and to begin again. You should know that where you are today is not where you ought to be. You should aspire to rise to your next level when you realize that your position of borrowing and lack is not where you supposed to be and that you need to stand up and confront the challenges.

You need to take the right decision right now and stop meditating on your sorry case. The prodigal son took a right decision by quickly running back to his father in restitution. *You are where you are today because you failed to take the right decision or you kept on dragging your feet*, procrastinating action on issues that can affect your life while forgetting that you are the architect of your own fortune. This is the best time to take a wise decision and act promptly. You need to do something about your life and all other things that concern you. You need to make a tough decision. The tough decision the prodigal son made was that he decided to get back home.

What are the right decisions you need to take today that will push you to your next level? Is it going back to school, getting married, doing away with all bad friends, looking for another job, changing your location, desisting from spending extravagantly, *stop buying things that cannot add value to your life, or stop staying longer on the phone about issues that do not matter to you?*

I challenge you through this medium that you need to do it now. This is the best and the right time. Life is about decisions and choices. It is either you make a better choice or allow life, society, your job, or even your boss at work to make a choice for you. *Your job will dictate to you when you can have your breakfast or lunch.*

Making a decision is not easy. Your family, friends, and people around you will mock you. Make a decision to move to the next level. It is better you take an audit and review your life and marriage once a while. You don't just struggle in marriage. You don't hang out with dropouts. You can do better than that. There is a room for you on top. It is too congested down here. *The journey to the elevation is personal.* You have to be responsible for your life.

In order for you to arise, you must refuse to love sleeping too much. You must wake up. Many would say, "I need my eight hours." Why are you sleeping for eight hours straight when you have a lot to do in your life? You need less than eight hours of sleep out of twenty-four hours if you really want to make it. Some will say, "I need to sleep in the afternoon." Why must you sleep in the afternoon at your age? Time and age are not on your side. You have wasted much more time in your life. This is the time for you to redeem the time. You must buy back the time you have wasted. Proverbs 20:13 tells us you must not love sleep or else you will be in poverty. Poverty is not only when you don't have money. *You are said to be in poverty when you are not where you ought to be. When you are telling stories when your colleagues are spending money, you are in poverty. You are also in poverty when you can't meet the needs of your family and the people around you. When you are dodging phone calls because you have nothing to offer the callers, you are in poverty.* When creditors are always calling and embarrassing you, you are in poverty. If you summon up courage and do one or two things about your life, you will see that you are bigger than what you are now. Life may be a lot easier than you thought if you wake up and arise on time. At this age and time, you are still talking about drinking, womanizing, looking for jobs that pay ten dollars an hour, waiting for the government to pay your salaries, relying on unpaid pensions, expecting your family abroad to send you money, or relying on the properties or little wealth that your parents left that are not even enough for the family to rely on, divorcing and complaining about one thing or the order, you are in poverty. When will you get out of your sleep and slumber? The Bible says that *a little sleep will add to your poverty* (Prov. 6:10–11).

Focusing is another ingredient needed for you to rise up. You have to be focused on a particular thing. Don't be too busy in spending time on things that are not important. *Don't generalize your priority. Focus on a single important thing.* Focus on your profession.

Don't be a photographer and at the same time be a mechanic. Some are general importers and exporters. They can sell cars today and sell shoes tomorrow. Next week they want to open a restaurant. Next month they are writing a proposal on selling yams. They will say they are general contractors. There is nothing like general contractors. *There is a need for specialization so that people will know your areas of specialization and seek your service.*

Stop jumping up and down. Stay on track. Try to do just a particular thing. *Don't be distracted by placing your hand on so many things.* It is true that multitasking is fine. Many people preach it, but let all your multitasking be focused on a particular thing that will eventually yield good results. Set your priority and do what you have a passion for so that without much money, you can easily do profitably. *If you have passion for book writing, leave the car selling for the car dealers and leave container/shipping business for people that have passion for it.* Stop shipping junks in the name of business! Enough of slimming pills when you are not born to be a model. Don't copy people; be real to yourself.

If you have a will, there is always a way out. *The reason why many people are not successful in what they are doing is just because they don't have a will or the determination to pursue things to the end.* The prodigal son discovered that the food he was eating was not what he was supposed to be eating. He was determined to go back home to his father and make an amendment. In uke 15:18, the prodigal son started with "I will arise." *The worlds* I will *are procrastinating and contemplating words that set a lot of people back till today.* I will do this and that. Many keep saying this without doing anything. But in Luke 15:20, he arose. There is a big difference between "I will" and "arose." Determination makes the difference between the two. The prodigal son did not only determine to do, he actually rose in action.

When you are at the "I will" stage, you can still change your mind. "I will" are procrastinating words that prevented many to reach their goals in life. *Procrastination is a destiny destroyer.* Look at how many things you have procrastinated since the beginning of the year alone not to talk of when you've grown up as an adult. Many immigrants planned to do so many things when they first got to America and the Western world without real action to support the plans but see where you are today by not acting on your plans. Many who proposed to pay off their debts by learning and cultivating financial discipline but are still spending money on things that are not profitable or do not add values to their lives will remain in debts. In addition, many who charge most of their clothes, shoes, and jewelry expenses on credit cards will remain in debt for a long time for lack of financial discipline. Tell me, where is the financial discipline you promised at the beginning of the year? When are you going to stop and arise?

You promised to go to school, and the school session is almost over without you being in class. When exactly are you going to wake up and face your challenges and stop being a slave for other people? You as a husband, you do not enjoy your wife because of her job as she spends most of her time at work. *Why don't you invest on the wife's future for better remuneration and freedom?* Throw away "I will." Many of us have a lot of "I will" projects hanging in our houses. Please do something about them.

Conquering of fear is another way of arising. Many want to arise, but the fear of the unknown may grip them. They say, "What of if it doesn't work?" But why don't you try "What of if it works?" *Focus your attention on "if it works" and not on "if it doesn't work."* Invest more time in being optimistic and being positive. Let your faith work for you positively. *To conquer the fear, you need to cut off some friends, because some are dream killers.* When you share your dreams with them, they will always say negative things about your dream. They may say, "What you are about to do is not for people of color. You have an accent. Your speaking English is not fluent." Some will say, "Have you ever seen anybody prosper with this kind of business?" You should ignore such people.

You need to associate with people who can lift you up and encourage you to achieve your goals. *Excellence has no color, so if you are successful, people will be forced to learn how to pronounce your name, and they will pronounce it by force.* All your mistakes will always mean to be a logo and style. People will listen to you because they know they need you. But it takes a man who has conquered fear to attain that level. The prodigal son conquered fear by going back home to

236

his father. He met his promotion. He would have died in poverty if he did not conquer his fear. *What is waiting for you at the other side of your fear is promotion and success that may be beyond your imagination.*

Forgetting about your past and learning to move on is another area you need to concentrate on in your attempt to arise. If the prodigal son was thinking about the money he used to have, the life he used to live, the friends he used to hang out with, he would have not been able to go back home to his father. Looking at his past would not have allowed him to agree to want to be living as a slave in his father's house. Imagine the prodigal son deciding to go back home and live like a slave. He had learned how to eat the humble pie. He humbled himself to go back home and to live a humble life as a servant.

At times in life, you may have to go back to where you said bye-bye and begin again if that is where your star will shine and if that is where your destiny or purpose is. Many immigrants ought to have gone back to their original countries because of their poor conditions despite the existing opportunities in the Western world. There is a place called "there" and another "here." "There" may be where your destiny will shine. But if you stay "here," poverty may be in the corner because you are in the wrong place. *All your blessings are in a place where you are supposed to be.* If you have been turned down in different places before, but because of pride or ego, you refused to go back where your destiny will shine. It is time for you to go back and fulfill your destiny.

KNOW YOUR ASSIGNMENT

I t takes someone to know the assignment at hand before he can be successful. If you don't know your assignment in life, all assignments will look like it to you. *If you know your assignment, you will know what your needs are.* Many don't understand what their needs are. No matter what your needs are, if it goes with your life assignment, God will surely provide them. *Every gift that God gave to you is tied with your assignment in life.* God will give you all the resources needed to fulfill your goals if you know your given assignment in life.

Your assignment in life may be the area you are suffering on currently. It is left for individuals to be sensitive to their time, environment, and conditions in detecting their assignment. If you are waiting on the Lord for a baby, your assignment may be to do things related to the baby. In case you are under any sickness or plague at one point in time, your assignment may be to find a solution to such sickness. This might be what will showcase you to the world, put you in position, and end your suffering. Nature or natural things might not put you in position, but your assignment will always put you in position.

In the course of doing your assignment, you must not let anything be a big deal to you. *You will be stress-free if nothing is a big deal to you.* Many a times when you are possibly not able to clearly know your assignment, you may be under stress. *Where you will get to in life is determined by your assignment.* That was the case of Esther in the Bible. Esther's position and circumstances did make her to be the best and the chosen one among other women, but she was finally chosen by the king. It is not about Esther but the assignment placed on Esther. *Don't bother much about yourself or your present situation but about your assignment.* You may not operate effectively on your assignment if you are not in the right location for your assignment. *Where you are will determine your assignment and how effectively you will perform in your assignment.* Your assignment may require you to stay in a place that may not interest you, but never mind. Just stay firm and be focused.

Avoid Instant Reward

It is important to know that in life, there is a law of natural progression. This is the law of order. Every living thing is bound by this law. Any man aspiring to be great would not want to jump over this law. In relation to time and seasons, raining, dry and winter seasons do come at their appointed time. Snow cannot fall in summer; while the excessive heat cannot be experienced in winter. Things follow the natural law of order of natural progression. It is very unfortunate that people are used to a microwave style of life. We live in the world where people expect results immediately, now or never. *Microwave actions are not always good. Although it may look faster, it will not last.*

In the past, marriage involved lots of processes before getting to the childbearing stage. But nowadays, childbearing comes before many marriages. Many people have children before their weddings. A lot of people don't even want to get married but only want to have children. *It is natural to plant and watch the plant to grow and mature before the harvest time!* Many would choose not to plant but harvest because they are in a hurry! Many people do not want to work but want to get rich as quickly as possible. *Many want a result or harvest right now as people are getting used to a microwave style of life.* Microwave food temperature is temporal; when the food cool off, they lose their taste. Many prefer to use slimming pills instead of exercising their bodies and eating good food. Many use performance-enhancing pills whenever there is competition rather than constant practicing what they are good at doing.

The desire to get rich quick prompted many impatient people to play lottery for windfall wins, which never come! Some others have become prison candidates for robbing banks or by using their positions to embezzle public funds to enrich their families and friends. Some ladies go into prostitution in their efforts to get rich quickly. The love of money makes many people commit serious offences. *People are deceived when they see life as movie scenes whereby one can begin and finish a human life cycle within two hours.* In the movie scene, a baby can be born, get married, pass through some challenges, become rich, and later die within two hours.

One thing we should always remember is that it takes a short time for the actors to rehearse a movie. That is the reason why movies do not have a long life span. *Life's endeavors are not movies; they are not dramatic at all.* The amount of time and resources you invest in a particular venture will determine how big your harvest or your dividends would be. In real life, it is not possible to accomplish the life cycle as short as possible. *It is so sad that human beings want to put on little efforts and expect to get big results in a short time as in a movie.*

Civilizations have made it possible for people to do things and get the result instantly. For instance, it's possible to reach your loved ones or friends across the ocean in a minute. You text, fax, or e-mail another person at the other end within some few minutes. It is also possible to get instant news, cash money from ATMs, get fast food and other information needed instantly. Within few minutes, frozen food can be ready for consumption with the help of microwaves. We have come dangerously close to losing touch with reality and believe we have access to a fast and instant life. Human life is not like that. We have to go through those steps in a sequential order in order to fulfill our destinies.

In reality, in order for you to successfully achieve your dream, you must properly obey the law of natural progression. The challengers are not making tough choices but making right choices consistently. *It is easier in life to make the wrong choice that can ruin one's life than to make the right choices that will shape one's life for good.*

One of the greatest challenges for individuals today is making the right choice and expecting instant reward for whatever they do.

In the movie, it is very easy for James Bond, the actor, to drive a car at over a hundred miles per hour and jump out of the car when the car is in motion without getting hurt! He may also decide to bomb a whole city without thinking about the lives and financial cost or implications. Similarly, an African movie actor may decide to fight lions with just a knife and still conquer the lions, while pastors in the movies can cast out demons with mere waving of hands on demon-possessed people. The movies had been programmed to be so within that short time.

If making a right choice is dramatic in nature, you will get immediate reply. The truth of the matter is that the right and the wrong choices you make in real life at the moment will have little or no noticeable effect on how your day goes for you, tomorrow, the next year. There may be no applause, no cheers, or screams. Waking up in the middle of the night to study what people will need or think about how to invent new products as in the case of Apple and other inventors may not be natural. Spending your time in going to school or learning one business or the other may not be fun. Spending your money to attend seminars and to train young employees may not be easy, but they are required investments for a better tomorrow. *Those undramatic actions you are taking now will definitely affect how your life will turn out to be in future.*

In life, *making the right choices and taking the right actions may not be easy and can also be very easy.* People around you may even not notice when you made the choice. Those who noticed it may not care about it. Likewise, it may not even have an immediate effect on you or around you, but over time, the result will be made clear to you and all other people around you. *One thing that is 100 percent sure in human endeavor is that the right choice you make today will, over time, make you move higher and higher on the ladder of success in your life.* The wrong choices and actions taken will have the negative effects and ruin your future. Either way, there will be consequences for decisions made. *You just have to be careful about whatever decision you may choose to make in life.*

RECOGNIZE YOUR HARVEST

*T*here is nothing you ever need in your life that God has not placed into your life! There is nothing you want to become that God hasn't wired you to become. *You may fail to become who you want to become because of shared ignorance* of what those things are, or the rich deposit of God in your life, which are meant to take you to the position you ought to be. Ignorance is a very dangerous thing. In Psalm 73:22, David said, "So ignorant was I, I was as a beast before him." Solomon said in Proverb 19:2, "Also that the soul be without knowledge is not good." It is important for you to find out the importance of God in your life.

It took eighty years for Moses to discover that God left something in his hand that could change his life forever. When God wanted Moses to lead the Israelites, Moses began to give all sorts of excuses why he would not be able to lead the people. He gave excuses such as "I got nothing," "I am a stammered," "I am too small," "This task is too much for me," etc. But God asked Moses what was in Moses's hand. It is what was in Moses's hand that he eventually used. Many of us in life don't know what we have in our hand that can bring out our fortune. Things in our hands are not limited to what we are physically holding; they include the talents which God has given us.

In Exodus 4:2, God said, "What is in your hand?" Moses said, "It is a rod." Moses did not think that the rod had any significant value until God asked him to cast it down, and he did, and the rod became a snake. In real life, there may be so many things in our hands that we may joke with because we don't even know what they can turn into if the right efforts are applied. The major problems many human beings have today are that people are ignorant of what God has deposited in their lives. The difference between success and failure, life and death, wealth and poverty, good health and sickness, making it and not making it in life lies on how we recognize or use what we have in our hands. *When God deposits something in your life and you don't recognize it, it becomes problems for or to you.* Whatever is not recognized cannot be celebrated. *When you don't celebrate what you have, it might not be useful for or to you.*

There are natural laws and spiritual laws. Law of gravity says anything goes up must surely come down. It is only Jesus that defies that law. But in the real sense, if you don't understand certain laws and you work against it, you may eventually kill yourself. For example, if a man falls from a ten-story building, he will die. The law of reproduction demands that you reproduce what you are. You can't plant a mango and reap a pineapple. Likewise, *you cannot put in hours of sleep and laziness and expect to make it in life.* Whatever you want to produce or what you want to be in life required efforts in having the right seeds and making relevant investments. *Law of seed demands that whatever you have in your hand and sow today will produce what you will have in future.*

Law of recognition teaches us that everything we need in life is already deposited in our lives and merely waiting to be discovered. There are so many things settling or deposited in our life today that we do not see. May God open our eyes to see what God has deposited in our life in Jesus's name. Law of recognition comes to play when Jesus was nailed on the cross. There were two thieves, one on the left and one on the right. One of the thieves recognized Jesus and said, "I know who you are. Please remember me in your kingdom." He ended up in paradise while the other one who failed to recognize Jesus and yelled at Jesus went to hell. The difference between the two of them is the simple word *recognition*. It is possible for you to be in the midst of millionaires, helpers of destinies, and opportunities and don't recognize it. *The difference between what you get and what you do not get is in your recognition or nonrecognition of what God has for you.*

The law of recognition literally activates the law of elevation and promotion. David recognized the anointing of God upon Saul, and he gained the kingdom. Saul refused to recognize the anointing of God on David, and he lost the kingdom. After all, Saul was a boss, but his lack of recognition of David's anointing made him lose his own anointing and kingdom! *When you recognize what God is doing in your life, it can move you from obscurity to prominence.* Zacchaeus, a short man, recognized the power in Jesus and ran ahead and climbed a tree in order to see Jesus. When Jesus got under the tree, Jesus ordered Zacchaeus to come down to be blessed. Furthermore, the woman with the issue of blood recognized the power in Jesus and fought her way in the crowd to touch the garment of Jesus Christ. Jesus felt the touch and healed the woman.

Recognition can move you from where you are now to greater places. There might be many who worked in various offices and positions of power without being recognized until they retired or left their positions. After retirement, many have been called for higher service because of the recognition of their past work and integrity. Many people under recession fail to recognize or identify several opportunities which can be better utilized by them to improve their lots or reach their better economic goals. Many are into business, while some are working in government offices and various organizations but fail to identify the opportunities around them. They instead keep bothering and relying on assistance from members of their families abroad while some keep blaming their families for their misfortunes instead of accepting the responsibilities and using their God-given talents to achieve their dreams. You need to recognize opportunities in your immediate environment and tap to it for your good. *Recognition could be the difference between poverty and fortune.*

Harvest recognition has to do with our Christian life, our daily and secular dealings. In the Christian world today, many who give offerings and tithes but whose financial situation does not improve tend to question God on the veracity of the scripture. Luke 6:38—which says, "Give and it shall be given to you"—is not true! Many behave as if they have given more than enough and want God to give evidence that are compensated for their generous gift. *Majority quotes related scriptures about the harvest of what they had sown. Many felt they have not received financial returns for the offering they had given!*

Some thought they have not yet received blessings in certain areas where they hope to receive blessings. Many who received blessings may still complain that what they had received as blessing for their giving is less than what they gave as tithes and offerings. *God will always reward you for your giving no matter how long because God is not a man that he will tell lies.* He confirms this in Numbers 23:19. He will always do what he promised to do. The problem with most people is that they fail to recognize their harvest. God has done so many things in their lives. What is left for us as human being is to look back and appreciate what God has done in our lives. If we can recognize what God has done in our lives, we will stop complaining. *Complaints will never help us achieve our dreams.*

What many people failed to recognize is that the way of God is not our way as in Isaiah 55:8. God always has multiple ways of solving problems. The problem with many people is that *they look one direction to find solutions to their problems.* If they fail to see a solution the way they thought possible, they tend to conclude that God had not helped! As a result of this, *many fail to engage in activities that will better improve their lives.*

Lack of harvest recognition makes many people to be ingrates. In other words, men's short memory may cause men not to be grateful to God at all time. This may as well not let them recognize the harvest. Some people praise God when things are going well with them and complain when situations are bad or uncomfortable. This was the case of the Israelites in the wilderness. When they had food, they sang praises to God, but when they were in need, they changed. They queried Moses for bringing them out of Egypt for destruction.

Many of us tend to think that God is not faithful to us in rewarding or giving during the critical times when we lack and when we are in serious need of money to pay some bills or meet some certain obligations. Many believe at a critical time that they have overpaid the Lord with their giving! *We should not emphasize much on what we cannot have or get now. We should remember what God has done in the past and be hopeful about what he will do in future.* If we can do this, we will appreciate the blessing of the Lord and think how we can apply those blessings to work for the fulfillment of our dream.

People are so myopic by focusing on what God has not done in their life and failing to see the opportunities around them which they can use as a ladder to achieve their dreams.

If, for instance, a couple who got married and had a baby after ten months complained that God had not given them a financial breakthrough, such a couple should be reminded of some couples who had gone through fertility procedures called IVF for five times at the rate of $15,000 each before they became parents. For a couple that gave birth naturally, God has given the complaining couple $75,000 by calculation.

There are many whose lives have been saved from a series of terminal diseases and dangerous situations. Such people should be grateful to God and count their blessings or recognize their harvest. *God does not owe anybody anything.* We should better understand what God had made us pass through in order to save us from all dangers.

CHANNELS TO YOUR DREAM FULFILLMENT

*W*rite down your dream. You need to make your dream physical by writing it down. Your dream and aspiration must not only be in your mind or your brain, or else your dream will just be like a wishful thinking. There is a need to involve your senses and actions. In other words, *you need to make picture of your dream.* Speaking your dream aloud is even better, but still, the dream cannot be fulfilled if you fail to write it down. *The moment you write down your dream, your dream starts to become real since you have a clear picture.* That is the more reason why the construction engineers usually have a picture and plan of any building or structures they want to build in the site before starting the project. This makes the project specific. At the end of the project, any structure built different to what was drawn in the original plan is considered to be out of the plan.

Start planning. It is very easy to have a dream, but the major challenge is to have a proper plan on how to achieve the dream. There are lots of evaporated dreams for lack of planning. You need to come out with a plan that will shift you forward from your dream's starting point. *To plan is not so good enough, but you need to follow up the plan with all your heart, might, and sincerity.* Planning without follow-up is better compared with a student who get an admission to a school of his choice but did not work hard to gain a certificate. Getting admission only will not earn him the required certificates.

What will give him the certificates is to attend the classes and fulfill the entire requirements needed to get the certificates.

Don't make the mistake of waiting to get the perfect plan. Why? *Planning only cannot get you to your destination. Planning is just a starting point for your dream to come through.* That is why planning is so important. *If you lack planning, it means you lack a starting point; you lack a foundation.* A building without a foundation will surely crumble. First start with a plan and then go through the processes required to execute the plan needed for your dream to come to life. *Your starting plan is not the plan that will eventually get you to the top. It is just a foundation and starting point for your liftoff.* A first plan will eventually lead you to the second, third, and fourth plan depending on the level of plans required to achieve your dream. It is good to have a plan to start with.

Never hold on to your past. One thing I know that is common to everybody in life is that while walking, you either look down or look straight ahead. I presumed that *those looking straight ahead are looking ahead for their future, while those looking down are looking back at their past.* Studying those looking straight ahead, you will see that they are always walking faster, because they are always in a hurry to get to their various destinations, which I will like to call the future, because they know what the future has for them. They can see and move away from all obstacles in their ways. They don't want any delay. While those walking with their head bowed down and not facing where they are going tend to hit or collide with objects which may waste their time. Those walking with their faces down presumably are holding on to their past. *Holding on to the past creates fears in the mind.*

It is not a bad thing to revisit your past. *It is what you do with your past that matters but not the past itself. There are two things you can do about your past. You either hold on to it or let it go. Although, you cannot totally ignore your past, but is better for you not to hold on to it. You hold on to your past when you let your past mistakes or inadequacies pull you down.* The worst damage you can do to yourself is to hold on to your past. People who are successful may not ignore their past, but they do not hold on to the past. They use lessons from their past as ladder to their next level or as a foundation on which they build their future. On the contrary *most unsuccessful people tend to focus and hold on to their past as an avenue for people to have pity on them and to seek for attention.* One of the characteristics of unsuccessful people is for them to live with one foot in the past and the other foot in the future. While talking about their past, they will say, "Only if things had been in this or that way, I would have been successful in life." And while making references to their future, they will say, "If I can get this or that done, or when this or that happens, I will surely be successful." They completely forget and ignore the present, forgetting that only what they have in possession is their present. *It is the decision you make at present that will determine your future. A driver driving a car cannot rely on the rearview mirror to move forward.* No matter how fast you are, when you put yourself in reverse gear, you will not move forward.

An average human being has in common two questions to ask himself. "What is right and what is wrong?" Unsuccessful people tend to focus much on what is wrong than what is right. The question "What is wrong?" is always on their lips every minute of their lives. *Successful people do not have time to hold on to what is wrong; they don't keep malice.* They always let go whenever there is disagreement or words of confrontation with others. Not because they believe these can cause harm to them or maybe they are cowards, but for the simple fact that they don't have time to waste and do not want anything to slow them down in achieving their dreams. They are very busy moving closer to their future than to be moving away from it.

The shortest route of getting yourself up the ladders of success is for you not to hold on to your past by not letting it pull you down. In order to fulfill your dream, you should only make references to your past to make corrections of past mistakes. You can also take responsibilities for your past misdeeds and errors you've made. *Your best friend in life is your future;* you own the responsibilities of nurturing and feeding your future. *You have to be addicted to your future for your dream to be fulfilled.* Remember, I said in the beginning that a dream is a "clear picture of a better future." When you do have a clear picture of your future and you carefully and consistently invest your time into that future, you will surely achieve your dream notwithstanding the ridicules and shame you may meet on the way

You need to be careful of what you spend your time on. *It is very clear that you can't change the past. You can only influence the future.* It is your choice to rather be influenced by something you can't change or change something you have capacity to change.

Pay the price. Anything in life that is worth having is worth working and paying a price for. In case you are not willing to pay the price for whatever it is you want, you should have it at the back of your mind that *the price of neglect is far costly than the price of commitment.* For any dream you have, there are prices to pay. The price may involve giving up something. Achieving one's dream cannot come and will not come cheap. The quality of your dream will determine the price to pay. The price you pay may be proportionate to the result you will get. Your dream may be worthy of billions of dollars, but that does not mean you have to pay for it at once with your personal bank check or your lifetime savings.

Lack of understanding of how to pay price for one's dream made a lot of people lose their dreams. Many gave up their dreams when they see the estimate of what their dreams will cost, forgetting that paying the price for one's dream is not a onetime action. It is something you can embark on progressively. It is not a credit-related issue. *You can pay for your dream by installment with a penny a day.* Many may wonder how. A penny a day may not necessarily be monetary. It means different things to individuals based on the circumstances surrounding everybody's case and situations with time.

To some people, a penny a day may mean letting go of some pleasure for the purpose of pursuing a lifetime event. *It may mean that you forgo the purchasing of some unproductive materials or things like clothes and jewelries.* It may be giving up some junk food and other habit for the sake of our health in order to live long to fulfill our dreams. *It may be cutting off some friends who are not inspiring or not add values to our lives.* It may require you to form the habit to let go or give up your right to be right by not exerting control over any conversation for the sake of good relationship.

Paying the price for your dream may involve hanging on to your present car or house instead of buying a new one in order to avoid possible pressure which the payment for the new may bring on you.

At a point in my life after my bachelor's degree, at my first place of assignment during my National Youth Service Corp in Nigeria, I realized that my primary field of career which is plant science may not land me where I am projecting to be in the economic world on time or forever. I quickly made a U-turn after my one year of National Youth Service Corps program, with God and so much efforts, with productive advice from people who mattered. I found myself in the graduate school of business in two different universities, both in Nigeria and in America, which eventually got me back on track.

Is the price small? No! For a guy like me who had spent most of my prime time in the laboratory studying plants and some microbe's behaviors to suddenly switch to business school doing accounting, managerial, and business courses at the highest level and attending business seminars, it involves a lot of time and sacrifices. But I knew the sacrifice would pay off eventually. How? I was able to meet with many executives in different departments of many companies during the course of my study. Likewise, my internship took me to four European countries where I met with different people and saw how things were done there. *At any point of these, journeys I kept seeing the need for me not to work for people but with people.* I got the deep sense of the fact that a *job will earn me a living but business will earn me a fortune. Likewise, I discovered those who made things happen do not have regular working hours as they work as long as the business demanded.* They don't punch cards in or out like many workers did. Furthermore, I discovered that if we can think like the 5 percent who are the wealthy, in a matter of time, we will be part of them. But if we think like the 95 percent, which is an average person, we will remain average.

I also discovered that *billionaires invest today and buy a lot tomorrow, while a poor man buys a lot today and pays more tomorrow.* Failure to pay the price you need to pay for your breakthrough may forever cause you to be a permanent pillar or support for other people's dream while your own dream is left inactivated. *The price to pay for your dream to come to reality may not be too much or hard as many people thought.* The price may be to reduce your sleep or let go of some junk food that may cause fatigue in your body or cost you a lot of money. The price may also involve doing away with some of your friends that are not productive or going along with your vision. Going to school and updating yourself may be the price you need to pay to move you forward. It may involve cutting down your expenses by not buying what is not necessary.

It's sad to see that *many have much jewelry made up of gold with monetary values in their closet, looking for funds for their petty business,* when they could have converted the jewelries to investment money. There are other people who waste their funds on buying different kinds of clothes for other people's birthday parties and other functions while working two to three jobs! (*Common to Africans in the Western world!*) Relocating from your present base to where good things are happening may be the price you have to pay to move you forward. In some cases, if your fiancée does not share your dream, it is better you don't go ahead with that marriage. It is better to find your dream before you find your spouse, or else your spouse may throw a spanner to your wheel of progress. The truth of the matter is, "There is a bigger price to pay for not doing it than the price for doing it. The price of neglect is much more than the price of discipline," said Jeff Olson, the author of the *Slight Edge. If you don't figure out something in which you can be successful at, you may remain a rolling stone.* The price to pay for negligence can be catastrophic.

Make constant visits. It is very important to always visit your dream on a day-to-day basis. This is the reason why it is important to have the picture of your dream by writing it down. Writing it down will give you the opportunity to visit and read it every day. *Looking at your dream every day will wake you up and move you closer to the helpers of destinies who can help you fulfill the dream.* It is important that you keep yourself constantly and repeatedly focused on your dream. *Failure to get focused on your personal dream will make any other people's dream look like your dream.* Do not learn how to play basketball because your friend is prospering in choosing basketball as a profession when you are wired to be a singer.

Surround yourself with your dream. *Let the awareness of your dream be on your face by looking at your dream every day.* No doubt, opposition will come. The impossibility spirit and the people surrounding you might be telling you that you "can't do it." This dream is too much for you to fulfil. Why even bother yourself trying such a big deal like this? Nobody has ever done this in your family! Nope, it will never work! Don't you think about the financial implication of what you are doing? By the way, how would you market your idea? *You will be bombarded with extra negative thoughts.*

What you can do and need to do at this time is to surround yourself with your own yes. *Surround yourself with the possibility messages that tell you that your dreams are real.* Having your dreams clearly spelled out on paper, in most vivid and specific terms possible with a very tangible concrete timeline, provides you with an environment of yes! For your goals, dreams, and aspirations.

It is so amazing that as soon as you set your goals, life has a way of putting its own activities in your set dreams calendar. Different kinds of unforeseen events will start to show up. If you decide to sit down, fold your arms, and focus your attention on these unplanned events and circumstances, which I call *distractions*, you will never fulfill your dreams. But when you focus attention on your dreams by surrounding yourself with goals that will lead you to your dream, with the right philosophy, you will come out with the right ideas that will lead you to the right path to your dream's fulfillment. *All you need to do while on the right path to your dream fulfillment is to keep following the path.*

Until you are seriously committed to your dream, there will always be hesitancy. There's a tendency for you to draw back. This is where many people miss out in life. Majority quit at the junction to their breakthrough due to lack of commitment. *As soon as you are committed in doing what you know how to do best, every other thing will fall in place for you.* W. H. Murray in *the second Himalayan Expedition said,* "*Whatever you can do, or dream about, you can begin it. Boldness has genius, power and magic in it.*"

Looking at your dream, it may look too big for you to accomplish. But remember, it is doable. *Try not to start the journey to your dream fulfillment in a big way.* You can start small by figuring out the first step. Rome was not built in a day, and the journey of one thousand miles will start with a step. Little drops of water make ocean. *Remember that every step you take or every decision you make will lead you somewhere. It will either break or make you.* It is either build your dream or build someone else's dream. Your steps will either move you away from the masses (poor) or move you closer to the masses. You are the architect of your own fortune and misfortune.

Integrity. This is the quality of being honest and having moral principle. Integrity should be a watchword for anyone trying to be successful in all areas of life. *Integrity involves doing things legally and maintaining highest moral standards.* John D. MacDonald once said, "Integrity is not a conditional word. It doesn't blow in the wind or blow in the weather." *A person of integrity does not tell lies, he is not involved in any shady or unlawful business*, and he is trustworthy and reliable.

Lack of integrity will make people not be able to prioritize their time and end up making wrong decisions. Freedom makes many people lose their integrity and the ability to do little things which can add value to their life.

In order to be successful in life, you need to ask yourself some important questions like *Can I hold on to the integrity of doing the little things I ought to do every day irrespective of who may be watching or directing me?* Am I a trustworthy person who people can rely on for business transactions? What would people say about my character? Can I maintain necessary discipline when nobody is watching me? Remember, whatever you do today matters in future. *Where you are today is a result of what you did yesterday. Whatever you chose to do as your daily habit will either lead you to either success or failure.* You have the right to choose. Take note of your daily habit. It will surely work for your good.

People who want to be independent by choosing to have personal business should be people with integrity. This is because it is the way you hold yourself as an independent person that will make or drown you. You should on your own do things at the right time without anyone urging you to do exactly what you are supposed to do at the right time even though nobody may query your authority. Lots of people tend to get intoxicated with freedom to the extent that they don't even bother to do what is right or expected of them to be done at the right time, and they forget that *success demands slow and steady action over a period of time.* Integrity is not limited to the business world alone; it can be useful in reshaping your health, behavior, personal development, and your perceptions of things around you. *Integrity requires commitment, discipline, and a desire to maintain a respectable standard.*

Understanding and forming the habit of doing one thing at a time consistently with good attitude and *integrity will make your life go up like that of the 5 percent of the people that are making it in life today.* If you are in the camp of the people that procrastinate and can only function whenever they are motivated, who can't sit down and think on their own simply because they don't have people who will shout at them, your life will surely be like that of 95 percent of the majority who live paycheck to paycheck.

Remember, *5 percent of the populations that are successful are the groups in category of CEO of companies, inventors, investors, and people in Wall Street. They are the few people who control the resources that are supposed to be for the rest 95 percent of the population.* These 5 percent of the populations might not have been born with integrity, but they must have built their integrity. With integrity, they will live happy lives and leave fortunes for their younger generations. The other 95 percent of the people may live their lives unfulfilled, always angry, crabby, and with bad thoughts.

Take responsibility. John Boroughs once said, "A man can fail many times, but he isn't a failure until he begins to blame somebody else." You should learn and be ready to take responsibility for everything you do in life, however bad or good it is. *Taking responsibility in life will set you free of all odds. It will also give you opportunities to correct mistakes.* You will hold on to your power when you accept responsibilities even when others are wrong. Taking responsibility is one of the best characters that can be displayed by any person who want to fulfill dreams and promise. Acceptance of responsibilities makes a great difference between a successful person and unsuccessful one. "The predominant state of mind displayed by those people on the failure curve is blame. The predominant state of mind displayed by those people on the success curve is responsibility," said Jeff Olson.

In life, people will experience negative things and make mistakes, but it is how they are managed that will indicate success or failure. Certain things may happen which may be beyond our control, but it is not about the problem that happened but how one views and handles those circumstances that happen to you. This makes a lot of difference between success and failure.

The people in the category of 5 percent in life which are the successful people usually don't blame anybody for their wrongs. They don't have excuses. They know that making mistakes is not a dead end. They know the importance of moving on when the situation is bad. They know that nobody can do it for them. They learn how to live by their mistakes. Despite mistakes, they still set their standard high. They do understand that the only limitation they can have in life is themselves. *Successful people know that it is not what happened to them that matters but how they handled what had happened.*

Those who are in the category of 95 percent which are the poor people are known to shift blames on people around them. Some blame their location as the reason why they do not prosper. Some blame their parents, families, and relations abroad. Some blame coworkers. They usually express regrets about the schools they graduated from. They make excuses about their spouses and many will even blame the weather! They are the set of people who don't see anything good in life. They are full of backbiting, gossiping, and envy. They have an association called free readers association. They read newspapers every day for free at the newsstand. After reading and digesting the paper, they analyze most of the news and articles in the newspapers. They blame the government and all the people in power for any problem. These set of people don't see anything good about life.

Successful people believe they are the sources and architects of their own misfortune. They appreciate the circumstances and people around them without pointing accusing fingers to anybody. They take responsibility for whatever they do. *One of the best attitudes of successful people is that they are willing to take risks, accept responsibilities, and focus on their goals.*

THE POWER OF
SIMPLE THINGS

D o you ever realize that there are two sides to the coins of life? It is possible for people to be in the same environment and may or may not feel the same way or in are the same mood. Have you ever found time to sit down and ask yourself why some families are happy, fulfilled, creative, and loved by everyone that comes across their ways as they live close to one another and give out generously, while there are other families out there who are angry, hostile, living in poverty, and always seek for help, complaining, criticizing, and seeing nothing good about life? Why is it that many never seem to manage their time and resources to stay in good shape?

Why is it that some people are swimming in debt day in day out while some are making money every second even when they are sleeping? Statistic shows that 95 percent of the people on earth are poor while rich people are just the 5 percent. Many retirees find it difficult to live a good life at their old age. Despite hard labor at their younger age, only a few of them live to their expectation or live a fulfilled life at an old age because many lack financial security. Only about 5 percent of the population live to achieve their goal in life financially, spiritually, materially, and health-wise.

The question remains, What are the interesting things that the successful 5 percent of the populations are doing that make them fulfill that the other 95 percent are not doing? Is it their career, education, dressing, ability, character, who they know, or people around them? The answer is no! *What successful people are doing that always keeps them on top are simple things like focusing, persistency, risk taking, self-discipline, self-confidence, and so on. These are very easy to do, which everyone can do.* The question now remains, if it is easy for anyone and everyone to do, how come only 5 percent are dedicated in doing it to their advantage? The answer remains, *"Simple things that are very easy to do are also not easy to do, despite anyone could do them, and many will not do them."*

In the real world, rich and the poor have the same characteristics. They both have to walk, eat, talk, laugh, and go to bathroom. They both drink the same clean water, though in different containers. Rich men have their family and friends to take care of while poor people have their families they take care of at their own level. At times, they both play golf and have a good time in bars. Basketball players and the spectators with cheerleaders are both on the field during the game. They were both in the same arena having the same pressure and anxieties about who would win the game, but their take-home is different. People who are rich read lot of motivational books and business journals while poor people may also read those books and journals, but still their outcome are different.

Chief executive officers of a company and the cleaners in the office were both in the office at the same working hours, and most likely they were using the same elevators or stairs and lunchroom Monday to Friday. They all have the same hour in a year to work with. They all utilized these hours one way or the other by engaging in those actions they do think are not significant which eventually will have effects on their lives. In a real sense, successful and unsuccessful people both do the same basic things at every hour of their lives. Yet, *the thing successful people do take them to the top of the ladder while things unsuccessful people do don't add values to their lives. The difference between the two groups is in the level of their awareness and understanding of those things they do.*

Both rich and the poor people see the problems in their communities and what people lack. Guess what? They have different interpretations about what they see. While the rich men do the follow-up to what they see and read and use it as ladders to their next level, the poor men do nothing about the information they have collected.

Rich people see problems in their environment as opportunities to make money by finding solutions to those problems. Poor people see problems as mountains that nobody can move.

It can be assumed that, everybody will like to be successful since everyone wants a better life. This of course requires great efforts and depends on the choice made. It may be easy for anyone to choose not to smoke cigarettes or drink alcohol in order to avoid cancer and other lung diseases. One can also abstain from fornication to avoid sexually transmitted diseases. This is by choice that is open to everybody. The right choice will involve discipline and the consideration of consequences of their actions and inactions. One of the reasons why many people may not do the simple and significant things that are very easy to do and which can transform their lives may be the feelings of the absence of immediate consequences of their actions or inactions. *The dangerous consequences of inability to do those essential things will include failure in life and missed opportunities for success.*

Failure to go to school while you are young and able to study to become a professional may not have immediate consequences as long as you still have the capacity to run around and do hard and unskilled jobs, but it will definitely have consequences at the later age when you will not have the strength to do hard work or you may not have enough funds to finance your old age. *Spending on jewelry and clothes (uniforms for occasions) may not have immediate consequences, but the consequences will show up later by the time you don't have the ability to work and you realize that the money you spent on jewelry could have been enough for you to do a lifetime investment!*

Riding expensive cars obtained on credit when you have no stable source of income may not have any significant meaning to you now until you realize that the car value is depreciating every single day. Your payment on the car is not reducing while your ability to work overtime is reducing!

To have many children may seem not to be a problem when a man is cheating around with different women, but it matters when it comes to bear the responsibilities of taking good care of those children. Likewise, a woman with many kids with different men will not feel the impact immediately until the reality of being a single mom with many kids start to set in.

If you pay for and attend seminars that will lead to your break-through, it will not have any consequence today. *Your decision to stay indoors, burning the midnight candle, working on your dream while your mates are partying around may not have an immediate consequence,* while your refusal not to charge to your credit card things that are not economically important to you may not bring a social recognition. But at the end you will be better off than others who went partying and acquiring credit over credit on unproductive ventures.

Success is not like acting in a movie. It is not dramatic at all. Success is built in a progressive manner. Success is a process and not a destination. It is something you experience gradually over time. Likewise, failure in life is a gradual process. To become successful or a failure involves the same gradual process. You may not get a reaction, comment, or feedback from people while you are pursuing your dream. *Feedback on your success and action will come when you have succeeded or failed. In success, a pupil will commend you while you will be mocked or laughed at when you fail.* They will either say it to your face or in your absence.

Many people are carefree about their state of health. You see people mixing up and drinking sugary food all the time. Would diabetes strike you immediately? No! It will definitely happen inasmuch as you continue the consumption of sugary products. It is a gradual process. Many people live close to the gym and always walk past the exercise bike. *Many live next door to the city parks where they can take a walk, but they don't have passion for exercise.* For the fact that nobody will challenge them for not exercising and because the result is not immediately visible, taking exercising seriously will not be a priority for them. Many don't take their state of health seriously until doctors recommend certain foods or exercises for them. Consuming pounds of food which contain butter every day will not have immediate consequences until later when a heart attack may strike.

Overall, what you do today matters. The major difference between successful people and the unsuccessful person is that the successful people do little things right and identify opportunities for a better future. The little things that will make your life better in life, which will secure your health, and make your dream come true are so simple and very insignificant. Nobody will notice or even applaud you because they may make no difference initially. They will look as if they don't matter, but in the real sense, they do.

DEFINE YOUR POSITION

In order to make headway in life, one must know exactly where one is or where one stands. One should not deceive him/herself. Everybody in life should define exactly where he/she belongs to. This is very necessary in measuring your level of success or failure in life. You cannot be in the middle or stay neutral. You are either cold or hot; you cannot be lukewarm. You can either be in the category of successful people in life who are 5 percent of the population or be in the level of 95 percent who are in the "not enough" categories.

Knowing where you are (your location) is important in determining the type of help you will need, where, and when to get help. For example, somebody stranded on a highway who needs help needs to tell the Rapid Respond Square or other sources of help the exact location or the nearest exit where he needs help before he can be located for the help needed. Otherwise, he may not get the required help on time. What I am saying here is that you cannot be neutral. You are either going down or going up. You are either improving your life or diminishing in value. *You either learn lessons that can improve your life, or you are far away from learning.* If you are not working toward improvement of your career, health, and family life, you must be working against it. You know yourself better. You need to be honest with yourself about where you belong to. This will help you in working toward your dream.

Looking at your personal development, how do you think people will rate you? Will you be on the high or low rating side? Are you learning more about yourself, the situation around you, and the trend of events in life? What are you doing in relation to getting new ideas, skills, and improving on the old ones? What about your moral behavior? Is your character improving or depreciating due to frustration and inability to focus on things that can promote your dream?

Is your financial life in order? Are you living on paycheck (salary)? Did you have any savings for your future and that of the family? Do your daily life activities depend on credit whereby you have to borrow to live your life? Are you able to invest for your family's future with the little income you are earning? Or are you just living a life of hand to mouth? Are you projecting to have financial freedom any time soon?

How about your relationship with others? Are you still hanging out with the old friends that will not add value to your life, or have you stepped up in hanging around those that can improve your life? *Are you still in the company of the dream killers or dream promoters?* Is your association with your present friends still ending with drinking and womanizing? Are you planning to mingle with the successful guys who can bring positive change to your life? What about your families, your children, parents, brothers, sisters, and others surrounding you? Are they growing up in the way they should grow? Are they improving financially, or are they in poverty? What can your family and the people in your community say about you? Are you a role model to your family or a black sheep? *What kind of impact is your life having on the world around you? Is your presence with them making any difference in their life?* Do you have any plans for the next ten years of your life? What do you want people to remember about you as your legacy after you have gone to the great beyond? Do you want to die fulfilling destiny through your sharing the good ideas in you with others, creating jobs for people, making people happy, and using your talents positively? Or *do you want to die loaded by not fulfilling destiny by holding on to resources meant for millions of people to succeed, by not being able to write the articles for the magazines or the books which are supposed to have helped transform people's lives, by not creating jobs for people who would have been managers and directors through you. The choice is yours.*

Adding together all your professional accomplishments and your career, personal life, your relationships with others, and your connection with God, how would you rate your overall value or the full meaning of your life? Will your grading fall between excellent, average, or below average? To be honest with yourself, you need to know where you really belong to without any doubt. You must be kind enough to do yourself a favor by telling the truth. Failure to tell the truth may lead to your disadvantage because telling the truth and being honest with yourself may be the turning point where your life will be changed forever.

I always feel sorry for many people who take the issue of life like the end of a semester's exam, whereby they can group together before the exam and do the tutorial related to the exam. This makes them have ideas of what to expect in the examination hall. In this case, if they have questions in the tutorial that goes with the exam questions, having done well in the tutorial can make them pass the exam. Inability to study the tutorial very well may eventually lead to their failure. Ability to study the tutorial very well will put them on the success row. But life is not like that. Nobody can predict or have an idea of what will happen in the next minute. That is why it is important that you contribute your best while you can. Many also compare life with movies which has parts one and two, whereby the film producers put everybody watching the movie in suspense at the end of part one in order for them to watch part two. In the movie, it is possible for the audience to have the full knowledge of the movie by watching part two regardless of which part of the scene they missed in part one. Likewise, the whole life circle can be reached within two hours in the movie. This means you can be born, go to school, get married, get rich or poor, and later die within two hours. But the truth of the matter is that life is not an exam or movie. *Things about life are not dramatic. Life is for real. Try to be real and specific with yourself. Take a look at your life and tell the truth about where you really belong to.*

The good thing is that it is never too late for you to adjust yourself and take productive steps toward fulfilling your dreams. Where you are now is your present with your past behind you while you are facing the future. *Remember, you have capacity to change your future while you absolutely have no control over your past.* You can decide to turn your life in the direction you want. You may choose to let it go either up or down. *You can either go forward or backward; it is not possible for you to move in two directions at the same time.* The past is not by any way equal to the future.

What should be important to one is to understand to spindle pendulum into the side of success, since things needed to be successful in life are in and around the individuals who should try as much as possible to use them for necessary empowerment to his advantage. *When one is empowered, the achievement of success will be assured.* It is a pity that many do not know the difference between the genuine success and mere success. That is the more reason why many rest on their oars by merely achieving success in one area of their lives. *A genuinely successful life will involve success in the areas of family relationship, career, and in the spiritual life.*

Genuine success has the capacity to move from one generation to another generation. One success affects the other positively. *When you are improving positively, it will be easy for you to get attracted to other successful people.* You will be friends to many relations. Successful business associates will come around you. People who are well-to-do in your community will rally round you. *Success has many friends.* When you succeed in reaching out positively to other persons through your interactions and words of good advice and encouragement, you will touch such life and possibly change such life for good. *A single life you change may also change another person's life for good.* You have the choice to turn around the life of people around you and your community for good. It is never too late for you to start. Start now.

BE INFORMED

Ignorance can simply mean a state of being uninformed, lack of knowledge, or lack of information. It is also a state of being unaware of things or situations around us. Ignorance can shut down the wheel of progress if not checked on time. Therefore, for one to fulfill one's dream and destiny, you must seek knowledge. There is an adage which says, "Ignorance of the law is not an excuse." What you don't know, you don't know.

One thing I discovered is that *this world would be a better place to live in if only we can embrace change that will improve our understanding and knowledge that really matters in our environment.* Life can be better enjoyed if we could educate ourselves on critical matters that will improve our knowledge. Many people believe they are the masters of all knowledge and therefore behave as if they have nothing to learn from others to change their positions on any matter, even when they are wrong in all perspectives. They will ignorantly and arrogantly hold to their faulty conclusions or position on given matters. They will always ignore all wise counsels and hold on rigidly to their faulty perceptions or wrong views of issues. Anybody in this state of ignorance will never fulfill his/her destiny in life. It is advisable that we should improve our knowledge in order to achieve our dreams.

Our wrong assumptions and conclusions on various matters and fellow human beings based on poor reactions and judgments on hearsays about somebody or event without even cross-checking the information collected from a third party can destroy relationships and make one lose good advice. Many people have missed opportunities because of their ignorance. *The sure path to failure is when a man is ignorant and yet rejects every opportunity to obtain relevant knowledge.* Many remain ignorant because of their inability to differentiate between reality and illusion and because they often fail to seek the truth because they are afraid that others may ridicule them, and they continue to hold on to their faulty positions in order to protect their ego from being bruised. *Ignorance is so dangerous that what you don't know and you don't know that you don't know can easily hurt or kill you.*

For the fact that you don't know that you are a diabetes patient does not mean it will not kill you if proper care is not taken. Because you don't know how to swim doesn't mean that you will not drown if you jump to the pool of water. Simply because you can't see "do not enter" or one-way traffic signs that are boldly written is not an excuse for you not to get a ticket from police if you get pulled over after passing through such traffic signs. That means you need to study and know your immediate environment. Know exactly what is going on there and be part of every action that is necessary. *Knowledge is power. Knowing something or a lot about your environment and what you are dealing with on regular basis will save you from danger.* Keeping yourself informed with the latest technology and on other current affairs will do you good in reaching your goals in life.

One of the quickest ways of attaining our goals in life is to constantly check our ignorance gauge on issues at hand and swiftly move on to improve our understanding of matters at stake.

Mind Your Thinking

Thinking is visualizing a thing or imagining it. It is also calling to mind certain things or remembering it. It has capacity to concentrate on a matter. Every day of your life, you keep thinking about one thing or the other. You spend your life thinking; you think about thinking itself. You think about small and big things. You think about this and that. But the important thinking that should be in your mind is for you to think like a champion. As you think in your heart so is he (Prov. 23:7). *Your life cannot make any progress if you cannot do qualitative thinking. Thinking makes you apprehend and consume certain ideas.*

You should learn to think in a way that a champion can be made out of you so that your life can experience progress. Thinking makes you determined or estimate what you should do or achieve. *You cannot think without envisioning. You see pictures in your mind, where you want to go, what you want to achieve, and how you want to go about it.* Thinking makes you reckon what a particular matter will be. It is quite important for you to work on your capacity to think, not only to think alone but to think in a right way. Thinking involves meditation. *If you want to succeed in life, you need to learn and know how to think like a champion, not like a loser.* Thinking is not just important, but it is important for you to become what we call champion. Thinking will allow you to have things in your life that can promote you to your next level.

Thinking like a champion involves you thinking progressively. You must develop new things in your mind every day. *Progressive thinking is what moves you in a direction to be successful.* Progressive thinking requires you to learn, unlearn, and relearn. In other words, you learn new truths; you unlearn old things which you are used to, and then learn new things that will promote your life and destiny. Progressive thinking is a necessity for succeeding. Many people do not always find progress in life because they blame others for their misfortune. *When you always find excuses instead of acting or working and you lack progressive thinking, your life may not change for good.* Without progressive thinking, you are likely to be unsuccessful.

Thinking progressively alone cannot lead you to your promised land. In other words, in conjunction with your thinking progressively, you must be constructive enough about your thinking. Constructive thought is one of the prerequisites that can make you achieve your dream. *Your thought is what you become. If you cannot change your thought, you cannot change your life.* This is where your life is being determined. This is where your lives are either made or broken. *When you have a constructive mind, you see more than what it is happening.* You develop an ability to see the future. You will see beyond your nose. *When you have a constructive thought, there are possibilities that you will fly higher than your peers.*

A man with inventive thinking does not wait for things to happen. He goes out and gets things done because he knows that nothing in life happens by itself except when someone makes a decision to make it happen. If you really want to achieve what God wants you to become, you must be do more progressive thinking than your peers and be determined to do something different from your colleague. You must be many steps ahead in your thinking. *Inventive thinking will make you ask questions about what to do and why to do it.* It will also make you go further to find solutions to identify problems while your colleague may be finding excuses for not acting.

You make up your mind to invent and to really have breakthroughs. *Until you question the regulars of life, nothing tangible happens.* You must think outside the box and be creative. *Get out under the ceilings and see that there are lots of stars in the sky.* The ceiling has a limit for you, but with sky, you are limitless. Decide in your heart that you don't want to be just a regular person like the multitude. You must dance to the order of creativity. The Bible gave us the idea that

God is a God of creativity. *You don't want to live a life of consumption but a life of production and creativity.* All the amenities we are enjoying today are the products of the thoughts of people like us. We don't have any excuse not to be creative in life. I challenge you today with this medium to rise and be creative so that your life's destiny and dream can be fulfilled or achieved.

Never rely on your certificate as your yardstick to measure success. Having degree certificate(s) does not guarantee your success. Many degree certificate holders are poor in life for so many reasons. "If somebody offers you an amazing opportunity, but you are not sure you can do it, say yes, then learn how to do it later!" said Richard Branson. *School rewards people for their memory. Life rewards people for their creativity and ability to solve problems.* School rewards caution; life rewards daring. School hails those who live by the rules; life exalts those who break the rules and set new ones. *Being top of your class does not necessarily guarantee that you would be at the top of life.* The world is filled with poor graduates, but it has rich opportunists.

Kevin Ngo said, *"If you don't make the time to work on creating the life you want, you are eventually going to be forced to spend a lot of time dealing with a life you don't want."* Your certificates and degrees are meant to help you garner the experience and expertise needed to fulfill your dreams; they are not your destination.* I have watched pitiably many graduates with degrees and certificates languishing in poverty, looking for jobs that don't exist, while people with keen eyes for opportunities reach the pinnacle of success in the most unlikeliest of ways. Do you have a graduate or degree holder around you who is poor? I bet you have, as they are everywhere. I have a very painful truth to dish out to graduates out there: *Your degree or certificate is not the cure to poverty; the cure to poverty is your ability to see and seize opportunities.* There are several reasons why degree holders are poor. Many university and college degree holders are poor and remain poor because many don't think beyond their certificates. Albert Einstein said, *"Education is not the learning of facts, but the training of the mind to think."*

Have you ever heard of the creativity term "think outside the box"? One of the major reasons why most graduates are poor is simply because they cannot see and think beyond their certificates. I have seen engineering graduates work as bankers. I have seen medical doctors with great skills in web and graphic designs. I have seen lawyers that are very dexterous with finances. The list is endless. The basic truth of life is that *the skills needed to be much sought after and become more successful in life are not really found within the walls of the classrooms. Your certificate is just a proof that you are teachable*; it does not suggest what you are totally capable of doing. *You are full of possibilities when you think beyond your degrees and certificates.* Many university graduates prioritize their certificates more than their gifts and talents. It is advisable not to leave your gifts dormant while pursuing and hunting for jobs with your certificates. There must be a complementary balance in the pursuit of your passion and the search for jobs. *Everybody is gifted for something, but the winning edge comes from our ability to work on our gifts and bless the world with it. The very best way to develop yourself is in the direction of your natural talents and interest.* To live a fulfilled and impactful life, you need to work harder on your gift than your job. You need to discover your gift, develop it, and sell it. Don't bury your talent with your certificates. The certificates of many graduates prepare them for a world that no longer exists. It has been found that most of the skills taught in schools are becoming obsolete in the present world. The world has changed a lot, and so have people's needs. It is sad to know that the present form of education does not prepare students for the future. Graduates are becoming an endangered species in the face of a changing world.

The African archaic methods and approaches of learning are preparing graduates for a world that no longer exist, as we are churning out degree holders every year with certificates that have face value but no intrinsic worth. Most African institutions are filled up with lecturers and pseudo-educators with lecture notes, methods, and approaches that have lost relevance in a changing world. *Majority of the university graduates nowadays know less about themselves but more about things.* Certificates and degrees don't reveal people to themselves; they at most measure their IQ (intelligent quotient). There is no recovery without discovery. *A poor man is simply someone that has not discovered himself. The more you discover about yourself, the more you realize the treasures hidden deep within you.* We all carry inside ourselves latent treasures that can only be unveiled through self-discovery. *Certificates and degrees have killed and are still killing the initiatives of many certificate holders.* Degrees and certificates can close people's minds to ideas while initiatives open it up. If you are not careful, your degrees and certificates will close your mind forever. *The purpose of education is to keep your mind perpetually opened toward limitless possibilities.* Fred Smith saw an opportunity for overnight delivery of anything anywhere in the United States (US) and ultrafast delivery anywhere in the world, and FedEx was born. It will be interesting to know that Fred Smith got a grade C in a Yale economics class for an idea that the professor belittled as unworkable. Smith's company became the first American business to make over $10 billion in annual profit. Beginning with just 186 packages delivered the first night, FedEx now delivers to over two hundred countries using over 6,030 aircraft; 46,000 vehicles; and 141,000 employees.

Degrees and certificates have positioned a lot of people to look for jobs and not for opportunities. *Certificates and degrees prepare graduates to look for jobs and not open their eyes to life-changing opportunities.* You are not poor because you don't have a job; you are poor because you are not seeing and seizing opportunities. *Being POOR is simply "passing over opportunities repeatedly."* What keeps people ahead in life is not their education or degrees; it is simply the opportunity that they seized. *Jobs may be scarce, but not opportunities. If there is a problem to be solved, there will always be opportunities.* It is a waste of your education, exposure, and experiences if after you graduate from school, all you think about is searching for a job. An enlightened and educated mind should be able to see and seize opportunities. Certificates and degrees prepare people to look for security and not to take risks. You must be willing to make mistakes and take breakthrough risks. Taking risks and learning from mistakes help you in knowing what works and what does not. When Thomas Edison was being questioned by a journalist on how he felt for having failed for 999 times before getting the idea of the light bulb, his response stunned the whole world when he confidently said, *"I have not failed 999 times. I have only learnt 999 ways of how not to make*

CREATE A DESIRED FUTURE BY WORKING ON YOUR OWN DREAM

a light bulb." Many graduates and degree holders are becoming progressively poor because the skills required in the modern world to get rich are not taught in schools and institutions. By 2025, we would lose over five million jobs to automation. That means that future jobs would look vastly different by the time many people graduate from the university. Future jobs would involve knowledge creation and innovation, and people that are only equipped with skills found in the classroom would be a misfit in an ever-changing world. Skills like critical thinking, creativity, people's skill, stem skills (like coding), complex problem-solving skills, etc. are central to living a more comprehensive and productive life. It is advisable for graduates and students in institutions of higher learning to think wide, deep, and outside the box. Take volunteer jobs and don't be afraid to navigate fields that are different from your field of learning. Your future career would require you to pull information from many different fields to come up with creative solutions to future problems. *Start by reading as much as you can about anything and everything that interests you.* Once you get to college, consider double majoring or minoring in completely different fields. It would pay off in the long run. Don't limit yourself to the classroom; do something practical. Take a leadership position. Start a business and fail; that is, a better entrepreneurship. Contest an election and lose. It would teach you something political science would not teach you. Attend a seminar or read books outside the scope of your course. *Think less of becoming an excellent student but think more of becoming an excellent person. Don't make the classroom your world but make the world your classroom. Step forward and try something extra. Invest in something you believe in.*

YOU ARE UNSTOPPABLE

To achieve success, one must be prepared to squarely face opposition forces on the path to success. *Remember that turbulence does not affect things on the ground but things at the high altitude.* The airplane does not face turbulence while on the ground but in the sky. You should expect that *your challenges will be directly proportional to your greatness.* That is to say, the greater your achievements, the greater the challenges. Life and situations around may work against your wish and destiny in life. Sometimes our weaknesses and some personal problems may be used to attempt to pull one down. Lies may be fabricated, and gossips may be created to discourage you from achieving your goal, but as much as you remain steadfast in what you are doing, you will definitely be unstoppable in achieving the goal. *If you make up your mind to succeed, nothing can stop you. Even the worst tragedy cannot stop you.* The greatest fears you have kept in mind will not be able to stop you from achieving your set goal. The financial pit you may fall into and the secret pains inside you that makes you cry day in day out cannot stop you once you are determined to succeed.

Whenever you fall into a pit, you can simply turn the pit into PIT, or *preacher in training*, and move ahead to fulfill your destiny. The giants and the law in the land which posed as obstacles to your progress will not be able to stop you once you know what you are doing and are consistent in doing it. No event, no history. *Sometimes a mistake you made on the way may become a miracle for success at the end.* Success in life is not about mistakes made but is about how you handle the mistakes and the lessons learned from such mistakes. If you missed a particular job or contract simply because of the little or major mistakes you made, you should never give up. This is because *the mistake you made will be a lesson to another person and an experience for you to help others and to prepare better for the future exercise.*

Time may not be on our side, but it can't stop us. Tribulation may want to stop you from achieving your destiny; calamity will want to raise its ugly head. *There are some people who don't hold your conviction and who do not hold your belief just because they know you are different and they can't stand it.* They will do everything possible to try to belittle you. Mind you, those who tried to belittle you will end up being little as soon as you step up to your responsibility and succeed. *You should believe in yourself and have it in mind that nothing can stop you from making waves. Never be intimidated by any challenge or confrontation. They are bound to happen.* All problems in life come with solutions. Never allow challenges to discourage you and make and keep you in custody. Feel that you are born to be great and that nothing can stop you. *You are an arrow that has been shot at a target. An arrow shot at a particular object will complete its mission when it hits its target.* Therefore, you must hit what destiny has in stock for you before you are considered successful in life.

All difficulties thrown at you will always be stepping-stones inasmuch as you are working fervently to support your personal dream. *Challenges are meant purposely to bring you closer to the purpose of God in your life. So don't be discouraged whenever challenges emerged.* It was a challenge that took the biblical Joseph to prison. The woman who set up Joseph by telling lies against him did not know that she was doing Joseph a big favor. If adversity made people walk away from you, and if your friends had despised and forsaken you, you should not worry as such things may work to your advantage. Adversity is meant to reveal the heart of men; adversity will make you know those that are truly on your side. Don't expect your roads to be smooth all the time. You should expect some potholes and detours on your journey to success or else you may not know those who are for you or against you.

Fire allows you to know if there is a snake in the wood. At times, it is good to put fire (challenges) around you. By so doing; you will know friends who have true love. *If you don't have problems, you will not know that some people can run from you. You will not know that some people you call your friends may have two faces. Without adversity, you will not know who your friends truly are from those who are just taking advantage of you.* A friend in need is a friend indeed. You must know that there are people who are set to use you. There may be users in your vicinity, even among your friends. The good news is that they can't stop you from reaching your goals. Just be careful.

The level of your attack will correspond with the blessings you are to carry. If adversity attacks you, it is a sign and a pointer that you have something special that is worth stealing from you. It is left for you not to let intimidation and challenges steal your success from you and rob you of the achievement of your dream. There is more to your future than you know, and you should therefore not be discouraged. *If your future is bright, you should not expect an easy or a free ride to your success.*

The reason why you may have so many attacks is because you are uncommon and anointed. Uncommon people are resented by common people, while pure people are resented by impure people. Lazy people don't like diligent people. Unserious-minded people don't like serious-minded people. Don't fool yourself by having the belief that many people will like you. Somebody somewhere may be waiting for your downfall. Some others may be waiting for you to come and borrow money from them. Some may not want you to succeed; while others may find faults in what you have not achieved. That is why when they tell you either jokingly or seriously that you have a better future ahead of you, you should better claim it rather than reject it. They may call you all manners of names like millionaire, problem solver, the man in charge, and so on, only in a bid to mock you. You better claim them because those names will work for your good. Regardless of the names and labels they stick on you, they can't stop you from reaching your goals once you remain committed and focused.

Many a times fear may steal the purpose of God in someone's life. Past experience of failure may pull one back when one wants to try a new thing. Moreover, the spirit of fear in one may be telling one not to try it because one cannot do it and can't see if one has seen anybody who has successfully done the task in the family. All may predict failure, but you should ignore such discouraging comments and go ahead and do your things according to the purpose God has ordained you to do. They can only bother you but shouldn't stop you.

Stop running around trying to please anybody. Stop trying to explain your vision to people. Some of them may even not like your idea or your-self. They may not be interested in your achievement. Therefore, there is no moral reason why you should be explaining to them where you are heading to. If people say you are nothing, that does not mean that you are nothing in the real sense. You know who you are. Keep your dream to yourself and nurture it. Many times, it is good to travel alone. Nobody or no challenge can stop you because you have an uncommon purpose. You may be little in your own eyes, but you may be a solution to somebody's problems. Nobody can stop you. *Never allow anyone to define your purpose. When people can define you, they can classify you. When they can classify you, they can nullify you.*

When you begin to come into your purpose and you don't fit within the regular, you definitely have messed up somebody's opinion. When you mess up somebody's opinion, that somebody will likely hold you down within their little parameters, forgetting that you are more than who they think you are because your level has changed. They cannot hold you into ransom because you have become more than their classification of you. They can't stop you because you have been predestinated. Nobody can stop or toy with your destiny. Your destiny is already fixed; nothing can stop you.

Stop bowing to adversity, tribulations, and people's opinion. The wind of life may blow you around, but you will definitely arrive at a fixed end. Before you were formed in the womb and give birth to by your mother, the Lord already knew you. So no adversary or human being can reform you or prevent you from fulfilling your destiny. No way! Before, Dell, Apple, and other computer companies manufactured the computers. They foreknew the computers, and therefore they put different software that could perform different functions in the computers. The same way, when God created you, because he foreknew you, he put prosperity in you. He inputted your wife, your children, your house, and all things that will be commensurate with your destiny in you. As you are living, you are just discovering them. It is already in the package. Nobody can stop it.

People may take something physical away from you and fight what they see, but they can't stop your destiny. Where you live doesn't matter inasmuch as you know that God has put all these packages in you. If you live in the desert, you will still prosper. At this level, it is not where you are (desert) that will determine your destiny but what has already been planted in you. You are already carrying your destiny and purpose; you will surely arrive at your destination safely. Nothing can stop you. *The reaction of your enemy is just on the impression of you, which he has and cannot change your achievement.* Therefore, nothing can stop you from fulfilling your destiny. People have the rights to hold opinion about you. You have the privilege not to believe or agree with such opinions. Don't let people's opinion hold you back. Your later end shall be so bright. Your dream will come to reality as you are unstoppable.

TURN CHALENGES TO OPPORTUNITIES

O n many occasions in life when many people face several challenges, they may feel as if life is ending and meaningless. In some other times, many people may feel that people around them are making life difficult for them. These challenges may make many affected people to be weary of doing what they should do or procrastinating over activities that if addressed can lead them to their success. *Achieving dreams has to do with coping with challenges. It is a challenge that makes the champions.* There is no champion without a story of challenges. No matter how good you are as a boxer, you must get to the ring and fight before you can be declared a champion. Don't bow down for challenges. Many give up and run away at the junction to their breakthrough. *God can use problems and challenges to wake you up.* For example, in Acts 12:25, when Herod first kills James, the church kept aloof. But when Herod grabbed Peter, the early church saw the need to wake up. Suddenly, they realized if they did not do something, Herod would kill all of them, so they began to pray. It was a problem that led Joseph to the prison where he became an interpreter of dreams. Until then, Joseph was a mere dreamer and servant before he finally got to the palace.

Many times, problems can turn to what will lead us to discover our potential. For example, Philip never knew he had the potential to be a great evangelist until the church experienced intense persecution that scattered the disciples/apostles. Even before then, he thought it was just good enough for him to be an outstanding deacon. However, when his friend and fellow deacon Steven was killed and Saul was throwing Christians into prisons, he ran to Samaria and brought the joy to the city after he led them to Christ.

It is possible for you not to understand your potential or the talent you have until you are confronted with challenges. *We should not run away or bow down for our problems or challenges. Instead we must be bold and courageous to face such challenges till we are able to solve the problems.* We should remember that "no event, no history." No examination, no promotion to the next grade. *Without problems, we may not know the ability we have in us!* It was because of the problem the Jews had with Goliath that brought out the young David to face and kill Goliath and made David a hero.

If you don't know where you are going, anywhere you get to looks like it. If you know your ultimate goal, you will know when you have reached the goal. There are rooms for unlimited improvement and advancement as you journey toward the goal. What does it take to move from one destination to another? The simple answer is your ability to work on your set goals or dreams. All that is recorded in the Bible are things we can get if we passionately work for them. The Lord said that Abraham would get all he could see, and it came to pass. Likewise, in the physical, *you can get or be all you can see and want to be if you know how to go about it and know exactly what to do.* The reason why many people are stagnant is because certain fundamental demands are ignored. Whatever you see and believe you can become is possible. *When you see it, you are empowered supernaturally to become it. You can be silent on what you heard but you can't be silent on what we have seen.* The more the opposition about what you see and believe, the stronger you become about the things you have seen. Eyes that are looking are many, but the eyes that are seeing are few.

What does it mean to see? It means to see because it will terminate your doubt. Paul said in the Bible, "The eyes of our understanding being enlighten" (Eph. 1:18). Understanding is the eyes in with which we see. *When our eyes of understanding are blocked, we can't see.* What you can't see, you can believe. Your faith and belief come up naturally when your eyes of understanding open up. *Understanding is what differentiates success from failure. Depth of understanding deter-*

mines the level of greatness. The Bible says that "people perish for lack of knowledge" (Hosea 4:6). If you must get there, you must play your part. *It does not take time but choice to prosper if you know what to do.* Likewise, *it doesn't take time but truth and knowledge to experience changes.* It does not take centuries but a right choice to change for the better. *You need to see further so that you can arrive faster.*

We should know that it is God's will for us to be gainfully and profitably employed. We must therefore try to have good business and jobs that are profitable to enable us to eat and live well. In 2 Thessalonians 3:10, Paul advised, "If anyone will not work, neither shall he eat." We must therefore not be idle or lazy. *Many people can be jobless because of the bad economy, but we hold the promise that ours will be an exception.* In Genesis 47:15, there was lack but in verse 27, with God there was abundance. We must be living with the consciousness of our peculiarities and not let the bad or negative news on the television, newspapers, or what we see outside determine our economic situations. *We should remain dedicated to God and our dream. In other words, we must remain attached and dedicated to God in all things.* We should not let challenges disconnect us from God. While challenges can definitely bring frustration, our strong connection with God, other people, and our dream can ensure success and improvement. We should be connected to God's words. Isaiah 3:10 shows us that we shall be eating from our doing and not be dependent. If and when we give God the best, God will make us prosperous or will prosper us. We need to look to God alone. Our *inability to trust God may become a barrier in our effort to reach our destiny.* We therefore need to keep our focus on God alone. Nobody can match what God has in stock to offer us. Whatever we desire, we shall have when we work and pray. Whatever our hands have to do to prosper us must be done efficiently.

Our warfare determines our success. When we have proper understanding, we shall know how to approach our challengers. Never see yourself as someone based on what you are but on what you want to be. *Genius is 1 percent inspiration and 99 percent perspiration. Anybody can wish for riches and most people do, but only a few people who have definite plans plus burning desire to succeed will gain sustainable wealth.*

Challenge is the mother of provocation. You can't be provoked if you are not challenged. Something must irritate you for your provocation to aggravate. *What will make you succeed in life is at the back of the door, you must be irritated and get provoked before the door can be opened to you.* Many at times, people misunderstand provocation to be a bad thing. No! *Not all provocations end in disasters.* If you are not provoked or irritated by your present situation, you may not move to the next level for sure. Challenges should make you productive. Don't bow down for your challenges. You should exercise your provocative right or power to fight back your challenges. Challenge and provocation are like five and six. Positive provocation gets things done faster than expected. It brings about immediate or fast results. Although, the result may vary.

I was watching TV one day. What I saw really caught my attention. A boy of about five years old was playing outside with his cat. Suddenly, a dog ran to a little boy and bit his leg. As the boy was screaming and trying to escape from the dog, his pet cat playing outside with him ran toward the dog and challenged the dog with an attitude that was provocative. Eventually, the dog ran away from the small cat that was fiery looking.

There was a road car accident that happened some time ago in one of the major highways in America which involved a boy and his mother. As the car somersaulted, the mother who is the driver of the car dropped off from the car. Suddenly the woman realized that his son was trapped under the car with his arm being pressed down by the weight of the car. The woman quickly got back to her senses and provocatively and single-handedly lifted up the car and saved her son before she got help. She was later asked how she was able to single-handedly lift up the car on her son. Her response was, "I was provoked to see my son dying." She got irritated and was provoked. This triggered her ability to lift up the car alone as the last result for her son's survival.

Those who are positively provoked on any matter or issue has learned to use it for their benefit and the benefit of others. *There are some blessings and breakthroughs you will never achieve if you are not provoked.* The provokers around you are on assignment to push you into your destiny and favor. There are many dream haters who may come around you, and you are thinking that Satan sent them around you to set you back. The truth of the matter is that if God did not permit them to stay around you, you will remain the same. I usually tell people that not all people who hate or mount pressure on you meant it for bad. Many are for good in disguise.

You don't have a testimony until you defile the prediction of those who said you will fail. You don't have a testimony until you defile the prophesy of those who said you can't make it. You don't have a testimony until you prove wrong the bad thoughts people had about you. *No testimonies until you rise to attain the level of what God has for you.* You don't have a testimony until you frustrate the token of a liar. You don't have a testimony until you embarrass those who said you would never rise. You should make the prophesy of the bad people not to come to pass by not giving chance to distractions standing against your progress.

Don't waste your time thinking and worrying about bad people anymore. Instead, study and embrace them and use them for your good. No doubt about it, your provocation will rise after you have tried so many things that are not working for you. This is good for you because if things had worked for you earlier on as planned, you would have settled for easy and worthless things. Don't worry. A day will coming when you will thank your provokers, because where they will push you beyond your imagination. *If you can't afford or you don't want to leave your comfort zone, someone else has to push you out of your comfort zone so that you can attain a position that no one has ever reach in your family and communities.* That is what your provokers do. That is their duty.

How your father spent his life shouldn't be your cutoff point. Your brothers and sisters are not the barometers to measure your own progress, your community, or background. Where you come from is not an issue in determining your progress. That is why challenges and provokers provoke you to push you to your normal position where you can attain your destiny. Life is tough when you are facing problems that you know nothing about or you don't know the way out. But mind you, it is even tougher when people are rejoicing on your problem. People would go to any level of texting or gossiping about your predicament. *Many people prefer you to be useless simply because they want to use you as an illustration or a case study.* They want to refer to you as the same person in the same place. They want you to keep quiet. There are times when people look at you, size you up, and mark you down. They've forgotten that man looks outside when God is looking inward. You will excel if you use them for your good.

Provokers are all around and everywhere, even in the church and our various places of work. Many people believe they are in the position to tell your story. They talk about the time you were in primary school, when you have only one pairs of sandal, when you borrowed money from them, when you were not married. They wonder why you are now flying around the world. They want to know the source of your finances. They might be thinking you have someone who is backing you up somewhere. But what they don't know is that the dream you are carrying is not physical. *When they are feeling sorry and sober for you, there is a miracle in the motion. Please work on your own dream and stop letting people use you as a tool for making their fortunes.* Provokers will provoke you to your breakthrough. When you have not been provoked, you pray with swag or styles. But as soon as you are provoked and face challenges that are ridiculous, you will increase the pace of your prayer.

Many don't want to leave or shift gear from their comfort zone until something pushes them. *Don't stay too much on your comfort zone because where you think is your comfort zone is not comfortable compared with your next level.* But you may not know what is ahead of you until provokers force you out of your comfort zone. What determines your coming out of your comfort zone and the rate at which you will run out of your comfort zone will be determine by what is chasing you. *A man chased by a lion will move out more speedily from his comfort zone than the man who is chased by somebody with an ordinary stick.*

Due to your provocation, many will call you all manners of names. They will say you are too provocative, you don't usually rest, you are a disciplinarian, and yours is too much. Mind you, *you can't change how people treat you or what they say about you. All you can do is change how you react to their opinions or comments about you.* Don't worry yourself about their comments. What they want is for them to keep you on the same spot. They want you to keep borrowing money from them. *They don't want you to do anything apart from placing you on salary every month.* They don't want you to see beyond your nose. They don't want you to come out of your roof in order to prevent you from seeing the sky. Remember, God already built what you will need to succeed in you. It is left for you to discover it.

You really need adversaries and challenges for you to have a break-through. These will make you sit tight and see opportunities around you. Your challenges which can provoke you to your victory can be that thing which is bothering you that you always remember when you wake up in the morning; it can be something you are still waiting or crying for. Have it in mind that not all challenges come from the devil. *The best secret to success is to find a problem and solve it.* Don't always run away from problems. *The problem you noticed is the problem that makes the world noticed you.* Some challenges will change your level.

Your provocation will lead you into process. All finished products once went through a process. Although going through process may be painful, you need process to get things done or cooked. To make cake or bread requires going through different processes of mixing and putting it in oven at high temperature. But when it gets done, everybody is happy. The same principle applies to gold and other jewelry we are wearing today. They all went through painful proce-dures before they're ready for use. In the physical, it is painful when somebody you have helped lets you down. It is painful when you were ridiculed or rubbished in town either because of what you know little or nothing about. It is painful when those you fed and clothed come back later and mock you. It is painful when your confidants or those people you show love to come back and let you down.

It is very sad when your manager, supervisor, or team leaders are frustrating your effort at your workplace. But for the fact that you have bills to pay at the end of the month, you decided to endure.

Whatever chaos or trouble around you will finally work for your promotion, blessing, lifting, and testimony. After all the processes, you will definitely manifest your destiny in life. *Don't be too in a hurry to pass through the process that will take you into greatness.* Success and greatness is not achieved by feelings or emotion but by timing. *Your tears cannot activate your success and promotion.*

Don't let reactions of people or situations around you deprive you of your success. Some people and situations around you will be pushing you or laughing at you, but don't let them push you out of your success. Some may not believe in what you believe, but don't let anybody change your belief. Keep your focus; it won't be long. They will push you into your testimony. You are closer to your breakthrough than where you are coming from (lack and poverty). It won't be long. It is a matter of time. *Don't quit at the junction to your breakthrough. Always remember that your present situation is not your final destination.*

Those who always run away from challenges never enter into their breakthrough. They will never fulfill the promises of God for their lives. *You need provokers to set you on fire for your success.* If there are no challenges, you may not be able to sit right. Without challenges and provocation, many will not wake up to things that can promote their destiny. *If you are not pushing back, you may not move forward. Retreat is necessary for advancement.* Provocation and challenges will definitely prepare you for your advancement if carefully handled. Don't be satisfied with what you're not supposed to be satisfied with. When your provocation is over, breakthrough and promotion will follow. You will have another name when you achieve your breakthrough. *In the aftermath of your provocation, you should establish that business which you have developed in your mind. You should write the magazines and books you have been contemplating about.*

You should help people you are destined to help. Make the breakthrough telephone calls you have been procrastinating on for long time. Try to execute the innovative ideas you have in mind a long time ago. Go to the school of your choice to improve your knowledge. *You should aspire to put people at work. Be an employer and not an employee.* This medium is to let the readers of this book know that most of those provocations are orchestrated to promote your life and to fast forward you to your destination. You will not die without fulfilling your destiny in Jesus's name.

UNDERSTANDING CONSTANT LAW OF WEALTH CREATION

I n life, there are laws that guide our actions and things. These laws are constant and cannot be changed. For instance, the laws guiding the force of gravity in physics which says, "Anything which goes up must surely come down" cannot by any means change. There are laws of floatation, Archimedes' principle, the law of aerodynamics, and so on. In the physical realm, there are laws to be respected in order to achieve success. When such laws are appropriately applied, things begin to happen. By the way, what is a law? A law according to Wikipedia "is a statement of fact, deduced from observation, to the effect that a particular natural or scientific phenomenon always occurs if certain conditions are present." Laws can also be referred to as principles that make things happen. For example, the gravitational pull around us makes it possible for us to walk around without falling. Once a law guiding a particular thing is put in place, it makes things work in a certain way.

There are laws which guide wealth creation. These laws are so simple. But as simple as they are, they will not work in your favor until you take them seriously and apply them. Until you are able to apply these laws, there would not be a change. Many people think that walking or hanging around people who made it or reading business books or the success stories of those who made it in life is enough to make them successful! Many Christians believe that staying under anointing and receiving prophetic blessing are enough for them to become successful even if they don't take further action toward the realization of their dreams. This is a wrong approach. *Things will not fall in place until one takes appropriate actions. Making it in life cannot depend only on anointing. It entails working smart and getting focused.* It is about making profitable use of opportunities around you. It is about stopping procrastination and start acting. There are some constant laws of wealth creation in life that, if judiciously used, can bring about divine success.

The law of creative mentorship. The law of creative mentorship encourages you to study those who have been creatively successful in their chosen field. *Study those who have done what you want to do so that you don't have to waste your time, money, and resources in reinventing from the scratch again.* It is not easy to find a new Bill Gates or Steve Jobs. Creating new ideas might not be easy. We can study the sets of pioneers and learn more from them. Look into how they applied various principles that work for them into their daily lives. When you do this, what took them many years to learn, you can learn and master them within a short time.

Whenever you buy an inspirational book, you should know that you are not just buying a book but the personal experience of the writer of the book. When you buy an audio tape or video of successful people, you are not just buying words but the experience. It means you are buying all the ideas and the experience of several years.

Burning desire law. The motivation to acquire wealth must be accompanied by a desire for wealth creation. You must have a burning desire to be successful and fulfill your dream. *To be successful in life will not come cheap.* You must go the extra mile ahead of your peers. Your desire to become great will arouse you and remind you that you are staying too long on the same spot, and that you can't afford to be going on in life as a poor man and that you have a lot of responsibilities to shoulder for your family and communities at large.

Having a burning desire to succeed is irrespective of your location. You can desire to succeed at any location or spot you are in. Opportunities are all around everywhere. It is your duty to open your eyes of understanding and notice the opportunities. When you are truly ready to move to the next level, nothing can stop you. The bigger problem and challenges with many people are on how to decide when, where, and how to start the action.

Law of definite of purpose. You must have a well-defined purpose for why you are looking or working for money. *Money is like a vapor or gas. It can come and go at any time.* If you don't have a particular purpose for having the money, you may misuse the money or get ruined by the wealth created with the money. *Money has no definite control or characters of its own self. It takes and imitates the characters of its owner.* The money in the hands of drug dealers will be used for drugs. It will be called drug money. While the money in the hands of investors will be used for investments. On the other hand, the money in the hands of a hungry person will be used to buy food. In other words, *money in your hand will be used for whatever you have in mind as priority as at the time you are in possession of that money.*

It is very important for you to know why you really want the money which you are hustling for. Is it for helping people who are in need? Is it for your immediate family's need? Do you want to build churches or school with the money? Maybe the money is for investment or foundation creation. Whatever reason why you are trying to acquire the wealth, you need to have it in mind before you finally get the money or else you may squander the money.

If you desire sustainable wealth that makes a difference, it has to be the type of wealth that can change and impact the life of others for good. Enduring wealth is the one that comes with the motives of enriching others in some way. *Real wealth is when you have empowered the helpless without the intention of receiving anything back from those you've helped* even though there might have been some of those helped who may be capable of paying back what were invested in their lives. Fingers are not equal. As a wealthy man who has the capacity to help others in time of need, you should not expect any direct returns. You can extend the hands of help to widows, orphanages, and set up charity organizations that can pay school fees. The more you reason and act on these lines, the more likely your wealth will increase. In case you become tired, some of those you've helped may come to your rescue.

Law of entrepreneurship. Majority of the wealthy people become wealthy by starting and building their own businesses rather than working as salary earners. *Many wealthy people started by building their own enterprises and with faith in the success of their enterprises.* There are some who inherit their wealth. It is true, but their parent who started the businesses must have been creative and hardworking to ensure the success of their established companies. While it is good to have a good job with a good pay, remember that salary is fixed. *To be an entrepreneur is not about you being able to pay your bills. It is not about making sure your immediate family is all right. It is all about you being blessed and being a blessing to others around you and you making a difference in the lives of others around you.*

It is in being an entrepreneur that you can create wealth using your skill and available resources to follow your vision. You need to know how to create space and volume of what you are about to produce. Without you being able to create and produce in great quantities, you will be limiting your capacity to serve. *It only takes an idea to have a breakthrough.* With a viable single idea as an entrepreneur, it is possible for one to influence large number of consumers of products. Say for example you have an idea of manufacturing cars in one of the third world countries but you don't have the financial backing to make it possible. Do you know that you can contact and convince a car manufacturer like Toyota to come and build a car company in one of the rural areas of the chosen country of your choice? Part of the deal you give to Toyota may be to guarantee that the company through the government may be able to operate tax-free for a specific time and be protected against unfair competition from other car makers!

Manufacturing companies like Toyota in rural areas will improve or provide social infrastructures and employment for the people in road constructions and other service industries like hotel and restaurants and in mechanics and other technical workshops. Hospitals and schools will also spring up to serve the people. All the services are attendant benefits from the idea of an entrepreneur.

All you need is for you to have a breakthrough in one area and learn how to manage the resources by investing the resources in different areas of the economy. At this level, you need management skills to sustain your wealth. The first company will eventually give birth to other companies. That is one of the secrets of how wealthy people create chains of wealth.

The law of small beginnings. Is it not amazing to see that some entrepreneurs who started with small or little capital may be more successful and do better than those that started with large capital? *If you start big, you may fall big, and you are putting your resources in a big risk.* When you start small, you lower your risk. When you start with a big capital, it means you are not hungry. You might end up hiring people you are not supposed to hire, rent spaces you don't have to rent, or pay lots of overheads that are not necessary. Although, the amount of capital required to start a business depends on the nature of the business. What is big for one may be small for others. It is left for the entrepreneurs to determine what is big or small for them. *Law of wealth accumulation demands that you start small in your respective business or else you may not know how to handle your resources.* You need to have the hunger for starting small. When you start small, you will be able to monitor the daily operations more effectively and make the operation efficient.

It saddens my heart to see people going on holiday with the equity cash out from their mortgage refinance. Many spend this money within a month and spend more than ten years to pay back, forgetting that the $10,000 taken from the mortgage refinance is enough for them to become millionaires if well managed. Many finish school and get salary upgrades, only to go and lease new cars from car dealerships and start a fresh car payment with huge interest. Many will mortgage new houses and pay for the next thirty years. Some borrow $10,000 and pay back close to $100,000 because of high interest. Many use borrowed money to renovate and equip their houses. Many do this because they think there is every possibility that large amounts of money would still come. They did not even think of investments, however small the investment may be. Many despise their little beginnings. This is the genesis of their reproach. *Not that God is not providing for many of us but due to lack of wisdom, many have squandered the money meant for their breakthrough.* Most successful enterprises started small. You should remember that inside your seed, there is a harvest. Don't despise the small beginning.

The law of courage. You can never succeed in any business if you are afraid to fail because of what people will say. *Your willingness to risk failure and disappointment is a measure of your desire for you to succeed.* You better let them say whatever they want to say because if you fail, they will talk. If you succeed, they will also talk. Why are you then not taking positive action about your life? Why must you be stagnant and take chances to fail? *Thomas Edison, who invented the electric light bulb, tried and failed 99,999 times before he finally succeeded at the ten thousandth time!* People asked him what really inspired him to move forward and continue to try despite the fact that he failed *99,999* times. His answer was that *he did not fail. He only learned 99,999 ways how not to conduct electricity.* Failure is a matter of perspective. *Failure is a better teacher.* If you have never been through something, you will not know how to overcome it in the future. Your willingness to be courageous and take risks to fail is better for you than not to take the risk. Life itself is a risk. *Not doing anything is a risk itself. By doing nothing, your destiny is at risk.* There is something in your life waiting for your discovery. An old man in Kentucky, United States, discovered a modest recipe for a popular fast-food group. That recipe has given rise to the popular *Kentucky Fried Chicken*, which eventually transformed the life of the old man and the lives of others. At the age of sixty-five, the man pursued his vision and made a success of it. Today, the name KFC is popular not only in the USA but all over the Western world.

The law of confidence. Confidence is very crucial in whatever we do in life. Confidence helps you break through in whatever you do. Philippians 1:6 tells us to be confident in all things. *We can become whatever we want to be in life provided we are confident that we can.* Philippians 1:6 tells us that God has begun a good work in us. That good thing started in us right from when God created us. There is no challenge that you are passing through that the Lord who began the good work in you doesn't know, and he knows that you will pass through once you persevere and have faith.

When you have confidence, you will be empowered to face very squarely all problems. What builds the confidence in you is when you truly know who your God is, what he can do, and what he has done. You will be confident enough if you know and believe what you have.

When going for an interview, you must have confidence enough to face the panel In order to answer the questions reasonably well and to present yourself as a relaxed person. Confidence is one of the keys to making your breakthrough in life. Without confidence, you will be compared to a fancy car without an engine. *Confidence makes you stand out and get noticed in the crowd.* With confidence, you can go places. If you are confident enough, the sky will not be your limit. *Your demonstration of confidence can open the door of opportunities for you!*

The law of risk. It means *no risk, no success. Little risk, little success.* Although, there is profitable risk and foolish risk. You should learn to know that there is a calling and purpose for your life. Your money is meant for investing in your family business and not to be invested on clothes and other conspicuous spending without real economic returns. *Clothes may make you look smart, but looking smart may not bring you economic returns you demand.* To be smart, you must have what is called delayed gratification. That is to delay your enjoyment. For example, reading for examination while others are celebrating and making merry. On the other hand, you are investing your money while others are buying things of no future values.

The law of unusual positives. This law requires one to be positive in whatever business one choses to do. One must feel positive, think positive, etc. For example, when people do not expect much from you or look down on you as a person who cannot be successful in any business, it is for you to remain positive about yourself and discard the negative opinion of you by some people. It is necessary for you to stay positive about all the actions you take. Sometimes you may make wrong decisions and your goods or service may not sell or may not pull the crowd as originally envisaged. On such conditions, you must remain positive, because *if you got it wrong this time, you may definitely get it right the next time. You should therefore not give up or be discouraged with what people may say about your decision.* If you failed more than one time and you tried to correct your mistakes, not crying over the past failure, you are better off than the person who has not made any effort for the fear of failure.

Every time there is a failure, what you need to do is to simply sit down and write down the possible reasons why you failed. You need to be extremely positive whenever you are about to embark on any project in life. You will no doubt hear people calling you different names. That is common and normal. You will see people who are ordinarily not qualified to talk to you or face you in all circumstances, criticizing your ideas or your projects. You must ignore them because the vision you have is bigger and more important than their negative attitude. Moreover, you must believe that *your dream is bigger than your present situation and is bigger than what you may be going through. Never give up or abandon your dream because positive attitude is necessary in fulfilling your dream.*

The laws of persistence. This is the law that encourages you to hang on to your dream and the faith you have in your dream. *You should believe that if you persist long enough on whatever you are doing, you will succeed.* Your persistence and determination will surely bring success in the long run. There is nobody who has reach the pinnacle of success in life that has not met with one stumbling block or the other during the course of trying to reach the top. But what eventually led them to the top and kept them there is their persistency. They refused to bow down to opposition. We should know that there is no royal road to prosperity. *To be a wealth creator or to fulfill your dream, the importance of persistence and determination cannot be overestimated.* Many may stand to challenge you and set up competition against you just to frustrate you, even if they don't know where they are going. But the only key that shuts their doors is persistency. They may tend to bring down your standard, but it is your duty to stay focused and be persistent in whatever you know how to do best. *Don't be intimidated by the negative actions and judgments of other persons on you.* You should know and understand what you are called to do. Be at your best all the time. The ability to apply all the laws that have to do with wealth creation effectively will surely lead you to success and will push you to where God wants you to be.

Having understood the laws that back up wealth creation, it is essential for you to have the right strategies to make the laws work for you. *Having the right strategy is the critical key to and for success.* It is not enough to just read or study the Bible and other motivational books, but we must act on them. You must also be ready. A man will not be given what he is not ready for. That is the reason why it is not good to invest in somebody that is not ready for business. All they will do is to wreck all the money and time you have invested in them. When the business nosedives, they will invite you back to come and resurrect the business again. *Don't waste your time in riding along with any individual that is not on the same page with you in business in terms of readiness.* How would you explain the situation whereby you invested in somebody who agreed to run a boutique or restaurant or any other petty business only for you to visit the shop unannounced at noon and found the store is still locked just because the attendant considered himself to be the boss over the business! It requires special skills to run a business, to pass an exam, and for a pastor to efficiently manage a church. It is to be noted that *giving money to start a business to a person who lacks the minimum required skill to run a business is a sure road to failure.*

There are stages in business formation. At each stage, discipline is required. At the beginning, when there may be no income or when the profit may be small, prudent spending is advised as at other stages even when the business is operating profitably. Going through the barrier of business worth thousands will give room for the businesses worth millions and billions. But in a situation whereby you spend all the initial money you realized when your business is at the hundreds stage, or peradventure you eat your capital at the initial stage, your business and economy will be in jeopardy. *No business will grow without strategy.* It is left for you to develop a strategy that will work for you based on the business you are creating. It is highly important for anybody who wants to start a business to have some strategic plans to be use in forming and running the business.

Creativity. Being creative is not just about talking about problems. It involves finding possible solutions to identified problems. In order to be successful in whatever business you are doing, you need to be creative. The answers to your questions are in your creativity. The way out of your present predicament is in your creativity. *You need to be creative for you to move up above your peers.* You have to be creative for you to get out of box. You cannot see beyond your nose if you are not creative. Everything around you is a seed. Nothing around you has arrived as a finished product.

The book you are reading now is from trees. The clothes you are wearing is from cotton made on the field. The glasses you are wearing are from sand extracted from the sea. Ditto to all the glassware you are using to drink or serve food on your dining table. The designer shoes and belt we are wearing are from hides and skins extracted from animals. I guess what you only do with the animals that come across you is to kill and eat both the meat and the skin. The fancy auto tires are from rubber materials from the farm. *You are surrounded by seeds and creative ideas which you can nurture to mature products. Be bold to work on what you can* do to nurture your seed/idea, and let it germinate and grow to maturity stage for harvesting.

You can only get paid for your contribution. Without contributing, the only option left for you is to pay before or after enjoying the benefit rendered through other people's contribution. You need to think very deeply on your idea. If television will not allow you to think, it will be better for you to switch it off. If it is your daily job, you should try to change the job. If it's your friends that constitute a hindrance to your rational thinking, it is advised that you should do away with such friends.

Find a place where you can be alone to think. It may be in your room, place of work, in the library, even while driving. *Find a place whereby you can be alone for a couple of hours to be devoted to thinking and reflecting on issues of living. It is not good to be in the midst of the crowd all the time.* Crowds may choke your thinking and ideas. At times you need to be away from your spouse for some hours in a day. Don't let the phrase *"what God has joined together"* disturb you from having a quiet time to think about your life and destiny. *You need to let your spouse know that you need to have some time alone for meditation.* This is not about loving one another or not; it is about your future and the future of the entire family. *We are told that many rich men and women don't sleep eight hours like many poor or average people do.* They keep thinking of how to solve people's problems. *You cannot be wealthy until you are able to provide or invent what solves people's problems. You cannot know or discern solutions to people's problems by following the crowd.* You must, first of all, think before acting. This is what will eventually showcase you to the world.

Having a job with a salary will not let you solve people's problems. Your creativity will allow you to find answers to many questions. *Creativity will allow you to meet those that matter in life.* I have said it earlier that *creativity is about thinking about solutions to issues.* Have you ever sat down and thought about any particular problem which needed solutions in your community or in the world today? *You can solve such problems by conceiving positive ideas on possible solutions.* Somebody first thought of the telephone, and today many people enjoy the use of the telephone to communicate across the globe. In the same trend, it was somebody who thought about the computer. The computer is now a household name in the modern world. The CD, a way of recording memories in both audio and visual versions, was invented by James Russel in the late 1960s. His discovery had spread throughout the modern world. The airplane was an idea by some people who wanted to travel by air fast and safe. We can also start something which can benefit the future generation rather than waiting to enjoy the fruits of the good and hard labor of others mentioned above.

Innovation. Innovation can be described as the ability to think of a better or easier way of performing a task. This creates your ability to think outside the box. *Innovation makes you take your thinking to the next level. Innovation is the use of new methods of doing things differently from what everybody has been used to.* Innovation gives solutions to problems. You should always learn to ask what is the answer. How do I do it? That is innovation for you. Stop grumbling and complaining like other people do. *You should see things in different ways from the multitude.* Try to ask questions and be sensitive to the environment you are in. There are opportunities which may be flowing around irrespective of your location. *You can only see available opportunities if you have a creative mind. It is a creative mind that will enable you think of what you can do differently from others.* If things are not going on well with the people in your community, it is your creative mind which will enable you find solutions to such problems to meet their identified needs. *Innovation will showcase you in your world and will let you meet people who matter.* You must exhibit innovative thinking for you to move ahead in life.

Space. This is your level of readiness in doing what will move you forward to your next level in life. The space you have created will determine the level of your breakthrough. The Bible records the promise of God to bless the work of our hands, fill our basket, and our storehouse. These three models of blessings are all entrepreneurs on their own. But you must have space to store these blessings before they can become manifested. These types of blessings are not the type you can store in a lockup shop or carry around in the trunk of your car. *When you have no space to accommodate what will push you ahead in life, life will become impossible and difficult for you.*

You should go beyond the mentality of selling goods in your car or buying from another person who brought the goods directly from the factory. *Think of having your own designs and trademarks.* Create space for yourself by having your own warehouse and get distributorship, not a lockup shop with limited space. *Think about a bigger facility than a car trunk sale.* If you can't think big, you can't grow big. It is time for you to stop calling people to come and see what you are selling in the boot/trunk of your car. Show them the bigger facilities for your business.

SEE YOUR FUTURE

I t is very important in life for you to see a bright future ahead of you. As a businessman or woman, you should see yourself as an owner of a franchise or importer and exporter who move goods around the world. As a musician, you should not see yourself as belonging to a band that plays only in the local areas but as one who organizes many concerts and plays in many cities and places.

As a medical doctor, you should stop seeing yourself as a physician working in just a local clinic working many long hours in order to make the ends meet. It is better to create your own business by building your own clinic, participating in some medical researches, and contributing research reports in professional journals/magazines. A pastor of a church must see beyond pastoring congregations under the basement or in tent, but he should rather see himself as belonging to a mega church and addressing various conferences in many cities and states.

Do You Know That

Where you are today is a result of the thought you had yesterday. Where you are going tomorrow is a result of what you think about? If you can think and act like the 5 percent who are the wealthy, in a matter of time you will be part of them. But if you think and act like the 95 percent, which are the average people, you will remain average. Live a life of just enough, base life on 401(k), cooperative or retirement money, or loans and social security is not just enough. Bankruptcy can affect your retirement savings. You should think about the effect of bankruptcy in Detroit on 401(k) and retirement savings during the 2008 economic recession. When we think like billionaires, we will step into where God wants us to be financially. Whatever is in our hearts will create the world we live in. If average is in our hearts, average will produce itself. If it is abundance, it will also produce itself.

The Bible says God will bless what is in our hand because the remote is in our hands. That is why we have the best TV around us, and we pay on cables. We place our hands on different latest phones. That is why we have Bluetooth and pay lots of bills. We have the key of new car which is on credit. That is why we pay car notes. pe Place our hands on big houses. That is why we pay lots of mortgage, and we can't sleep in the house because we work two to three jobs. What does it profit a man who bought a house that cannot sleep in the house more than two times in a week because of huge mortgage and other utilities bills? If we put our hand on investment, God will continue to bless us.

When you know how to learn, every step you take will be a step toward success.

Many stars and celebrities make millions of dollars but still live and die as poor people because they failed to invest in profitable ventures. Some others later file for bankruptcy. A borrower is a slave to the lender. The big car you drive, the big house you live in, and the designer clothes you wear as an average person does not portray you as a millionaire in America and in other developed countries. But they increase your burden and make you restless as you think how to get out of the debt you have put on yourself.

If ten years ago, after paying your bills you had fifty dollars in your account and today when you are making twice as much you still have the same balance in your account, you should check yourself to find out why you are where you are. Unless you change your act by investing in an investment, you may remain the same or worse in the next ten years.

Unless we change our thinking, no matter how much we make, we will still be in poverty and cannot be rich.

By working for people, you will make a living. When you're working on your business, you will make a fortune.

Your boss will never feel comfortable to see you competing with or getting richer than he is.

You should plan beyond your job.

Billionaires work smart; poor people work hard.

It is possible to work hard and not work smart. Hard work is good, but working smart is better. People who work harder and not smarter tend to die sooner.

Only people with jobs have working hours. They punch in and punch out.

When there is a work to be done and there is not enough wisdom to do the work, it could be boring and laborious. It could take a long time. It could also can bring a lot of wastage and even injury. Investment and not labor produces wealth.

We need to employ God and give him work to do in our life and let him know that at the point of the risk taking and all the time, he is in control. The Bible says God will direct our steps and actions but not our sitting and inability to take action and risk. No angel will come and drop money in our pocket or credit our account with money. We should look for opportunities and take risks. By the time we begin to take some steps, God will direct our steps and show us the direction we should go. He will lead us through. One step will lead to the other, and one connection will lead to the other. We can't grow if we can't get out of our comfort zone or tent. Not that we will not fail, but not retrying will make us a failure. But we can always bounce back if we keep trying. That is why rich people are rich. Rich people know that failing does not make you a failure, but never trying at all does. Poor people believe they have a 90 percent chance of failing. They have the mind-set of believing that there is a lion in town that can devour or kill them. The question to ask is who identifies the lion, and who proves that the lion is looking for them, if at all, in town?

Poor people see risks as something they can't afford to take while rich people see risks as something they can't afford not to take. Rich people see life as a window of opportunity, and the window of opportunity will only open for a while. After that, it disappears. An average poor man reads one or less self-motivated book in a year while rich people read an average of two to three different books in a week. The wealthy know that wisdom is a key to abundance. Therefore, they have a desire for more information on every area of business, ranging from stocks, real estate, and other businesses.

We live in an information age. It will be tragic to live without information during this age. The man who wondered out of the way of understanding shall remain in the congregations of the dead (Prov 21:16).

Rich men don't waste time listening to senseless radio programs in their cars. Instead they listen to audio books or CDs comprising business-oriented discussions. Rich men believe an hour of driving listening to jargons in the car is equivalent to five hours a week, twenty hours in a month, and 240 hours a year wasted. An hour of listening to good tapes in the car is a bonus. When they come out of the car, they come out with their senses, and they feel good and develop the confidence and believe they already gained something for the day even when their day has not started. Poor people think self-help books and tapes are the last solutions to problems, but rich people see it as road map and the beginning of a solution to the problems. The reason being that poor people don't practice what they read in the book or what they hear in CDs. But rich people do. To be on top, you have to improve your skills and knowledge. We must be ready to accept change and do things a bit different from the way we normally use to do things.

Poor people seem to allow their time to be wasted on unproductive ventures such as watching unproductive programs in the television, texting unproductive messages, wasteful texts on Facebook, and other social activities like parties. Rich people have different ways of thinking about time. They value their time and will rather spend it on something profitable.

A poor man may believe that money and jobs are the most valuable assets, but a rich man will say, "I can get money, but I can never get more or regain my time." A wealthy man considers time as his most valuable asset and believes that an opportunity lost can never be regained.

You can steal a wealthy man's possession but not his time because he believes time wasted cannot be regained. Pastor Adeboye and the other reputable anointed men of God and people in Fortune 500 cannot joke with their time.

The CEO of the company spent visually the same time as their employees at work per day. The difference is what they spend their time on in building and promoting themselves.

Rich people have an agenda for the day, weeks. and even months so they don't just go all around without marked engagements. Wealthy men just will not do things that will waste their time. They don't cut lawns, wet grass, and wash their cars themselves. They don't do handiwork in their homes. Instead, they use such time to think about what will fetch them millions and spend little money on those things they don't want to do themselves. Rich men read business papers at car washes while their cars are being washed. Rich men see business opportunities coming. Rich men look for ways of solving problems financially. They think of ways to solve the problems related to their business, while poor men run away because they believe they don't have solutions.

Rich men will never give up. They learn the principles of falling and rising. They look at problems as mountains that can be removed, while poor people see problems and challenges as mountains which put an end to their progress because they are afraid to move close to or beyond the mountain. Rich men see problems as mountains which can be useful, so they look for opportunities in or around the mountains. They also see problems as mountains which can be used positively for their own advancement. For example, David was not popular in Israel until Goliath came to the scene. God used Goliath's strong head as a mountain to bring David to the limelight. We should not run away from the mountain which God may want to use to advertise us. Unfortunately, many people give up and run away at the junction to their breakthrough because of fear of the mountain! Rich men see problems as tools that God uses to wake men up.

Rich people put their families first before anything. They usually think about how to better the life of their kids. Majority of rich people think about how not to leave or accumulate debt for their kids, while many of the poor people have nothing on ground for their families. Poor men allow their kids to struggle right from the beginning. They teach kids on how to build credit so that they can be fit for future loans. Rich people don't allow school loans to weigh down their kid's future. I heard someone saying he was trying to pay his student loans on time so that it will not affect the student loans approval for his kids in future.

Rich people would rather find a way to establish their children in one business or the other rather than making them employees.

Life is the most difficult exam. Many people fail because they try to copy others, not realizing that everyone in the examination hall has no same but different questions to attempt.

Recommended video. Watch the video of *SC Featured* Richie Parker (Hendricks performance).

BRIEF SELF INTRODUCTION

The author, Idowu Kotila, has a Bachelor of Science degree in plant science (Botany) from University of Ado-Ekiti, Nigeria, in 1996/97 session. He proceeded to get a postgraduate diploma in financial management and accounting (PGDFMA) in the year 2000 from Obafemi Awolowo University, Ile-Ife, Nigeria. In October 2014, he graduated with a Master's in International Business (MIB) from the Graduate School of Business and Technology, University of St. Mary's Minneapolis, Minnesota, United States of America.

He attended different seminars and workshops on personal improvement and economic empowerment. He worked in various disciplines in America before finally choosing to encourage people on the need for them to be skillful and enterprise for their future benefits. He runs small personal business and founded a nonprofit organization called African Education and Health Initiatives (AFEDHI). It purposely to gives back to the less privileged communities in Africa in the area of academics and basic health care and to help orientate and unify the African communities in diaspora (www.afedhi.org). Facebook address;" African Education and Health Initiatives".

He is the publicity secretary for the organizing committee that hosts the vice president of Nigeria, His Excellency Professor Yemi Osinbajo, for a town hall meeting with the Nigerians in diaspora in the state of Minnesota, USA, and its environ in August 2018, which gave birth to the initiatives known as Building a New Nigeria.

He recently wrote a book titled "Survive the Recession". It was written to suggest how to find spiritual and practical solutions to family finances. He is currently working on other books and magazine called "Global Achievers". He is married to Kemisola Kotila and blessed with three wonderful kids—two girls and a boy. They are Hannah, Abisade, and Adeteniola Kotila. To God be the glory.

CPSIA information can be obtained
at www.ICGtesting.com
Printed in the USA
JSHW020031040621
15513JS00003B/42

9 781647 014018